MAYOR OF THE SKIES

D1715447

ISBN:14637283x
EAN:9781463728311

Front and Rear Cover illustration by Peak 7 in Deerfield Beach, FL

Printed in the U.S.A.

Visit our website: stephengravett.com

MAYOR OF THE SKIES

STEPHEN GRAVETT

For my wife and many friends who read my novels: I appreciate your faith in my stories. To my good friend Chuck Schwaderer, who once again read this book a chapter at a time and offered invaluable feedback: thanks a million. Thanks to our Veterans: as one, I understand.

PROLOGUE

Alain Secur and Kyle Anderson were waging a personal war against each other. As the two largest condominium builders in Miami Beach, they found that the scarcity of buyers caused by the real estate bust of 2006 threatened their economic survival. They valued each customer more than gold. Their styles varied dramatically, and for one, his methods of finance made him more vulnerable than his rival. Eventually he would renounce his title as Mayor of the Skies and seek asylum in the bounds of poverty.

CHAPTER ONE

June 3rd, Present Day

Reginald Gambrel, the new head of the Southeastern Division of DEA stationed in Miami, was invited on the Coast Guard cutter Emilia by Commander David McCall. McCall and his staff were interdicting a possible cocaine haul in the drug-familiar waters near Cuba and the Cay Sol Bank. Gambrel's staff had targeted the expected drug deal based upon hard intelligence gathering that had begun four months prior from an unusual tip. The tip's origin was not through normal street channels. Generally tips came from a rival cartel or a pissed-off ex-business partner or some anonymous middleman. This tip, however, came from a trim carpenter doing renovations on Gambrel's house in Coconut Grove. Upon endless verifications from the strange source, the lead got traction quickly as being credible. Phone taps, informants, and solid police work confirmed the plan. The cutter was headed to a rendezvous point with a small Bahamian freighter, where Coast Guard crews packing their weapons would board the freighter for the remainder of its trip—if allowed. The freighter's routes and its habits were well known by drug operatives in the area and would not draw their attention. On board the freighter were two special armored cigarette boats with high-speed capability and dozens of deck-mounted guns.

The *Emilia* was an hour away from its rendezvous in the late afternoon summer daylight, fifty miles southeast of Miami. The ocean was flat

1

calm, and the shimmering, deep-blue water made for a smooth, almost idyllic, cruise. At Reginald's side was his assistant, Jack Enzi. At that moment they were mesmerized by an unusual sight off the port side of the cutter. Hundreds of flocking birds were diving around a long, narrow Sargasso weed line that looked like a golden oil slick. In the middle of the weed slick was an unknown object, possibly a lumber pole or wood plank. The fury around the site was unusually brisk by marine standards. Hundreds of larger fish torpedoed the small baitfish beneath the slick, while birds dive-bombed the bait ball from above. Larger fish and small sharks chased the medium-sized fish from below. Occasionally, a slow-moving, gray fin would appear from below the slick and charge the wooden object. The weed line was in the direct path of the cutter, and as it began to dissect the golden slick, a sickening sight became obvious to Jack and Reginald. The object was not lumber, nor was it a cooler bobbing on the surface.

"Oh my God, Reg, it's a body," blurted Jack in disgust.

"I would say part of a body, "said Reg, intending to be accurate and not sarcastic.

"Jack, get your ass up to the wheelhouse and get this boat stopped. The drug interdiction is officially canceled."

Randal Penn, special agent for the Miami headquarters of the FBI, was just getting ready to leave for home. He had worked until 7:45 p.m. that evening, concluding another twelve-hour day. Penn was loading his briefcase with files for his homework when his BlackBerry rang. The caller ID came up Reg Gambrel. Prior to coming over to the FBI, Penn had been Reggie's boss at DEA. *Probably wants to hit South Beach for a cold one,* he thought as he hit the accept button on his BlackBerry.

"Hey, boss, it's Reg…"

Rand interrupted his former star pupil and said, "Where do you want to meet?"

"No can do, good buddy. I'm on my own gig right now, offshore with the Coasties."

"Oh," said Penn. "What's up?"

"We just pulled a half-eaten body from the sea with a couple bullet holes in the head. We were headed on a drug deal near Cay Sol—practically ran right over it."

"Well, aren't you lucky? I guess we won't be having that drink," said Penn, curious and disappointed.

"Sorry to do this, but this one's for you, man: international waters, murder, kidnapping—the whole trifecta. Gotta feeling you'll have this one by morning."

"Thanks, Reg. Any ID?" asked Penn.

"No. Pretty messed up. Female, thirty-five to fifty years old, red hair. It will be a tough ID."

"OK, just get it to the morgue later tonight, and I'll take a look tomorrow. Keep it under wraps from the junior officers and crew as best you can," Penn said.

"I know the drill, boss. Will do."

"Whatya doing about your big drug bust?" asked Penn

"This will take precedence; you know that. It's canceled."

"Oh, so you're on your way back? Call me tomorrow and scan the report over in a PDF. I want to pick your brain on something else, too," said Penn.

"Good night, Rand."

Miami Developer Kyle Anderson was sitting in his waterfront mansion alone on Biscayne Bay in Miami Beach gazing across the turquoise waters at several of his past high-rise luxury condos. Fate and skill had smiled on Anderson, as most of the glass gems had been successful. His thoughts turned to his wife. His marriage to Sheila had been a love-hate relationship since they met and married right out of high school thirty-two years ago. She had been his first construction secretary. He sat on the terrace watching the sun disappear as the shimmer from the bay's waters turned fire red. Just then the phone rang. He fumbled for his cell phone. At last—it was Sheila, his wife.

"Hey, honey, where are you?"

"Don't you remember? Pedicure, facial, and massage today in Aventura? Suzy's?"

"Yeah, yeah, I forgot. Just worried. See you soon; love you, babe."

"Hey, I'm doing this for you so don't fall asleep on me tonight or you'll miss something special," she said seductively.

"Don't worry; that won't happen. See you soon."

After the call, Kyle reflected on his latest bout of memory loss. He was stressed out over his new, mixed-use, urban in-fill construction project in Miami Beach. Lately he had suffered through an ugly recession that had reduced his lofty company to a handful of people. The drought was understandable for this part of the nation. Like Las Vegas, Arizona, and other parts of Florida, condominiums and housing in general was off by 65 percent since 2006. Rapid sellouts, investor buyouts, multiple flipping, and high-octane sales were replaced in Anderson's vocabulary with terms like foreclosure, short sales, deed in lieu of foreclosure, and vulture sales. Unfortunately there was very little upside in profits associated with those terms. But Anderson was still kicking, and his new mixed-use project and his relatively small inventory of existing condos would get him back on the map. Sales were improving, too. He was also suffering from extreme competition from Alain Secur—short for Alphonse Secerrini. Secur had changed his name years ago just prior to developing his first real estate development in Rahway, New Jersey. He witnessed Italian developers in the northeast drawing extra suspicion from nearly everyone, including the IRS and homebuyers. What worked best was his move to South Florida the following year.

Secur seemed to be just a step ahead of Anderson the past five years. Most of his good fortune came from a ready source of financing from a New Jersey pension fund, always eager to loan Secur nearly 100 percent of the development costs. Like Anderson, Secur was mainly a high-rise condominium builder. Secur was fortunate to have wealthy partners because no matter how many or how few pre-sales he had, he always broke ground right after his permits were approved. Unusual for this business, it drove his competition crazy. Secur also seemed to have a sixth sense about where Anderson was building and often got to the best sites before Anderson had a chance to submit a contract. No matter how confidential and secret Anderson kept his intentions, Secur got there first almost every time. Anderson had his own feelings about New Jersey pension funds loaning money to an Italian developer from the northeast with a new, French-sounding name. He reluctantly accepted his competition's fortunes of superior financing but questioned his clairvoyance.

CHAPTER TWO

T he following morning Randall Penn was sitting at his favorite deli in South Beach awaiting the man who had replaced him at DEA. It was like old times. Their last big bust together had started at this same table. Penn was sipping hot tea and reading the sports section of *The Miami Herald*. Across from him lay the glistening ocean of the Atlantic. Already the pretty ladies in their thread bikinis were strolling the beach hoping to be discovered, gawked at, or swept off their sandy feet. Not far behind were the hounds—tattooed young men flexed and tan with their tongues hanging out, trying to look cool. Palm trees stood still as Penn gazed at the calm, lake-like ocean beyond the people of South Beach. The *Herald* reported the Miami Dolphins were two weeks into training camp and already three of their top players were injured. Penn turned to the financial section and was shaking his head in disgust, oblivious to Reg's presence.

"Hey, boss, whatya so upset about? You lose money in the stock market again?"

Penn looked up with a strange stare. "What? Oh, hey, Reg. You startled me. No. I stay out of those rigged games," said Penn. "Those damned Dolphins are at it again. Three players going on IR, and the season hasn't even started. How can you be out of shape in Miami?"

"South Beach, Joe's Stone Crabs, and the Bahamas. That should do it. What do you care anyway? It's been that way forever. Now, the Heat—that's different," concluded Gambrel as he moved to his seat across from Penn.

"I suppose you're right. Seems we've had this conversation before. So how goes it as my replacement? Any big busts besides the one you missed last night?" asked Penn, looking over his newspaper.

"Well, nothing like the Gianno bust, if that's what you mean, but the one last night may have proved interesting—a purported Mexican cartel way the hell over here selling their poison. New kids on the block, I guess. What happened to the good old days when it was just the Colombians and the Cubans?" said Gambrel.

"I guess it won't be long before we get them into our crosshairs as well," said Penn as he finished his paper, looking Reg straight in the eye.

"I haven't got much time, Rand, so I'll get right to it. Last night we found a young woman half eaten, bobbing in the middle of a weed line in the middle of the Atlantic. Two shots to the head with a small caliber gun."

"What makes this so unusual? We see this occasionally," said Penn, leaning in closer to Reg so patrons would not hear.

"Good point. This seemed different, though. Pretty girl in an expensive dress and a string of Mikimoto pearls still around her neck. No robbery, that's for sure," said Reg.

"Now that seems a little out of place. Without the bullet holes, it's your typical drunk person overboard."

"Exactly," Reg said.

"Well, I appreciate your pinch hitting for us. Presuming you found her in international waters, I guess it's our baby now," said Penn.

Reg said nothing but nodded as he drank his coffee.

"I presume the body is in the morgue? Anything else I should know?" asked Penn.

"Not really. No ID, the body was bloated, and part of the left leg and torso had been munched on by sea creatures. I could see this was a well-maintained woman, both physically and financially. No wedding ring. The medical examiner is working on the forensics right now. It's still hush-hush. You can determine how you release it publicly."

"Well, I won't be able to stall too long. Thanks, Reg, I'll get right on it. Gotta go. By the way, anything else you have in your gut on this one?"

"Not really. Just unusual. I think whoever did this had money, boats, and maybe too many women."

"Did anyone ever tell you that you take after your old boss in the smarts department? Exactly what I was thinking. But why?"

"That's your job now, Rand. If I find out about anything else, I'll call you. We'll get that drink soon, too."

With that, Gambrel gave Penn the typical thrust hug and departed.

High above the city of Miami in his Claughton Island office, Alain Secur, f.k.a. Alphonse Secerrini, was enjoying the scenery while drinking his double espresso and reading *The Miami Herald*. Next would be the *New York Times* and the *Wall Street Journal*. It had been a tough four years for the normally successful condominium developer. His world and its normal operating style were no longer relevant. But in Florida it was the same for everyone developing and building residential and commercial projects. Only rental apartment builders and a few fortunate government contractors building the shovel-ready infrastructure projects with Washington stimulus money were thriving. The same old contractors who built roads and bridges got all of the government work. With the fall of Fannie Mae and Freddy Mac and all the new financial restrictions put upon banks and other lenders, the building business nationwide was in the toilet. While Secur's golden goose with New Jersey feathers had loaned an abundance of money for new projects in the past, the large sums Secur owed with no new buyers in sight turned that tap dry. Worse yet were the carrying costs on interest, developer-owed HOA fees, and operational costs to keep the company afloat, which Secur was now paying from his personal funds. But even his substantial reserves were beginning to get low, with no relief in sight.

The buzzing of his intercom interrupted his depressing thoughts. "Miss Michel to see you," said Janice Pardee, Secur's secretary of twenty years.

Secur rose from his desk, straightened his tie, and pressed the intercom button on his phone. "Please see her in, Janice."

A single click on the button by Janice acknowledging the request sent Sandrine Michel into the man cave of Alain Secur. As she entered, Secur, as always, was in awe of her beauty. She was French, tall, and slender but

9

curvy, with medium-cut blonde hair. Her stunning, blue, piercing eyes and square jaw depicted a Swedish goddess, but she was all French and very sexy. Dressed professionally in a navy blue suit slightly open at the top, she exuded confidence.

Sandrine had been born in France and worked at her father's construction company near Toulouse before meeting a carefree, successful restaurateur in Palm Beach. After a torrid, cross-oceanic relationship, she finally moved to the US to be with her lover full-time. Eventually the flames subsided along with the romance, and Sandrine sought work in the international city of Miami. She began working for Kyle Anderson ten years ago, dating on and off. She was Kyle's assistant for six of the ten years, rising rapidly the past four years. While initially smitten by Anderson, his solid marriage and devotion to his wife gave Sandrine countless fantasy moments at home alone but no male companionship.

Five years ago at a Broker's Reception in Miami Beach, she met the attractive Italian developer with a French name. Secur fell madly in love with Sandrine almost immediately and pursued her endlessly despite his long-standing marriage to his wife Alicia. However, the feeling was not mutual; at least not right away. Secur was relentless. He finally took her to bed after three months of presents, flowers, diamonds, and fancy dinners. Sandrine fought being mistress to a married man, but eventually the handsome Italian won her heart. She was certain the romance would quickly run its course and she would be single once again. But she became even more attracted to Secur, and her role eventually changed into a formidable partnership with him. And she could not minimize the sex—steamy, hot, Italian-on-French sex. They were like college kids fucking everywhere and anytime—in his office, in the car, nearly in public, in luxury hotels, in boats, in planes, in his construction trailer—everywhere. The relationship was never volatile, yet it had smoldered hot for over five years.

Before Secur spoke, he double-checked to see that the intercom button was off. He could not afford anyone to know about Sandrine. Confident they were safe, he grabbed under her dress gently, squeezing her ass as he kissed her deeply. His erection was instantaneous as Sandrine pushed off gently, looking down to see that Secur had an embarrassing bulge in his pants.

"Down, boy. Plenty of time for that later," she said with a guilty smile. She adored the effect she had on him.

"It's been almost two days," he said, wide eyed.

"Uh huh, two days without me, but you're still shacking up with Alicia. You remember—the woman you are married to?"

Secur's face turned crimson as he struggled for a comeback. He thought better of it and let the remark slide. The truth was, he loved his wife as well—only differently. He quickly changed the subject. "What brings you to the lion's den so early, my dear?"

"While I love you very much, I am here because I have not heard from my sister in over three days."

An uneasiness gripped Secur as he spoke. "I am sure she will find you soon. You know she is the wild one in your family."

"Alain, I wish you would not say that. She is just not as selective as she should be sometimes, but she is my sister," responded Sandrine, head down, withdrawn and worried.

"All right, I didn't mean anything by it. I know sooner or later she will come up for air—so to speak," correcting himself. He wished he had not used that term.

"Alain, three days is a long time to hold your breath. I'm really worried this time. I despise her boyfriend, too."

"Tell you what. I'll put out some feelers and see who may have heard anything. OK?"

"Well, I guess so," she said as she moved in to kiss Secur good-bye. Instead, she squeezed his butt and pushed him gently away, playfully smiling.

"Put that dog back in his cage; we'll settle this tonight. Please help me find my sister." She turned quickly and was out the door seconds later, leaving Secur hard and wanting, standing in front of his desk.

Moments later Secur pulled out his untraceable cell phone and dialed his banking friend Biagio.

11

CHAPTER THREE

Randal Penn was meeting with the medical examiner reviewing the latest morgue victim. Once the body had been cleaned and prepped for the autopsy, the critter bites were not as ominous looking as when Sonya Michel's body was first pulled on board the cutter festooned with seaweed, fishing line, and small crabs. Reg's pictures were pinned on the wall behind Penn as he carefully walked around the steel gurney comparing the pictures as he viewed the body. Exam rooms always gave Penn the creeps. He had seen many dead bodies, but the pale, naked body on a steel gurney wearing nothing but a toe tag made it more personal. The ancient rooms with old fluorescent lighting and the medical smells of an autopsy were an unpleasant duty of his calling. Dr. Grey Wong, the medical examiner, always seemed so cheery and eager to see outsiders in his den of corpses. *Creepy*, thought Penn.

Penn got right to the point. "Can we assume she was killed by the shots to the head?" It seemed like a stupid and obvious remark, but not in the business of murder—and from the looks of it, this was a contract murder, or at least meant to look like one.

"I'd say that's a safe bet, Rand. Twenty-two caliber—two went in and none came out," said Wong, speaking through his face mask.

"Had to ask. Time of death yet?"

"No, but soon. I'm working on it."

"How old do you think she is, Doc?" questioned Rand.

"Guessing thirty-five years, six months, and ten hours," Wong said, half serious.

Rand smiled. "Yeah, sure."

"Somewhere between thirty-five and forty-five. I'm guessing closer to thirty-five."

"Anybody claim her yet?"

"Nope."

He went through his one hundred questions as Wong patiently answered most of them. Penn was considered to be one of the most thorough and relentless investigators as head of DEA before joining the feds. The FBI was drooling to get him when they learned he wanted something in law enforcement more challenging and high profile than drug smugglers. He was a bit of a fame whore, but he loved the chase and all that came with it.

Penn had a law degree from the University of Pennsylvania—cum laude. After several years with a large Wall Street law firm, he resigned the year before he thought he was due to make partner. The partner who originally recruited Penn to the firm and cared for him like a son leaked the news that he would be passed over for partner and asked to leave the firm after the announcement. It was not because of his stellar work gone bad, but rather that he took several weeks off to help his ailing father into hospice, staying with him his last days. Big law was a sick, unyielding business run by cold, overworked lawyers, and their rules were not flexible. It was better for Penn that his trusted mentor explained why he would be passed over. The mentor hoped Penn would quit upon hearing the news. Penn resigned within weeks, politely unloading his considerable workload to others so no client was left untended. From that moment he knew law with another big firm was not for him. He applied to DEA and was on a plane to Washington the day they received his application. After several years with DEA, Penn resigned once the FBI accepted his application. For him it was about more action and bigger challenges. His final bust at DEA with Gambrel was a monster event, leading to numerous arrests throughout the country and the Caribbean. The bust brought down a class action fraud engineered by a leading Dallas attorney and benched forever the smartest smuggler in the eastern United States.

Content that he had a good grasp of the initial autopsy, Penn left Dr. Wong to dictate his findings. As he left the morgue, a *Miami Herald* beat writer rushed him as the sliding doors opened into the mid-day sun. At first Penn was startled until he recognized Lane Smith, a respected police reporter he had known for over six years.

"I got nothing for you right now Lane; no ID, no name, no motive. You scared the shit out of me back there lurking in the shade," said Penn with a slight smile.

"Sorry, man. Hey, what's this I hear about a pretty lady floating in a weed line like a discarded chum bag?" said the usually blunt Smith.

"Wow, what university taught you to talk like that? I am really impressed," blasted Penn, dishing the trash talk right back. Reporters loved him.

"The University of Take My Money and I Didn't Learn Crap," Lane fired back.

"Now you're talking. I went there, too."

"Seriously, Rand, what's going down? I got my sources, so don't bullshit me," said Lane.

"OK, no bullshit, no comment."

Lane said nothing.

"OK, that's not nice, sorry. Your sources are partially right, but I have to prepare a press release or my friends at the *Sun Sentinel* and the *Post* will give me a load of shit. They already think you work at a desk in my office. I'll send it to you first, but I can't give you much lead time. Promise me this: you'll call me right after you get the release so the story you heard is accurate. You got part of it right, but there's more to this," explained Penn.

"Thanks, Penn. Hey, I hear your old partner at DEA is tracking Mexican smugglers near the Bahamas."

Penn strolled to his car without looking back and responded, "You've been smoking too much of the product you are writing about."

"Is that a confirmation, Penn?"

Penn shot Lane a behind-the-neck bird as he disappeared into his Black Tahoe. Driving away, he sorted out his remarks for the upcoming PR release. As a sensitive person, he could not imagine how many people reading about this murdered woman the next day would panic, thinking the mystery woman was a missing wife, daughter, or child—worst part of the job.

The next day Kyle Anderson came to work only to find his top assistant, Sandrine Michel, barging through the lobby doors to the parking lot and bouncing off of Kyle's shoulder crying uncontrollably as she sped to her car. Caught off guard, all he could say was, "What's wrong, Sandy?"

She glanced back and looked at him briefly without saying a word. She backed her car up quickly, almost hitting his Jaguar with her Mercedes. Smoking her tires out to the street, she was gone in an instant, leaving Kyle literally in her dust.

Anderson bound into the elevator and rode it to his penthouse office, determined to find out what had happened to Sandrine. Instinctively he did not call her. Someone close to Sandy was in trouble, and she would be incapable of rational conversation. He suspected something had happened to her sister Sonya. He knew of no other close relation Sandrine had. Anderson knew Sandrine at work as a professional. She occasionally shared brief stories about Sonya—often in unflattering terms. He did not know Sandrine's boyfriend but knew she dated or had a steady guy. She was a very private person. He liked it that way. Anderson was secretly attracted to her but felt better of it—financial preservation by avoiding a divorce. He believed for a while she felt the same, but over time they kept their hormones in check.

The elevator doors opened into the offices of Anderson Development LLC. Janis Hart, Anderson's loyal receptionist, was in tears behind her station. As Anderson approached her, he casually looked at the front page of *The Miami Herald* sitting on her desk. In bold headlines it read, *UNIDENTIFIED SOCIALITE FOUND MURDERED AT SEA*, with the subtitle *pearls and expensive dress intact*.

His face blanched as he stood speechless above his sobbing receptionist.

"Sandrine went to see her sister's body at the morgue," managed the receptionist.

Anderson listened in slow motion and initially did not respond. The response registered seconds later as he recovered. "It says here unidentified. How can she be sure it's her?"

Janis was still weeping uncontrollably. Finally she responded, crying between words. "She gave Sonya pearls last Christmas and knows she loves red dresses. How horrible to drive to a place almost certain your sister is that woman. If it is not, that's bad too," said Janis.

"Janis, I want you to go home. I will get Karen up here to do your job today. I know how close you were to Sandrine. If she calls you first, call me and fill me in. I'm going to the morgue to see if I can help her." With that Anderson picked up the paper, tucked it under his arm, and headed for the elevator. Two minutes later he was in his car, headed for uncertainty.

CHAPTER FOUR

The phone rang in Penn's office on his private line.

"Hello, Rand, it's Dr. Wong. We have a positive ID on the lady in the red dress and pearl necklace."

"Go ahead, Grey."

"Name is Sonya Michel. Her sister, Sandrine Michel, identified her about five minutes ago. I'll e-mail her contact information over after we hang up."

"Grey, what can you tell me about Sandrine's demeanor and her conversations with you in general?"

"It's all on tape, which I will send you with the other information. Do you want a brief summary now?"

"Yeah. You know, the basic points and your observations, if you have time," asked Penn.

"Sure. The sister was pretty broken up, as you can imagine. She obviously had a pretty good idea it was her sister on the drive here. That had to be tough. I hate it when that happens," complained Wong.

"Go on," prodded Penn.

"Her sister identified the dead woman as Sonya Michel. She's thirty-seven years old, no diseases. Cause of death multiple bullets, twenty-two caliber to the head at close range, no other physical damage other than suspected shark and crab bites; estimated time of death approximately thirty-six hours ago. She did not drown; DOA into the ocean. That's about it," repeated Wong expounding on his earlier conversation with Penn.

Rand said nothing.

"You there, Rand?" inquired Wong after a few moments of silence.

"Yeah, just thinking. Will you be there in the next thirty minutes? I'm headed over now," said Penn.

"Come on over. I will be here."

Twenty minutes after leaving his North Miami office, Kyle Anderson pulled into the morgue parking lot, dazed and confused by what he saw. Sandrine Michel was crying in the arms of Alain Secur, his closest rival and a fellow Miami developer Anderson detested. He quickly pulled into a parking space where he would not be noticed, got out of his car, and peered from behind a tree, continuing to observe Sandrine and Alain. The parking lot had only a handful of cars parked in it. Anderson feared he would be seen. Just then a man in a black Tahoe pulled in beside his Jaguar. As the man exited his car, he gave Anderson a long, serious stare. Only then did Anderson come to realize how suspicious he must have looked. He noticed the man had a small recording device in his hand and appeared to be speaking into it as he observed every car's license plate in the lot, his included. Anderson knew the man was a cop of some kind, and he would soon be hearing from him. *Damn it*, he thought, *this will be embarrassing.*

Anderson had seen enough and quickly returned to his car. He watched in his rear view mirror until the cop approached Sandrine and presented his ID to her. Then, while she was distracted, he slowly left the parking lot and headed back to his office. The morning had been surreal. He wondered how the next few hours might play out. It could not get much worse, he reasoned. His thoughts were no longer about Sandrine's well-being, but about the consequences and what his future actions should be over what he just saw. Anger welled up inside of him as he mindlessly drove through traffic considering one dark scenario after another. He could not shake these thoughts. *What to do next*, he worried.

Penn thought the couple looked scared momentarily when he presented his ID to them. He spoke softly to the woman. "Excuse me, miss, are you

Sandrine Michel? My name is Randall Penn of the FBI," said Penn as he held his ID and his credentials in plain sight for thirty seconds to be sure both people had time to see he was the real thing.

Sandrine whimpered a soft, "Yes."

"I am so sorry about your loss, Miss Michel, but this is a police matter now. I don't expect you to answer any questions right this minute, but I was here to see the medical examiner and I wanted to let you know who I am and that we are vigorously pursuing the perpetrators."

"Mr. Penn, nothing is more important to me now then finding Sonya's killer. I will be happy to speak with you right now if you like."

Penn was surprised but pleased. "Ms. Michel, the first hours of any investigation are critical. The faster we get on with our work, the more likely we are to find the people involved in this homicide. I appreciate your willingness to cooperate like this, but if you need more time..." said Penn as the question hung in the air.

"I'm OK; now is fine."

"There is an office inside, or you can follow me to my office uptown," Penn continued. He then turned to Secur standing sheepishly behind Sandrine. "Sir, may I get your name for my records? Are you a friend of the deceased as well?" said Penn quickly, looking Secur in the eye. He could see the man was surprised.

"Huh? Well, uh, no, not really. I am not a friend of the deceased. I am here to support my friend Sandrine," said Alain, uncomfortable with the situation.

"Your name, sir?"

"It's a, huh, Alain Secur. S-E-C-U-R, no E at the end."

"Fine. I will need to be alone with Ms. Michel for a few minutes. You may wait inside or leave if you wish. However, I will need to speak with you eventually. May I have your phone number and address?" asked Penn.

"Uh, are you sure, detective, uh, I mean inspector, uh..."

"It's agent, sir, and yes, I am sure," said Penn with a smile.

"I don't know anything, really, and I barely knew her sister," explained Alain as he handed Penn his business card.

"It's strictly routine. You'd be surprised what we find out. Every nugget of evidence helps us solve a case. I am sure you understand," assured Penn.

21

Now Alain felt stupid and thought how suspicious he must have sounded. Just then Penn spoke.

"It's natural to feel that way. We understand people's reluctance, but we appreciate your help."

Penn saw Alain's relief once he returned his information. Secur checked with Sandrine to see if she wanted him to stay; she did not. He was on his way back to his office five minutes later. He complimented himself as he left the parking lot about not being too affectionate to Sandrine in the presence of Agent Penn. That would stir questions he did not want to answer.

Penn carefully escorted Sandrine back into the building, finding an open conference room three doors down from the entrance. Within seconds a receptionist arrived to see if they needed anything. Two coffees were ordered as Penn put his recorder on the table in full view of Sandrine. He could see she was a beautiful woman, even in her emotional state.

CHAPTER FIVE

P enn sat across from Sandrine and arranged his recorder. Normally agents interviewed in twos, one as the scribe and the other as the steely-eyed agent constantly watching the eyes and movements of the suspect. But Sandrine was not a suspect at this time, and the recorder was for Penn's accurate account of this meeting. He stirred his coffee and gathered his thoughts. He wanted to give Sandrine a moment to compose herself. After so many interrogations, he knew to take his time and be respectful of what must have been one of the worst mornings in Sandrine's life. The grieving was just beginning, and here he was, a complete stranger about to question her at the exact worst moment. But that was what he had signed up for, and fleeing criminals waited for no one. He cleared his throat.

"Again, Ms. Michel, I am sorry for your loss. Before we begin I would like to offer you the free use of our EAP section at my office, which deals with victim support and counseling. You may always call me, but often it helps to speak with another female in that division. Will that be all right, Ms. Michel?"

"Please call me Sandrine," she said, getting her strength and resolve back. "And yes, that is very nice of you and the FBI."

"Well, Sandrine, there is no rush. I must be thorough, but you may stop me at any time. The more details you can give me, the better chance we have of catching the criminal or criminals."

"I understand, Mr. Penn. I will do my best."

"Let me get the formalities out of the way, Sandrine. First, you are voluntarily meeting with me, and I will use this recorder. It's just easier and more accurate for me to recount and re-examine back at my office."

"I understand," said Sandrine.

Without hesitation Penn spoke. "Your sister Sonya was how old?"

"Thirty-seven last month."

"How often did you see her or speak with her?"

"We spoke every day, and I saw her a couple times a week. We were close."

"Please feel free to embellish your answers if you think it would be helpful," Penn instructed.

Sandrine nodded without speaking.

"Was she missing for long, Sandrine?"

"We had not spoken in two days, so naturally I was worried. Then today when I saw the newspaper, I gagged uncontrollably because I just knew it was her. I always worry about her."

"Was that worry due to love of a sister, or was she with the wrong crowd?"

"Both, I think. Well, I know I loved her, but I did not always approve of her men friends."

"Was she dating anyone? In particular, anyone you disliked?"

"Yes."

"Yes you knew him or yes you disliked him as well?"

Sandrine hesitated momentarily, then answered, "Yes to both."

"Who might that be?" Penn lightly pressed, seeing Sandrine was hesitant.

"A man from New York named Biagio LoPrendo."

Penn blinked in surprise and fell back in his chair. His old law firm in New York represented the LoPrendo family interests in real estate throughout the New York boroughs. It had to be the same people. But Biagio did not ring a bell. Maybe he was younger. The LoPrendo family was well connected to most of the unions and their pension funds. They used some of

24

their own money and most of the union's money to finance their real estate development arm in condos, office buildings, and rental apartments. If you were late paying rent, you would not want to live in a LoPrendo rental apartment complex. Penn remembered some of the stories he had heard from his law partners who closed many of the LoPrendo deals. He never could figure out why his firm represented a suspected mob family whose business interests may not have been 100 percent legit. Money clouded the judgment of most attorneys, he remembered.

Penn continued. "How long had she been dating Mr. LoPrendo?"

"About seven or eight months."

"Do you know how the two met?"

Penn could see Sandrine recounting moments in her mind. She saw Penn waiting for an answer.

"Uh, no. Yes, now I remember. She was out with some friends at a bar in South Beach, and this guy across the bar came over and introduced himself. My sister did not always make the best decisions," she said.

"And this was about seven or eight months ago? Can you be more specific? For example, middle or beginning of a month, the month, the restaurant, etc.?"

"Well, let me think."

"Take your time; any detail may be important," said Penn as he gave her a tissue to wipe her new tears.

"I think it was that steakhouse near Joe's."

"Smith and Wolensky?"

"I think so, yes."

"Good. Did you ever meet this guy Biagio?"

Sandrine hesitated as Penn studied her body language. She asked to go to the bathroom and left to gather her thoughts. Penn could sense the conflict and was beginning to wonder if Sandrine was an innocent bystander or afraid of possible repercussions; maybe both. He quickly walked outside and dialed his office on his cell phone. He asked for his assistant, Ronnie Feldman.

"Good morning, Ronnie. I've got just a minute, so I'll make this quick. Get me any wants and warrants or any information you can on a New Jersey or Brooklyn guy named Biagio LoPrendo. Next, the same for an Alain Secur.

Finally, run these six tags for me and get me their owners," Penn read the numbers as he finished and returned to the conference room. Sandrine was sitting erect in her chair, ready to resume. Her staunch posture did not go unnoticed by Penn. He sensed a confession of sorts coming.

Before he could speak, Sandrine began. "Mr. Penn, I'd like to clarify something I stated before our break."

"No worries, Sandrine; that's why we take breaks. It gives one the time to recall more details. It is very common, and I appreciate your candor," said Penn in a disarming tone, hoping to further ease the way for more difficult revelations to come. It worked every time.

"Is this conference in strict confidence?"

"Are you fearful of something or someone?"

"In a way, yes. First, the man you saw me with is more than just a friend. He is my lover of over the past five years, and he is married—obviously not to me."

"Go on; don't be afraid. I've seen this before."

"I assume his wife probably knows, but it's one of those Italian marriages—open for the man but closed for the woman."

"Are you French, Ms. Michel?" Penn's tone was becoming more formal.

"Yes, I am. My family's originally from Toulouse. Why?"

"Alain Secur sounds French, not Italian. What am I missing?"

"Very astute, sir. Alain changed his name many years ago when he was building and developing real estate in New York and New Jersey. His real name is Alphonse Secerrini, but he felt an Italian name in that area was a negative. Apparently the mob was very much feared at that time in that area. Anyone with an Italian name was assumed to be shady."

"I understand. Is this just an alias or a real name change?"

"Oh no, he changed it legally over twenty-five years ago. This is now who he is."

"I presume this is the same Alain Secur who develops high-rise buildings throughout Dade County?"

"Yes, that is he."

"Goes by the alias of *Mayor of the Skies*?"

"Yes, that too," giggled Sandrine. It was her first smile in over thirty minutes.

"How interesting. Anything else you may want to disclose?"

"Yes. My sister met Biagio at Smith and Wolensky, but I was there with Secur and Biagio that night. She was at the bar when we walked in, and we stole her from her friends."

"OK, so you know the origins of this romance. No problem. Can you be more specific on the date?"

"It was just after Thanksgiving last year."

"Did you approve of Biagio? Check that. Did you like Biagio for your sister?"

"Not really. He was all flash and dash. Typical womanizer."

"Did they ever fight? Did he ever hurt her?"

"No, Sonya was a sweetheart. She would never give a man a hard time. But still, with a name like Biagio LoPrendo and coming from the New York area—I was fearful."

"Understandable. Sandrine, are you currently employed, and where?"

Penn watched as Sandrine's face turned a rose red. He wondered, *is she holding something back?* "I work at Anderson Development LLC in Miami Beach."

"So you work for your boyfriend's competitor. Is that correct?" Penn was so surprised that his question bordered on being inappropriate in tone.

"Correct."

"I meant nothing by that. I assume everyone is OK with that," mumbled Penn, looking down in embarrassment.

Sandrine said nothing.

Penn had the urge to ask if Anderson knew Sandrine was dating Secur. He really doubted it but did not want this honest flow to be truncated by one bad question. He would eventually find this out anyway, so he continued his light questioning.

As the interview progressed, he became enamored by Sandrine's beauty. He gave her some friendly advice about what she had told him, reminding her to call him with any new facts that might come to mind. He also gave her the card of a friend of his at the FBI who did special counseling for victims of crime and their families. He could tell she was still in shock, and her confidential revelations contributed to even more stress. He thanked her, gave her his card, and returned to the building to finish up his interrogations with medical examiner Grey Wong.

CHAPTER SIX

Kyle Anderson was both furious and compassionate with Sandrine. His temper was vented somewhat on the ride back. It had been a furious morning thus far, and he knew it was unwise to make hasty decisions, especially when an advantage could be gained by a calm, well-thought-out approach.

His office building was straight ahead. Every time he approached the modern glass tower overlooking downtown Miami and the surrounding canals and bay waters, a sense of pride surfaced and he would think, *I built that beautiful structure.* Kyle entered the private executive parking spaces in the adjoining structure. His parking spot was close to the elevator nearest the building entrance. There were no names on the spaces—just numbers on the curbs for security reasons. He quickly parked, entered the building, and took the elevator to his penthouse offices. When the doors opened, he was surprised to see Janice still at her post. She looked composed.

"I thought I told you to go home and sit this one out," said Kyle.

"I know, Mr. Anderson, but I need something to keep my mind off what happened and stay to help out. Was it her sister?" said Janis, avoiding Kyle's question.

"I'm afraid so."

Janis began to cry again. It was short lived, and she stopped. Kyle felt guilty knowing that Janis had stifled her tears so he would not order her home again.

"Are you going to be OK?"

"Yes, I had prepared for that, but still it's sad. I will be fine; don't you worry," said Janis in an upbeat tone.

"I'll be in my office, but unless it is Sandrine, I am not available today. Tell them I am out of town until tomorrow. I need some think time without interruption," said Kyle, striding to his office.

Once inside his cavernous office with windows taking up 270 degrees of wall space, Kyle felt secure for the moment. As he gazed out at his favorite sights, he paused to observe the activities at certain locations. Chalk's seaplanes were in a line on Watson Island. One was rolling out of the water, presumably full of people just in from the Bahamas. Farther south, a cruise ship was leaving for a fun-filled Caribbean voyage. Container boats were unloading their wares at The Port of Miami. Behind and to the west, small freighters steamed up the Miami River loaded with God knows what. The sights of business unfolding at mid-day in Miami. The visual cruise from his glass penthouse calmed him and lowered his pulse. Now he could think straight with controlled emotions.

The Sandrine revelations were endless as Anderson played "what if" for one possibility after another. The most negative came to mind first: *Was she a traitor to me and my company? How long had this been going on with her and Secur? Did this explain why over the past five years I was beaten out of every site Secur and I competed for? Was she merely dating him and still loyal to me?* One thought after the other, Anderson pondered ideas, sometimes giving Sandrine the benefit of the doubt and sometimes crushing her with harmful thoughts and profanity.

He pulled up his Word program on his desktop PC and decided to make a list of possibilities, limiting the entries by priority to the ten least likely scenarios. Then he highlighted the top two: *was she a traitor giving information to the enemy, or was she dating in full confidentiality of Anderson Development business?* Regardless of the one he would eventually act upon, he decided to investigate both at the same time, concluding that the truth would eventually surface. No longer naïve, he would watch Sandrine with his own eyes and others he would retain to follow her day-to-day routines.

Penn's next meeting with Dr. Wong was about an hour long. Aside from shark, crab, and critter flesh wounds, it was another murder victim dumped in the ocean; most bodies caught the Gulfstream and headed into northern waters, never to be seen again. There were two significant differences in the ballistics of the two head wounds; they were high on the top forehead and into the hairline by several inches. In addition, there were rope burns and flesh indentations around her ankles.

Wong pointed to the entry wounds and remarked, "Here you can see that someone would have had to point the gun down while looking into her face."

"But we've seen this before, Gray. Kneeling victims get shot like this all the time," said Penn, speaking as if professional hits were a routine event.

"Rand, most are in the rear of the skull. These entries are from the front heading downward toward the brain stem in the rear, such as this angle," said Wong, using his pen pointing the directions he described.

Dr. Wong continued, "I think there were several suspects involved in this murder. Here's how I think it went down. Time of death puts it around 3:00 a.m. I believe the victim was initially bound with rope around her ankles and thrown into the ocean alive. The natural reaction would be for her to spread her arms to tread water in a vertical position. Then they fired down on her head to make certain she was dead. This way, no DNA in the boat."

This scenario seemed eerily familiar to Penn. "Well that's quite a stretch Doc," he said.

"Before you came over from DEA, I had another case nearly identical to this, but the victim was the chief building inspector of Miami Beach at the time. Same caliber, same wound location, same rope marks."

"Now I remember. They never solved that case either, did they?" Penn said as the coincidence surprised him.

"That's right, Rand, but all fingers pointed to Alain Secur, although no one could prove it. He had a solid alibi," said Wong.

"What do you mean all fingers pointed to Alain Secur?" asked Penn.

31

"It was well known this inspector had it out for Secur. He was one of the few honest ones, and he was disgusted that Secur had all of the rest of the inspectors in his back pocket. He was saving millions by cutting corners, and I guess this inspector was about to go over everyone's head to the state's attorney.

"So what did the state's attorney say?" asked Penn.

"The guy was murdered before he ever met with the state's attorney."

"Thanks, Gray. I need to get back to the office. My number one, Ronnie Feldman, has sent me several texts, so she needs answers. Are we all done here?"

"Yeah."

"Can you do me a favor? Send over the file on disc for the building inspector case. I see a coincidence here that bothers me."

"Me too. I will get them to you later today along with the disc on Ms. Michel," said Wong as he bid Penn farewell.

Penn left the building with a thousand unanswered questions swirling in his mind. On this summer day in late morning, a warm breeze smacked his face. The tropical smells of Florida filled his nostrils as he strode to his Tahoe. His thoughts shifted to the windswept palm trees obeying the wind in unison and the puffy white clouds against a piercing blue sky. He thought about the still-sweltering summer days of haze in New York, where he had been an unappreciated lawyer not long ago. *Glad I am here*, he reminded himself. In south Florida your thoughts were never far from the beach or the ocean. *The ocean*, he thought as his mind switched to the Sonya Michel's murder.

Penn headed back to his office. The traffic was brutal heading north from Miami. He was a dozen or so miles from his FBI haunt in North Miami Beach near another mad scramble of twisting intersections—The Golden Glades Interchange, affectionately called the "spaghetti bowl." It loomed between Penn and his office. One wrong turn here and you could end up in Naples.

Penn was certain Sonya had been murdered because she knew something someone else did not want her to disclose. She gave her life for that unfortunate set of facts. The astute remark by Dr. Wong of another similar murder years earlier was upsetting as well. Random murders and crimes of passion were usually tied to jealousy, anger, vendettas, and gang wars—all routine, unfortunately. But once the perpetrators were caught, order generally came to the lives of those involved. But serial assassinations of seemingly innocent people were a declaration of war by the FBI, and Penn especially. South Florida was still a little bit like the O.K. Corral in many respects. Political corruption, drug and gang wars, illegal aliens, break-ins and white-collar scams were still part of the tropical landscape, just less noticeable with more and more people living in the area. Penn was determined to review the cold case and compare it to Sonya's homicide. He was looking forward to meeting with Ronnie Feldman and diving into the solution to this case. Penn parked his Tahoe and walked quickly into his office, looking forward to seeing Ronnie.

CHAPTER SEVEN

S andrine returned to her apartment at the Portofino Condominium but decided first to walk South Beach. Just a block from the ocean and one of the most beautiful beaches in Florida, it was perfect for times like this—a need for solace and grieving. The waters were pure turquoise and clear as the blue skies above. The sun was overhead, and the warm temperature was subdued by a mild ocean breeze. For a weekday it was crowded as tourists from all over the world set up their sun worship venues beneath umbrellas and cabanas. Sandrine decided to walk near the water, where the incoming waves lapped over her feet. She stopped to take it all in. The lazy scenery was cathartic. Seagulls and sandpipers shared the skies and the beachfront. Paddle boarders were taking advantage of a flat, calm ocean. Small boats and yachts were coming and going from the cut to her south, and the profile of freighters offshore steamed by at a crawl miles off shore. An otherwise idyllic day was marred by the brutal death of her sister, and *for what?* she thought. In between thoughts of her childhood came thoughts of why she had died and at the hands of what person.

As she took in all of the beauty before her, Sandrine began to think more resolutely about why anyone would want her sister dead. To her horror she realized that this was a targeted professional murder, with her sister as the intended victim. What had her sister known or done that made her that dangerous to someone? She was reluctant to look through Sonya's personal belongings for fear of finding a telltale clue. *Maybe later*, she thought. She began to focus on reasons. She eliminated her sister's doing anything to upset another human being. It was not her nature. She was a free spirit but a warm and kind person. So she must have known something, reasoned Sandrine.

Just then her phone rang. It was Alain.

"Hello, darling, what are you doing?"

Sandrine decided to play it close to the vest and answered, "Nothing, dear. Just walking to my apartment."

"May I come by?"

"If you don't mind, I want to be alone."

"I understand, sweetheart. How did the interview go with the feds?"

"Alain, don't talk like that. You sound like Al Capone. He was a very kind FBI agent, not a fed."

"OK, I'm sorry. I didn't mean it like that."

"Listen, honey, I need to go. I'm drained," said Sandrine suddenly, not wanting to talk to Secur anymore.

"I understand, but what did he ask you?"

Sandrine hesitated. She was not going to discuss anything about the contents of any FBI meetings. She felt a little vulnerable, not really trusting anyone except agent Penn.

"Are you still there, Sandrine?"

"Yes, Alain. I can't even find the energy to talk about that. I'm sorry. I will talk to you later. Good-bye."

Sandrine had never cut Alain short before. She surprised herself. She surprised herself again by walking north to the Delano Hotel and stopping in for a cocktail at the lounge by herself.

"May I help you?" asked the waitress.

"A double Cosmo, please."

The following day Kyle Anderson left his home, driving the relatively short distance from his Star Island Mansion to his office on Biscayne Boulevard. Traffic along the McArthur Causeway was light early in the morning darkness as he headed west toward downtown Miami. He first saw the cranes in the Port of Miami appearing as empty iron soldiers lit up like giant Christmas trees. The docks adjacent to the causeway were home to numerous Goliath cruise ships. They would not be back until Saturday. Directly before him through his windshield were the concrete mountains of Miami, bright and bold in the darkness. He had helped build those silent monoliths.

Now, though, he was oblivious to his surroundings. He drove by rote memory to his planned destination. All night he was haunted by the thought of Sandrine being intimately involved with his closest competitor and Star Island neighbor Alain Secur. Anderson lived on the southwestern corner of the island two doors south of Julio Iglesias and overlooking the city of Miami and the cruise ships at Dodge Island. Secur lived on the northwest side of the island next door to the old Elizabeth Taylor home; his view was toward Miami Beach. Just enough separation so they never saw each other.

Driving his silver Jaguar, he began to recount his last five years. Before Secur had become the Mayor of the Skies, Anderson had owned that title. Then, five or six years ago, Secur had outmaneuvered Anderson on eight to ten sites in the condo-rich A+ neighborhoods on Claughton Island near the Mandarin Hotel and a fertile residential area just north of the Rickenbacker Causeway along Brickell Avenue down from the JW Marriott and Four Seasons Hotel. Anderson was forced to seek alternative sites north of the Venetian Causeway in Miami and Aventura in North Miami Beach. Occasionally he got lucky on a site that was considered an inside deal. Two such deals had occurred within the past four years, and these A+ locations were strong competition to Secur—with Kyle the more successful. The other eight were strong B+ sites but not with the prestige or higher profit margin potential where Secur developed most of his projects.

It hit him hard—*five years ago I hired Sandrine*. Once that revelation surfaced, he could not stop thinking about the coincidence. He perseverated on it. As he arrived in the parking garage still in morning darkness, the bright lights inside the garage stunted his thinking. Once he adapted to his new surroundings, his thoughts returned stronger than before. He had to stay calm in order to lay a trap for Sandrine. It would not be easy for two reasons: Sandrine was smart, and he was impatient. In fact, his urge was so great to immediately confront her that it was all he could do not fire her on the spot.

His thoughts did spark a rational note of irony. While Secur had secured those A+ sites with higher margins, more density, and taller buildings, the recession had made his exposure and loan liabilities much larger than Anderson's. Anderson pre-sold his units with greater down payments and would not start a building until he was 65 percent pre-sold. He also had more of his own equity in each deal. He had to because his banks required it. This had actually saved Anderson's company in the recession. Secur, on the other hand, had the very cozy Teamster financing that, over time and due to early successes, had become lax and careless from a financial under-writing point of view, lavishing new money on Secur whenever he requested it. From a selling standpoint, Secur required less money down from his purchasers, which gave him a competitive advantage in sales volume but not in quality of the buyers. On some of his buildings, he started construction with zero pre-sales. Just before the crash in 2006, the quality of his buyers could be classified as subprime—a curse word bandied about by nearly everyone describing the mass failure of US real estate and banks. *So maybe Sandrine has done me a favor, albeit inadvertently,* thought Anderson.

CHAPTER EIGHT

"**M**r. LoPrendo here to see you, sir," buzzed Jamie Pardee, Secur's executive assistant.

"Please show him in, Jamie." With that, Biagio LoPrendo, entered the cavernous glass menagerie of Secur's palace. LoPrendo was a swarthy, short, well-built spark plug. He was impeccably dressed in a blue Brioni suit. His shoes were shiny like his manicured nails, and his confidence was beaming. He gazed into Secur's eyes with intensity and purpose—intimidation was always a side effect of his persona. As Secur offered him a seat in front of his desk, he remained silently mindful of the purpose for this visit. Today that purpose was to square up family and Teamster business.

"Shall I get you some tea or coffee?" offered Secur, feeling the pressure already.

"No thanks, I'm good."

Knowing why LoPrendo was there confused Secur's normal conversation style. *Should I attempt the usual pleasantries, or should I sit back and let him start the beating?* thought Secur. He had some issues to press himself, but alas, LoPrendo began in his usual blunt way.

"I think it's time for you to begin some asset sales, even if it involves personal assets," began LoPrendo in a calm, matter-of-fact tone, dropping the bomb and waiting for a reaction.

Secur knew what that meant: his home, his cars, his vacation house in Montana, all worth millions. It was now or never, thought Secur. "Speaking of assets, one of yours has created an extreme liability to me, Biagio. I think you know what I am talking about."

"Let's not get into that here," warned Biagio.

"Here or there—it doesn't matter. Your thug murdered my girlfriend's sister. My God, she was your girlfriend. Now who's bringing the heat to where?" Secur said as he returned the pressure to LoPrendo.

"It was an accident; it could not have been helped."

"What fucking accident? She was pushed overboard and shot twice in the head. Explain 'accident,' Biagio." Secur was livid as his own Italian temper began to rage. He carefully backed off. "OK, whatever it is, we have to circle the wagons and deflect this," Secur said in a lower, constrained tone.

"She was about to go to Sandrine and spill the beans about the payoffs, drugs, and the Mexicans."

"Jesus, Biagio, can't you learn to have sex without running your mouth?" said Secur.

At first Biagio said nothing, and then he answered, " Is that why you thought she was whacked?" He gained back the momentum and said, "Fuck off, pal; you've got yourself on my bad side already, thanks to all your unsold and resold condos. The Teamsters and my family want that finished concrete sold, and we want some of your cash, too." LoPrendo was back in control.

"I'm doing my best. I've tried every trick in the book. People are buying food and gas, and that's it. Everything else is being put off indefinitely. This ain't no recession in real estate; it's a full-blown depression. You know that. You know what I'm doing. You've been my copilot on every move. Nothing shady is going on here, Biag," pleaded Secur, hoping to turn the conversation into something positive. Biagio was his friend, and he hated it when they argued like this.

"OK, agreed. I'll sweep Sonya under the rug; don't you worry. But my ass is as close to the fire as yours. I got major heat from bad guys all around—family, too," explained LoPrendo.

"Let's get planning," suggested Secur. Common sense was returning, and he wanted to seize the moment.

"Amen," said Biagio.

"As you know, we have started to see a nice surge in Latin American buyers from Mexico to South America and every country in between, thanks to our expanded marketing efforts in those areas and our lowered prices. Venezuela and Brazil are particularly hot right now—folks are always trying to get their cash out of there, now more than ever. Then we have local cash vultures cutting tough deals that we normally would not take. With this week's closings, I expect to send four million up to your guys," said Secur.

"While I appreciate the effort and applaud your tenacity, four million is like paying the minimum monthly charge on a large credit card debt. Alain, you owe us around $400 million, remember?" Biagio reminded Secur.

"I know, but this will snowball; you'll see. First the Latin Americans, then the locals and Europeans, just like before."

"Not this time. This recession is different, and it's not going to change quickly. Our government is inept, and the country is broke. I don't see it falling that way. But forget about me; my lenders don't believe it either," concluded Biagio. He continued before Secur could respond. "Further, the next group of buy-out vultures is getting restless as well."

"Let them go to hell, Biagio, after what the last two vulture funds did to us. Is your memory that short?" blasted Secur once again. He pleaded with Biagio, "Besides, if I use them, the discount I will have to sell out for will be substantially below your mortgage."

"My lenders are ready for that eventuality, Alain. Don't kid yourself; we know when to cut our losses. It's time to move on."

Secur had accumulated thousands of unsold units three years ago when his original buyers flaked out and walked from their insignificant deposits, leaving LoPrendo and his Teamsters holding worthless loans with virtually no repayment. The fact that all condo developers from Miami to California had lost their asses in this same recession did nothing to assuage the impatient Teamsters. Secur, sensing defeat, decided to make a deal with the devil; only at first he thought it was an angel from heaven. He secured a deal with two hedge funds formed specifically to acquire distressed real

estate at vulture prices. Unfortunately for Secur, these cats were sophisticated and made you bleed for their money. And that they did. Primestar
RE Ltd and Bird of Prey LLC combined forces and entered into a bulk sale
agreement to purchase all five hundred units in a monolith on Brickell
Avenue called *Shimmer*. The name came from Sandrine. She was going to
suggest that Kyle Anderson use it on one of his glass towers in South Beach,
but he failed to close on the land, foreseeing doom in the marketplace that
Secur had ignored. The land was now for sale for $6 million with no takers.
Anderson knew better than to spend $100 million for glassy vacant apart-
ments that no buyers wanted with borrowed funds from large banks capable
of inflicting financial ruin on his firm. Unfortunately, Secur had not learned
to temper his greed.

In the end the pre-closing inspection team, consisting of savvy engineers
from Prime and Bird of Prey, found so many code violations at Shimmer
that Secur reluctantly cut a deal with the devil. Secur could hardly refuse
the huge discount of the already-discounted price offered as a take-it-or-
leave-it deal just prior to the closing. His bribes to nearly every building
official to cut corners and save money made the building a construction
disaster. Prime and Bird of Prey closed on the buildings, but only after
they secured a secret deal with the city to pay for a portion of the costs to
repair what could be fixed easily without ripping the building to its studs.
In addition, they hired the best engineering firm to certify the building
structurally sound and substantially in compliance with the South Florida
Building code.

The final bullet was an extremely expensive fifteen-year insurance policy
covering the entire building, which was obtained to protect Prime and Bird
of Prey from any and all potential latent structural liabilities that the Home
Owner's Association's sleaze ball attorneys might try to extort at a later date
when they eventually found out the building was crap. All courtesy of the
city of Miami Beach, whom Prime and Bird of Prey threatened to expose
to the state's attorney if they did not pay for all due diligence costs. When
the two hedge funds and their blue-blood MBAs, Ivy League lawyers, and
experienced engineers were done with Secur, he was lucky to receive a small
check at the closing rather than having to write one himself just to get rid

of the building. Needless to say the Teamsters were not happy, and Biagio was suddenly thrown into the same bull's-eye as Secur for making such a careless decision. Secur learned a valuable lesson: vultures leave no meat on the bone.

Secur and Biagio finished their discussions with a plan to deal more carefully with the next vulture fund, which was currently interested in purchasing a four-hundred-unit project near the Four Seasons Hotel called Glisten and a larger tower consisting of six hundred units nearby called Claughton Towers. Nearly one hundred of the combined thousand units were sold and closed, so there was some small repayment of the acquisition and development loan to the Teamsters. Both men agreed that they would not be caught off guard on this vulture transaction.

Anticipating the same strategy, Secur had lawyered up with one of the best construction law firms in the state and was about to select an international engineering firm with experience in countries that routinely bribed officials to get work completed in a timely fashion just so they would know what to look for in Secur's towers. They proactively drew a line in the sand for themselves to prevent another vulture rape and another deal with the devil. Satisfied with their game plan, Biagio and Secur agreed to have a drink later that evening to discuss the Sonya Michel incident in Fort Lauderdale out of view of the Miami crowd. For the moment Biagio dropped any further conversation about Secur's selling his personal assets. He had Secur's personal guarantees anyway. If he wanted to, he could force the sale. When and if it was necessary for Secur to begin liquidation, Biagio had the ace.

CHAPTER NINE

"Hey tiger, don't just stand there wasting that manly impulse. Get your ass in here so I can satisfy that urge." Penn was caught so far off guard that he burst out laughing, nearly dropping a fine bottle of LaCrema Pinot Noir on Ronnie's doorstep. Ronnie was dressed in a skimpy lace thong and a transparent short teddy chemise that did nothing to hide the large nipples sitting atop her luscious breasts. While her townhouse was an end unit partially secluded from others, she was, after all, an FBI agent sworn to high morals, so she had looked twice before jumping Penn's bones. She put her arm around his neck, pulling him into the house as he continued his deep laughter, brushing the doorframe with his uncontrolled hard-on.

"Sorry you missed me today, sugar, but a woman can't wait forever," she said with her hands on both hips.

By now she was bare chested, wearing only her black lace thong. Ronnie Feldman had beguiled Penn ever since the day she transferred from Dallas with her buxom beauty, blonde hair, and 5'10'" Texas-sized stature. Her perfect hourglass figure, accented by her large, natural breasts and slim hips, dazzled every male in the North Miami FBI office. She had graduated from Texas with a degree in criminal science. The next four years she served on the Dallas PD, specializing in forensics and crime scene investigation.

She was forty years old and was once divorced (high school sweetheart), with no children and a love of practical jokes. Ronnie had been with the FBI for over fourteen years, eleven years in Dallas and three years in Miami. She was assigned to Penn the day she arrived. By now it was well known throughout the office that the two agents were lovers, but they rarely fooled around at the office—at least not where others could see. Tonight they would blow off some steam, have passionate sex, and discuss the Sonya Michel case over dinner. That's what FBI couples do.

Penn was barely able to put the wine on the counter before Ronnie had pulled him by his tie into her bedroom. He never fought her urges for sex; no sane man would.

"Your mine tonight Randall, so get naked and put that woody to work."
"I love it when you talk dirty to me, babe. By the way, I'm wearing a wire. I'm arresting you for sexual harassment. You have the right to remain silent while I screw your brains out," said Penn, smiling at the woman he loved.

They locked lips while Penn hustled from his clothes and seconds later dashed under the covers for their pre-dinner mini-orgy. They exchanged tender words as Penn rubbed her body softly, his fingers becoming familiar again with her soft skin. They made passionate love for the next forty-five minutes. Penn satisfied her two times before they finished in a heap of sweating bodies, lovingly exhausted but completely fulfilled. After they finished and washed, they slipped into matching FBI robes. Ronnie had sewed the FBI crests on the robes as a joke. Penn had begged her not to fearing that somehow word might reach the office providing fellow agents with plenty of material for humorous retaliation; which finally did happen. They wore them proudly to dinner.

"What's for dinner, babe?" asked Penn.
"You just had the appetizer. Did you like?"
"Yum."
"I made spaghetti and meatballs. I can heat them up if you're ready," said Ronnie.

"Is this one of those old Jewish recipes from Texas?" remarked Penn with irony in his tone.

"Listen, buddy, there's plenty of Jews in the deep old heart of Texas. You want barbeque instead? I make a mean pulled pork sandwich and collards," she said lovingly, taunting Penn, squeezing his ass in fun.

"Pulled pork? Are you kidding me?"

"You've seen me eat hot dogs at the Heat games, Penn. What's the big deal?"

"You are one special package; never a dull moment, that's for sure. And I love every bit of that tall Texas body, mind, and soul, too." Penn leaned over to kiss his love.

Penn was Lutheran, and Ronnie was Southern Jewish with a twang to her accent. Two of the secretarial women in Penn's office were Jewish from New Jersey and Queens. To hear the three of them talk by the water cooler was a hoot. They all got along famously, with Ronnie definitely affecting the others' cooking habits.

They finished dinner on TV trays, surfing between Fox News and ESPN. The Marlins were on tonight against the Reds. Feldman showered first, then Penn, and they settled into casual clothes. They each had sets of clothing for all occasions at each other's homes for moments like this evening. Evening sleepovers were becoming more common between them.

Tonight would be an all-nighter, reviewing evidence from the Sonya Michel murder as well as the Artone Gomez murder with the identical MO six years prior. Ronnie had fished out the file before coming home. Her thorough research and forensic skills made Penn's job easier. Two years earlier, during an evening study session at the office and with both sets of hormones raging, the big bang occurred that eventually brought the two together, the lawyer from New York and the Jewish cop from Dallas. During that meeting Ronnie reminded Penn that she remembered him from her Dallas PD days when Penn busted the famous Dallas lawyer Sean O'Neil. O'Neil and a slug from Fort Lauderdale named Vincent Gianno had the most unbelievable web of racketeering, murder, and pharmaceutical fraud she had ever witnessed in one case. Dallas PD was a participant in the case, and thanks to her forensic investigation, they were able to solve the DeFrane murder in Dallas as part of the Gianno/O'Neil racketeering, murder, and dope smuggling case. Their destiny seemed preordained.

"Here it is, Rand, the Gomez autopsy. I reviewed it earlier, and it is definitely similar. Why a building inspector, though?"

"I'm not sure, but I doubt that Gomez was an innocent bystander. The more I read about Secur and his lenders, the clearer my focus becomes on his methods. Did you know Alain Secur changed his name from Alphonse Secerrini? His financing comes from several chapters of the Teamsters union in the Northeast. One in Rhode Island and another in Brooklyn," said Penn.

"I would not want to owe money to those guys. And all those empty buildings—that's some serious debt."

"Now you're talking, sweetheart," Penn remarked.

"Somewhere in this is murder and betrayal; I smell it too," Ronnie said, lounging back into the couch and looking to the ceiling for more inspiration.

"Here's one for the books. Secur's girlfriend is Sonya's sister, and she works for Kyle Anderson. The two developers hate each other. Anderson cannot know, can he? Why would he tolerate that?"

"That's what I love about this job. We represent the dead no matter what turns up. Trust me, we are going to find those bastards and put them away for good—for Sonya's sake," said a determined Ronnie. Penn knew she was disgusted by any murder, but when it involved innocent women, her determination ratcheted to the highest level. He looked on and smiled.

"Where did the trail end with Gomez, and who did we question?" asked Penn.

"It was definitely a clean, professional hit. No witnesses. Everyone who had a possible connection or reason to kill this guy had an ironclad alibi, as you would expect."

"You got names on that list?" asked Penn.

"For starters, Secur. He was a lame suspect. However, according to the file, he was with Biagio LoPrendo when Gomez was slain."

"Who else?" prodded Penn.

"Some guy named Moto Seanu, a Samoan illegal who was working in Miami at the time. We never could find out his employer or his whereabouts. Seems he gave us the slip and went back to Samoa. Nothing much after that. Piss-poor police work by our guys, if you ask me."

"It happens, darling. We cover as much ground as possible with a small number of agents, and sometimes things fall between the cracks. Every one of our guys works his ass off. Thank God for our cyber guys and our firepower. Those are our game changers," Penn said, concluding his brief documentary.

"I know, dear, but this guy Moto should have been followed more closely."

"Well, do this then. Run a passport sweep and see if the guy's been in town recently. Patterns do repeat. Who else is on that list?"

"Huh, that's funny—Kyle Anderson. Says here that Anderson Development LLC had complained constantly about the building inspector. Seems that Gomez failed a bunch of inspections on Anderson's jobs, costing delays to the projects. Anderson showed up one day during an inspection that failed. He called him a no-good spic looking for a handout and ordered him off the job. Gomez called the police, and Anderson was arrested for threatening a city official. He was released and not charged since the alleged threat was never corroborated. I'm not liking this Gomez cat," concluded Ronnie.

"That's always a problem down here. One of this area's great weaknesses—graft, bribery, public corruption. I'm not minimizing it; it's just constant," said Penn.

"What conclusions are you drawing from all this, honey? I'm starting to think Secur and maybe Anderson should be visited real soon. Secur's financial problems are certainly well known."

"Yeah, I'll say three quarters of the empty condo projects are his," said Penn.

"None are Anderson's," said Ronnie.

"What about that list of license plates in the morgue parking lot I asked for? Can I see that, please?" requested Penn. Ronnie reached in into the file and handed him the list.

Penn scanned the list of names and then said, "There it is: Kyle Anderson's silver Jaguar. I knew it." Penn blurted the name as if he had discovered an unusual fact.

"So what? He was there with Sandrine, probably to console her. According to Anderson's website, she is his assistant. Perfectly normal, wouldn't you say, Rand?"

"Assistant, are you kidding? She was romantically embraced in the parking lot by Alain Secur while Anderson was hiding behind a tree watching the events unfold, being sure not to be recognized. That's why I copied the license plates in first place. To see who this creepy guy was staking out the morgue."

"Huh? Oh, that's not right. He must have just found out about those two. What could that be about?" asked Ronnie.

"We're going to find out; that's for damn sure, babe. All right, let's get together our list of people for questioning. Then I'm going to bed," said Penn. His thoughts were whirling once again.

"Me too," said Ronnie, leaning in to give Penn a wet smooch on the lips.

CHAPTER TEN

I t had been three days since Sonya's murder when Sandrine finally showed up for work at Anderson Development LLC. Now it was different for her. She had always been able to justify her position at Anderson, even with her love for Secur. And, of course, the perks she received in exchange for key confidential information was an entitlement and huge conflict of interest. She felt dirty. Her past betrayals made her feel cheap and unworthy. She knew her world was about to change. Secur's fortunes were changing for the worse day by day. She noticed his lack of drive and the loss of optimism. He was becoming like the rest of the country: disillusioned, disappointed, deprived, and hopeless. But he was different, too. He owed hundreds of millions of dollars to his lenders. He of all people needed to get up and stay up, no matter what.

She was also aware of a different element of friends. They were rough around the edges, secretive and aloof. Sandrine was smart, and she had grown up in the real estate business in France. Big money is always at stake in real estate development, especially at Secur's level. But big money came from only so many sources. Most of those places were good, but the alternatives were always messy. It was the day after Sonya's murder that Sandrine began to replay her life with Secur, carefully noting the people, places, and things she had experienced. The people had changed for the worse, and the conversations seemed less friendly, even threatening at times. The trip through history had raised suspicions about what Secur might know of her sister's murder. *Is he completely innocent?* she wondered.

Just then, Anderson leaned into her office. "Can I have a word with you?" was his simple request.

"Uh, yeah, sure. I'll be in in a minute," Sandrine said in a dreamlike stupor.

Kyle ignored her forlorn look and returned to his office. Sandrine became aware of her lethargy and promptly pulled herself together walking the short distance to Kyle's office. Approaching Kyle's personal secretary, Joan Evans, Sandrine nodded hello and awaited Evans's reply.

"Sandy, dear, I am so sorry for your loss. You go right on in there. Kyle's expecting you," said Joan.

"Thank you, Joan, you're so sweet," remarked Sandrine as she passed with her head lowered.

She entered Kyle's office, which employees affectionately referred to as the man cave. It was decorated in minimalist modern with lots of glass and a large section of wall space whose centerpiece was a seventy-inch flat screen TV. Flanking all sides, top, and bottom of the TV was Kyle's "*I love me section,*" with pictures of Kyle fishing, meeting celebrities, and accepting awards; commendations; certificates; family photos; and an autographed Heat jersey from Dwayne Wade. His desk was merely a thick piece of glass supported by twin chrome and bronze sawhorses—attractive but a bit ostentatious. Kyle watched every step Sandrine made to the chair facing him. Behind Kyle was a large round clock with an inscription on its face that read, "Time is Money."

"Welcome back, Sandy. We all missed you here, but we understand you needed the time. I am truly sorry for the passing of Sonya, especially under such circumstances. If you need anything, you just let me know."

Sandrine began to cry as her guilt forced a momentary collapse in front of Anderson.

Kyle sat somberly behind his desk, recognizing the source of her grief. He knew why she was crying, and to a certain degree, it made him feel better. *At least she has a conscience,* he thought. He had decided not to tell her what he knew; instead he was going to get information by stealth and misdirection and toy with her. He had mixed emotions, too. Aside from her espionage, she was an excellent nuts-and-bolts executive. Her bidding skills and job site organizational skills were the best he had ever seen in his twenty-five years in the business. She was a skilled communicator and was always on top of her game. But every time he replayed the scene of Sandrine in Secur's arms at the morgue, he winced in mental pain. He walked around the desk to comfort Sandrine. Unexpectedly, she rose and hugged Anderson hard. Before he could say anything, she spoke in sobbing inflections.

"Kyle, you have been so good to me, and I don't deserve it. I appreciate all the chances you have given me, the advancements, your mentoring, and your honest work ethic." She stepped back and looked Kyle in the face and kissed him gently on the cheek. "I must resign, effective this minute. I'm sorry. Good-bye." And she turned, walking out.

Kyle scrambled to stop her and ran in front of her, stopping her at the door. He spoke while holding both her shoulders as she raised her head from shame. "If you mean all of that, then you owe me this. Don't do this right now—please. I don't want you making drastic decisions while you are grieving and confused. Take whatever time you need. Call me; let's go somewhere to talk, but please don't leave like this," said Kyle, surprised by his compassion. He now knew what he had forced from his mind so many times: he was in love with Sandrine.

She smiled and again kissed Kyle, but this time on the lips. "OK, I'll try my best."

His fate was sealed.

CHAPTER ELEVEN

*"What part of 'Make the body disappear' did
you not understand, Moto?" asked Secur.*

He and Moto Seanu were meeting in a dark corner of the Mia Kai restaurant's Molakai bar. The Mai Kai had been open for nearly fifty years. At one time its lush gardens, waterfalls, and superb Polynesian food made it a must for every tourist who came to town. The locals were loyal, too. They had solid entertainment every night consisting of a Samoan drum and tribal dance routine that had entertained diners for years. But the old Mai Kai was not like it used to be. It was in disrepair, and the gardens were tattered and not as lush as before. Still, it was a favorite spot to have a drink and not be noticed. Moto had worked at the Mai Kai for the last three years under the stage name of Tuku Silei. Secur had decided to meet Moto an hour before his meeting with Biagio at a nearby steakhouse.

"It could not be helped, Alain. Two separate cigarette boats running without lights were coming toward us very fast, man," said a nervous Moto.

"Do you know how this will look?" said Secur, red faced.

"Relax, man. That was because we didn't use enough weights."

"First, it may be different to you, but to me, a body was supposed to disappear in the second largest ocean in the world, and miraculously it was found floating in the Gulfstream," said Secur.

"OK, dude, I get it. What do you want? A refund?"

55

"No. I want to know what Sonya told you," queried Secur.

"Dude, she was peeing her pants. She didn't say shit the whole time," said Moto. He stood up, looking down on Secur. "I'd appreciate it if you don't come in here again to discuss your business. Now if you will excuse me, I gotta get to work." With that Moto disappeared behind closed doors, leaving Secur to his thoughts and his Mai Tai. Secur slurped down his rum drink and headed for the valet.

Less than two miles from the Mai Kai was the elegant Ruth's Cris steakhouse, site of the Biagio/Secur meeting. Biagio was seated in a secluded corner when Secur arrived. The room was aromatic with the smell of garlic, butter, and prime beef wafting between tables. Secur shook hands with his friend and lender.

"What looks good, Biag?" asked Secur, sliding into his seat after telling the waiter to bring the wine list.

"About nine hundred condo closings going smoothly in the next couple of weeks and more after that," kidded Biagio. He had finished half a glass of wine waiting for Secur to arrive and was in a light mood even though the topic tonight was serious. Biagio had grown to admire and like Secur, and he detested differences between them.

Secur managed a lopsided smile, then a chuckle. "Amen. Me too, Biag. I just saw Moto," continued Secur.

"And?"

"He said they were jumped by two cigarette boats running dark in the Atlantic that night. It spooked him, so there were no weights applied. Basically he ran away liked a scared, three-hundred-pound Samoan," said Secur.

Biagio smirked, and that made them both laugh as they conjured up the mental picture of that amusing sight.

"We can't use him anymore. He's becoming a liability," remarked Biagio.

"I understand, but what and when?" said a surprised Secur. He was not used to the casual business of murder that Biagio and his family took as commonplace. After all, he was a builder and developer.

"I'll take care of this. Leave it to me," answered Biagio. He could see the wheels turning in Secur's head. He had to keep him focused a little while longer.

"Why exactly was Sonya hit?" asked Secur.

"Alain, my dear friend, she was my lover of eight months. Do you think that was easy?"

Secur needed to be careful how he answered that question. He was on thin ice with just about everyone in his life.

"I'd like to know a little more about what was about to go down that made her so dangerous. If you don't mind," asked Secur in a quite sincere tone.

"Certainly. Sonya was a wonderful, beautiful free spirit. More fun than any woman I have been with. But she was very pragmatic and idealistic. I stand at blame for letting her beguile me and seduce certain things from me in the heat and passion of the moment."

Secur interrupted, sensing the reason before Biagio could explain. "Not the Mexicans. Tell me you did not leak that source during mad, kinky sex. Please, not that."

"Relax, Alain. No, I said nothing about your slimy Mexicans. She seemed to know about them already. I thought you may have somehow mentioned it," answered Biagio, staring into Secur's eyes as if to prove his innocence.

"Me? I rarely talked to her. And Sandrine doesn't know, either," Secur mentioned quickly to exclude his lover.

"Look, she had to be silenced," said Biagio.

"How do you know she did not tell Sandrine? Sandrine has refused to see me ever since Sonya died."

"It has only been three days, for God's sake. The woman does not need your sex. She needs time to grieve. Don't you know anything about Italians?" said Biagio as the added wine made him more conversational and animated.

"She's French, Biag, remember?"

"French, Italians, they're all the same."

"We'll see. OK, how are we going to pay the Mexicans on this next vulture sale without your Teamster boys coming in with their bean counters and finding the shortage?" asked Secur.

"That is the real problem now, is it not? Why do you think I asked you to start selling your assets? I can't cover it all," added Biagio.

"How are the Mexicans doing? Those crazy bastards will cut your head off for a nickel...uh, peso," said Secur.

"We discussed this before, remember? I warned you that dirty money carries dirty consequences. But you insisted we use them against my advice. Sell the assets, Alain, especially the jet and your home. It's fashionable again to be humble," said Biagio.

Secur was beginning to get flush, and his heart rate was spiking. He saw no way out, so he repeated his previous question. "Again, Biag, where do we stand with the Mexicans?"

"They're restless, just like the Teamsters and every other person or entity that loaned money to your company. Personal guarantees don't mean the same thing to the Mexicans. It's more as if they own your soul."

That had an ominous sound to Secur. He knew what Biagio was saying was true, but it had an aura of finality to it once it was spoken.

"OK, I'll sell it all, but you have to have my back on this, Biag. I cannot give away these goddamned condos right now, let alone sell any. Surely they know I am trying," said Secur, dripping sweat from his forehead.

"Of course, Alain, I've got your back. Just get it under control. You concentrate on this upcoming vultures closing, and I'll handle your flank. We'll get through this. Selling your assets is a step in the right direction. Now let's order some steak," said Biagio.

Biagio could see for the first time that Sonya's death and the Mexican threat were deeply affecting Secur's state of mind. He had to stay close and get him through this. Without Secur, regular business and vulture sales could not happen. Biagio dominated the rest of the meal, talking about baseball, women, food, and wine—anything but Secur's current situation.

CHAPTER TWELVE

I t was 2:30 in the afternoon, and Penn and Ronnie were in the conference room reviewing the Sonya Michel case and any operational support that may be required. It was obvious after their homework the night before that strange relationships in this case needed to be quantified, understood, and investigated. The FBI, and Ronnie in particular, were skilled at uncovering facts that painted a picture that would eventually lead to the arrest of criminals. While every case was different, skilled detective work was still detailed and calculated. Penn and Ronnie began to list the people they needed to interview and the goals of each interview, including the exact type of data they were looking for; not all were suspects. In the case of Sandrine Michel, the two main questions would be why are you involved with a married man who happens to be the number one competitor for the boss you work for, and do you know who would want to murder your sister. From these basic questions, others would flow, and there was a host of other, less important questions that could yield gold as well.

"Let's start with Kyle Anderson. How do we feel about him, Ronnie?"

"I've done some research with our sources in real estate and banking this morning. He has quite a reputation, mostly all good. He is very conservative in his approach to financing his residential towers."

"How so?" asked Penn.

"Patience, my sexy bomb; I'm getting to that," she said, making Penn blush. "According to my sources, he does not leverage his projects with overburdening debt. He has at least 50 percent of his own money in every deal, and for condominium contracts, he asks for at least a 35 percent deposit from all buyers, sometimes more. Fannie Mae requires a minimum of 20 percent down on all condos. He never starts a building until 85 percent are pre-sold. His lawyers are tough as nails, and they do more than keep the deposit money if someone walks from a deal; they sue for specific performance and are successful most of the time. He allows a small number of investors into his deals, and he requires affidavits attesting to a buyer's status—very tough, I'm telling you, Penn. He has the highest closing percentage of any condo developer in this recession, and none of his projects have defaulted," said Ronnie as a fascinated Penn absorbed every word. Penn fashioned himself as somewhat of a real estate expert. At the height of the market in South Florida, he flipped two condo units he had bought as investments and made two times more than his salary. Other friends he knew had done the same thing but invested their profits in more units, only to lose everything one year later. He took his earnings, paid the taxes on the gain, and never looked back. What he had just heard about Kyle's disciplined approach impressed Penn. Secur's financial problems were in the newspapers almost daily, but nobody ever wrote about Anderson's misfortunes. He was boring and successful. *No story there*, thought Penn.

"That is quite impressive, considering every other developer has leveraged himself out of business, leaving banks holding millions of dollars in unsold units," said Penn.

"Anderson is highly respected in the real estate brokerage community, donates to a dozen charities, and sits on several bank boards. In short, Mr. Penn, your everyday model citizen. Did I say he was married with four kids?" said Ronnie.

"What did you find out about our boy Secerrini, or should I say Secur?" asked Penn.

"Mr. Secur is not such a nice man. He hates working with real estate brokers and has been sued numerous times for not paying agreed-upon commissions. He either runs the poor brokers out of attorney money defending his suits, or he loses if a strong broker takes him to the finish line. We know he cheats on his wife, and all of his buildings are practically empty. He has been known to start a building totally on instincts without one pre-sale."

"Not one?" asked Penn.

"Not one legitimate pre-sale. He does sell to relatives and investors with skimpy deposits and counts them as pre-sales," clarified Ronnie.

"What else?"

"You want more?"

"Yeah. How does he get lenders to agree to those loose terms?" asked Penn.

"That is the most unusual part of his business model. Most of his money comes from Teamsters, with very little of his own equity invested. Apparently, in the go-go days when everything sold and flipped, he made this group a lot of money. He became the man with the Midas touch and earned the nickname 'Mayor of the Skies'."

"I remember reading that in the papers. The business editor gave him that nickname," said Penn.

"Anyway, as he became the fair-haired boy for his lenders and investors, other Teamster chapters jumped on the bandwagon. He had too much money chasing too few deals, so he did what every other developer does when he has money burning a hole in his pocket—he bought more land, built more high-rises, and began to believe the hype," said Ronnie.

"He's been in the hole for over two years now. I can't imagine the Teamsters being this patient," added Penn.

"I know he had to vulture out one building. Not sure how well he did, but one of the firms that bought him out was called Bird Of Prey LLC. That can't be good."

"Where are you getting all this stuff?" questioned Penn.

"Digging it out of the net and public records. I got our financial boys working on the figures as we speak. I'm sure he's just barely making the interest payments with whatever he sells. Do you remember when I told you I looked at some of his units because the price was so unbelievable?"

"I remember," agreed Penn, not really sure he did.

"The building's quality was horrendous, so I got scared. There were no residents living in the project either," said Ronnie.

"We need to find out what's keeping his ship afloat financially. I have a friend who knows the guy who owns Vulture Assist Realty LLC. They specialize in marketing the last few units of the developer's inventory once the sales force is closed out by the builder. We'll go together. When he lays eyes on you, he'll open up like a broken dam," kidded Penn.

Ronnie was blushing. "FBI clothes aren't real sexy, Rand."

"Wear one size smaller."

"Uh huh. With my luck the SAC will see me and call me down."

"I'll clear it," reassured Penn.

"Are you serious?"

"Sort of. It's for me too," chided Penn.

"I'll see you tonight. Try to keep that thing in your pants until then, wild man."

"OK. Speaking of hot chicks, what about Sandrine? Where does she fit into all of this? Victim? Conspirator? Unwitting accomplice?" asked Penn

Ronnie looked through her notes, struggling to give Penn a good answer. Sandrine had been harder to check because of her low profile. Nothing on the net and nothing in the public records except her home on the tax rolls.

"I don't know much about her except that she lives in one of Anderson's condos. Looks as if she got a good price on it, too. At this point I would have to say you're half right. Victim for sure, but unwitting with no accomplice tied to it. I think she has wedged herself into an uncomfortable corner. Having never met her, I drew some of my conclusions on your report about the meeting you had with her. Our tails tell me she has not seen Secur since her sister's death."

"Yeah, I tend to agree with that assessment; every word of it. By the way, who's tailing her?" asked Penn.

"Melnick is on her. Let's concentrate on Secur and all that surrounds his world. I can't wait to hear what your Vulture company guy has to say. Those guys are always full of good intel."

Penn excused himself for a meeting with the special agent in charge (SAC), Jim Thorne, as Ronnie Feldman continued to work on her investigation outline.

CHAPTER THIRTEEN

Alicia Secur was a stunning Italian American woman. Fifty-two years old, slender, and shapely, she could be mistaken—and often was—for a woman a dozen years younger. She was the first in her family lineage to be born in America to immigrant parents from Florence, Italy. Her parents had settled in Brooklyn, in an area known as Flatbush. In the early days, it was populated by Jews and Italians, but it later gave way to mostly island immigrants from Jamaica, Haiti, St. Lucia, and African Americans. Her parents moved to Little Italy on the island of Manhattan in the early seventies, when she was only six years old. Her official reason for leaving Alain Secur at home in Miami was to visit her mother, now ninety-one years old and living with Alicia's older brother in Queens. That is what she told Secur.

But the real reason was a secret meeting with Luciano LoPrendo, Biagio's uncle. Luciano, known as Luc, was in charge of legitimate and not-so-legitimate family businesses. He was not involved with the New York and New Jersey Teamsters, as his son was. In truth he had no interest in speculative real estate like condominiums and other to-be-built spec buildings. He only owned buildings that were sure winners. Many he bought as half empty still produced enough income to pay the bills. He had no financing on any buildings, having paid off the mortgages years ago. He considered his nephew to be a careless real estate professional and a horrible lender's representative. Alicia had become his eyes and ears over the past four years, ever since real estate values in South Florida and everywhere else began to plummet. This downturn and Secur's inept handling of the situation made his small investment and those of his friends worth less than the A & D loans used to construct the empty monoliths, meaning his condos were worth less than the loans—far less. Her husband Alain was oblivious to the close ties enjoyed between his wife and his friend's powerful uncle.

Secur's ever more public affection for Sandrine and the indiscretions he barely hid from Alicia had pushed her over the edge. She showed no sign to Secur that she knew, but it was difficult to share her bed with her whoring husband while keeping up the guise of a faithful, old-world Italian wife. She considered her alliance with Luc self-preservation mixed in with a bit of revenge. As things had progressed ever more badly for Secur, it looked like the right move for her. Today's meeting was called rather quickly as the murder of Sonya Michel had reached Luc LoPrendo. Alicia entered Luc's office in south Manhattan prepared to give him the latest update on her husband's failing empire.

"Alicia, how wonderful to see you. I trust your ride on the commercial jet was not too unnerving," Luc offered.

"Of course, Luc. First class is always fine for me. I don't expect you to send the company jet every time, especially now," Alicia remarked. She was smarter than Secur would ever know. She had grown up with wily businessmen as family members afraid of nothing, including killing off the competition or a delinquent deadbeat. She had patiently bided her time watching her husband's greed, ego, and lust grow out of control. The moment had arrived for her to get even, and Luc LoPrendo was happy to assist. Luc was feeling heat from his friends in the Teamsters to do something about their losses with Secur. He had warned them against lending on speculative projects far from home. He chastised them for not having the best loan documents or basic pre-sale requirements as standards for their loans. Yet, despite his warnings, they had eagerly jumped into the hot Miami condo explosion; now it was about to fizzle. They all now sought his help, but for them, full financial recovery was out of the question.

"I must say I admire your willingness to help us find a solution to this mess. I see that Alain's lover Sandrine lost her sister this past week, presumably to something Biagio and Secur did not want her to know," confessed Luc.

The remark stung Alicia, but she had dealt with the *"other woman syndrome"* for so long, she let it go.

"Alain still does confide in me, but on this one he never mentioned a thing. He still believes I know nothing. I think it was horrible what happened to that woman," said Alicia.

"He's not going to make it, you know?"

"I know that, and everyone else does too, but he still holds out hope that all of a sudden the skies will open and thousands of buyers will fall from above, ready to buy his condos at the old prices. Can you believe that, Luc?"

"No, and I doubt he really believes that. His miracle will never happen," said Luc.

"What do you intend to do?" asked Alicia.

"I'm not sure. But I am getting serious phone calls from dangerous people who want me to intercede on their behalf to liquidate what we can, take the losses and lick our wounds, and move on. We thought that would begin happening on the recent deal with the two hedge funds, but your husband's buildings were so poorly constructed that we barely received twenty cents on the dollar when all was said and done. Now there are a couple of more vulture funds circling two of his projects looking to buy in bulk for deep discounts. My friends at the Teamsters don't want a repeat of the last sale," said Luc.

"Are they aware of the Mexicans, Luc?"

"No, and I am having trouble verifying just what their involvement is. Do you have anything else to add from before?"

"Just that they provided mezzanine loans on a couple of the towers," answered Alicia, not knowing exactly what mezzanine financing was.

"Mezz loans? Well, they can say good-bye to that money. It sounds as if they're worse underwriters than my nephew Biagio. Come to think of it, that was probably blood money based upon what they could and would do to someone who was dumb enough not to pay back the funds. Your husband must be in dire straits; not very smart either. If you are going to borrow money from Teamsters and Mexicans, you better damn sure have a plan to pay it back, with interest. Lord have mercy on your husband," said Luc with a disgusted look on his face.

"That bad, huh, Luc?" answered Alicia.

"Afraid so, dear. But let's talk about your future," said Luc with a solemn look on his face. "First you will lose all your assets once this house of cards crumbles, so be prepared. Cars, boats, most of the proceeds from the sale of your home, jewelry, paintings, and your vacation home will all be liquidated to pay the outstanding debt. Any uninsured jewelry you own that is not of some record move to a safety deposit box under my name; I will help with that, and you shall have the keys. The insured jewelry is of record, and your creditors will press you hard for its surrender. Don't get cute; give it up. Start building a cash reserve, but be careful. Tracing cash is easier today. Take sums under $3,000 at a time. Put that in a bank box at another bank. Find a friend to rent the box for you, but you keep the keys. Do not try to shift marital assets out of your joint name into yours; it's already too late for that. That's called a fraudulent transfer, and you can get in trouble if you try. I will be down in two weeks on some R and R, and we will go over this again. About ten days into my vacation, you will get another call from your brother about your mom: get up here right away; it's important; she needs you—that kind of thing. You will come back with me on the company jet. Not long after that, things will probably turn bad for Alain. I cannot have you there if the Mexicans want their money. You'll be kidnapped for the money or murdered as retribution. I promised your father I would look after you when he died, and I intend to do so. Any questions?" said Luc.

Alicia was shaken. Luc was direct as always, which meant he knew what he was talking about—which scared her even more. She gazed at the rich wooden floors, losing herself in the safety of the beautiful wood grains.

"Alicia, Alicia, are you all right?" questioned Luc, startling her.

"Yes. Luc, is it safe for me to go back now?"

"Certainly, my dear. I have some men already there watching over things, and watching over your husband. They have been instructed to watch over you as well when you return. I have my man's name and cell phone for you, just in case he is not at the airport to meet you. Stay close to him at all times. I know the temptation may be to question Alain's protectors about his whereabouts with a certain woman, but please do not do that. He has been instructed to keep his distance and avoid contact with you at all times. Clear on this?"

"Yes, absolutely. My father would be very proud of the great lengths you have gone to protect me. I do have one more question, maybe two. Who else besides the Teamsters and the Mexicans loaned money to my husband?"

"The Teamsters are big boys, and in the end, they will not be a problem. Their pension has suffered losses before—risks of the business. The Mexicans, especially if it is drug or conflict money, will want to set an example if they are stiffed. I am certain Alain knows this and will prioritize all monies to them; I would if I were him. Myself? I have less than $200 thousand of family money in his projects; most of it is Biagio's money. But against all my wishes and attempts, Biagio managed to talk about a dozen tough Italians, if you know what I mean, into investing millions of dollars of their money in these projects. I have no control over them, but they are pressuring me to assist in the return of their capital. Each of those men invested in spite of my personal plea not to. The addiction of this last real estate cycle was worse that heroin. Had I recommended those investments to them, I would probably not be here today," said Luc as Alicia felt herself drawn into the personal horror story that was now part of her life.

"May I say that it has not been wonderful seeing you this time," chuckled Alicia, using humor to cover her fright. "I am grateful to have you as a friend. Thank you so much, Luc."

Alicia left Luc's office and was driven to her brother's home in Queens. The trip to her brother's seemed like an instant in time. All the way there, her thoughts replayed the entire conversation with Luc. She could not get the meeting out of her head. By the time she reached her destination, she was no longer afraid. She had resigned herself to a life without Alain in the very near future. Self-preservation and planning now occupied her ambitions.

CHAPTER FOURTEEN

Penn and Ronnie were enjoying a mid-morning bagel and coffee at their FBI offices. It was the third straight morning Penn had followed her to work after staying over the previous night at her townhouse. It did not go unnoticed at the office. Just married screen savers were posted on Ronnie and Penn's computers on behalf of the FBI Cyber Group. Heart-shaped cookies were in the break room, and a bride-and-groom plastic cake statue resided on a small cake beside the cookies. The FBI lovebirds were used to the symbolic sarcasm. They could give it right back as well. Ronnie called everyone to the break room. She was standing next to Penn. Once everyone arrived she promptly shoved a large piece of cake into Penn's mouth, getting most on his face. She smiled sarcastically at everyone in attendance without saying a word and walked through the surprised crowd to her office. Penn stayed behind to clean up.

The crowd stayed behind, kidding Penn relentlessly before dispersing. Soon thereafter the office returned to FBI decorum. Penn went to Ronnie's office to see if everything was all right.

"You OK, honey?" he asked gingerly.

"Not really. I may seem like this tough little Jewish girl from Texas, but it gets a little old with the Cupid stuff. Let's just move in together and make it what it is. You rent, I own, so it's easier for you to come to my place. OK?"

"Whoa, baby doll. Let's slow down. It's not that you're not right; I've thought about it, but let's discuss this when we are both less emotional. I think we're ready, but let's do this away from here," reasoned Penn.

She wrapped her arms around Penn's neck and gave him a short peck on the cheek when a strange voice startled them both.

"Would you two get a room?" said SAC James Thorne, their boss.

Penn and Ronnie spun their heads so fast they bumped each other in the temple.

"Ouch, that had to hurt," observed Thorne, unable to control his smirk. He continued, "Come to my office immediately, please."

Within two minutes Penn and Ronnie were sitting in Thorne's office after he had motioned them each to a chair. Thorne had joined the FBI's New York office right out of Columbia Law School. He could have his pick of any assignment he wanted in reward for his thirty years of service. Rather than retire he had himself assigned to Miami five years ago for the weather, the fishing, and the international intrigue. He was still in great shape, tanned, and good looking, resembling movie star James Brolin. His wife and he were empty nesters, with older children living in various cities around the states. Thorne and his wife dined at the best restaurants, attended charity functions, traveled, and relaxed at the beach whenever possible. He was silently reading a single sheet of paper, and when finished, he peered over the page at the two of them.

"Your buddy Reg over at DEA just sent this to me. Remember those suspected Mexican cartel members smuggling drugs in the Cay Sol Bank area? They are no longer suspected smugglers and are a man or two short right now," said Thorne.

Penn and Ronnie looked at each other and sighed a breath of relief, seeing that their office affections were not the reason for Thorne's invitation. Thorne was surprised Penn and Ronnie had not heard.

"Seems your friend sent this interoffice memo to me for distribution rather than to you, Penn. Your boy's following the regs just fine. I would have thought he would've at least called you," said Thorne.

"What's in the mystery letter, sir?" requested Penn in formal terms. He was not surprised that his old assistant was by the book; that's how Penn had taught him to be.

"Apparently, their second attempt at a bust was tipped off by someone minutes before they arrived at the drop. One of the Mexican runners took off from the mother ship with a full load of dust thinking he could outrun the supersonic bullets of the Coast Guard guns. Dumb sonofabitch. The Coasties blasted his transom with their deck gun, and the idiots, now dead in the water with no power, opened fire on our boys. In a search of what was left of the Mexican shooters, they found a piece of paper with the name of Alain Secur on it and the address of his home and office in his pants pocket," said Thorne, shaking his head.

"I don't suppose this idiot had any ID on him?" asked Ronnie.

"No, of course not. However, his mates in the boat were so afraid after seeing the effects of the high-caliber gun impacting the chest of one of their men that it didn't take much to get them talking."

Penn began to chuckle.

"What's so funny about that, Rand?"

"I've seen Reg interrogate suspects. It makes me uncomfortable watching the poor perps squirm—he gets some of them crying. I'd shit information too, sir," said Penn.

"Anyway, one of the Mexican grunts said this guy, or what was left of him, was an assassin looking for Secur because he wasn't paying back his loans to the cartel. According to the grunt, he was just along for the ride that night when the DEA raid occurred, and that's why he decided to try to outrun the Coasties and Gambrel's boats," said Thorne.

"Does this guy Secur have a death wish? What's he doing borrowing money from these kinds of people?" asked Ronnie in disbelief.

"Ronnie, how many times have we asked that same question about other bad guys whose careers we've put to an end?" asked Thorne.

"Point taken, sir," she said.

"What can you tell me about your progress on the Sonya Michel murder and all that goes with it?" inquired Thorne.

"We have an appointment to interview Sandrine Michel today. We're meeting her informally at a coffee shop in Bayside," said Ronnie.

"I was practically mugged by Madam X in the parking lot last evening. Our little hooker snitch informant had some interesting info for me regarding the troops we're now investigating," revealed Penn.

"Yeah, she loves my boy here because they used to date," kidded Ronnie.

Thorne smiled broadly, watching a red-faced Penn give his girlfriend a dirty look.

"She was damn good, too, babe," said Penn, which immediately quieted Ronnie. "She told me that she had heard that Secur was in trouble with the Teamsters from New York, and he was getting ready to sell his house and other expensive toys—or else."

"Penn, please tell me what all this has to do with Sonya Michel. Is Secur a suspect? I read your report. It said he had an ironclad alibi within the range of time she was murdered. What's this got to do with anything?" pressed Thorne.

"We have a theory that someone inside the Secur organization wanted Sonya dead before she could tell someone what she knew. And that this information would be detrimental to his company or to him," contributed Ronnie.

"So you're saying Secur might be involved after all? Let me understand something. He's already nearly bankrupt, he cheats on his wife and she knows it, he's borrowed money from violent groups of people, and he has to sell all of his assets. Is that right?" asked Thorne.

"That's correct, sir," said Penn.

"Explain to me this. What else can possibly hurt this guy? And why murder someone for more bad news that probably isn't going to matter anyway?" asked Thorne.

"Just this, sir. He has three or four real estate hedge funds chasing him right now wanting to liquidate nearly all 1200 units he has left in his four remaining towers at discounted prices. He believes this will get him back enough capital to settle with his creditors, step back, downsize, and await better times," said Penn.

"I have our accountants working the numbers sir," added Ronnie.

"OK, I'll give you a little more time to pull this together, but don't turn this into one of your old DEA capers. You're FBI now, Penn, and this is about an American citizen murdered in International waters. Leave that other crap to Reg. Understood?" said Thorne.

"Yes sir, I understand," said Penn as he and Ronnie rose from their seats to leave.

"And for God's sake, stop French kissing her in this building."

The two left blushing and smiling as they returned to Penn's office. They had a busy day ahead of them. They were due to meet Sandrine at noon in Bayside and had an appointment with Miami's top condo broker in the late afternoon. Thinking back, Thorne had made a fair point about Secur's motive to murder Sonya, thought Penn. Maybe their theory was wrong.

CHAPTER FIFTEEN

Miami Condo Vultures LLC was part of a new cottage industry spawned by an overbuilt real estate industry that left in its wake thousands of unoccupied condominium units from Miami to Las Vegas and even parts of California. Marty Burns was at the right place at the right time. He was a cocky young brat broker who started his selling career at the age of twenty eight in Miami just at the beginning of the condominium-building boom. Times could not have been better for him then. With everyone from janitors to housewives owning three to four condominium contracts that were sure to be flipped before closing to the next sucker, Marty had a loaded gun full of sellers and buyers. His first year in the business, he made $500 thousand in commission revenue without breaking a sweat. The following year he hired several good-looking women, most of whom had just acquired their real estate licenses. By year two he had a harem of aggressive, good-looking young women sucking deposit checks out of married and single guys whose hormones completely blocked all common sense. That year he raked in $1.6 million in commission dollars and formed his own firm called Condo Magic Realtors LLC. By his third year, he had hired several very smart and extremely attractive gay men to round out his roster. They proved no match for mothers and single women. They also brought in the wealthy gay crowd from Miami and Fort Lauderdale. The third year saw twenty-four associates bringing to Marty

Burns $2.9 million in sales commissions. His personal record was flipping one penthouse in a Kyle Anderson project on Biscayne Bay four times in eighteen months, an exception to the rule even during those times. He, like everyone else, thought the market would never end. Then came year four.

It was obvious by the spring of 2006 the market had tanked. In fact, looking back, the statistical end came officially in July 2005. But summers were traditionally slow, and even though 2005 was much slower than the previous three years, denial had taken hold. People were sure that the Thanksgiving bump would occur as usual, leading to an early successful season for 2006. A late November hurricane swept across the Gulf and destroyed any Thanksgiving optimism as tourists and snowbirds stayed away. By March of 2006, nothing was happening when it should have been. A majority of Marty's sales flaked out before closings, flips were not occurring, and people were walking from their deposits. Some developers had sold 90 percent of their buildings to investors who were hoping to flip their units before closing. The pool of suckers had run dry. Banks got skittish, and pending projects with pre-sales were stopped. Within months it was obvious that the meltdown had begun. Fort Lauderdale, Tampa, Las Vegas, and parts of California experienced the same pain. Marty scrambled to make sales, and when he did, very few ever closed. He cut his staff and began three solid months of doing nothing but collecting data on as many distressed condo projects as he could find. He became an overnight expert in vulture sales. He knew that 25,000 empty units in the greater Miami metropolitan area spelled a long and frustrating wait for the thousands of investors who did close hoping to rent their units waiting for the storm to pass. The sensible investors took their hit and sold at discounted prices to whoever came along. Armed with statistics and a confidence that markets would be depressed for some time, he persuaded condo owners wanting out that it would be a long, painful recovery. Nearly half scoffed at him the first year after the meltdown, claiming he was wrong. The market had never missed two years, and they could wait it out, or at least so they thought.

The following year, with the market still in free fall, only 35 percent scoffed at Marty. By year's end, Marty finally changed Condo Magic Realtors LLC into Miami Condo Vultures LLC. The name was risky but effective. In the fourth year after the plunge, only 10 percent failed to agree with Marty that this was a lengthy market depression. That year 90 percent of the people Marty pitched for listings at vulture pricing agreed with him and listed at unbelievably low prices; they persuaded their friends to list with Marty, too. From that point on, he never needed to go on listing appointments as investors and desperate sellers flocked to his offices. If sellers wanted too high a price, he turned them away. Gone was the staff of trophy girls and young, good-looking gay men from the go-go days. He kept a couple of trophy girls who had weathered the storm and several hard-working, successful gay men. His nucleus of six people relied on splashy Internet ads, Twitter followers, bloggers, and a phenomenal website showcasing thousands of available units. He was making almost as much money as before, with less work, easier sales, and lower overhead. When interested prospects showed up at his office, 85 percent of the time he converted them into buyers. Suddenly everyone was looking for a cheap deal. Marty, now thirty-six, was more polished and mature and less cocky. He had aged a lifetime in just six years and was now a respected condominium expert. Hedge funds, newspaper reporters, other brokers, and banks sought his advice.

"Good afternoon, Marty. Thanks for seeing us on such short notice," said Penn, meeting Burns at his downtown office.

"Soldiers, veterans, and law enforcement folks always get my undivided attention," said Marty. Penn already liked the guy.

"May I introduce my partner, Ronnie Feldman," said Penn.

"Ah, yes, we spoke on the phone briefly," remembered Marty. Ronnie had set up the appointment.

"We would like you to keep our discussions confidential if you could. I think you will see why," said Penn. Marty agreed with a nod.

"We are working on a case that requires background on two developers. They are not accused of any crime and are not people of interest now, but their experiences in the market may lead us to the real suspects," said Ronnie, trying not to sound too clandestine. Fortunately Marty was enamored by her good looks and frontal curves, hearing only about half of what she said and nodding yes just the same.

"Anything I can do to help. Who might these two developers be?" asked Marty bluntly.

"Kyle Anderson and Alain Secur," said Ronnie. Penn was noticing Marty's engaging nature and decided to let Ronnie call the shots. They were an interchangeable duo, so it didn't matter who asked the questions.

"How interesting, number one and number two. Today I'm not sure who is which," answered Marty, somewhat surprised.

"What can you tell us about Anderson?" asked Ronnie as Penn took notes as today's scribe.

"Very solid, good reputation, conservative, works well with brokers, and builds a quality product."

"Where does he rank in your mind?" asked Ronnie.

"He used to be number two, but I'd have to say now he is the class of a very small, successful field."

"What makes him number one now?" she asked.

"It's a little like the tortoise and the hare. He is very methodical in everything he does. He only allows 10 percent of his building to be sold to investors. He takes a 35 percent deposit, not 10 percent or even 20 percent, as Fanny Mae requires. I have never seen him start a building until it is 65 percent sold, often 70 percent. He invests his own money and has very few partners. None of his buildings are in trouble, and most have been turned over to the Home Owners Association. All of his HOAs are financially sound. I don't think I have ever heard of an HOA suing him at the point where they take over. That's incredible itself," said Marty.

"Does he sell at a discount?" asked Ronnie.

"Oh lord, everyone in this market has had to discount, Anderson included. But here's the difference and another reason he's tops. Because of everything I just said, his units are the first to sell and the easiest to sell. I have people now calling specifically asking for Kyle Anderson buildings. Most important to me, his organization has never stiffed me on a commission," said Marty.

Penn finished his writing and nodded to Ronnie. She took the pen and pad, deferring to Penn as he began his questions. Marty saw the switch and was slightly disappointed

"The obvious question is, what about Alain Secur, in your opinion?" posed Penn.

"Like Kyle, we're business friends too. Unfortunately he is in free fall right now," said Marty.

"Meaning exactly what?"

"He's the rabbit of the two. While Kyle is deliberate and conservative and uses his own money for equity, Secur is just the opposite. In 2003, 2004, and part of 05, Secur was leveraging himself into thousands of new units with many different partners. Some of his partners are not the nicest people, either. He would take any deal on one of his condos with very little money down. Some of his buildings had nearly all investors as buyers. Many of those investors signed cash contracts with no financing contingencies because they could never qualify for a loan anyway—no staying power. They all thought they would flip the unit before the buildings were finished. He's got two or three buildings right now that are totally empty— every single person who contracted to buy has walked from the deposit," said Marty as he reluctantly criticized his friend.

"I can see this is bothersome—he's your friend after all. It would bother me too, but this information is for our internal use and only a handful of people will see this report, certainly not Alain or Anderson, for that matter. Why don't you tell us what worries you as his friend instead of me trying to pinpoint the right question. Take your time," said Penn as Marty noticed the admiring look on Ronnie's face while she stared at Penn for a brief moment. He saw the love in her eyes. Marty took a drink of water and prepared himself for Penn's question.

"The rumor on the street is that Secur's lenders, Teamsters from New Jersey and New York, are pissed at Secur and want him to bulk sale his remaining units, pay them what he can, and move on. I understand that Glisten and Claughton Tower are next to go if the new bulk buyers are satisfied with their due diligence. That is not a given, by the way, since his last bulk sale went badly due to quality and code issues," said Marty.

"What does badly mean exactly?" asked Penn.

"He contracted to sell in bulk at one price, but the quality was so bad and the code violations so severe that the bulk buyers re-traded the price way down just before the closing," said Marty.

"Re-traded?"

"They forced him to discount the agreed-upon price because the build-ing was misrepresented. They could have walked, but Secur agreed to their aggressive pricing because he was desperate to get the cash," answered Marty.

"What can you tell me about the buyers?" asked Penn.

"Typical vulture funds. They are set up with investors for the sole pur-pose of acquiring distressed real estate, in this case condominiums," said Marty, pausing for a moment and then continuing. "Here's what I find odd, Mr. Penn. The discounted price was too low in my book. Weeks before his big sale, Secur and his banker, a gentleman named Biagio LoPrendo, approached me to list all his empty units. The banker seemed very satis-fied with what I told him about pricing. In time I could have gotten about 25 percent more than he did in bulk. But a week after they were here, Secur called and told me he had a bulk buyer; I wished him luck. Yesterday he called me and asked if I would list his mansion on Star Island..." said Marty, ending abruptly. *Had he volunteered too much?* he wondered. *What kind of trouble is Secur in?*

Penn noticed that Marty had stopped talking. He knew what had hap-pened. Penn diagnosed the guilt right away. "It's OK, Marty. Your friend is not in any immediate trouble with us. As I said, he's a perimeter person with some issues. Issues we plan to discuss with him very soon."

"I know how that goes, Mr. Penn. Do you have anything else for me?" asked Marty

"Yes. Are you going to list his house? And why do you suspect he is selling at this moment?"

"I don't do well with big mansions. We're not geared for it, and I would do him a disservice by taking his home as a listing. Don't get me wrong; someone is going to make a lot of money selling that home. Priced right, it will go quickly."

"Apparently he needs the money," said Penn, stating the obvious.

"He does. That's why I recommended Skip Johnston over at Christie's in Miami Beach. For the record, Penn, all major developers, with few excep-tions, have had to sell their homes, boats, and cars to stay afloat in this bastard of a market."

"Have you ever met a woman by the name of Sonya Michel, Mr. Burns?" asked Penn.

"You mean Sandrine Michel of Anderson Development?"

"No, her sister Sonya."

"No, but if she looks anything like Sandrine, I sure would like to. Is she in any kind of trouble?" said Marty.

"Unfortunately she was murdered several days ago. We are looking for a reason why she was killed and what she might have known," Penn said. He watched Marty closely, and so did Ronnie. *Could this guy be involved?* he wondered.

"That's awful. Sandrine is a wonderful person. I assume her sister is cut from the same cloth," said Marty, shaking his head and looking at the floor. Then he quickly looked Penn in the eye with a fearful look. "Is Sandrine at risk?" he asked.

"We don't believe so," assured Penn. They finished their interview and left their cards. They thanked him for his time and left. Within minutes of their departure, Marty reached out for Secur on his cell phone. The number had been disconnected.

CHAPTER SIXTEEN

Penn and Ronnie were driving south to meet Sandrine. Once they were on the road leaving Marty Burns's office, Ronnie gently reached over and stroked Penn's upper thigh. He gave her a funny look as if to say, *What, right now?* She read his mind and spoke. "My place is nearby. You got time for a quick one?"

"Jesus, Ronnie, do your hormones ever rest?"

"Not when I'm around you, big guy," she kidded, mocking Penn.

Penn had been thinking about discussing Burns's interview, but her touch had distracted him.

"Seriously, honey, can we talk some business?"

"OK, you win, stud."

Penn laughed. This woman had so much energy and wit. He could never be mad at her; besides, he loved her dearly.

"Thank you, dear. What was your impression of Marty Burns?" Penn asked.

"I think he is forthright and sincere. I also think he has nothing whatsoever to do with Sonya's death. I also believe he is very concerned about his friend Secur and may not have given us all he had," she said.

"I didn't see it that way. His eyes told another story. I think he bears watching," reflected Penn.

"I was taking notes, but you could see his soul. I'll defer to your good judgment." Just then Ronnie felt an urge. "Penn, turn in to that Wendy's; I gotta pee. Would you like a Diet Coke?"

"Sure."

Ten minutes after stopping at Wendy's, they pulled into a Cuban coffee shop near Brickell Avenue just down the street from Secur's project called Glisten. Ronnie had set the meeting hoping a neutral site would make Sandrine more comfortable. When they arrived Sandrine was seated in an end booth. She had a forlorn look on her face, her cheeks were drawn, and she looked uncharacteristically disheveled. Ronnie whispered to Penn what she observed as he nodded agreement—both noticed her demeanor. Ronnie stepped ahead of Penn and greeted Sandrine first.

"Hello, Sandrine. Sorry we had to do this so late in the day," said Ronnie in a soft, reassuring voice.

She half smiled, nodded to Penn, and said nothing as both agents sat across from her. The shop was not busy, and they were away from those few patrons in attendance. Good ambience for a confidential interview.

Penn began. "Sandrine, you look tired. Would you rather we do this another time?"

"No, I'm fine," said Sandrine so softly that Penn and Ronnie could barely hear her. For this discussion Penn would be the scribe, and Ronnie would conduct the interview.

"I have been staying at my apartment down the street most of the day, just sitting around mourning my sister's death. It's tough when you are alone. Two people are out of my life, one by violence and another by my choice," she said in a low, steady, conversational tone. It was evident to both Penn and Ronnie that she was emotionally unsettled.

"Have you been by to see our people and share some of your grief with our trained professionals?" asked Ronnie, bending down to look Sandrine in the eye.

"No. Truthfully I forgot until you just reminded me. I thought I could do this alone, but I'm not sure anymore," she said with a fatalistic edge in her voice. Ronnie looked over at Penn for any ideas. He had none.

"Why don't we call it a day, get you some help, and do this when you are more at ease and less stressed?" Ronnie said.

Sandrine raised her eyes level with Ronnie. "No. I need to do this. I cannot let my sister die in vain," she said in a firm tone.

Ronnie yielded. "All right, then, let's go at your pace. Stop me at any time. You said you lost two people. I presume you are no longer in touch with Alain Secur. Is that right?"

"Yes. I have left him—for good."

"Has he tried to contact you?"

"At first, he tried. The last time I saw him was after the meeting with Mr. Penn at the morgue. He called several times. At first I spoke with him, but later I stop answering his calls. He has not called in days. I miss him, but my conscience won't let me see him."

"Your conscience?"

"Yes. I feel so dirty now. Kyle Anderson has been so wonderful through all of this. I betrayed him for a married man whose business decline in some way, and I don't know how, contributed to Sonya's death. I just know it," said Sandrine.

Again Ronnie glanced at Penn—no response. She decided not to pursue Sandrine's suspicions right away. She did not want to lose her. Despite Ronnie's forensic skills, she was considered one of the FBI's best interviewers. She massaged her conversations, never letting her interviewee feel trapped or guarded.

"Are you able to work much at Anderson Development?" asked Ronnie. A simple, innocuous question requiring minimal thought.

"Not really. I feel guilty working there after spying on Kyle. He is such a smart developer to get through this. How did I make such bad choices?"

"Love does that sometimes. But you now realize what you have done. You can still make it right," said Ronnie. She could see her questions were helping Sandrine cleanse her guilt one word at a time.

"You're kind and smart, Ronnie. Some guy will be lucky to have you," said Sandrine, oblivious to Ronnie's relationship with Penn.

Ronnie thought twice but did not say anything about Penn—*this is not the right time*, she thought.

"Well, thank you. Someone as beautiful as you must know what she is talking about," said Ronnie, surprised to see Sandrine stand and walk out.

She was not leaving; she came across the booth and hugged Ronnie, sobbing on her shoulder. Ronnie returned the hug. A minute later she put a hand on each side of Ronnie's face and kissed her gently on the forehead. Sandrine returned to her bench.

"Sandrine, let's try some more questions. If you let me, I think it will help you release some things bottled up inside you," said Ronnie.

"I agree. Fire away."

Ronnie fumbled through her notes to let the moment settle in. Then she began. "So you have guilty feelings about Kyle and loving feelings for Secur, and you are grieving for your sister. Can you see how this might create the state of mind you are in?" she said, not letting Sandrine answer as she continued. "Any person sitting in this booth would feel just as you do."

"I suppose you're right, Ronnie."

"You mentioned you felt Secur may have had something to do with Sonya's death. How so?"

"Oh, just a hunch. Certainly he did not have a direct, purposeful involvement. I know Alain too well, but lately he has been around some people who look as if they could kill someone in an instant if you said the wrong thing. Sometimes I was scared," she said, awaiting Ronnie's next question.

"What kind of people?"

"People whom his lender representative, Biagio LoPrendo, brought to some of the dinner meetings we were at. They were New York types who looked like mobsters. Then of late, dark, sinister-looking Mexicans with heavy accents, unshaven and unsophisticated. I left one meeting because they kept staring at my breasts—you know how women know that look?" said Sandrine as Ronnie returned her nod.

Ronnie saw Sandrine looking and feeling much better—*a fighter*, she thought. "From what you are saying, it appears that everyone who loaned money to Secur is now looking for their money, and there may not be enough to go around. Is that a fair statement?" asked Ronnie.

"There is no question that this is now happening. I think Alain has inadvertently started his own Ponzi scheme among his lenders and his investors. I heard this morning from one of my sources that he is selling his house, his boats, his jet, and even some of his prized artwork. A sure sign that the end is near—figuratively speaking," she said, smiling for the first time.

"With all of this going on, how did your sister come into harm's way? Do you have any idea?" asked Ronnie, posing the questions she needed but could not until now—Sandrine was ready.

"She was dating Biagio, Alain's friend and the lender representing the Teamsters," said Sandrine in a normal, steady, confident voice.

Ronnie would press harder. *This lead could have legs*, she thought. "How long had they been seeing each other?"

"Just about eight months."

"I presume you and your sister doubled with Secur and Biagio a number of times?"

"Yes, on a few occasions."

"What were they like around you and Secur?"

"My sister loves a good time, and so did Biagio. He was always nice to her. But I had that woman's intuition that there was a dark side to him back in New York. I never confirmed it, and it could be me trying to protect my sister."

"That's normal and admirable," said Ronnie noticing that Sandrine spoke of her sister in the present tense. She could feel her grief. "Let me pose something to you. You're a professional in the business, and you know how it works. We have heard that Secur is like a riverboat gambler. He's all in or not in at all," Ronnie said and paused.

"Go on. I'm listening."

"Secur gets his buddies to buy units to meet his pre-sales. And maybe he doesn't tell his lenders they are bogus pre-sales. Now he gets Biagio, and because he's Secur's friend he knows they're bogus too, but he goes out to get the Teamsters to make the loans anyway because he doesn't see that the market is about to crumble. Secur succeeds with the first few deals and pays everyone back their money plus interest. A trusting relationship begins, but so does Secur's greed. He pulls the same stunt on his next building, but instead of one building, he convinces his lenders, now lathered in success, to come up with money for two or three projects. Each of these new projects has artificial buyers counting toward his pre-sale requirement, or maybe by this time his investors think he is God and give him the money with fewer pre-sales than before so they can start the buildings right away. Now the market tanks, the pre-sales walk, sales become nonexistent, and Secur has several see-through buildings with no homeowners. The interest clock is ticking, so Secur needs fresh blood in the way of new capital. No one in New York will lend him any more money because they cannot see a way out. He becomes desperate and seeks money from the drug cartel, loan sharks, or other high-interest, illegal money guys. After all, they are the only source left, and they know he'll pay or he and all his relatives will have a very bad day. Then, during all this, your sister learns something she shouldn't—and that is why she is removed," said Ronnie as Sandrine stared in disbelief.

"How do you know so much about my business?" she said.

"I am in forensics; we have consultants and a network that has access to every endeavor one can dream up. If someone is doing it, we'll learn it. This is what we do." Ronnie said with pride.

"I am afraid I reached the same conclusions, probably that day in the parking lot when I was with Secur at the morgue with Mr. Penn," she said. "It is the only possible solution. But what did she know?"

"Sandrine, let's call it a day. I want to call our people at EAP and have them talk with you so you can get well quicker and get on with your life. Let Mr. Penn and me noodle over this information and get back to you in a few days. I'll treat you to lunch, and we'll tie up any follow-up questions I have at that time. Can we do that?" requested Ronnie.

"Sure. It would be my pleasure. You have helped today more than you will know," said Sandrine.

Penn and Ronnie bid Sandrine good night and headed for Ronnie's townhome for take-out, sex, and vegetative TV. This had been a busy but fruitful day as their puzzle began to show possibilities. Tonight not a word about this case would be reviewed between them. They were exhausted.

CHAPTER SEVENTEEN

Biagio LoPrendo was in Fort Lauderdale having dinner at an exclusive beachside restaurant. Sitting across from him was his Samoan bodyguard, Moto Seanu. They were situated in a private room generally reserved for large parties. The room was full of expensive wines racked along the back wall, providing an expensive and attractive backdrop to patrons peering through the sectioned, glass double French doors. He had paid for the room for the whole night, but the wine and gourmet dinners would be extra.

"I don't feel safe here anymore," started Moto. Biagio sipped a wine as he listened.

"It's partly your fault; you completely blew the burial at sea. And since it floated into international waters, the feds are now on the case," said Biagio.

"Bullshit. You need to keep your fucking mouth shut when you're fucking your woman. What were you thinking?" answered Moto, slightly raising his voice and becoming animated. Fortunately the room was closed off, so no one could hear.

"Yeah, I screwed up. I couldn't let her warn her sister, though," said Biagio. He knew he had screwed up. Moto had terminated Sonya's life on his orders. Biagio had actually cared for her deeply, but his own well-being was hanging in the balance as one bad decision after another manifested itself upon the inept financier. It was he who had recommended Secur as a worthy investment risk for the Teamsters and a few unwanted friends of his uncle. The pressure to perform was weighing heavily on him. Biagio was actually more pressured than Secur. It was as if the recession gave Secur an honest excuse for failure, but the same forgiveness toward Biagio was not extended.

"My Uncle Luc is coming down in a few days, and I have no answers for him. His friends are not nice—they hate to lose money," whined Biagio.

"I have my own problems, and I cannot get involved. You asked me to do a job, and you paid me well. I thank you, but I am out of here in the morning," said Moto.

"Where will you go?" asked a surprised Biagio, feeling now more than ever he needed Moto for protection.

"I cannot tell you, brother. I'm a person of interest, but no one knows my name. Let's just say I want to keep it that way."

"What am I going to do? I need protection. You're my friend," pleaded Biagio.

"I know it sucks, my friend, but I'm not going to jail for you. When this cools off, I'll reach out for you." With that Moto disappeared into the busy crowd walking along A-1-A.

Biagio sat in disbelief, alone in the wine room, staring out into the crowded restaurant as his friend disappeared. He tried to think positive, but if these next two vulture sales did not succeed, his safety would be in doubt. *I probably have seen Moto for the last time*, he thought.

Kyle Anderson was in his office working late. The past two weeks, he had engaged a private detective to follow Sandrine and report to him her every move. He knew he could trust PI Jack Sanders because he was his cousin. Jack was over six feet five inches tall with receding blond hair and the typical PI paunch just above his belt. Kyle had given him the elevator fob to his penthouse offices so he could make these late-night meetings after Sandrine and the regular employees had left. He was sitting in a chair that made him look even bigger than he was, directly across from Kyle, who was finishing up an international phone call to Buenos Aires. Kyle spoke jobsite Spanish, but his greetings and good-byes sounded great.

"Hey, Cuz, how's it going? So our little turncoat has been quiet and loyal the last two weeks, huh?" said Kyle.

"As I told you before on the phone, very little activity of any interest to Anderson Development LLC has occurred. She has stayed close to her apartment, met with the FBI crew a few days ago, and has come here to work occasionally," said Jack.

"She seems to get stronger every day. She's doing a wonderful job with our Latin markets. That was Raul Cruel in Buenos Aries just now. He couldn't say enough about her energy and her follow-up," noted Kyle.

"Are you still going to let her go when she gets better? I mean the grieving thing?" asked Jack sympathetically.

"Had you asked me that question last week I would have said- absolutely. But call me a sucker for a pretty gal; I'm not so sure now. She is throwing herself into work like never before—and she was great before," said Anderson.

"You can't trust her, and I'm not going to tail her for the rest of her days here if you decide she stays," noted Jack.

"Of course you're right, Jack, but I keep thinking, or wishing, that she would come forward and give me an explanation that would partially explain her behavior, which we know is not likely to occur," said Kyle.

"Look, I can plant a GPS monitor on her car and download her whereabouts every day if you like. It will save you some bucks."

"No, don't do that. Stay with her another month as you have. I'll figure out by then what I want to do."

"Hey, how's business?" asked Jack, switching away from Sandrine.

"I can't believe what a comeback we are having. Thank God for the Latin buyers. They want to get money out of their countries and still see Miami as the place to be. It's as if we were a huge Spanish theme park flooded with visitors," said Kyle.

"I see a lot of guys with empty buildings starting to make sales. There are actually lights on at night in nearly all of the buildings that used to be dark. Secur's buildings aren't doing so well, though. What's up with that?" asked Jack.

"Good question. He's certainly not known for his quality, and his last bulk sale was downgraded pricewise for that reason. Stuff like that gets out to the public, and it taints your properties. We sure as hell let our future customers know his construction sucks. All's fair…you know?" said Kyle.

Jack lifted his huge frame from the small chair and bid his cousin farewell. He was efficient and candid, never staying beyond business when meeting in Kyle's building. He delivered his report, spoke his piece, discussed perfunctory pleasantries, and was gone. Kyle was left in thought as his private line rang. "Leaving now, honey," said Kyle to his wife.

CHAPTER EIGHTEEN

S andrine was meeting Ronnie for lunch near FBI headquarters at one of the many restaurants along NE 163rd Street, sometimes referred to as North Miami Beach Boulevard. It was a major six-lane east-west thoroughfare and easy for a tail to lose himself. Jack Sanders was several cars behind Sandrine. She was unaware of the tail. Three cars behind Jack was Ms. Feldman. Ronnie by instinct and experience had picked up Jack a few miles back. By her good fortune, she was running just behind Sandrine. Noting the tail, she phoned Sandrine's cell phone. Sandrine picked up after the third ring less than a mile from the restaurant.

"Sandrine, it's Ronnie. Listen carefully; don't react. I want you to go by the restaurant by about four blocks. Once you go by, move to the left lane gradually and make a U-turn at the light. Don't look in the mirror now or when you turn. I think someone is following you, and I just want to make sure. Just do as I say, and I will see you at the restaurant in five minutes. Good-bye." And that was it, as she left Sandrine to wonder.

Nervously, Sandrine followed Ronnie's exact instructions. She pulled over and turned around as instructed.

Jack Sanders did not take the bait, but he did go one turn up and made a U-turn ahead of Ronnie who was now following him. He would easily catch up to Sandrine's red CLK 350 Mercedes convertible—an easy target. Jack loved following red cars.

Ronnie did exactly what Jack did, noticing his car to be a white Dodge Challenger. The parade of cars was back in line, this time heading west back to the restaurant. As Sandrine pulled into the left turning lane, Ronnie eased up behind her in Penn's Black Tahoe.

Jack Sanders went by Sandrine, thinking that she had missed her turn and was now at her eventual destination. He doubled back once again and turned into the same parking lot where Sandrine was parking her car. Once in the strip mall parking lot, Sanders spotted his target but failed to notice Ronnie's Tahoe, parked three hundred feet away from Sandrine, observing him.

Ronnie watched as Sandrine walked into the restaurant. As she opened her door to join Sandrine, she carefully scanned the parking lot, picking up the white Dodge Sanders had arrived in. As he stepped from his car, Ronnie noticed the man was large and tall. She had already taken the plate number and would not make a scene with the stranger following Sandrine. It was dangerous, and she knew she would eventually find out who this person was. She spoke into her voice recorder, saving valuable information while walking to the restaurant, apparently unnoticed by Jack. When she opened the door to the restaurant, Sandrine's face was fleece white with a stunned look in her eyes. "Ronnie, what was that?" she said in fright as Ronnie quickly signaled her not to talk any further.

"Stay calm; it's no big deal. I will tell you at the table. First, stay right here. I want to call this in to Randall right away." With that, she went outside and casually called Penn on her cell phone. He answered the phone and before he could say hello, Ronnie explained in detail where they were and what had happened. She gave him the plate numbers and asked Penn to text her who it was as soon as he could. Then, without being on the phone more than two minutes, she hung up her phone to gather up Sandrine, still in shock inside. They were seated immediately at a table Ronnie requested, looking out at the white Dodge. They could not be seen from outside.

"This is crazy, Ronnie. Who would want to follow me?" Sandrine asked.

Ronnie had to play this defensively. "Sandrine, is there something you are not telling me?" asked Ronnie with a straight, confident voice.

Sandrine said nothing as the waitress took their drink order. The restaurant was one of a hundred chains sitting on a small out parcel of a main strip mall. It was surrounded by hundreds of parked cars in a sea of asphalt, a common sight along this busy highway and most of South Florida. As Sandrine sat silent, Ronnie looked outside to see who might be looking back. She glanced to the exact spot to confirm the car following Sandrine was still there—it was. A large man was sitting inside reading a newspaper. Ronnie's phone began to vibrate. Penn's text came to Ronnie's phone: *Sanders Detective Agency-owner Jack Sanders.*

"Do you know a Jack Sanders?" asked Ronnie, breaking the silence.

"Yeah, why?"

"Apparently he is the man following us. I got his plate number and sent it to Penn, and he just sent me a text telling me who that white Dodge sitting over there belongs to," said Ronnie, growing impatient with Sandrine. "Now what the hell's going on?" she said, eye to eye with Sandrine.

Sandrine hesitated; she was relieved but upset with Ronnie's sudden attitude. "Jack Sanders is Kyle Anderson's cousin. Kyle occasionally has him go to jobsites dressed as a subcontractor to spy on subs and his own superintendents to make certain that everyone is doing what they are supposed to be doing. He's scared of getting inferior work and poor job leadership. Jack once worked as a superintendent for Kyle. Damn good, I'm told. But what's with the attitude, Ronnie?" said Sandrine.

Ronnie ignored the question and asked Sandrine, "Why would he be following you?"

"I don't know. I guess Kyle is worried about me," she answered. Just then it hit her—*unless he knows.*

Ronnie watched her face carefully for clues and sensed immediately that she had just now discovered the reason why Sanders would be following her. "Why should he be worried about you? You're just Secur's girlfriend, right? And you work for his number-one competitor, whose brother-in-law or cousin is now following you," said Ronnie sarcastically.

Her sarcasm was not missed on Sandrine. The waitress arrived to take their order, and Ronnie quickly brushed her off.

Sandrine gathered her thoughts. "OK, I'm sorry. I'll tell you what I know. I think Jack is either watching to see what I do next with Secur because somehow Kyle has found out I'm a traitor, or he wants to protect me from Secur," she said, staring down at her lap.

Now Ronnie believed her. "Is that everything, Sandrine?"

"Not exactly."

"All right, then, let's get it all out on the table. You need to level with me," said Ronnie, less demanding.

"I know this is awful, but just before Sonya was killed, she texted me a message. She must have done it in the dark under stress knowing she was about to die because there were so many misspelled words," said Sandrine, her eyes beginning to tear.

"Go on. This is important for the case and for you to get this out."

"I know, Ronnie, and you and Penn have been so good to me. Why do I do this to people?"

"It's OK. This is normal. Don't you think Penn and I see this all the time? Now go ahead let it all out," said Ronnie, soothing Sandrine.

"I can only imagine her last few moments. It frightens me to think; on a boat late at night knowing you're going to die any minute. At least she figured out what she was being killed for," said Sandrine as Ronnie handed her a tissue for her tears.

"How so?" said Ronnie.

"She only sent me a few words, but I think I know what she wanted me to know. The message read, 'Your friend killed Gomez.' She must have waited for the message to go out and then threw her phone in the ocean. I never received it with her personal effects."

"And it was never found by our crime scene crews as well," contributed Ronnie.

CHAPTER NINETEEN

"Get out the files on Artone Gomez, sweetheart. We have homework tonight," said Ronnie on her cell phone, leaving the Sandrine lunch.

"It's still out; I never put it back. Why, what's going on with him?" asked Penn.

"Sandrine finally spilled the beans at lunch. What a piece of work."

"Yeah, I don't trust her. She's a pretty face with lots of secrets behind it," remarked Penn.

"Hey, watch it, buster, or this pretty face will get after you," fired Ronnie, kidding her lover.

"Just stating the facts, dear. Did you think I had not noticed?"

"OK, back to the case. Are you in the office?"

"Yes."

"I'm ten minutes away. I don't want this on the airways. See you soon to explain," said Ronnie. As she drove through traffic, her mind was spinning. *Why did Secur kill a building inspector? She did mean Secur, right?* He had enough money to bribe the entire building department—*hum, maybe he did,* she thought. She quickly arrived and spotted Penn waiting outside.

"Hey, babe, what you doin' out here? Can't wait to see me?" she laughed.

"That's it; you caught me. Actually, it's a nice day. Those four walls were telling me to take a walk, so I thought we could walk and discuss your newfound information. By the way, good work," said Penn as he leaned in to kiss Ronnie's cheek.

"Good idea," she said, returning the kiss. She began telling Penn her story right away. "As luck would have it, I pulled out onto 163rd Street as Sandrine's red Mercedes was headed to our destination. There was a string of cars ahead of me. Sandrine drives like a man, weaving in and out of traffic. Ahead of me I see a car that appears to follow her every move. That's when I got the tag number for you. I confronted her with the name Jack Sanders. Then she tells me it's Kyle Anderson's cousin."

"What the hell is he doing following Sandrine?" asked Penn.

"Long story short, Rand, she begins to open up. We're not sure exactly why Sanders was following her, but since Kyle now knows she's a traitor, he is either concerned about further corporate espionage or concerned for her well-being—or a little of both," she said.

"So that's the story you waited until now to tell me?" asked a surprised Penn.

"No, darling, that's the window dressing. Sandrine begins to see my impatience and decides to level with me. The night Sonya was murdered, in fact, moments before she was actually killed, she sends a four-word text to Sandrine. It said, *Your friend killed Gomez*."

"Wow. Which friend, Ronnie?" asked Penn, catching Ronnie off guard.

"Why, Secur, of course," said Ronnie, wondering now if it was Secur

"Kyle, it's Jack."

"Hey, Cuz, where are you?" asked Kyle.

"Sandrine just had lunch with that looker from the FBI."

"Oh, that one. She's gorgeous. That might be my next job," answered Kyle in a light mood. Then he continued, "So what happened that can't wait until tonight?"

"This may be my last night. My cover is blown. By dumb luck that FBI gal was behind me when I was following Sandy. You know how Sandrine drives, so it wasn't hard for her to figure out who I was."

"Are you sure she saw you?" asked Kyle.

"Yep, I'm sure. When Sandrine was leaving, the FBI gal hesitated, wait-ing to see if I would follow Sandrine. When I waited she had no choice but to go ahead of me. That hesitation told it all. So do you want me to con-tinue?" asked Jack.

"No. Not for now. Lay off her for a while. Let me think," said Kyle.

"Hey, how come you're in such a great mood?"

"I just got this week's sales report. We sold thirty units to various fami-lies from Rio. I hardly had to discount any of them. That puts me within fifty more sales of being completely debt free. All gravy after that," said an exuberant Kyle.

CHAPTER TWENTY

Secur was in his office working late. He had just sent his secretary home when his private line rang. Only a half a dozen people had that number.

"Alain, it's Marty."

"Marty who? You mean Marty Burns, the guy who used to sell my condos?" answered a sarcastic Secur. He had not heard from Marty in two weeks, and it had been months since he had brought him a deal. Secur was upset. Burns used to sell more of his units than any other brokerage firm. But now—zip.

"Alain, it's tough out there."

"Cut the shit, Marty. I see other guys selling. *The Daily Review* just had the story about Kyle Anderson's deal with a family from Rio. They bought thirty units, and I see you brokered that deal."

"Yes, I did. But Alain, that negative pub you got from the bulk sale hurt you badly. The brokerage community does not have a lot of prospects these days. You know how easily they spook, so they go where they think they can make the quickest and easiest deal. Brokers are not complicated beings. They go where the deal with the least resistance is. You need to rehab your rep a little bit and get your quality up," said Marty.

"So you're now telling me my business. Why are you calling?" asked an upset Secur.

"I'm returning your call of last week," answered Marty.

"What? You expect me to remember why I was calling a week later with all that I am going through right now?" Secur replied, now livid. He hung up and sat at his desk, deep in thought. His world was spinning out of control. He owed everybody money, and none was coming in. His bulk sale was set to close in three weeks, and he was nearly out of cash. At least his home was getting action from the brokerage community. His art collection would sell fast. The boat might take a while. Just then his new cell phone vibrated. He looked at his screen to see who it was—"MEX." *Great,* he muttered to himself.

"Armando, good to hear from you. How are you?" Secur winced as he answered.

Armando Nacion was the Mexican equivalent of Biagio LoPrendo. While he represented investors seeking to loan money, his interest rates and collection methods varied greatly from Biagio's. He was more modern in one sense: all of his transactions were paperless but accurate to the penny. He was born in Cuidad Juarez, across the border from El Paso, Texas. His English was impeccable, and his manners were very American. His lifelong ambition had been to become a Ciudad Juarez police officer. This he did for fourteen years until one day he needed extra money for his wife's heart condition. There were no medical benefits with his job, and he had already drained his savings. At that moment he made a life-changing decision to break the law. The Trinolea cartel ruled Juarez and was always preying on police officers needing money. Once word got out about Nacion's needs, a Trinolean street captain contacted him and told him the hospital bill was paid.

At first he had second thoughts and tried to resist, but he could not. The next day he resigned from the Juarez Police Department. His wife and young son were moved to Trinolea turf on the west side of town so they could be protected from competing cartel factions. Nacion was smart. His brains and flawless English moved him quickly to the top of the cartel. He knew money, money laundering, and financial investments, handling all of the cartel finances. Thanks to him much of the cartel money had been cleaned and was earning legitimate returns on a host of traditional investments around the world. Real estate in largely Spanish population sectors was his specialty. Miami was such an area, and the Trinolea cartel had moved off the Florida coast, importing their drugs into Florida and the Bahamas in a variety of ways. They needed to clean some bucks, and Secur was ripe.

Alain Secur was a good customer for the Trinolea cartel. Nacion's affable manner made Secur feel comfortable even though he knew it was poisoned fruit. In the nicest way possible, Nacion explained to Secur that his interest rate was 15 percent and it was due every month, payable to a local Miami bank partially owned by Nacion's cartel. There was a five-day grace period on his loan, which now totaled over $39 million. The money was not secured by any collateral, and Secur spent it on Claughton Tower's and Glisten's carrying costs. He owed his next installment to Nacion in just over two weeks.

"Hello, Alain. How are you today, my friend? I am in town staying just down the street from you at the Mandarin. You wanted to speak with me, I am told?" said Nacion.

"Yes, Armando. Would you be available now?"

"Now? Yes, of course. I'll meet you in the lounge in twenty minutes."

"Perfect," said Secur.

Secur called down for the valet to bring his car around. He was driving a pedestrian Mercedes E-550 nowadays. His car collection had been delivered to an auctioneer three days before as he and Alicia were down to a two-car family—instead of nine. Within minutes he was stepping into his car for the short hop to the Mandarin. It was so close he could have walked from the Banco Santander building, where his penthouse offices resided a short distance west of Claughton Island and his current destination.

He strode through the Mandarin lobby and immediately spotted the immense body of Nacion. When he raised his large hand to wave to Secur, his 6' 5" frame looked three feet taller. The men greeted each other and headed for the bar. It was 9:00 p.m., and the lights of the city and the bay as viewed from the lounge were impressive. It was cool outside, so each man gathered his drink and walked outside along the waterway near the seawall. They spotted an empty bench and sat down to talk business amid the soft lighted Miami sky line. The silver ripple of Biscayne Bay created by the full moon relaxed both men.

After they clinked glasses, Armando spoke first. "You have such a beautiful city to live and work in, Alain."

"Yes. A nice setting here tonight," said Secur, wanting to dive into the conversation but knowing it was not the Latin way. Nacion would lead.

"You see that red-and-yellow light to the southeast across the bay? That is the condo building I now have a spectacular residence in," said Nacion.

Secur hesitated with his answer as he absorbed the sights and sounds of bayside Miami. He could hear the gentle patter of water hitting the seawall beneath their feet and the muted sound of fish splashing along the surface. Even the loading cranes on Dodge Island had lights glittering on their steel bones. Nacion ignored Secur's silent vigil and spoke. "How is Alicia and your son Bennett?" asked Nacion.

The mention of his family members by a dangerous man like Nacion made Secur angry, though he could not show it. It was intended as a veiled threat, and Nacion knew Secur would interpret it as such—mission accomplished.

"They are fine, thank you. How's your family doing?" answered Secur calmly.

"They are fine, but I don't see them enough. Alain, shall we skip the small talk and discuss why you wanted to see me on such short notice?" said Nacion in a calm, even tone, glancing up at the stars.

"Certainly. I have a payment due in two weeks, and I won't have the money by then. What can we do?"

"What would you like to do, Alain? A deal's a deal," said Nacion, still glancing at the sights as if not concerned by Secur's announcement.

"I would like a two-week grace period for free with no additional interest," requested Secur.

"You are a businessman; would you agree to a deal like that?" asked Nacion, now looking Secur in the eye.

"Yes I would if someone promised to pay off the entire loan at that time. Do you think that would be worth an abatement of interest for fourteen days?" asked Secur, now glancing at the stars in the night sky.

"I see, an interesting proposition. I'm quite happy to hear that, though we are a little worried about your continuing ability to pay."

"You won't have to worry much longer. So what do you think, Armando?"

"From your lips to my ears, amigo. What happens if you cannot pay after fourteen days?" asked Nacion.

"I don't anticipate that occurring. But if it happens, as they say, I guess we will cross that bridge when we get to it," said Secur, wishing he had not used that term.

"Tell me why you believe you will be able to pay in full all of the sudden with this extension. By the way, we will miss your business," said Nacion, trying to project optimism even though he doubted his client could deliver what he had just spoken.

"I am in the final stages of negotiating a bulk sale of two properties: that one right behind us and that one just to the right of the Four Seasons Hotel. As you can see, excellent locations," said Secur, pointing to Claughton Towers and Glisten.

Nacion took time to observe each as a brief silence hung in the air. "All right, assuming that sale goes off without a hitch and you have your money, where do we fit into your repayment plan? The Teamsters have very large loans there, and the proceeds will not be enough money to pay us both, if I calculate correctly. I know of the bulk sale. Nine hundred and thirty units sold just like that?"

"You've done your homework."

"Yes, and I know this as well: you'll probably get around $190 thousand per unit, or $176 million total. After fees and closing costs say you net $170 million or so. You owe the Teamsters $250 million, which I am sure you negotiated down somewhat. So, amigo, were does my group figure into this little financial disaster you have created?" said Nacion to a surprised Secur.

Secur was surprised even though Nacion was off slightly on the real numbers. *Shit. I cannot bullshit this guy*, thought Secur, choosing his response carefully. "Impressive, Armando. I can see why you were chosen for this line of work with your organization. I should hire you when I get back on my feet," he said as Nacion smiled at the compliment. "But I have made many millions for the Teamsters when times were better. They are willing to take a substantial write-down. Beyond that, I am in the process of liquidating some assets. These are good assets, and I have a pledge from the Teamsters that I may carve out what I owe you from the sale for the pledge of cash from that asset pool," said Secur, relieved that the conversation was going well.

"Well, then, as I said before, Alain, we will miss your business. I like your plan. Will you join me for dinner? I promise no business will be spoken." Nacion requested.

"I would love to," answered Secur.

They left their tranquil post and adjourned to the elegant surroundings of the Mandarin Hotel.

CHAPTER TWENTY-ONE

Penn was on his way to South Beach to meet Gambrel at Izzy's Deli. It was their favorite coffee shop for morning relaxation. In their days together at DEA, Reginald Gambrel and Randall Penn could be spotted there four mornings a week. Gambrel was at an outside table when Penn arrived in his usual coat and tie.

"Look at you all spiffed up. Big day in court?" said Gambrel.

"No. Interviews today with a couple of bad guys."

"Yeah? Who"

"Alain Secur and his lender, Biagio LoPrendo," said Penn as he sipped his coffee.

"They sound like a couple hoodlums," remarked Reggie sarcastically.

"That's all you and I deal with, and to what do I owe the pleasure today of your presence at our historic breakfast spot?"

"I thought you might like to know I'm now chasing Mexican smugglers—ruthless group of guys, too. They may not be as smart as Gianno was, but they are tough. They'll shoot you dead if they can," Gambrel said.

"OK, thanks for that bit of information, but I'm not in DEA anymore, remember?" kidded Penn.

"We're doing much better without you," gamed Gambrel right back at Penn.

"Enough. What is it you really want to tell me? I'm a little pressed today."

"Word on the street is that the Mexicans are loan sharking big money, real estate, stocks, and gambling."

"Enterprising group. Did you say real estate?" asked Penn as another light went on. Then he continued, "Real estate takes big bucks. Cash in big quantities is difficult to move. Have you heard how they are doing this?"

"Do you know how many Spanish banks there are in Miami?" asked Gambrel, leaning in.

"Tons, I guess. Latins buy a lot of real estate. To some it's a means to get cash away from their tax-happy dictators."

"Exactly, Rand. My guess is that their main banks are in Mexico and they funnel funds through their American branches electronically. The dirty money from there gets scrubbed up and loaned as legit funds here, virtually untraceable in a cyber-sense, you see," said Gambrel. Penn was quiet, taking in what Reggie had just said.

"One more thing to check out. Reg, I think you're on to something, thanks. Hey, did you ever bust any more of those guys?" asked Penn.

"Working on it."

"I read the report you sent me several days ago on Sonya. Was there any rope around her arms and legs? Doc Wong said she had rope marks, but your report said no rope was present. Is that true?" said Penn.

"Yeah. No rope, but I couldn't tell preliminarily about rope marks with the bloat when we found her."

"OK, thanks. I gotta get going. Keep me in your salsa loop, gringo," kidded Penn, leaving for his office.

Minutes later Penn was driving north on I-95 when his mobile rang; it was Ronnie. "Hi, babe, you headed in?" she asked.

" I am, and I look spectacular. Tell the ladies at the office I'm in my blue suit and red power tie, and I'm available for pictures on my lap."

"You disgusting old man, you can't even handle me. But I promise you that I will let them know what you just said. That should be good for a laugh."

"What do you have for me—business wise?" Penn inquired, wishing he had not said how good he looked to Ronnie. Now he would have to stop and get muffins and bagels to minimize the hazing.

"I've been working the Gomez murder file pretty heavily. Secur and Gomez had a very public feud."

"I am aware of that. It's widely known."

"Yes it is, but his alibi the days before and after the body was found floating off Fort Lauderdale is ironclad. Too good."

"What's your point, Ronnie?" asked Penn.

"I've done some checking. His alibi is ironclad because he was with one guy the whole time. How convenient. Both create the alibi by being with each other."

"Are you going to tell me who the guy is? Or should I tell you, sweetie pie?" chided Penn.

"OK, Mr. Hunk in the Blue Suit, who is your choice?"

"Biagio LoPrendo," Penn answered.

"Bingo, Penn. You've been doing my job," said Ronnie.

"I'm seeing this the same way as you, Ronnie, but try this on. Gomez was five years ago. When did Secur and Sandrine start hanging out? Isn't that what young people call fucking each other today?" said Penn, thinking of another possibility.

"OK, so now, what's your point? You think Secur was with Sandrine during all this?" she asked.

"Think about it, babe. No one knew of this relationship. She hides it pretty well today, doesn't she?"

"Yes, she does."

Penn continued, "Chances are the investigation team doesn't even know Sandrine was a possible friend because back then, nobody did. Do you remember how she told you how she was swept off her feet and could not resist Secur? It's perfect. She is with him so Biagio can say he was with Secur, and no one knows the difference. Sandrine would never know Secur lied to the police, assuming he did, to protect Biagio. Biagio is just too close to these two murders, and the MO looks identical."

"Good police work, Penn. I think we have ourselves our own little devil's triangle."

"I'm coming up on the Golden Glade. Anyone there yet?" he asked.

"Looks like Secur is just getting out of his car. I'll warm him up till you get here, partner. When is Biagio due in?" asked Ronnie, looking out the window as Secur was arriving.

"Around 2:00. I wanted to leave plenty of time for Secur. I figure we can do a summarization of Secur's answers at lunch and be ready for Biagio after that."

"Good plan. I like it. I think we're on the right track, Penn. I smell it."

"Me too. See you in five," said Penn, ending the call and exiting 95 at 163rd Street.

CHAPTER TWENTY-TWO

Kyle Anderson was about to have a late breakfast with Sandrine at a quiet restaurant at Bayside, overlooking Biscayne Bay. His plan was to talk about work and see where the conversation might go. He was growing less angry with her over the secret Secur defection. While he was hoping for a confession born out of guilt and loyalty, he would not be disappointed if it did not come. In reality, many of the sites where Secur had eventually bested Kyle had proved better off lost for Anderson Development in the end. They were trophy sites demanding expensive buildings on small plots at very high prices. They required taller, more expensive buildings, so both the trophy location and a trophy building befitting of the site meant higher construction costs and not necessarily higher profits. Fortuitously Anderson had settled for B+ sites that still had good views and good locations, but his conservative nature was to build less expensive, shorter buildings, concentrating on great value. His business plan was being rewarded despite the economic paralysis in real estate. The new wave of Latin buyers had seen to that.

His architecture and amenities were stellar, and his quality and reputation brought numerous referrals. Referrals were the cheapest and most coveted sales to have, delivered by happy customers for free; no expensive ads or promotions needed. The presence of ever-increasing, referral-based buyers allowed Anderson to save hundreds of thousands of marketing dollars over a five-year period. Since this money was originally budgeted and part of the money the banks loaned him, Anderson merely converted the unspent funds to a special interest reserve fund. These monies allowed Anderson to carry his buildings deep into the recession without any additional corporate financial stress. Except for a few bank-encumbered units, he was now beyond break-even on each of his remaining projects. Every unit left in inventory had little or no debt. His carry was nearly nonexistent, yet every sale generated 100 percent revenue to Anderson Development. So as he approached the table Sandrine was already seated at, Kyle Anderson had no worries and was a happy developer. He had rationalized Sandrine's bad judgment.

Breakfast this morning was at Bayside, a project in an area near the first concerted effort of the downtown Miami revitalization planned many years before. Located just south of the Miami Heat's home court, the American Airlines Arena, It had preceded the renaissance of South Beach and had gone through times of uncertainty and tenant turnover in the earlier years. But today the beachy, two-story, pastel buildings were full of healthy retailers and great restaurants. Kyle had picked one of his favorite bistros directly overlooking the Miami Marina from the upper level. The outside views were spectacular. Anderson never tired of the international flavor of Bayside. The green waters of the marina were full of boats, yachts, and water taxis. In the distance, mammoth cruise ships docked at Dodge Island set the near views just a few hundred yards east. Framing the cruise ships in the distance were the multi-colored high-rise condominium buildings on South Beach; some built by Anderson and some by Secur. The mid-morning was warm yet dry as the crowds began to fill the pink-and-turquoise-painted shops flanking the water. Smells of salt water wafted and mixed with the aroma of food generated by dozens of restaurants getting ready for the day and night ahead. The smells reminded Anderson of the wharf in San Francisco.

"Hello, Sandy, sorry I am a little late. Marty Burns brought in three contracts as I was leaving. Great prices with hardly any discounts. Unusual after the beating we have had these last five years."

"That's great news, Kyle. It does sound strange to say 'hardly any discounts.' I'll bet we are one of only a few condo developers anywhere in this country to be able to say that. Great leadership by you, Kyle," she said. She wasn't sucking up to Kyle; she meant it. Her guilty conscience was alleviated since her spying was over for good. The rationalization cleared her mind.

"It was a team effort. I just chose the right folks to help me do this," he said, dodging the credit as he always did. He could see Sandrine was fidgeting as he spoke.

"Kyle, I don't know how to say this, but I must resign from Anderson Development." Her tone grew quiet as she finished a shocking sentence that caught Kyle completely off guard.

Kyle said nothing at first, trying to process what had just happened. *Was this her self-inflicted punishment?* thought Kyle. He stared at his water glass, unable to come up with the right thing to say. *Is this a blessing or a curse?* he wondered.

Finally, Sandrine, seeing his hurt and confusion, spoke further. "I see you are wondering what to say. So let me make it easy on you. Due to my sister's death, my mixed emotions and lack of focus, I believe I would be a hindrance rather than a help to your wonderful company going forward," she said with a tear forming in her right eye.

"I don't see the lack of focus, Sandy. You've thrown yourself into work these last couple of weeks like nothing I have ever seen. That cannot be a reason—at least in my mind," said Anderson. He thought he had convinced her before that staying was best for both of them. Now he was pissed off that she was leaving and that he had not seen it coming. He would miss her; he knew that. He could forgive her. Before that day in the parking lot, he had thought he might have even loved this woman. Again he sat silent, thinking, wondering what to say.

"Thank you for those kind words, but my mind is made up," she said heavily conflicted. Tears were streaming from both eyes onto the tablecloth like rain. She could not contain herself. She rose from her seat, walked around to Kyle's left, leaned over, grabbed his head in both hands, and kissed him hard on the lips. "I love you," she muttered, then turned and left the restaurant, sobbing all the way to her car.

Kyle could feel the look of other patrons upon him, each one boring a hole through him with his or her thoughts. Their thoughts, however, did not matter. He watched her leave, wondering if he would ever have the opportunity to see her again. Suddenly, he wanted her. She had said it: "I love you." He had thought it, too, no denying it. His mind was spinning. He had come to this restaurant wanting her to confess her transgressions, and now he was numb with love. *What has just happened?* he thought.

CHAPTER TWENTY-THREE

Alain Secur and Randall Penn completed their reintroductions to each other and were headed to the conference room where Ronnie was already seated. Today Ronnie would be taking notes. Penn was careful to seat Ronnie on his left side so Secur did not feel surrounded. Secur had decided to dress down for the interview, wearing an open shirt and sports coat. He came alone, sans attorney, because he had agreed to speak for the good of the case, which meant the good of Sonya and Sandrine. He had not seen Sandrine in over two weeks, since their meeting in the morgue parking lot, and he was lonely and confused.

"Good morning, Mr. Secur. Are you comfortable?"

"Yes, by all means."

With that, Penn dove right in. "Alain, I saw you embracing Ms. Michel in the morgue parking lot when we first met. What is your relationship with Ms. Michel?" asked Penn very matter-of-factly.

Secur was not expecting such a quick start. "Is this really important?"

"I spent a lot of time preparing for this discussion today, and I have a chronological direction that depends on your answers, so it is important for me to keep this just to one meeting. I hope you understand?" said Penn, leaning in with his head cocked to one side. *What a fuck-off this guy is*, thought Penn.

"If you must know, she is my girlfriend, mistress, or lover. Whatever you want to write down," answered Secur, slightly agitated.

"How long have you been together?"

"About five years."

"May I presume you knew her sister Sonya?"

"You may, and I did," answered Secur, keeping his answers as short as possible.

"Did you get along with Sonya? Did you see her much as well?"

"We were friendly. At first she was not happy with her sister going out with a married guy, but inevitably that passed. When it did, we occasionally double dated."

"Did Sonya date a lot of men, or was she a settle-down-with-one-guy woman?"

"When I first met her right after Sandrine and I began seeing each other, she seemed to go through a guy about once every three or four months. But recently, I had introduced her to one of my single friends, and she was with him for eight months or so."

"What was your friend's name, and what can you tell me about him?"

"His name is Biagio LoPrendo. He is actually one of my lenders on several condominium projects I own. I believe you are speaking with him this afternoon."

"I am. How did you two meet?"

"My wife and her family are from New York, and her family was close to Biagio's uncle, Luc LoPrendo."

"Did Biagio loan money directly to you, or did he represent banks, hedge funds, or investors?" asked Penn.

Secur asked for water, and Penn picked up on the stall. He had seen this many times before. Agents would wager with Penn at which question the infamous water stall would occur.

Secur sipped the water and cleared his throat. "Biagio is actually a dealer's representative. He represents pools of investors placing their money in various investments," Secur said, knowing Penn would ask who. He continued, "In this case most all of the money has come from the Teamsters. They like me, and I have made them money over the years, so they keep loaning me money on my projects."

"Even in this economy, Mr. Secur?" asked Penn.

"No lender in any condominium project today, knowing what they have seen happen these last few years, would have made those loans in hindsight. Real estate is risky and prone to these kinds of business cycles," said Secur, avoiding a direct answer.

"So the answer is no?" said Penn.

"Yes. The answer is no."

"Thank you for your candor. You said that the Teamsters lent you most of the money. Who loaned the rest?" asked Penn, wondering what other suckers Secur had beguiled.

"Luc LoPrendo and some minor investors on my wife's side provided some additional funds," said Secur. "Mr. Secur, might I offer an observation? You can answer it if you want. The facts are self-evident in this case. If I were a builder in these times and had borrowed money from the Teamsters and reputed members of organized crime like Luc LoPrendo and his cronies, I would be extremely concerned if I could not sell the hundreds of units that stand vacant in my buildings. What's your plan, Mr. Secur?" Penn decided to launch a missile into Secur's little story.

Secur reached for the water and took a gulp. "I am unaware of the personal status of Luc LoPrendo, or his friends, for that matter. Besides, what does this have to do with Sonya?" pressed Secur.

"Before I came to the FBI, I was an attorney for a large law firm in Manhattan. That firm represented Mr. LoPrendo in his real estate deals. I can assure you where there's smoke there's fire. I would be very careful. I say that because you are right about this market. It sucks, and to some extent and it is certainly not your fault. People like that don't care. Be careful," said Penn, leaving Secur to squirm.

"I appreciate your concerns, but my relationship is very open with them and I have made them aware of our challenges."

Penn ignored the rhetoric, knowing it was a lie, and continued. "Anybody else loan you money on your projects?"

"Nope. That's it," said Secur, hoping that Penn did not know of the Mexicans. He would deny it, knowing it was a felony to do so.

Penn decided to discuss Gomez. Secur was ready. Penn could see Secur was lying about certain facts, but he really felt the meat of his interview was coming up. "Mr. Secur, about five years ago, a building inspector who had been giving you problems on your projects was found murdered in virtually the same fashion that Sonya Michel was recently murdered. Did you know Artone Gomez very well?"

Secur again reached for the bottle of water as soon as Penn finished speaking. "Yes, I knew him. He was trouble; always had his hand out. The difference was that if his underlings tried to extort us, we could at least go to him to deal with those kinds of issues," said Secur.

"Uh huh," agreed Penn.

"But once the chief guy comes forward with the same behavior as his subordinates, then it becomes a problem. Whom do you go to?"

"Did he try this with everyone?" asked Penn, becoming amused with Secur's rationalizations.

"Kyle Anderson threatened the bastard and threw him off the job. He was arrested for doing that but was eventually cleared. Same guy," said Secur as Penn neared the end of his questions.

"Mr. Secur, where were you June third, the night before Sonya was murdered?" asked Penn.

Secur was visibly shaken. He was silent for a while.

"Mr. Secur, June third, please," repeated Penn.

"I was at home asleep," answered Secur in conflict with his conscience. *Did he say the evening before they found her?* he was confused. His alibi with Biagio was for the night they found her. He then realized the actual death was the day before.

"Was your wife with you, in case we have to verify this information?"

"Yes, she will."

Penn wound down the interview asking assorted timing questions and light informational questions that produced no stress. He and Ronnie thanked Secur and showed him to the door. They reconvened in the conference room to recap the short session.

"How many times did you catch him lying, Rand?" asked Ronnie.

"For sure about three times. There is someone else loaning him money, I suspect. I think his alibi may be shaky, and he probably had some other answers that stretched the truth. But I don't think he killed Sonya; however,

I think he knows who did. This guy is a dirt bag, sweetheart. I can feel it," said Penn, staring at Ronnie's beautiful face.

"How much time before Biagio gets here?" asked Ronnie.

"Honey, we can't have sex here. It's forbidden," kidded Penn.

"You wish, Rand. I'm hungry; let's get some lunch at the Avenue Deli. I'm craving corned beef."

CHAPTER TWENTY-FOUR

Penn and Ronnie were returning from lunch in Penn's Tahoe. It had been a working lunch, going over the Secur morning interview and getting ready for the upcoming Biagio interview. Ronnie shared new Intel with Penn about Biagio. Both agreed that Secur and Biagio made a questionable tandem. This afternoon they hoped to expose facts that might make Biagio stumble and admit something he otherwise might not volunteer.

"Honey, Secur is somehow involved in this murder. I don't believe he was present, but he may have sanctioned it. There is any number of bad things in his life that he is desperately holding onto by a very thin string."

"I like the way he hesitated when you asked him where he was the night before the murder. He doesn't know the actual time of death, so he told us where he was the night we found her in the ocean."

"Or so he says," said Penn.

"Let's see how LoPrendo answers some of the same questions. I'm sure Secur was on the phone to Biagio the moment he was out of sight of this building," said Ronnie.

They walked into their office together and saw Biagio sitting calmly on the sofa in the waiting area. Penn and Ronnie would cordially welcome

Biagio to the building in an attempt to diffuse any immediate tension or nervousness.

Penn strode decisively toward Biagio with a warm smile. "Mr. LoPrendo, how nice of you to take time out of your busy schedule and visit us here today. My name is Randal Penn."

Ronnie waited behind Penn as a slightly surprised Biagio stood to shake Penn's hand. Before Biagio could answer, Ronnie extended her hand, peeking behind Penn. "And I am Mr. Penn's assistant, Ronnie Feldman. How do you do?"

Biagio quickly shook Ronnie's hand, uncontrollably staring at her breasts. At Penn's advice, Ronnie had worn a blouse one size smaller than normal. *It's not fair*, she thought.

"Nice to meet you both," answered Biagio.

They settled into the conference room where only hours before the pair had grilled Alain Secur. As planned, Ronnie sat directly across from LoPrendo with Penn now to her right—their shoulders were nearly touching.

"Mr. LoPrendo, again thank you for being here today. I am sorry for your loss. I know it must be hard under the circumstances," said Penn as Ronnie silently nodded. This, too, seemed to confuse Biagio. He had probably expected a more direct approach after speaking with Secur earlier.

"I can hardly believe it myself. We loved each other so much," said Biagio

"We'll keep this as short as possible, " said Penn with his best poker face, followed immediately by a nod from Ronnie.

"Thank you both."

"Mr. LoPrendo, how long had you known Ms. Michel—Sonya?" asked Penn, starting with the most obvious.

"We had been dating exclusively for eight months."

"How did you meet Sonya?"

"I was out one night with some friends, and she was with her friends, and before you knew it, we were talking to each other and hitting it off. She was smart, funny, and good looking."

"Did you ever meet her sister Sandrine?"

"Yes, she was dating my friend Alain Secur."

"Were you aware Mr. Secur was here earlier today?"

"Yes I was. We are good friends, and I am his lender—or should I say the lender's representative. We talk nearly every day."

"Were you with Sonya the night before the murder—the night before we found her?"

"No, she was out with her girlfriends, and I had a private meeting with Alain at his office. We had been preparing for his bulk sale to the two hedge funds. I was buried in last-minute details."

Penn gathered his thoughts while he glanced at his notes. He had one person—either Secur or Biagio—in a conflict. He needed to confirm later by asking the same question over and over but in a different manner each time. "Did you and Sonya get along? What kind of person was she?" asked Penn after the slight delay.

"Sonya and I had a relationship of convenience. I was in New Jersey and New York, and she was down here, but we spoke almost daily. And when we were here, we spent all our free time together. She was a doll, fun to be with. I miss her," said Biagio, this time with more sincerity.

"So you were with Mr. Secur the night before we found Sonya. Where were you the night we actually found her body?" questioned Penn.

"With Alain again, this time for dinner at Smith and Wolensky's in Miami Beach."

"Were you alone together, just the two of you?"

"Yes, it was a working dinner."

"When had you last heard from Sonya, and were you worried?"

"No, I was not worried at all. I routinely had to put in evening appearances with Alain to work through these hard times in order to recover some of our bank loans. I had told Sonya two days prior that I would not be able to see her for a couple of nights. Secur had to tell Sandrine the same. A routine occurrence," said Biagio, reaching for the water bottle and taking a short drink.

"When did you last speak by phone?"

"Two days before she was found. She had plans with the girls, so when that happened, I knew her schedule was set. She was a spa girl, and she was gone all day sometimes. I think that was one of the things she had planned," answered Biagio. He was beginning to sweat under his arms. He was not prepared for these questions. He asked if he might be excused to use the bathroom. He needed the break, and he needed to think. As he left the room, Penn and Ronnie left the room as well, heading to Penn's office for a quick halftime recap.

"He's fumbling badly. When are you coming with the hard stuff?" asked Ronnie.

"When we get back, I am going to pose some tough questions. He could leave, but that would be even more telling," said Penn.

"I have full-time tails on Biagio and Secur. I think something's going to happen these next few days," remarked Ronnie.

"I have your intel files. Where did you get this about the Mexicans?" asked Penn.

"Your buddy heard it on the streets."

"Reg?"

"Yeah, he called me just before Secur came in, and I forgot to mention it at lunch. Your big, blue eyes took away all my thoughts," she kiddingly said.

"Hold those thoughts for later. Let's get back to the room," suggested Penn, walking out of his office.

"Mr. Biagio, you represent the Teamsters, do you not?" asked Penn as the first question after the break.

"Well, I actually represent their pension fund operations in real estate."

"Like a loan correspondent."

"Yes, very similar. I am paid for placing and underwriting their loans to various borrowers."

"So, are you in first position as the lender on Secur's debt?"

"Yes, we only loan in first position. We do not do second mortgages or mezzanine lending, which is considered secondary financing to us."

"Do you allow second mortgages behind your first position?"

"Not unless we approve them first."

"Are you aware that Mr. Secur may have borrowed additional money on this project from another source other than your group? Actually a rather rowdy group of Mexicans?" Penn began to warm up Biagio's hot seat.

Biagio hesitated. He reasoned if Penn and the street knew this fact, he would look foolish denying it. *Damn it.* "Yes, I had heard. It was one of the discussions I had with Secur those nights during Sonya's absence. It was done without our knowledge," lied Biagio.

"Were you aware that other people besides your Teamsters, and now the Mexicans, have loaned monies to Mr. Secur?" asked Penn, taking delight in Biagio's apparent uneasiness.

"Who might that be?" answered Biagio, suddenly becoming coy and serious.

"Several folks from my old stomping grounds when I was an attorney in New York City. They are not considered to be the greatest proponents of law and order, either. Tough cookies, in other words—like your uncle Luc," said Penn.

"Yes to your question. I consider my uncle and some of his friends to be part of the Teamsters group. They were begging me to let them in. Remember, the Teamsters had a run of three great years with Secur. Word got out."

"I'm wondering if the Teamsters, who have cleaned up their house over the years, would want their pension money side by side with some of the Northeast's mobsters," Penn said. He had said the "M" word. How would Biagio react?

"I think it's safe to say there are no mobsters, just hard working Italians you feds like to demonize," said Biagio, now getting upset.

"I apologize. We feds tend to get carried away," said Penn.

"Accepted. Are we about done here?" asked a stressed-out Biagio. Lying was taking its toll.

"Not much longer, sir. You said earlier you met Sonya at a restaurant. Did Sandrine and Secur set that up?" asked Penn, knowing the truth.

"I, uh, it could have happened that way. Yes."

"Do you know a man named Moto Seanu? A Samoan man who used to work at a Fort Lauderdale restaurant?"

"No, can't say as I have." *Damn it,* thought Biagio as he answered. *I have to lie.*

"OK, how about Artone Gomez? A chief building inspector in Dade County, murdered in an identical manner to Sonya five years ago," pressed

Penn. Biagio was now squirming and constantly reaching for water. Penn had him on the run.

"Yes, I heard about his murder. No, I did not know him. Why did you ask?" said Biagio, struggling to maintain composure.

"It is a cold case so fundamentally similar to Sonya's murder that we think it may be by the same person or persons. So we are getting facts on that case. It was just reopened the other day. That's all," said Penn.

Biagio said nothing. Sweat trickled down both temples.

"Last question. You said the night before and after Sonya's murder, you and Secur were together both nights. Is that right?"

"Yes, it is."

"Mr. Biagio, I find some of your answers inconsistent with those of your colleague Alain Secur. I'm going to need to speak with you again once I confirm some discrepancies with Mr. Secur. That should be in a few days. When you come back, it will not be voluntary, and you may wish to bring an attorney," said Penn. He had started off diplomatically and finished with a bang.

Biagio was stunned and dribbled out a reply. "What do you mean bring an attorney?"

"Simple, Mr. LoPrendo. I intend to Mirandize you and formally question you about today's inconsistencies and the murder of Sonya Michel. I could easily have you come in and Mirandize you, and you would say nothing and call your attorney, and we would all wait around until he shows up. I'm really doing you a favor. You should appreciate it," explained Penn. He rose above Biagio and extended his hand once again, thanking him for his cooperation. Ronnie followed suit as Penn spoke. "If you will excuse us both, we are running late for our next meeting," lied Penn as he and Ronnie quickly left Biagio to find his way out. Penn had set the stage for an adversarial parting, knowing the next sessions with lawyers would be that way anyway. He felt confidant he had his man—maybe Secur, too.

Once in Ronnie's office, he spoke. "That little bastard did it. I know it."

"I have never seen a fish filleted so well. Penn, you got the FBI in that guy's head big time. A little bit of a gamble giving him so much information, but I can see it will pay off. I was impressed, big guy," said Ronnie.

"Did you appreciate my skillful interrogation, Ms. Feldman?

"I'll say," said Ronnie, giving Penn a pat on his ass as he left her office.

The final assessment of today's important interviews would be finalized over barbequed ribs at Ronnie's apartment later that evening.

CHAPTER TWENTY-FIVE

Kyle Anderson was a man conflicted. His world was in good shape in an economy that had destroyed many of his peers. His marriage was sound, and his kids were doing well. But the image and words of Sandrine two days before had left him wanting more. The risks were high, and he knew it. What he didn't know was anything about Sandrine, except for her work at Anderson. He wanted to know more even though the little cricket on his shoulder, his conscience, was telling him it was wrong and dangerous.

He was sitting in his office staring out the glass expanse at a tropical wonderland before him. He felt fortunate to have landed in this wonderful and exciting environment where so many of his life's pleasures had been realized—the wide bay that blended into the green shoreline and the orange rooftops beyond. Kyle gazed upon sailboats, cruise ships, freighters, seaplanes, and the throng of cars moving to and from their destinations. *What a life*, he thought.

His secretary's voice broke the silence. "Miss Michel on line one, sir."

Without responding, he hit the button and spoke uncontrollably, "I was just thinking of you. When I can see you again, Sandy?"

Sandrine said nothing. Anderson panicked with her silence. But then he heard sobs and crying.

"Sandy, are you OK? I want to come over and see you," blurted Kyle, but his timing was not good. His heart was overtaking proper etiquette for a mourning sister. Still nothing from Sandrine, so Kyle tried to explain his feelings. "I didn't mean it like that. I just feel bad for you, and I want to help you and…and…" He paused. "It may be more than just liking you. I don't know, but I feel protective of you right now. What does that mean?" bumbled Kyle, acting like a schoolboy with his first crush. Sandrine had that effect on men, not on purpose, but the whole package clicked with men—great looking, smart, forceful but reserved, and endearing to people without seeming condescending. It was a deadly combination that Kyle found hard to resist. He was not far behind her in all the same categories. His infatuation with Sandrine must now be obvious to her.

Finally she answered, softly at first. "Kyle, I meant what I said, but I'm not sure what I meant exactly. You have been a guiding light to me, and frankly, I have let you down. I'm sick about it. I've made bad choices before when I was emotionally tied to a man. I want to tell you, but I am ashamed. It's not like me. My sister's death has clarified my thinking and exposed the weakness in my moral compass," she said, starting to sob again as Kyle debated his next move.

But, in an instant he changed his mind and decided not to give her the easy way out. It would tell him a lot. Did she have the moxie to own up? "Now, now, it can't be that bad. I frankly don't know what it could be, but you have been an extraordinary executive for me. I mean this; you are a large part of our success."

Sandrine said nothing as Kyle's words only proved to further cast shame on her deeds the past five years. He gave her the opening.

"Will you see me again?" he pleaded.

"Yes." More sobbing.

"Would you consider coming back to work once we work through whatever it is you feel is stopping you?"

"I'm not sure. Let's just meet, but not here. A lunch somewhere quiet," Sandrine said, sniffling now.

"Call me when you are ready. If I don't hear from you, I will not bother you ever again," offered Kyle, hoping to instill some urgency with Sandrine.

"It will be in the next two days, I promise. I need some space right now, though."

"I understand. Good-bye, Sandy."

After the call Kyle was more in touch with his feelings and could see that it was wise for him to not be impetuous. The cooling-off period would be good for him. It would tell him his true feelings and let the hormones die down.

Uptown in North Miami, FBI special agent Randall Penn and his assistant agent Ronnie Feldman were on a conference call with Darren Jacobs from Penn's old law firm in Manhattan. Penn had asked him to check his sources in New York and New Jersey to see what was happening with the Teamsters and Luc LoPrendo.

"Thanks for calling, Jake. How's the hot summer treating you in the concrete jungle?" chided Penn, hassling his former friend.

"Like you are in a cool spot right now. What's the temperature, ninety-five degrees?" fired back Jacobs.

"But we have an ocean breeze and women in bikinis," answered Penn, getting a scowl from Ronnie.

"Hey, you still seeing that gorgeous Jew from Texas?"

"No, just an ordinary girl named Ronnie," answered Penn, which elicited a kick to his shin by Ronnie under the table, followed by a long moan from Penn. Ronnie covered her mouth while laughing, knowing how much that hurt. It was a lucky shot.

"Hey, Ronnie, I know he deserved that. How are you?" said Jake.

"Good, Jake. We Jews need to stick together," said Ronnie.

"I'm back," answered Penn, still doubled up in pain and shaking his fist at Ronnie.

"Whatdya got for us, Jake?" asked Ronnie, turning serious.

"Lots of stuff on the street about these characters. We have not represented them in years, so I can tell you more than I normally could," confirmed Jake.

"We appreciate that, buddy," said Penn.

"Luc is kind of on the hot seat, I'm hearing, Rand. He has assured his boys they will be made whole in the Miami condo investment."

"Can you explain *his boys*, Jake?" asked Ronnie as Penn nodded in accord.

"Not the Teamsters. They're on their own. He's got some of the Tucci boys breathing down his neck. They want either his real estate or some of his blood, I'm hearing," said Jake.

"Have you heard anything about Biagio LoPrendo, his nephew?" asked Penn.

"Very little. He seems to be the black sheep in the family. Uncle Luc got him the job with the Teamsters. Not the shiniest penny in the pile, if you know what I mean," said Jake.

"We agree with that, too," said Ronnie.

"Have you heard anything about some Mexicans involved in this?" asked Penn.

"No. But I'll ask."

"Anything else?"

"The Samoan you asked about. He is supposedly a freelance contract guy LoPrendo occasionally has a use for. He has not been seen for a while, though. Oh, here's one I almost forgot. Your guy Secur the builder, his wife was up here meeting with Luc last week. They were pretty chummy, from what I hear," said Jake.

"Interesting news. Hey, where do you get all this shit from? This is good intel. I still do pro bono for some unfortunate street folks who have more information than money to pay me. Quid pro quo, remember?" said Jake.

They said their good-byes, and Penn and Ronnie went about digesting and categorizing what they had just heard.

"What a maze of deceit," said a disgusted Ronnie.

"Nothing like the Big Apple for this kind of shit. Daily occurrence. Kind of makes you appreciate our little slice of heaven," said Penn.

"I think we have enough to start focusing on Secur, Biagio, and finding that Samoan. That to me is where the murderer or murderers will come from," said Ronnie.

"You're right, dear. It's late, and I want to go home, watch some mindless TV, and snuggle with my little Jewish gal from the Lone Star State," said Penn, rising from his seat, walking around Ronnie, and rubbing her soft shoulders.

CHAPTER TWENTY-SIX

Alain Secur was out of sorts and edgy. He was alone in his Star Island home, sitting in his office doing some calculations. His debt payoffs to the Teamsters and the Mexicans were due in two short weeks. Everything depended on the success of his upcoming two-part vulture sale. The Indians were circling the wagons, and Secur was nearly out of bullets. He could count on the Teamsters to write down their debt, but the Mexican money owed was blood money; pay up or be killed. He was now nervous because everything depended on his vulture sale going perfectly. His payoff with the Teamsters allowed for him to pledge his personal assets for the agreed-upon shortage they would not get right after the closing. The shortage, approximately $39 million, was earmarked for the Mexicans. All of Secur's significant assets were up for sale, and the total amount he expected from their sale exceeded the shortfall to the Teamsters. Biagio had negotiated this deal prior to the Teamsters' agreeing to terms on the restructured payout at a lower amount. Over the past few years, the Teamsters had made a handsome return on Secur's buildings in the heyday of real estate. They acknowledged this by allowing Secur this one discretion. Banks, REITs, and other real estate investors were all cutting deals in these times just to get out. It wasn't as if their thinking was out of the mainstream.

Secur, like most experienced developers, could run the numbers in his head; it drove his CFO nuts.

Glisten and Claughton Towers had 930 units for sale out of 1020 constructed. Secur was under a letter of intent with the vulture fund for $200 thousand per unit, or $186 million for all 930 units. Less selling expenses of $5 million, he would net $181 million. This represented forty-one cents on the dollar at today's already low sales prices, and it was below the replacement cost of the units if they were built from scratch today. The Teamsters' outstanding loan stood at $442 million. The entire proceeds from the sale would go to the Teamsters and friends of the Teamsters, less $39 million to the Mexicans. The $39 million owed back to the Teamsters would come later from the sale of Secur's Star Island mansion, his Feadship yacht, his expensive car collection, his condo in Ocean Reef, and some of Alicia's jewelry. These items totaled about $46 million in all. If everything clicked on sale day, he would be debt free after all closings with a little change left over. Now he began to relax.

It had been a strange couple of weeks for Secur. Sonya's death, which he was obliquely involved in, had alienated Sandrine. Now that Secur was back full-time with Alicia, she was noticeably aloof and home very little. He wondered where he would be two weeks from now. Hopefully it would be with Sandrine like old times and Alicia like old times. It was more of a dream than a reality, he surmised. *Time to plan a new life*, he thought. Just then the phone rang. It was Biagio with unpleasant news.

"Alain, we have a big problem."

"You think? We've had big problems for years. So many big problems that the 'big problem' phrase has no emotional effect on me anymore," answered a sarcastic and glib Secur.

"Hey, don't shoot the messenger, my friend. What's eatin' you?"

"Well, how about to start, I owe two separate, very tough groups a lot of money that I don't have. One of the groups will kill me, and likely you too, if they don't get their money in two weeks. I haven't seen Sandrine for weeks, and my wife is hardly ever here. Tell me what the big problem is, Biag, because I am numb to big problems," said Secur angrily.

"Moto is back in town, and he wants to see you and me now."

"Fuck him. He can wait like everyone else. Don't be a pussy, Biagio."

"Listen, Mr. Big Shot Developer, when Moto says he wants to see you, that's like the Mexicans wanting their money. If he says now, it is now. So I suggest you get out that house and meet me in Fort Lauderdale at the Mai Kai tonight. You getting this, buddy?"

"All right. What's he want? Did he say?"

"No, he didn't, and he wouldn't tell me when I asked," answered Biagio. He was glad to see Secur snap out of it.

"Great. Not another one of his cat-and-mouse conversations. The bastard wants more money."

"Maybe, maybe not," answered Biagio, giving thought to what Moto might want. He thought Secur might be right.

"OK. What time?"

"I'll see you there at 8:30. Moto is coming at 9:00. We'll talk about some business first."

Secur slammed his cell phone against his desk after he hung up. *What now?* he thought.

Penn had recon people on Secur and Biagio at all times. It was tedious and expensive work, but it was one of the most effective methods for catching bad guys. At 9:00 PM, Penn got a call at dinner with Ronnie. He stepped outside the restaurant with Ronnie in close trail. "Agent Delano, what can I do for you tonight?" asked Penn, hoping for some good news for a change. Ron Delano was one of Penn's most experienced shadow men.

"Agent Melnick and I are at the Mia Kai in Fort Lauderdale. Our suspects rendezvoused with each other here," said Delano, referring to Richard Melnick, another star agent adept at tracking and stakeouts.

"Are you inside the restaurant now?" asked Penn nervously, hoping he was not making a call from inside.

"No sir, I would never do that. I stepped outside, out of view. Melnick's inside," answered Delano.

"What do you have to report?"

"I believe the Samoan is meeting Secur and Biagio inside as we speak," said Delano.

Penn covered his phone and whispered to Ronnie that his agents may have found Moto Seanu. She smiled at Penn and nodded.

"How long have you been there?"

"About twenty minutes. I wanted to blend in for a while before getting up to call you," answered Delano.

"Good work. Here is what I want you to do. When they leave, I want you and Melnick to follow Moto. Use your two-man tactics and keep me posted. When he finally stops somewhere, I will send out a team to relieve you. Understood?" said Penn.

"Yes, sir."

Ronnie leaned closer to get an update from Penn. She could see a slight smile on his face. She knew it well. Penn hung up the phone, put his arm around Ronnie, and said, "Let's get back inside and have some dessert. Tomorrow is going to be a great day."

Secur and Biagio were sitting at a remote table in the fabled Mai Kai restaurant. In the background the stage show, featuring beautiful women and male dancers from Samoa, was underway. Jungle drums vibrated through the large room of diners, and fiery batons were twirled in rhythm with the drums and wild chants. Across the table from Biagio and Secur sat a melancholy Moto Seanu. The conversation over dinner was basically a review of each person's recent involvement in the Sonya Michel murder and reiteration of their alibis. After dinner, drinks were delivered, and Moto took the opportunity to promote his point.

"Look, guys, it's been fun, but I got to get out of here now. I feel the heat, and I don't want to be around this shit any longer. Biag, I like you as a friend, but I cannot protect your ass any longer. Alain, you've been a square shooter from the beginning, so I dig you too. But I got go now," said Moto.

So that's what this is about, thought Secur. *He wants a little traveling money.* He and Biagio just listened, saying nothing.

"I'm gonna need about a hundred and fifty grand to split, and it ain't negotiable."

"Who the hell are you to tell us what you think we should just up and pay you? I've been damned good to you. You just said so yourself," said an upset Biagio. *now it's going to get* ugly,he thought.

To his surprise, Moto stayed calm as he replied. "I expected that. Sometimes I can be blunt, so I understand your feelings. But I don't know any other way to say it but straight between the eyes."

"OK, Moto, you have done everything we asked, but we paid you what you requested, always in advance. We took a chance on you, but you delivered," said Secur, not wanting his friend to escalate a conversation with a known killer.

"Yes to everything you said. But because of circumstances beyond my control, I need to become invisible. I can only do that if I leave. Leaving means going through Canada over to Vancouver and taking a 'no names asked' tramp freighter home. That takes money, bribes and, well, shit—money," said Moto.

"OK, what's our guarantee you won't be back for more?" asked Biagio, calmer than before.

"Uh, oh, guys. There is a guy at the bar who is watching our every move and has been ever since we sat down. Why do you think I wore these sunglasses tonight?" said Moto. He immediately grabbed Biagio's arm. "I said don't look."

There was a moment of silence as Secur and Biagio glanced at the stage, taking a sweep of the bar trying to find the man Moto was speaking about.

"The guy by himself in the coat and tie hunched over his drink?" said Secur.

"Yes. Now stop looking."

"OK Moto, I get it," said Biagio.

"Is that a yes, then?" questioned Moto.

"Yes, it is a yes. Who the hell do you think it is?" asked Biagio.

"FBI is my guess. I noticed a guy tailing me the other day. They're watching us all is my guess, fellas," Moto said.

"What are you suggesting we do now?" asked Secur.

"Put the money in my account tomorrow and let me worry about the feds. I prepared for this tonight. I'll be fine," said Moto.

Moto rose without saying a word, pulled out a cigarette, and lit it as he headed for the glass doors leading into the labyrinth of plants and fountains surrounding the main building. He would not be back.

CHAPTER TWENTY-SEVEN

S andrine had not slept well in two days, ever since her conversation with Kyle Anderson. The less she was around Secur and the more she was around Anderson, it was obvious she had wasted five years in a relationship with an unethical, selfish, and corrupt man. She had told no one about Sonya's entry in her diary the day before she disappeared. She did not lie to Penn, but she would have if they asked her questions about Sonya's diary. Sandrine could tell from her writings that she was afraid of Secur, Biagio, and anyone connected with these disgusting prevaricators.

She was on her way to Fu Wau China grille in Coral Gables to meet Kyle Anderson. It was a little out of the way for each, but safe. The booths were high backed, and the lunch crowd was businessmen and women talking deals and company business in normal tones. She valeted her red Mercedes and saw Kyle inside at the hostess stand. It was a funky contradiction to see a Chinese restaurant in an old Mizner Spanish Mediterranean designed building. *Barrel tile, rough stucco and noodles*, she thought. She couldn't help herself when it came to real estate and design. One of her few addictions.

As she climbed two levels to a covered porch and the entry, Kyle, watching her in anticipation, opened the door from inside, greeting her with, "Hello, Sandy. They're just clearing our table." It was an awkward moment for both. *Should I kiss him? I want to, but where? On the lips, his cheek?* she wondered. Kyle felt the same, but being a gentleman he gave her the Jersey air kiss without really touching her. He did, however, hug her and took in the intoxicating sweet smells of this beautiful woman.

"Did you just sniff me, Kyle?" She smiled and blushed, knowing surely he would be embarrassed. A woman in earshot gave an approving nod to Kyle, wishing he had done the same to her.

"You caught me. The first thing I remember when we first met, besides your beauty, was how nice you smelled."

Sandrine could feel herself blushing, and she felt an urgent wanting for this man. "I am happy you said that. Sometimes men forget how a simple compliment can do so much for a woman's happiness."

The same woman standing near Sandrine seemed amused by the verbal foreplay and smiled again. Kyle saw her smiling and wished that the hostess would come to seat them. His wish was granted immediately as the blushing couple was directed to their booth. The two immediately picked up their menus, wanting to be ready when the waitress arrived to take their order. The waitress showed up seconds later with fried wonton chips and two waters. They ordered their drinks and lunch entrées at the same time. With that done, Kyle broke the ice.

"How have you been? Have you considered my offer?" he asked, diving right into the meat of his conversation. Sandrine was not stunned; she knew Kyle was direct, and she knew she was a valuable Anderson executive.

"In a way it will be up to you, Kyle. But first I need to tell you something. You may not be so ready to bring me back to Anderson Development."

Kyle judged how he should play out the next few moments of the conversation. He decided to let her confess what he already knew.

"I've made some bad judgments the past five years. Judgments that affected a lot of good people. You've heard me say I am ashamed of myself for these poor judgments without really telling you what they were. I will understand if you decide to get up and leave," she stated, looking down at her water. She continued. "The sites for Shimmer, Glisten, and Claughton

Towers would have been yours had I not discussed them with my boyfriend at the time. I betrayed your confidence," she said. She realized something was very wrong as she completed her confession.

Kyle was busy dipping the wonton into the sweet-and-sour sauce with hardly any attitude change as she dropped the big bomb. Finally he spoke in even terms. "I know," he said.

"You know? No you don't. You just want to get in my pants." She could hardly believe her own ears. *I said that. What an idiot you are, Sandrine.*

Kyle was caught off guard and could not contain his laughter. Now Sandrine was really confused.

"You told Alain, OK, I know?" said Kyle, smiling a little less.

"What? You knew? How? When did you know?" She was now starting to get upset, as if she had been set up. But before she could speak, their lunch arrived and the table went silent. In that split second, she reflected. *He knows; that's why he wants me back. That makes sense,* she thought.

"I was very upset. I wanted to fire you, but how could I? Your sister was just murdered. How did I know? I saw you at the morgue in Alain's arms, and suddenly a light went on. On reflection, by dumb luck it was a smart move for Anderson Development not to have taken those small, overpriced locations where the building costs were too high for the end selling prices we would have had to ask for our condos. When I lost out, I ended up at the B+ sites where the price expectations for the buyers were less. Thank God for that or I might have a bunch of vacant units like Secur," said Kyle.

Sandrine was quiet for a moment, taking in everything Kyle had just told her. Kyle studied her eyes. She was staring at her plate, moving her head as if agreeing with some silent conversation she was having with herself. Then she decided to talk. "You feel sorry for me; is that it?" she said.

"For the loss of your sister, yes; for you as a person outside of that loss, no," answered Kyle.

"What's that supposed to mean?" answered Sandrine, now more engaged. She was having second thoughts about this meeting.

"It means I think what you did was wrong, but you are incredibly good at your job. Now that all the cards are on the table and hopefully behind us, I need your brainpower. You are very friendly on the eyes, and I have had some kind of feelings for you ever since we first started working together.

Where that goes, I don't know, but we are in an incredibly difficult economy, especially in our industry, and I want you there with me to see it through. Does that help?" answered Kyle.

"I don't know whether to be flattered or disappointed. But I will come back. I miss my friends and you. But for now, let's just leave it at that. No you and me for starters. I admire your work, and I love how fair you are with your people, especially me, right now."

Kyle listened and said nothing. He knew she was right. It would not be a good idea to get involved. He also knew that might be easier said than done.

CHAPTER TWENTY-EIGHT

Alain Secur was determined to make sure his vulture sale would go off without a hitch this time. He thought, *How stupid could I have been to sell to a firm called Bird of Prey LLC? I deserved the screwing.* The new buyers, a company called Morgan Brothers REIT, had just finished their final inspections at Glisten and Claughton Towers. Secur had a team of condo inspection specialists sent over by Marty Burns. Burns always had his units and the documentation inspected by a firm in Hialeah call Ortiz and Sons Inc. They were starting today and would finish within three days. He was randomly inspecting about one third of the units because he could not afford to have them all reviewed. Marty Burns was calling to be sure that his guys had shown up. Secur confirmed that they had. They spoke for a short while.

After his brief discussion with Marty, Secur's secretary announced another caller was waiting to speak with him.

"Who is it, Jamie?"

"A Mr. Robbins with Morgan Brothers. Do you want the call, sir?"

"Yes. Thank you."

"Is this Alain Secur?"

"Yes, it is. Who is this?" said Secur.

"My name is Jason Robbins with the Morgan Brothers REIT. Do you have a minute to discuss our findings of the inspection of your two projects?" said Robbins. *Here we go*, thought Secur, *problems with the building.*

"I don't know how to say this, Mr. Secur, but I think you should know that we found Chinese drywall in 75 percent of the units. Unfortunately, this is not repairable for our REIT at a reasonable price. As you may be aware, Chinese drywall contaminates all metal surfaces and has the perception of never really being fixable once it has been removed and replaced. Under these circumstances there is no way we can go through with the purchase of your units. I'm sure you can understand the ramifications of the prohibitive costs to fix this problem, not to mention the PR nightmare that goes with any building having Chinese drywall," said Robbins, trying his best to be polite and calm. He must have known what a financial blow this would be to Secur. Alain Secur dropped the phone, fainted over his desk, and smashed his forehead on the marble surface.

Marty Burns was on the phone talking to his guys at Claughton Tower. They had just entered the building when one of Morgan Brothers' inspectors was leaving. Jack Pena, Marty's top inspector, had delivered the startling news to Marty at the same time Secur was getting the same bad reviews from Jason Robbins.

"Are you certain you heard him right, Jack?" repeated Marty, not believing what he was hearing.

"Yes, but I didn't believe him, so I looked myself. The AC coils in the affected units were just turning black, and the uncovered copper ends of the electrical wiring had already turned a rich black as well. Marty, I can smell the shit, too. I believe them. You know what this means, don't you?" asked Jack.

"I sure do, Jack. There is no need for you to waste Mr. Secur's money on an inspection that won't matter. Go to your other inspections and tell your guys not to mention this to anyone," said Marty. He hung up the phone and leaned forward on his desk, running his hands through his hair while bent over in frustration. *Poor Alain Secur. He's finished*, he thought. After a brief postmortem, he dialed Kyle Anderson's cell phone.

"Your old nemesis will never haunt your business world again," said Marty with his cryptic message.

"Hello, Marty. What has Alain done now? Left the country?" said Kyle, mystified by Marty's opening statement.

"Worse than that, Kyle. Inspectors supposedly found Chinese drywall in 75 percent of his units in both towers."

"No," said a stunned Kyle. He never took Secur's building talents very seriously. To Anderson, Secur was more like a real estate promoter with liberal lenders and any old general contractor who could slap up a building for him. He always cut corners.

"Yeah, afraid so. You know what this means, of course?" asked Marty.

"I cannot imagine the fallout. It will take at least a hundred grand a unit to strip the drywall, redo the electrical, install new AC ducts and air handlers, put in new drywall, give it new paint and new trim, and put all the cabinets and bathrooms back together—not to mention the money required to make the improvements and the cost of money, both new and old. He's finished, as you said," agreed Kyle.

"I got to go, Kyle. I have to figure out what I need to do with his listings in other buildings. Even though there may not be drywall issues in his other buildings, no one will take a chance on any Alain Secur properties. You know this business. Perception is reality," said Marty.

"Thanks for the heads up. Listen, don't tell anyone about this conversation. I mean no one is to know."

"Not a word, Kyle."

CHAPTER TWENTY-NINE

"Penn, they just hauled Alain Secur to the hospital from his office about five minutes ago," said Ron Delano, an FBI agent following Secur's every move.

"What happened?" asked Penn.

"I have no idea."

"Get with the guys in the van and see if you can tell from the tapes if something happened on the phone that may explain all this. Then call me back. Finish up your stakeout there and head to the hospital."

Moments later Melnick called Penn, this time from his surveillance stakeout of Biagio. Melnick was following Biagio at high speed, headed northwest toward the old Orange Bowl. He had called his men in the van to see what had transpired moments before Biagio ran to his car and sped away.

"Penn, it's Richard. Alain's wife called Biagio moments ago explaining that Secur had collapsed at his office and was on his way to Jackson Memorial Hospital in an ambulance. The guys in the van told me she was frantic on the phone with Biagio," offered Agent Melnick.

"I know. Delano called me from Secur's office. Did you hear why he collapsed?" asked Penn. Just then his phone beeped. The glass face on his phone lit up. *Delano.*

"Richard, I'll call you back. Stay on Biagio and get your van to the hospital. Track all of Biagio's calls. Ron Delano is on the other line, and he is also en route," said Penn as he pushed to switch calls on his Blackberry.

"Randall, I have the information on Secur."

"Go ahead, Delano."

"The last phone call to Secur was from a representative of Morgan Brothers REIT. He had just informed Secur that his inspection team at his two towers found Chinese drywall in 75 percent of the units. The line eventually went dead. It appears Secur, hearing that news, collapsed at his desk. Moments later on his cell phone, a woman named Pardee, his secretary, called 911," said Delano.

With that, Penn said a quick good-bye and summoned Ronnie Feldman to his office. She quickly arrived, sensing the urgency in Penn's voice.

"What's wrong?" she asked.

"Secur is on his way to the hospital. He collapsed after hearing from the vulture fund's inspector rep that his two towers are infested with Chinese drywall and the sale is off. Seventy-five percent of the total number of units are affected," explained Penn in a calm voice, a voice belying his tension.

"My God, you know what this means? All hell's about to break loose. The Teamsters and their friends will lose their entire investment. Worse than that are the Mexicans, who are expecting money right after the closings. Closings that will never happen. And then there are the friends of the Teamsters and Luc LoPrendo. Penn, a firestorm is coming."

"I'm afraid you are right," pondered Penn, thinking of how to catch Sonya's killer and the future killers of LoPrendo, Secur, and Secur's wife.

The ambulance arrived at the emergency room of Jackson Memorial Hospital, followed secretly by two FBI listening vans and two trained stakeout specialists, as well as by Alicia Secur and Biagio LoPrendo. By the time Secur was admitted, he had regained consciousness and was sitting up in bed behind a curtained area of the emergency room. He was momentarily disoriented, then embarrassed by the fuss. He had fainted forward, and his head slammed into the granite top of the desk in free fall. He sported a knot in the middle of his forehead and a nasty red bruise that by tomorrow would be purple. He had been knocked unconscious by the head butt to his desk.

It was 5:00, and Alicia Secur was on her way to Executive Airport in Fort Lauderdale to pick up Luc LoPrendo. His trip had been delayed a few days. Executive Airport was an out-of-the-way, medium-sized private airport in central Broward County a short drive from I-95 off Commercial Boulevard. It was five miles north of Fort Lauderdale International airport and close enough that many a beginning private pilot called to land at Executive only to be lined up at Fort Lauderdale International. Alicia had left her husband at Jackson Memorial Hospital after he was moved from intensive care. When he finally succumbed to his medication and was out to the world, Alicia decided it was safe for her to leave Secur in the good hands of the hospital staff. The nurse explained to Alicia that her husband would be out for at least six hours.

She pulled up to the Medallion FBO parking lot and viewed Luc's Lear 55 taxiing to the ramp. As she walked inside the fixed base operators' waiting area, the aroma of burned kerosene, otherwise known as JP-4 jet fuel, from Luc's jet stung her nostrils. The whine of the jet whirling at high rpms and the smell reminded her of more pleasant days when Alain and she would jet set around the world on their own jet; that jet was parked in a hangar in Opa-Locka, now for sale. The nostalgia continued as she chose a seat facing the glass window where she could see Luc deplaning. Alicia rose to meet Luc when he came through the door. He gave Alicia a large, Italian bear hug. She worried he had already heard the news about Alain and the Chinese drywall.

After they separated, Luc spoke. "My darling, how are you?" At that moment she sensed he had not heard. Better that she break the news than he hear it from one of the bad guys back home. Now was as good a time as any. "I presume you have not heard?" she said as she wrapped her arm around Luc's elbow to steer him to a quiet corner separating him from his entourage. The entourage sensed a need for Luc's privacy and left to pick up the rental car. Luc and Alicia would follow in her car.

"Heard what? I've been in the air nearly three hours," said Luc. Before she answered Alicia scanned the small waiting room, looking for strangers in earshot.

"Alain is in the hospital. He's suffered a severe breakdown," whispered Alicia.

"This mess has finally caught up to him, I guess," offered Luc.

"In a way, yes, Luc, but that's not the worst of it. My husband will recover, but his precious condominium towers are dead," she said. Now Luc looked her strangely in the eye. An unknown fear spiked his blood pressure in anticipation.

"Explain dead, my dear."

"This morning inspectors for the vulture funds found that 75 percent of the units in both towers that Alain is selling have Chinese drywall."

Luc's face turned red, and his eyes bulged as he attempted to control his rage. His worst fears had been realized. "Are you certain?" Luc asked, raising his voice in a controlled manner.

"Positive. Alain got the news via phone in his office while sitting at his desk. He fainted forward, hitting his head hard on the desktop. Jamie Pardee called the ambulance, and here I am hours later telling you," she said, feeling melancholy and dispirited.

"If he fainted, who told you?"

"A source who was notified at the site called me shortly thereafter," Alicia said, remaining vague, hoping Luc would not care whom her source was.

"My dear, I am so sorry for you. We will need to step up our protection of you immediately. You cannot go home, ever. Not until the dust settles and we see what will happen with so many bad guys owed so much money—especially the head-chopping Mexicans. I'm sorry; I didn't mean to say that," said Luc, deep in thought. He was calculating his next step. From the moment he had seen Alicia at the FBO, his well-laid plans were worthless.

"Oh Luc, I'm scared. Alain has no one to protect him. He's still my husband. I can't just leave him. And what am I to do?" she said, almost in tears.

"Your safety is now in my hands. Don't worry. But I will dispatch a team to watch Alain. Let's get out of here so I can devise a new plan quickly. Which car did you bring?"

"The black Navigator SUV, why?" she asked.

"They're fairly numerous down here; we should blend in. Just to be safe, I'll drive," he said as they moved outside and into the SUV.

As they pulled away he called his lead captain in the car ahead and instructed him to go north to Manalapan and the Ritz Carlton on the ocean instead of the original hotel in Miami where they had reservations. The Ritz was thirty-five minutes north of Executive Airport, located in central Palm Beach County in a quiet beach location. Moments later his captain called back and confirmed that a suite at the penthouse level was reserved under the name of Michael McEwan. *God Bless the Irish*, thought Luc.

CHAPTER THIRTY

Biagio LoPrendo was sitting in Secur's hospital room watching his friend fight his way out of sleep and grogginess. His head was moving side to side as the disorientation clouded his senses. His eyes opened just enough to see Biagio, and then his nose smelled his location. He realized he was in a hospital, but for what? It was dark outside his window, and he wondered how long he had been here.

"What am I doing here, Biag? Am I dreaming? What happened?"

"Rest easy. You're not dying; you simply fainted in your office and banged your head hard on your desk. It's just a minor concussion," he calmly explained, not wanting to excite his friend. "Can you remember what caused the fainting spell? Were you dehydrated? Are you diabetic?"

"No, I have no memory of what happened. I don't even know who I was talking to," explained Secur, rubbing the still-swollen knot on his forehead. Just then Biagio's cell phone rang.

"I'm with Secur at the hospital, Luc. Where are you? You sound like you're next door," Biagio said.

"I am in Broward County right now, and that is all we need to say over this line. How's he doing?"

"He has temporary amnesia about what occurred. What are you doing here?" asked Biagio.

"I told you I would be here just prior to the sale. Can you walk outside of Secur's room, please?"

"Sure. What's wrong?"

"Just do it now."

Biagio excused himself from a still-groggy Secur and went around the corner, far enough away that Secur would not hear.

"OK, Luc, please tell me what's going on."

The fact that Biagio had no clue what was going on made Luc irate. It was indicative of the last four years of Biagio's representing the Teamsters, his friends, and their money. Luc struggled to avoid an outburst. With calm reserve he spoke. "The vulture sale is over. That is why your friend fainted. The inspection team for the vultures found Chinese drywall in 75 percent of the units in both towers," said Luc, awaiting the gasping response from Biagio. Instead Biagio was speechless. He said nothing in his trance.

"Did you hear me, Biagio?" Luc repeated.

"How did you hear that before me? Is this a joke? It's not funny. How can you be sure?" peppered Biagio, not wanting to believe what he had just heard.

"I will tell you all of this when we meet. And I wish it were a joke," said Luc.

"What are we going to do? The Mexicans will kill him," said Biagio.

"Calm down. Reinforcements are on the way. Stay with him until my team gets there. You need to get the hospital to agree to allow our people to watch him until he recovers. Focus on just that and don't say a word to Alain. Understood?" said Luc. He was now in charge.

"How soon can we repair these units and get them ready to resell?" asked Biagio naively.

That nearly sent Luc into a tirade. "Biagio, sometimes I wonder how you got this far. Don't you remember the office buildings we bought in Hoboken containing Chinese drywall two years ago? We got the real estate for 15 cents on the dollar. It cost 50 percent of the total original construction costs to rip out and repair the bad drywall. All of the metal parts on the air conditioning units were black and had to be replaced, the drywall had to be stripped, flooring pulled up near copper piping, electrical wiring was mostly replaced, and on and on. Fortunately this was an office and not a home. If we were stupid enough to refurbish the units in Secur's two towers, the reputation of the builder and the perception and fear of any lingering consequences would make sales in a bad market nearly impossible. The vulture funds won't come back and take a chance like that. I see this disaster as a total write-down. This is like Lehman Brothers—going, going, gone," said Luc as Biagio himself seemed ready to faint.

"Write it down! You mean zero, nada? That's over 400 million in losses to just our guys, plus 39 million to the Mexicans," exclaimed Biagio, still in total disbelief.

"I don't want to discuss this anymore on this phone; you never know who may be listening. I have some *untraceables* we can use for the next couple of weeks. I will call you in the morning, and we'll pick a place to meet. Stay with Secur. When my guys get there, you're going to have to tell Secur the whole story. Don't let anyone hear you. He's going to see my guys, so don't make up some lame story. You got that, kid?" said Luc.

"Got it."

It was early evening, and Moto Seanu was blindfolded and riding in an old step van flanked by four men bigger and stronger than he. One minute he had been walking along the sidewalk near his Oakland Park apartment, and the next moment he was jumped, a large black sack was put over his head, and metal straps were tightened around him like an old whiskey barrel. Within thirty seconds he was lying in the back of a van or truck hearing only Spanish jibber and occasional laughter.

The ride lasted more than thirty minutes. Seanu's hearing was acutely aware of his changing circumstances. His Spanish abductors were now quiet, and the buzz of normal traffic was nonexistent. The roads were now bumpy, not smooth like before, and there was no stopping and starting as there had been in the city. *This is not good*, he thought. *I am going to be assassinated in the woods.*

The van stopped. He could smell charcoal lighter or some other fuel as he was lifted out of the van. It took four men to lift his plump, three-hundred-pound hulk from the vehicle.

FBI agent Orlando "Tony" Lopez had seen the whole Seanu kidnapping unfold as he was tailing the Samoan bad guy. Three nights ago Seanu had attempted to give Lopez the slip after his meeting at the Mai Kai. At the moment Lopez was talking to Penn after he had established the route the van and its abductors were heading. They were on US Highway 27 heading north into Palm Beach County. Lopez dropped back in order to avoid being noticed. This stretch of road was flanked on both sides by six-foot-tall sugar cane. Highway 27 was not a heavily traveled road, forcing Lopez to trail at a greater distance. He was certain he had remained undetected. If he was detected, he was heavily outmanned, and probably outgunned as well. Nothing new for this wily ex-military veteran, but worth avoiding.

"I cannot see exactly where they are turning, so I am going to lay back, turn off my headlights, and try to see where they turn off. Continually triangulate the GPS location of this cell phone," instructed Lopez.

"Tony, I know that area. Lots of big trucks up and down that road tonight, you can be sure. Be careful running dark. When you see them turn off 27, get as close as you can and give me your mark. Text it to me—no phone calls. Unfortunately I don't have anyone in the area I can send right now to back you up, so be smart and don't try to go it alone. I'll have guys en route as soon as I hang up, but you are an hour away," instructed Penn.

"Don't worry, boss, I'm not stupid. I will go beyond their turn-off by a mile or so and turn around and come back to within five hundred yards of their exit and wait to see which way they leave. I'll pick them up from there and track them back to wherever they are going," said Lopez.

"Sounds like a good plan. I'll text you every ten minutes to make sure you are OK. Keep that phone charged," reminded Penn.

Three minutes after Lopez and Penn finished their conversation, the van turned east onto a narrow dirt road. The moon was about three quarters full, so once his eyes adjusted to the dark without headlamps, he tracked his distance to the turnoff. He slowed for the moment as he approached the road, dialed Penn back, and gave him the mark. Penn could send a team in later that night with night goggles to determine where the kidnappers were and if this was their base of operations; or worse, where they were going to dump Seanu's body. As planned, Lopez went a mile north of the van's turnoff. His luck was holding since not a single semi- trailer truck had come from the north or the south during his trail. He coasted to a stop not using his brakes and made a wide U-turn heading back south. He cut the engine and coasted into place using the hand brake so his brake lights would not give away his position. He was almost stopped when his left front tire ran over an empty plastic one-liter soda bottle. He heard the pop, but he was sure he was too far away to be heard by the kidnappers.

CHAPTER THIRTY-ONE

Seanu was kneeling on the ground out in the middle of nowhere. He was surrounded by five dark-skinned Latin men with indifferent looks on their faces. For a moment Seanu took in the heavens and the skies above, beautiful on any other night, but this could be his last view of the heavens—a place he doubted he would ever see. A dull fire burned in a low flame in the middle of a large clearing. Fifteen feet from the fire was a single gravesite that Seanu was certain belonged to him. Next to that was a raised blanket that appeared to be covering something long and narrow. One of the five men came around Seanu with a flashlight and lifted the blanket for Seanu to observe. He shone the light on the uncovered image, and Seanu uncontrollably vomited on the man's shoes. He could not believe what he was seeing.

"Nice going, Moto. You puked on my shoes," the stranger remarked.

Moto was still in a trance as he saw the body of a man with his head severed and stuck under the armpit staring back at him with dead, empty eyes.

The stranger continued. "That's you if you don't do as we tell you. My name is Armando, and that's all you need to know. I found out today that one of my loans, a very large loan, will not be paid back because my collateral is infected. Do you know what I am talking about, Mr. Moto?" asked Armando Nacion. By now Seanu had accepted his fate and figured he would die here tonight, hoping not to end up like the gentleman next to him. And then, as he looked one more time at the misplaced face, he gasped uncontrollably. He recognized the face; it was one of his Samoan dancers from the Mai Kai, his friend Toomba.

"Oh, I see you recognize your friend. I'm sorry. This will be you if you don't do what we tell you. Do you hear me?" asked Armando as he put the barrel of his Glock under Seanu's chin, forcing him to look up at Armando.

"What is it you want me to do?" Seanu asked with a shaky voice.

Armando noted the childlike behavior of Seanu, who was weeping at the carnage beside him. "Stop whimpering. We're not going to kill you tonight. Maybe never," answered Armando.

"I'll do whatever you ask. Please don't kill me. I support my mother back home in Samoa. I am all she has." His voice tailed off.

After Armando relayed Seanu's response in Spanish, the other Latin men burst out in laughter. Seanu had become their little game for the evening. The laughter died as Armando raised his arm and then spoke. "You are a momma's boy, ey? We'll make you into a man. Listen carefully." Armando began to explain, "Today we lost a lot of money thanks to two friends of yours. These men promised to pay me back monies owed by next week. But as I said, their collateral, some nine hundred condominium units, are now useless piles of Chinese drywall. My sources tell me the units are nearly worthless even if you could sell them, which of course you cannot. These two friends must be killed and their bodies delivered to me. If you do this, I will let you live and I will forget that I saw you that night you dumped the woman in the ocean. I watched you that night as we went by. We were watching you the whole night. You are a sloppy assassin, Mr. Moto. I am not. Your so-called friends Mr. Secur and Mr. LoPrendo asked me to eliminate you that night. But we thought better and let you live," Armando continued.

As Armando Nacion revealed the truth to Seanu, it suddenly made sense. The strange way they had treated him after the murder. The uncomfortable meeting at the Mai Kai. *Those bastards*, he thought. He sized up his status and decided to stay cool and listen to Armando's ultimatum.

Of course he would agree, but his attitude tonight needed to change. His actions were being carefully graded by Armando.

Seanu decided to be flippant, showing less fear. He remarked, "I thought I recognized you."

It was not well received by Armando. "Do you think this is a joke, fat boy?" Armando said, riled.

"I'm here. Kill me if you want; I don't care. But I would like the job you offered me a minute ago. What are you paying me?" asked Seanu, bringing sarcasm to the discussion.

"How about I let you live? Is that payment enough?" warned Armando.

"I'll do it for a plane ticket home and ten thousand dollars. Surely you can afford that," proclaimed Seanu boldly. It may have worked, as Armando spoke in Spanish to his comrades, eliciting loud laughter when he finished.

"OK, fat boy, you have a deal. But if you fuck this up, I will personally go to Samoa and deliver your body parts to your mommy," said Armando. No one else laughed at the *mommy* phrase. Seanu expected that only Armando spoke English. *Could be useful,* he thought.

"You have three days to deliver Biagio LoPrendo and Alain Secur to me dead or alive, same price either way. I am a man of my word. Here is a nontraceable cell phone. Don't lose it. Carry it at all times; I'll be watching," said Armando. He cut the nylon cuffs from behind Seanu's back and handed him a shovel. After the remaining four men put the body into the grave, Armando gave one last command. "Bury your friend, and let's get you back to Miami."

Armando barked in Spanish to his men, "Where's Secundo? He was supposed to close the gate and come back to this site." The request went out but nothing came back. After a twenty-minute search, Secundo was nowhere to be seen, and Armando wanted to get out of the area before morning light came up.

"Leave him; he has a cell phone," said a concerned Armando. Secundo's disappearance was unnerving. He put all of his men on alert. Out here violent rednecks were as bad as Mexican cartel members. He expected that Secundo might have fallen prey to one of them or he may have been gored by wild hogs that roamed the area. He needed to leave immediately, and left Secundo to his own devices.

The popped bottle that Tony Lopez had run over as he parked along the side of US 27 did not go unnoticed, as he originally thought. But Lopez was a twenty-five year veteran in field operations, and he took nothing for granted; it was the reason he was still alive. After running over the bottle, he disembarked from his car with his night vision goggles and his favorite quiet weapon, a sawed-off baseball bat with a lead weight in the end. Lopez was six foot three and weighed 240 pounds. It could be lethal, but it was the best blunt quiet weapon he had tonight to disable a bad guy. Confident his last GPS to Penn had been received, he was outside his car thirty-five feet to the north, lying on the uphill swale of a drainage ditch running parallel to the highway. He suspected a man would be left to guard the road or at least warn Armando if anyone was coming. As he lay in the swale, several large trucks streamed by him with their headlamps illuminating his car for several seconds at a time as they passed. Since he was a good distance north of the turnoff, he knew that the car was not noticeable; the bottle pop on a silent night in the country was the reason he was in a defensive mode. He observed movement through his monochromatic night vision goggles; as he had feared, a man was crossing the highway with what appeared to be a gun in one hand. Lopez had locked all but one door; the right rear side was left open. The night was still dark enough so that Lopez felt comfortable enough moving closer to the car as the man, now a hundred feet south of his car, approached on the same side of the street.

Lopez was forty-six years old, in shape, and a veteran of many hand-to-hand altercations. The man approaching slowed as he got within fifty feet of the vehicle, crouching into a duck-walk position as he moved forward. Lopez figured he outweighed the medium-built man by forty pounds and knew he was a couple of inches taller. He began to feel more confident but stayed tense and prepared. The intruder was now directly in front of the front bumper, circling around to the passenger side front door.

Lopez had located himself directly behind the car, quietly leaning against the trunk. A sudden smash of the gun butt against the passenger side window sent glass flying in all directions. The man aimed the gun through the window and said "Stop" in harshly accented, almost undetectable English. Seeing nothing, he unlocked the door and quickly opened it, pointing the gun inside; no alarm. Lopez had pulled the alarm fuse before leaving the car in anticipation of such a move by the intruder. The man saw the car was empty and peered in to see what he could find. A bone-crushing blow from a lead-laced Louisville Slugger wielded by Lopez met the intruder's upper rear skull, spattering blood into Lopez's goggles. He immediately tore them from his head in time to see the intruder fall in a slump inside the car's front seat. Lopez reached to his belt, fetched his handcuffs, and cuffed the man behind his back.

Once secure, he rose from inside the car and scanned the surroundings for a second man. His eyes, partially adapted to the darkness, saw nothing. Lopez found his night vision goggles and cleaned the lenses. A final search through his goggles detected no movement. He continued to secure the unconscious intruder. He took his pulse—*still living*—then wrapped tape around his month and ankles and hauled the limp body into the back seat. A search of the victim's pockets revealed twenty dollars in odd bills but zero identification.

Ninety minutes later, as Lopez sat vigilantly in the front seat, he could see taillights coming from the side road turning onto US 27 and heading south, away from his position. He quickly started the car and waited a moment for separation from the van before he pulled out. He drove for a mile, inching closer to the van. He saw a crossing street ahead and quickly turned right, heading west for about two hundred feet, careful not to hit his brakes as he slowed down. Lopez quickly made a 180-degree U-turn, heading in the opposite direction back toward US 27. After turning back onto 27 in the same direction as before, he turned on his headlights and began tracking the van once again. He was three quarters of a mile behind the van. Feeling relieved, he called Penn.

"I'm heading south on 27 about half a mile in trail of the van. Are you getting my cell phone location?" asked Lopez.

"Yes. Can you converse?" asked an eager Penn.

"Yes sir. I have a bad guy in custody, unconscious, bound in the rear seat, head injuries. Can you intercept my position and have another crew track the van?" asked a tired and worn-out Lopez.

"Good job, Tony. At the next intersection two miles ahead, one crew will pull in front of you, and at the next intersection farther south, another crew will fall in behind you and flash their lights. They are all aware of the van description. When you get to Alligator Alley, go east to Fort Lauderdale. Do you know where Broward Memorial Hospital is located?" said Penn.

"Yes, sir, I do."

"I will be waiting for you there. Two state troopers are on their way and will escort you to the hospital once you turn onto The Alley. They are undercover, so don't expect the yellow-and-black cruisers. You'll know them. Great job, Tony. We'll debrief at the hospital," said Penn.

"Is Ronnie with you?" asked Lopez, strangely catching Penn off guard.

"Yes. Why?" Penn asked innocently.

"I'd rather look at her this morning than you while we debrief."

"You dirty old man. I'm telling her you said that."

"Bring a Spanish interpreter. I have a feeling this guy does not or will not respond to English interrogation," finished Lopez.

CHAPTER THIRTY-TWO

Armando Nacion was dead tired and in no mood to be nice to anyone, especially that someone who owed him a large sum of money. As he saw things in simple, non-emotional terms, his repayment generator was dead. Chinese drywall had struck the cartel. Back in Mexico, his bosses would not be happy losing $39 million, money that Nacion had vouched for as a good investment and a way to launder large sums of dirty money. Despite the high profit margins his primary product produced (cocaine) and the endless market of American users craving that product, $39 million was still a lot of capital to be without. At this moment he had no choice but to be pleasant with the person on the other end of this phone call, Biagio LoPrendo. It was just after 7:30 a.m. and not too early to call about something so important. He was driving south from Fort Lauderdale after dropping Moto Seanu back at his apartment in nearby Wilton Manors. Just before calling he stopped for gas and picked up two energy drinks and a cup of black coffee. Armed with mood stimulants, he felt a surge of energy, at least enough so as not to slur his words and sound tired and drunk.

"Biagio, its Nacion. I hear we may have a slight problem with the vulture fund. You realize my payment is due in less than two weeks? In full, by the way," said Nacion, polite and non-threatening.

Biagio had his canned response rehearsed and was finally glad to use it. He was not surprised by the call. He played along, proffering his own ruse. "I wish I had good news for you, but as you have probably already heard, the inspectors for the vulture fund found Chinese Drywall throughout both buildings," said Biagio, wondering how the truth would play out with this madman.

"Why can't we just fix the units and go back to the fund and give them a slight discount the second time around? I suppose I could take a partial payment until the repairs are done and the next sale occurs," responded Nacion. He played dumb knowing full well the ramifications of Chinese drywall repairs. He wanted to relax Biagio and keep him off guard, at least until Moto got to him.

"I wish it were that easy, Armando, but it costs way too much money to repair the individual units, and the buying public will not come back to a tainted project. Well, I shouldn't say they won't come back, but the huge discounts and increased warranty costs you will need in place to attract that type of buyer makes the repair unprofitable," said Biagio. He sensed that Nacion might now be more reasonable. *The truth is working*, he thought.

Nacion played along as he continued to reel in Biagio. "Well then, Biag, how exactly do we get our money back, and how do you unload the poisonous units?"

Biagio was ready with another canned remark. "I have heard that there may be companies today, including certain other vulture funds that specialize in Chinese drywall removal and renovation. They pay much less, obviously because of the large expense to cure the problem. But by virtue of their reputation and thorough post renovation warranty, they are much better equipped to handle the disposition of the infected product. But for you to wait that long, I have my own solution for your repayment at 100 percent on the dollar," said Biagio.

"How will you do that? Borrow more money from the Teamsters?" said Nacion quietly.

"No, they will wait for the next vulture sale," said Biagio, knowing it to be a lie. Nacion knew it was a lie as well but continued to play along. Biagio, now on a roll and certain Nacion was being cooperative, continued the lie even further. "Besides, Secur has been very good to the Teamsters over the years and has enough goodwill built up to weather this storm and come back another day," continued Biagio.

Nacion could barely control his laughter; an angry laugh it would be. "Well then, when shall I expect repayment? And make me believe you have a source," said Nacion.

"The exact date will be hard to predict, but Secur has listed all of his assets for sale, including cars, homes, his planes and boat, and his brokerage account. In all, $51 million to produce $39 million owed to you," said Biagio. He had inflated the real amount of the asset valuation for good measure.

"I see, and then I should be safe in this plan? A plan with a start date, but no exit date? Should I expect no interest on this amount, Biagio?" said Nacion with just a hint of disbelief.

"No. You shall be paid interest; however, we ask that the rate be lowered to 6 percent."

"Biagio, I appreciate your candor, I really do. I will call you in a couple of days to see how the asset sale goes," said Nacion. He heard enough to know there was little to no chance this would occur. He also assumed that the Teamsters were probably told the same worthless story. There was not enough money to go around. *Keep'em guessing*, he thought. With that, they said their good-byes, promising each to stay in touch with the other.

CHAPTER THIRTY-THREE

Penn and Ronnie arrived at the hospital mid-morning with intentions of debriefing a Latin male with a very sore head and an unwilling attitude. *What a great way to start your morning*, he thought, staring at Ronnie's cleavage. It did not go unnoticed by Ronnie, who often caught Penn looking below her neck. Penn knew what was coming.

"OK, big guy, watcha looking at, eh? I'm on duty, you know? This could be considered sexual harassment. I could literally have your job, Mr. Penn."

Penn was blushing with an ear-to-ear grin. "Baby, it's worth the risk. "

Ronnie was now blushing, as several doctors passed by just as Penn was commenting. She looked back to see if the doctors kept going or if they were sneaking a peek at her ass, as guys usually did. When she saw they were not, she pinched Penn's ass, surprising him once again. Somewhere inside the hospital, probably on their security cameras, someone was seeing a pretty good show. When they arrived on the third floor, they saw Tony Lopez at the nursing station. Two men from Penn's office were at the end of the hall, flanking the doorway to what Penn assumed to be the Latin outlaw's suite.

"Good morning Tony. Long night, huh?" said Penn. Penn could see the lines of fatigue on his face.

"Good morning, Rand, Ronnie. The perp is secure, so let's use the waiting room around the corner to interrogate him," said Lopez.

They commandeered the empty waiting room, and Ronnie took out her notebook and pen. For over thirty minutes, they peppered Lopez with questions relating to his experiences just a few hours before. They learned very little new information since everything except the short fight had been out of Lopez's direct observation; much of the debrief had already been discussed on various calls to Penn during the activity.

From there they went to see the Latin perp. He was resting comfortably. His head was bandaged heavily. The interpreter arrived with Penn and was reviewing a list of questions Ronnie had written for her. The Spanish woman was beautiful, and Penn hoped her looks would soften the prisoner. Information was important no matter how it was obtained. Penn and Ronnie provided the interpreter with a digital recorder. Initially they would not attend the meeting as long as progress was being made between the interpreter and the perp. Penn could see that the prisoner was groggy. He seemed to come alive when the vivacious woman came to his bedside and began conversing in Spanish. Lopez stood outside with Penn and delivered the play-by-play of the conversation in English. The interpreter was making extraordinary progress, which surprised everyone. The conversation had lasted about twenty minutes when the interpreter waved Lopez inside. Moments later Lopez returned with good news. Oddly, the conversational flow within the room continued and became one-sided as the prisoner, bound and shackled to the steel bed, began speaking in Spanish nonstop. He was clearly terrified and seemed relieved to be captured. He was younger than his weathered, unshaven looks. His dark eyes were sunk deep in his face, and most of his teeth were missing or rotted. He was quite personable, with no anger toward Lopez for the cracked skull he suffered. Lopez began to brief Penn and Ronnie.

"His name is Carlos Rodrigo Secundo. His family lives in C. Juarez and they will be killed if he does not work for the cartel at any task he is asked to do. It seems he has been asked to kill men from other cartels and agents against his cartel. This, too, he must do, or his family will be wiped out," relayed Lopez.

"Isn't his confession a death sentence? Why would he willingly tell us so much information?" questioned Penn.

"He looks at the FBI as some super law enforcement agency that he thinks can save his family in Mexico if he tells you everything he knows right away. He believes we can get to them before his boss can," answered Lopez as all three crowded around the door to Secundo's room.

"Has he given you the name of his boss?" asked Penn directly to interpreter Elaine Johnston. She was the Bureau's contract interpreter and was married to an attorney with the Dade County prosecutor's office. She was used to working with scared, underprivileged Latins from around the world. After the preliminary debrief by Lopez outside Secundo's door, all four adjourned to the quiet peacefulness of the waiting room to hear what Ms. Johnston had to say about her interview.

"Oh my God. What an incredible and sad story Mr. Secundo told me. He cannot be more than twenty years old, and he is being made to work and kill people for a man named Armando Nacion. Apparently Mr. Nacion is in some money laundering scheme for the Mexican cartel here in Miami; he is here with a team to collect their money or kill the borrowers," said Johnson. Her English was as perfect as her Spanish.

"What were they doing in the cane fields out west of Palm Beach last night?" asked Penn as Ronnie took notes.

"They had kidnapped a large, dark man, not Latin, and told him unless he killed the men who owe Armando the money, his family would be murdered back in his native country," she answered.

"Do you know what made this man so special that they targeted just him?" asked Penn.

"This particular dark, foreign man is friends with the two debtors. In addition to threatening him and his family, they showed him his friend who had been decapitated by Nacion. He was told that not only would they kill his family, they would also kill him the same way they murdered his friend," said Johnson, obviously not enjoying the conversation.

173

"What about Secundo? How many family members does he have back in Mexico?" asked Penn, fearful that children might be involved.

"He has a wife, two young children, and a mother, all under the watch of the cartel at a compound in C. Juarez, Mexico," she explained.

"My God, that's horrible," muttered Ronnie.

"Penn, can we let him go and follow him somehow, or implant a small radio beacon to track him?" asked Lopez.

"Any ideas, anyone?" asked Penn.

"When I struck Secundo, his glasses flew off his head. He was wearing those attachment strings that clip to the ends of the ear frames. We could plant a locator there," said Lopez excitedly.

"We cannot let him go, Tony. You've been watching too much TV. This guy tried to kill you, remember? A federal agent. We'll get Nacion some other way," answered Penn.

"How do we know this isn't one big lie to misdirect us? He may not even have a family," added Ronnie.

"Elaine, what do you think about his story? Is he telling the truth?" asked Penn.

"Yes, I think he is. He's not that smart, and he seems relieved that he told me his story. My guess is he thinks the great FBI and the United States of America will save his family. He also told me that Nacion would have probably killed him anyway because he—Secundo—could not stand doing the killings. In other words, he was not a psycho like the others," answered Elaine.

"Penn, why don't we bring Gambrel into this investigation and see if his DEA counterparts in El Paso have any ideas about this cartel?" requested Ronnie.

"Good idea, Ronnie. Elaine, did he mention the cartel Nacion represents?" asked Penn.

"El Trinolea. The Trinolea Cartel."

"Damn it," blurted Penn.

"What?"

"They are one of the most vicious groups along the border and central Mexico. Murder, kidnapping, political extortion, and slavery," explained

Penn. "Did he tell you where they live or where they stay in South Florida?" Penn asked.

"According to Sanchez, they have a mother ship of some kind forty miles off shore masquerading as a commercial cargo vessel servicing the Bahamas. He claims they are smuggling from the mother ship with numerous fast boats; he and a few handpicked soldiers move from house to house at random around Miami to avoid the authorities. Their weapons are already waiting for them when they move from one house to another. SUV's are swapped out after each new move. As I said, the kid was a wealth of information," said Elaine.

"What are we going to do with him now?" asked Ronnie.

"Quietly arrest him. No press. Attempted murder of a federal officer will be the charge," said Penn without hesitation.

"I'll call Reggie Gambrel and see if we can find out about his family. Elaine, get back in there and tell him we will try to help him but we need more information about the whereabouts of the mother ship, house locations, and what part of Juarez the compound is located. Mirandize him in Spanish and English, and be sure you have two of my men with you at all times. Lastly, at the very end, explain to him the charges against him and why. Everyone else back to the office except you, Lopez. Get some sleep. I'll see you in two days. Great job, everyone," said Penn as he left for his office with Ronnie.

Penn felt himself being pulled in several directions. Sonya's murder was still his main focus, but now he sensed more mayhem and possible loss of life. With the Teamsters and Mexicans not being repaid, Secur had put his life and the life of his family in jeopardy. But in Penn's mind, Secur and Biagio were people of interest in Sonya's murder and perhaps the murder of chief building inspector Artone Gomez. And now Carlos Secundo, the young Mexican slave, and his team of assassins joined the fray.

He turned to Ronnie and spoke, "When we get to the office, pop in and brief Jim Thorne on what we are doing and have the agents trailing the Mexicans report on the whereabouts of Nacion and Seanu. Fortify the troops so we can pick them up later. My guess is they dropped off Seanu so he can run down Secur and Biagio and kill them to save his own skin. I'm going to the hospital to visit Mr. Secur," explained Penn.

"Let the war begin," Ronnie said.

CHAPTER THIRTY-FOUR

Luc LoPrendo was getting an earful from some of Brooklyn's most notorious hoodlums even though he had warned them all about the soundness of boom-and-bust investing in Florida. "Pistol" Pecino, Vinny "the Vulture" Vendetto, and "Puny" Petruzzelli, a three-hundred-pound assassin, had all called LoPrendo in the past twenty-four hours. Bad news from Florida always traveled fast, with so many mobsters sprinkled among south Florida's finest neighborhoods. Some were calm, and others made veiled threats—threats that usually were acted upon. Luc felt uncomfortable for his own skin and for Alicia Secur's.

They were still using the Ritz in Manalapan as their base of operation, but the commute to Miami was wearing on Luc. Alicia had called Alain to let him know she was in hiding with Luc. He was relieved. *The Miami Herald* had picked up on the Chinese drywall story, and Secur's real estate career was effectively foreclosed. He went from being The Mayor of the Skies to The Chinese Devil in less than four days. Biagio had gotten Secur's power of attorney to liquidate his assets in favor of the Teamsters; Alicia's signature made it legal. Luc had dispatched his men to Secur's house to protect the mansion and all the valuables within from any Mexican intrusions. The Secur jet was flown to a small airfield in Tampa and was sitting in the same hangar as Secur's car collection, all of which would soon belong to the

Teamsters. Ten cents on the dollar was better than nothing. Luc was aware the Mexicans would want the asset money first, but he had equal firepower if a fight erupted. He also had a recorded first mortgage on Secur's personal and business real estate along with Alicia's and Alain's personal guarantees and a chattel mortgage on all of their personal property. His position as a creditor was perfected and superior. This paperwork was meaningless to the Mexicans, and Luc knew there could be bloodshed involving him and the Cartel members. He also knew they were violent, vindictive, and unpredictable. Luc's property credentials were civil and legal, but the Mexicans' credentials included murder, kidnapping, torture, and slavery.

Luc was sitting at the poolside bar overlooking the turquoise waters of the Atlantic Ocean having a cocktail with Alicia. He found her alluring and attractive and knew she felt the same about him. It was three o'clock in the afternoon as the westerly sun painted the puffy, anvil-shaped clouds a brilliant white. At the horizon thirty miles east, the cotton-white clouds merged with the surface of the off-blue ocean. As Luc and Alicia were conversing, a large flock of pelicans in perfect diamond formation swept low over the water, searching for their next meal. It was a quiet setting, with the slightest sound of small waves breaking along the shore. The serenity belied the impending potential for carnage and violence between the Mexicans, the Italians, and unbeknownst to both, the US Government.

"My dear, I hope you feel safe with me here, miles from our potential problems," Luc said, leaning close to Alicia. He put his hand on her hand.

Alicia accepted the gesture and felt warm to his touch. "Luc, you and your men have been very professional in every way. Under the circumstances I am quite happy to be here with you, but my thoughts are with my son Bennett away at school and Alain."

Since meeting Alicia during this crisis, Luc had become enamored by her sophistication and beauty. He appreciated her much more than Secur did. He was a widower and had girlfriends back in New York but only as a convenience and for sex; there was no connection with any of them.

"Alicia, I want you to know I find you very attractive, and while my role is that of a protector, I am hoping you may see me as something more romantic and sensual," said Luc in a confident and sincere tone.

It was one of the kindest and most straightforward pickup lines Alicia had ever heard. She began to blush, acknowledging to herself that she had similar feelings. "Luc, how wonderful of you to say such nice things. I admit I, too, feel an attraction to you, but with madness all around us, it seems misplaced?"

Luc felt emboldened and was flush with emotion, knowing she was attainable. He gathered his thoughts for an objection he wanted to overcome. "My dear, days of battle can be the most sensual of times. Nothing stirs the emotions more than the possibility that one or both of us might not return from combat, making sure that every safe moment is lived to the fullest."

After hearing that, her first thought was, *what a line of bullshit this guy has.* Yet it was nice to have a man curry favor toward her. It had been so long since she and Alain had felt like this that she was tingling with anticipation and visions of a sexual encounter with this handsome older man, her protector.

"My goodness, Luc, I had no idea you had these thoughts about me. It's a lot to take in."

"I won't push you, but I am relieved that my feelings for you are fully exposed," he said.

"Perhaps we should have an early dinner and see where this takes us," said Alicia, barely believing she had left a door so wide open for their eventual tryst.

"Meet me in the bistro tonight at 7:00," he said, holding the back of Alicia's right hand to his lips.

She was tingling and blushing as he rose to leave for his room. She sat still, watching as he left, admiring his body as he walked away. She was ready for the night.

CHAPTER THIRTY-FIVE

Secur was ready to be released from the hospital. He still did not remember what had happened to him the day he fainted and hit his head. Unfortunately, his friend Biagio had to bear the bad news about the Chinese drywall. At first he could not believe it, but then the story appearing in *The Miami Herald* confirmed whatever doubts he previously had. His protected whereabouts, and endless phone calls to his office had been hard on his staff as Secur healed in seclusion. Being isolated had its advantages, though.

Every day Biagio visited Secur. In addition, his wife called twice daily to check on his status. With his thoughts of Sandrine fading, he appreciated Alicia all the more. He hoped he still had time left with her to resurrect what once was. His wealth was nearly gone, and his stature was in serious doubt. Little by little he tried to collect his thoughts about how Chinese drywall had landed in those two buildings. He thought he had known better, but with all of the financial stress and the resultant disasters surrounding his failing empire, he was not sure and resigned himself to the thought that he may have missed something. Unfortunately, his director of construction had jumped ship to Kyle Anderson's company once the buildings were finished and Secur's empire began to fail even more. When the drywall scare appeared, Secur had run tests on his previous six buildings to see if they were contaminated as well. Fortunately, they were all clean.

Reflecting quietly on his forlorn status was actually a relief to Secur. The worst would be over soon. He had some personal monies put away for just this occasion, and he felt a new start would be a challenge worth pursuing. His pension plan would be safe from creditors. In all, he could count $6 million that he and Alicia could use for a fresh start. Biagio had given him hope that Armando might be amenable to a longer payout.

However, what Biagio neglected to tell Secur was that the Teamsters had plans to take the personal assets Secur had signed over to them and convert all of them to cash and keep the entire amount. Biagio did not want to upset Secur while he was recovering, so he agreed with Secur that those monies would largely be passed to the Mexicans.

Biagio was due to pick up Secur and drive him to a secluded Hotel in Naples, Florida, two hours west of Miami on the Gulf of Mexico. Because of the inherent risks from the unstable Mexicans, Biagio, despite Armando's assurances, had taken no chances with Secur's safety. He had arranged three separate limousines to meet at the hospital where Secur would exit the building. Two of Luc's men of similar size and bearing to Secur would be taken by wheelchair to a limo. Secur would take the third spot. Dressed alike in hooded sweatshirts and sunglasses, all three men would leave simultaneously, dispersing in different directions once outside of hospital grounds.

"Hey, pal, you ready for some R and R away from this town?" said Biagio as he entered Secur's room. Directly behind Biagio were two men dressed in the same University of Miami hooded sweatshirt that Secur was wearing. He exhibited a smirk and chuckle as he witnessed the drama Biagio had created.

"C'mon, Biagio. I don't need this kind of precaution. A bit much, wouldn't you say?" smiled Secur in reply.

"Better safe than sorry. Besides, it was as much Luc's idea as mine," said Biagio.

"Is Luc in Florida? Now?" questioned Secur, sensing his presence.

"Yes, he has Alicia with him in another city close by, and he has Bennett under protection at Dartmouth with his men. But let's discuss this on our way out of here," cautioned Biagio, watching the small crowd around them taking interest in their conversation. Secur picked up on Biagio's cue, and although he was desperate to learn more, he agreed to wait. The two Secur look-alikes took their positions in the waiting wheelchairs, and the entourage moved swiftly to the elevator. Five short minutes later, all three limos were loaded with human cargo and formed a single line filing out of the main parking lot. Once on city streets, each limo traveled in a different direction, with Luc's men and their firepower positioned in front and behind each limo.

Moto Seanu had not expected three Securs as he waited nearby in a grey SUV. One out of three was not good enough odds for him to risk being discovered by possible FBI agents. He was able to see how much more planning and manpower he would need to complete his mission for Nacion. He left the parade in a different direction as he headed west. As he left the hospital grounds, he noticed that different cars would follow him for a time before giving way to a new tail. He decided to go west to lightly traveled Highway 27. Once on 27 he could flush out his pursuers more easily.

Now alone in the limo with Biagio en route to Naples, Secur could no longer maintain his calm demeanor. Hearing that Luc and Alicia were together bothered him more than wondering if his son away at college would be safe without him. He knew that Luc had a secret affection for Alicia, and she was vulnerable to his charms. *How selfish to think of her first,* he thought in shame.

"Why is Alicia with Luc, of all people?" asked a frustrated Secur.

Biagio had known this was coming. He had been lucky to contain Secur at the hospital but, he was ready with his answer. "Who else might you suggest I have watch over her? A man working for Luc but a total stranger to Alicia?" said Biagio, now tired of the diva he was looking after.

"You know Luc would like nothing better than to get in Alicia's pants— he's fifteen years older than she is," exclaimed Secur.

"Luc made a promise to Alicia's father to watch out for her well-being. By the way, that might have included you, if you think about it," said Biagio.

"What's that supposed to mean? I thought you were my friend," said Secur.

"I am your friend and Alicia's too. You shouldn't be talking about jealousy and Luc. Your affair with Sandrine the past five years has not been as discreet as you thought. You must know that Alicia knows of your philandering ways. Right now I want you safe, your son safe, and Alicia safe. What's wrong with that?" said Biagio.

Secur listened to every word. His conscience could not dispute Biagio's reasoning and logic. He sat speechless, reflecting on how out of sorts his life had become in such a short time. He spoke quietly.

"You're right. I had that coming. I don't want to talk right now. Give me some space while we travel., OK?"

Biagio nodded yes. He decided to give Secur some time to think as he gazed upon the sea of grass and alligators from the limo. *If life could only be as simple as the Everglades*, he thought.

CHAPTER THIRTY-SIX

Reginald Gambrel was sitting in the conference room at FBI headquarters waiting for Penn to show up. Other agents popped in to say hello to their brother in arms from the DEA. The Sonya Michel murder had once again brought the two federal agencies to the same party.

"Good afternoon, Reg," said Penn from behind Gambrel as he entered the room without Ronnie. She was working on leads from their Carlos Secundo interrogation.

"Good afternoon back, Brother Penn. I hear your investigation is getting bigger by the week. Who's on first?" quipped Gambrel. If there was one thing Penn missed about the DEA, it was the more laid-back, hip group of guys he used to work with. He loved his agent team at the FBI, but they tended to be hung up on this coat-and-tie image. *Thank God for Ronnie*, he thought.

"Sadly, yes, my friend. Your sources are right on."

"Your little party is starting to spill over into my little piece of heaven, Rand. So I guess this is a good time to act together and put down these cats. Can you bring me up to date?" said Gambrel.

"I'm not sure where to start," said Penn.

"Try the beginning."

"The Sonya Michel murder has morphed into an incestuous who's who of potential candidates for criminal of the month and has opened a cold case closed five years ago."

"Hey smart-ass, I didn't say brief me in twenty-five words or less; give me a fucking break here, Penn. You got me all the way over here now. How about some people, places, and things?"

Penn laughed. He loved to push Reg's buttons.

When Reg saw Penn start to laugh, he knew he'd been had by his old boss. "Jesus, Penn," was all Gambrel could say.

"Sorry, Reg, I miss the banter. Can you tell?"

"I'm flattered, really. Now can we start for real?"

With that, Penn turned serious. "Ever since the Sonya murder, friends and players around her are showing up in dangerous places with dangerous people. We have a couple of people in our sights, but the distractions surrounding Alain Secur and Biagio LoPrendo pursuant to a failed bulk sale of condominiums has us running in different directions. A third suspect, a Samoan named Moto Seanu, may be the actual murderer of Sonya Michel. We have tails on all of them. Then along comes your Mexican smugglers, and Moto is kidnapped.

"Now this morning my agents find a gravesite west of West Palm Beach containing a Samoan dancer from the Mai Kai who was friends with Moto. The gravesite find was the result of our following Seanu, who had been kidnapped, presumably, by your Mexican friends. The tail that night on Moto and the Mexicans by my best guy, Tony Lopez, proved a windfall for us. Lopez clubs one of the abductors trying to sneak up on him from his observation post. We bring the perp back to a Fort Lauderdale hospital, where he proceeds to sing like a bird once he regains consciousness from the beating my guy gave him the night before.

"So now we have this picture in front of us, or at least so it seems. Secur, a possible Sonya suspect, owes the Mexicans a lot of money he borrowed on two of his condominium towers. Secur has a large real estate vulture fund ready to buy most of the units, pending a routine inspection of the property. The routine inspection shows Chinese drywall in nearly all of the condos, so the sale is canceled. Apparently, money from that sale was going to be used to pay off the Mexicans. The Mexican running the show here is a violent man named Nacion, according to our perp Secundo. Secundo claims he is a slave to Nacion and must do anything Nacion asks him to do, including assassinations, or else his family back in C. Juarez, Mexico, will be murdered by the Trinolea Cartel, his employers indirectly through Nacion. Do you want to hear more?" said Penn, reaching for a bottle of water.

"Crap, the Trinolea Cartel?"

"Yep, real bad guys," answered Penn.

"You got yourself a real barn burner, Penn. This makes the O'Neil-Gianno caper look boring. How can I help?" said Gambrel.

"By the way, have you been able to get anymore intel out of those guys you captured several weeks ago on that drug bust at sea?" asked Penn. He figured by now if Reg had gotten additional information, he would have been told.

"Naw, they got themselves a Spanish lawyer. We still have them in custody, but they're happy little clams right now. You know what happens. All of a sudden they don't have to worry, three square meals a day, a nice bed to sleep in, Spanish reading material, and new friends. To them prison is a predictable, carefree improvement over wherever they came from. They're done talking."

"Yeah, great country for those folks. Pisses me off, Reg."

"So again, Rand, how can I help?"

"I was hoping you could help me track down some safe houses the Mexicans supposedly have here in South Florida."

"How do you know they have safe houses here, Rand?"

"That little bird in Fort Lauderdale told us how they move around."

"What do you think this has to do with Sonya's murder?"

"I'm not sure. But ever since you found her body, my life has been full of murder, Mexicans, Teamsters, and a cold case from five years ago. You know the old saying in our business: there's no such thing as a coincidence."

"OK. For old times' sake, I will do it. But you owe me. Does Ronnie have a sister?"

"Afraid not. But she has got some great-looking babes at her temple. Shall I ask?"

"Yeah. Why not?"

Gambrel gave Penn a firm handshake and promised to deliver some meaningful intel as soon as possible. For Penn it was time to visit Secur again.

CHAPTER THIRTY-SEVEN

"I cannot get to him right now. He and Biagio left the hospital. They had three limos and three guys all dressed to look like Secur leaving at once. I couldn't chance being discovered," said Moto on his untraceable phone.

"I already know that, but that is not really my problem. I can do what you are supposed to do, and eventually maybe I will. But our deal was two dead and you go free with a little get-out-of-the-country money. Remember, Mr. Moto?" reminded Nacion in an intimidating calm and deadly voice. Moto had expected little sympathy. Unfortunately he had no clue as to the whereabouts of Alain Secur or Biagio LoPrendo and didn't know when he would.

"Do you know where he is?" asked Moto meekly.

"Yes, I do."

"Where are they? Don't play games. I'll run them down," answered a frazzled and desperate Moto.

"They are in one of three places: Naples, Ocean Ridge, or Tampa. We could not get too close because of the police escorts. But, those are the three separate destinations for the limos carrying your prey."

"OK, I have an idea. I'll be in touch," said Moto as the line on the other end clicked off before he could finish. He had no idea, and Nacion knew it. Moto scanned his mirror for a tail but there was no one following him on the deserted stretch of Highway 27. He breathed a sigh of relief, but his optimism and his life were short lived. A burst of gunfire from several automatic rifles coming from an oncoming pickup truck pummeled his windshield. His life was over before his car left the pavement, careening into a wide roadside draining ditch and sinking immediately into the murky, tannic-colored water. Gators and birds, startled by the sudden splash, left their banks for the safety of the water and the air.

Minutes later, FBI agent Tony Lopez passed the watery gravesite, unaware that his target was lying dead, out of sight below the waters next to the road.

Kyle Anderson was meeting Marty Burns for a quick drink at Joe's Stone Crabs. They were conferring about the likely state of Secur's ruined empire and whether an opportunity might be within their grasp.

"I don't know, Kyle, it sounds risky to me," said Burns, giving his opinion of Kyle's idea to offer ten cents on the dollar for all of Secur's contaminated inventory.

"Listen, I've run the numbers. At that price I can't lose. Look, here's the play. I take out the Teamsters for $42 million. I'll need to redo each unit at a cost of 85 to 100 thousand per unit. There are 690 contaminated units, so there's another 69 million to get the building completely up to snuff. Another five or six million for contingency and carry, and I am home free with 920 units at $117 million. The replacement cost new is $275 million. I can rent every apartment and still make a profit on the rental income while I hold the units for a better market sometime in the future. Don't you see, Burnsie? It's a no brainer," said Anderson, pumped up and excited.

"Yeah, but what about the stigma attached to a Chinese drywall building even after it's repaired? You can fix that building till the cows come home, but if somebody is spooked by the mere association of a smidgen of remaining Chinese drywall, you're no better off than Secur is right now," said Burns.

"Not so fast, Marty. There are strict procedures for cleaning up bad drywall. Second, there is an insurance company in Georgia that writes a policy against residual aftereffects. They won't write the policy unless you use one of their construction specialists who does nothing but Chinese drywall repairs. Finally, if I rent first at below market rates, the evidence of people living in the units with no problems whatsoever will erase the stigma over time. During that time, if the market comes back just a little, I figure I can clear 100 to 150 million in four to five years with all of the carrying costs paid by my renters. And you, my friend, are going to lease these buildings for me and make a small fortune yourself," said Anderson.

"Wow. If I didn't know any better, I'd say you had this planned all along," quipped Burns.

But Anderson was on his way out the door after a quick, "I gotta go."

Anderson saw the shape of Sandrine leaving the take-out section of Joe's and bailed from his conversation with Marty. He was able to come up behind her as she was walking back to her apartment less than two blocks away. He came beside her and stared at her face. She kept looking down and made space between the two of them. Finally Anderson spoke. "Sandrine, it's just me."

Recognizing the voice, and relieved she stopped, Sandrine looked at Kyle and smiled. It was an inviting smile, and Anderson's heart skipped a beat.

"Have you been stalking me, Mr. Anderson?" she kidded.

"No, not until about thirty seconds ago. Well, yes, just now. I mean I was having a drink with Marty Burns at Joe's, and I saw you out of the corner of my eye. So here I am. Is that dinner for two?" Kyle said.

"It could be, boss. What did you have in mind now that you found me?" kidded Sandrine. She caught Anderson off guard, and his faced blushed with embarrassment. In his mind this was the perfect setting for his not-so-secret desire to be with Sandrine.

"It could be if what?" inquired Anderson.

"I hate eating good food alone, so why don't you stop at the corner market, pick up a bottle of white wine, and join me at my place."

Anderson could not have asked for a better opportunity, and it took less than a second for him to accept. He stopped at the market and bought two bottles of wine and followed Sandrine to her building. Minutes later they were in the elevator headed to Sandrine's apartment and whatever else was to be. The banter stopped as they entered the elevator, as each remained silent wondering about the different scenarios that were about to unfold.

The only given was the spectacular meal they would consume. Sandrine's apartment was on the seventeenth floor of the Portofino Condominium, a project Secur had built and sold out successfully six years before. Anderson noticed the irony but said nothing.

Upon entering the impeccably designed interior, Sandrine took the wine from Anderson and moved to the kitchen, where she quickly uncorked the bottle, poured two glasses, and moved toward Anderson standing near the floor-to-ceiling glass sliders.

His gazed was fixed on the water view below. The building was so close to the inlet that it appeared they were in the ocean surrounded by shimmering, ice-blue water. Boats dotted the glassy surface like white fireflies leaving comet like trails as they moved. Sandrine tapped his shoulder, and as he turned to accept the wine, their eyes met and locked in silent anticipation. He accepted the glass and then took hers, setting both on a nearby table.

She accepted the inevitable, knowing a new love was about to begin. Kyle gripped her slim hips, pulling her to him as he slowly moved his lips to hers, kissing her gently at first. The early sensation led to a fiery, throat-deep kiss returned just as hard by Sandrine.

Sandrine pulled Kyle toward the bedroom, leaving two full wine glasses behind. Within moments of reaching the bed, Kyle backed away slightly and said, "Don't rush. Let's enjoy the moment."

This only excited Sandrine more as she quickly undressed herself. Standing completely nude and swollen with emotions, her nipples were hard and wanting. Kyle was still dressed, staring at the most perfect body he had ever seen.

Impatiently she began to undress her quiet lover as he succumbed to her desires willingly. Before he knew it, a wet, warm feeling from Sandrine's mouth engulfed him at the waist and completely excited his loins. She was a wonderful, well-schooled lover, he realized. Sensing his climax, she gently relented and moved to the bed, sprawling diagonally and exposing the perfect body Anderson could not resist. Standing naked looking down on her, he began to slide next to her with his head near her hips. He caressed her vagina and began to move across her thighs with his lips and tongue touching her along the way until he found the sweet spot of her body. It was stout and gorged as his tongue began to swell it even further. Her body arched, and a slight moan uncontrollably escaped her mouth. Near her climax, she pulled Kyle to her. He was inside her quickly, and the two thrust in rhythm until each had satisfied the other.

For several minutes they lay next to each other, staring upward at the bedroom ceiling, breathing hard, sweating and speechless. Kyle turned on his side as Sandrine turned her head. She smiled. Kyle broke the ice. "I've wanted to do that for five years," he whispered.

Her smile widened. "Me too," she said.

CHAPTER THIRTY-EIGHT

After eliminating Moto Seanu, Nacion was determined to find Biagio and Secur and deal them the same fatal reward. His finest warrior, Cisco Cavalarie, had determined by process of elimination that Biagio and Secur were at a swanky hotel in downtown Naples called the Suites on Fifth. The inn sat on the north side of Fifth Avenue in a toney section of restaurants and upscale shops just five blocks from the Gulf of Mexico. Naples was steeped in Mediterranean architecture and quiet by comparison to most east coast Florida cities. Real wealth from the conservative Midwest contributed to the low-key culture. Some called it boring, but unlike the pretentious East Coast, the old-money Midwestern residents kept the economy and banking business stable. Mercedes and Bentleys were replaced by Cadillacs and Buicks. People, especially the wealthy, kept to themselves—one reason Luc sent Secur and Biagio to Naples. Luc also knew the police chief, a stout union supporter and ex-teamster from New York. The chief would immediately notice any unfamiliar Mexicans appearing in his WASPY paradise. Luc also counted on the FBI to follow all three Limos, adding an extra layer of protection.

Biagio had been picked up early in the morning by two of Luc's men and was headed across Alligator Alley. Secur was being moved to a private condo owned by a friend of Luc's up the road about fifteen miles in beautiful Bonita Springs inside a gated community. Agent Richard Melnick had remained behind to tail Secur. But the gated community complicated security and surveillance for the FBI agent. He was reluctant to use his credentials to follow Secur, not wanting to alert anyone of his presence—at least officially. The quick-thinking agent pulled up to security and quickly flashed his ID and creds, hoping it would get him in without any hassles. Without asking a question, the guard admitted him immediately.

Pelican Landing was the community where Secur would be staying. It contained four championship golf courses and hundreds of villas, homes, and waterfront condos. Luckily for Lopez, he was able to just stay out of sight of Secur and still be able to see which direction they were headed.

Pelican Landing had only a few waterfront condos, and they were on an inland bay just east of the Gulf. Melnick saw Secur's vehicle turn into Bayview Towers at the westernmost extreme of the community. He noted the rear of the condo was positioned directly on the bay. Canoes and small skiffs were tied to a dock off the pool and recreation area adjacent to the bay. It was a spacious, green, beautiful security nightmare. *Who would pick this place to hide someone from professional killers?* Thought Melnick.

Penn was having a late breakfast with Ronnie in North Miami when his cell phone rang. The face of his phone signaled Agent Melnick.

"Good morning, Melnick. How's our guy doing?" answered Penn.

"Something doesn't add up here, boss. This place is not secure. There are multiple entry points in and around the community. Security is nonexistent. Biagio has sent just two guys to protect our boy," said Melnick.

"What's so bad about this place, Richard?"

"For starters, it's on a hidden bay with numerous groves of vegetation to hide in. The neighboring communities on either side are not gated, so someone could drive next to this place and literally walk in knee-deep water around the walls. Or, just come in from the bay in an innocent looking canoe."

"Most gated communities are just content to keep unwanted vehicles from roaming their neighborhood. I get it. But you're right. It sounds irresponsible. I'll get our local guys there to pitch in. Give me your GPS coordinates for now, and I will get some help in front and behind the building for you," said Penn.

Melnick felt relieved but still concerned. "You got someone on Biagio's tail?" inquired Melnick.

"Yeah. Agent Jackson has him covered. He's on the Alley coming across now," offered Penn.

"Any word on Moto Seanu, boss?" inquired Melnick.

"Nope. Lopez lost him on Highway 27 and has not seen him since. He didn't come home, and the neighbors have not seen him," said Penn.

"He's either dead or he gave us the slip," suggested Melnick.

"I was hoping he would lead us to the Mexican honcho. But you may be right. He may be dead. Call me with any updates or if you need anything else," said Penn as he hung up his phone.

"Do you think Moto has been killed?" asked Ronnie.

Penn hesitated before answering. It seemed he had been. "It's beginning to look that way, darling."

CHAPTER THIRTY-NINE

It had been a long day for Biagio as he pulled up to the Ritz Carlton in Manalapan that evening. He was about to meet with Luc and Alicia. He had traveled from the west coast after leaving Secur that morning and was feeling fatigued. His thoughts were with the threat the Mexicans posed toward him, Alicia, and Luc. His car was valeted and he strode through the refined lobby. As an avid architecture and interior design disciple, he usually meandered through elegant space like this observing the cache and theme of a room. Not today. He was purposeful wanting to see what, if anything, was occurring since the Mexican drywall abomination had left his buildings worthless.

Biagio spotted Luc sitting comfortably close to Alicia at the pool bar in casual wear. The vision of his close proximity to this beautiful woman and the flirting conversation told a story Biagio struggled with at first. Twenty feet from them, it made perfect sense. *Why not*, he thought.

Luc sensed Biagio's presence and immediately backed away from Alicia. Their expressions removed any doubt Biagio had about this newly formed couple. He was cool with it and pretended not to notice.

Before Biagio could speak, Luc stole the moment. "Biagio, welcome. You must be tired. How about a glass of champagne?"

"Good evening, Alicia. You are looking relaxed and beautiful as ever," said Biagio, smiling at her as he spoke. It was true, though. She looked alluring and flush with color. *Signs of a happy, satisfied woman*, thought Biagio.

She smiled and extended him a hand as she nodded her approval and welcome.

"Thank you, Luc, I could use that drink," said Biagio as he offered a firm handshake to his uncle.

"I understand you had an interesting day. How is Mr. Secur doing in Naples?" asked Luc.

Alicia showed no emotion. She was with Luc now and it felt good again to have a man who wanted her.

"He's fine, but later on with the business stuff. Not now, OK?" said Biagio, tired of the whole mess.

Luc nodded in agreement. For the next thirty minutes, the trio enjoyed one another's company, drinking champagne and peering east over the quiet Atlantic. Evening clouds were beginning to form in the August skies as the sun kissed their edges, giving a surreal orange outline to each floating body. Boats were moving at relaxed speeds, taking in the smooth ride over the turquoise-colored liquid highway. Beautiful bodies were packing up their beach gear after a pleasurable and uncomplicated day near the shell-bound beach. Taking in the symphony of sounds and sights momentarily erased the brewing financial storm from their short beachside party.

After another fifteen minutes, Biagio became anxious. He unsuccessfully tried to pry Luc from Alicia's charms. Finally he came right out with his intentions. "Uncle Luc, may I have a moment of your time?"

"Now, at this beautiful moment and with such pretty company at my side?"

"I thought we might dine together and Alicia would want to freshen up," said Biagio, hoping they would take his suggestion.

"Luc, I'll be in my room. When you two finish up, let me know our plans for this evening," Alicia said, moving from her seat and gathering her purse as she exited.

Luc was clearly upset at his nephew. He was beguiled and love struck with Secur's wife. He tempered his response to Biagio, realizing that what was old news to him was completely new to Biagio. His nephew would not miss the feelings between the two.

"As you wish, Biagio. Let's take a seat away from our guests." Luc paid the bar tab and they moved to a separate gathering area central to the patio area. Luc ordered another bottle of champagne as they carried their half-full glasses to the table.

Situated in their new venue, Biagio spoke first. "Secur was moved today to an estate on Marco Island by boat. He's in good hands. Even the FBI tail must have been surprised."

"Tell me how you got him free."

"It was cool, Uncle Luc. He snorkeled out about a half mile, and a cigarette boat came out of nowhere to scoop him up. The cigarette boat went out ten miles to a waiting sports fishing boat captained out of Marco, and the second switch was made there. He has a few throwaway, untraceable phones. I have the list of numbers and the days he will be using each phone. After three days we switch. Cannot be too sure," said Biagio, quite proud of his efforts.

"Well done, Biag. I should have you make Alicia and me disappear," responded Luc.

"OK, what's with you and Mrs. Secur anyway? For Christ's sake, she's twenty years younger than you—although you don't look your age," remarked Biagio.

"The last sentence saved your ass. Age is a state of mind, and I feel twenty years younger right now. Besides, it's only fifteen years, remember?" answered Luc playfully.

"Oh my god, don't tell me. You've had sex with Alicia, haven't you?" said Biagio.

"Yes, she's going to be staying with me for a while. Hopefully longer," said Luc, sipping a glass of champagne triumphantly.

"I can't say I blame her, and I am happy for you. She's been second fiddle to Sandrine for the last five years. No one can fault her. And she's staying true to her Italian roots by hanging out with an old fart like you, Uncle," offered Biagio, playfully raising his glass in a toast to Luc.

Luc chuckled at the remark, happy to see his nephew loosening up. "To business. Where are the Mexicans and Moto right now?" asked Luc.

"Nowhere I can swear to. But, Secur should be safe where he is for as long as we want," said Biagio.

"Where do we stand with the Teamsters?" asked Luc, now more concerned.

"That's another problem. They are livid, threatening to sue Secur, me, and probably the drywall company," answered Biagio.

"The drywall company is long gone, but you and I are still around. I'm as worried as you about my so-called mob friends who are lighting up my cell phone every thirty minutes. I finally left the damn thing in my room," said Luc.

"I hope plan B works out," said Biagio meekly.

"How do you plan to get rid of the Mexicans?" asked Luc.

"Pay them off, I guess. Hopefully they will be patient," said Biagio.

"I have some firepower if they won't," assured Luc.

"What are we going to do with Secur in the meantime?" asked Biagio.

"Good question," answered Luc.

CHAPTER FORTY

Kyle Anderson was working late at his office as usual. He was finishing a financial pro forma on two condo towers he was going to buy at distressed prices, renovate, and rent the apartments until the economy became more favorable. Then he would sell. He wanted to finish the numbers for his appointment with Marty Burns. Janice Hart, Kyle's receptionist, buzzed his intercom, announcing that Marty Burns had arrived.

"Please show him in, Janice. Thanks for staying late. I'll see you tomorrow," answered Anderson as Janice said her good nights to her boss. The tall wooden doors to Anderson's kingdom opened, and the iconic figure of Miami's number-one condo broker filled the opening. Kyle rose from his chair, awaiting Marty's arrival. They shook hands.

"Greetings from the glass menagerie," kidded Kyle. He and Marty had worked together for the last ten years, since before Marty hit it big. Kyle had also been a smaller fish in the business world back then. They had both grown successful together.

"Thanks, King Kyle. Just remember, I knew you when," remarked Marty.

"I would say the same about you. It's been good to grow together," affirmed Kyle.

"By the way, who was that beautiful babe you bolted for the other day at Joe's?" asked Marty.

Kyle could feel his face go flush red. He was married and had to keep his newfound relationship with Sandrine a secret. He stumbled for a cover story. "Ah, well, that was one of my top people who does a lot of marketing around here," answered Kyle.

"Of course. I thought I recognized Sandrine. It must have been important because you left me holding the check," said Marty.

"It was, and I am sorry."

"Whatya got for me tonight, Kyle?"

Anderson reached across the front of his desk and handed Marty his completed pro forma on Claughton Towers and Glisten. "I'd like your opinion on my strategy for these contaminated towers. If I can get all 920 units at ten to fifteen cents on the dollar, I think I can run them as rentals for several years, and then when times return to a more favorable condo market, I can convert them to condos and sell at near full price. The question is, can you get the rents I am projecting?" asked Kyle as Marty scanned the financials.

"At ten cents on the dollar, you are getting the land for free and the shell at 60 percent off. What are your renovation costs to get the drywall replaced?" asked Marty, looking up from the papers.

"Pretty smart, Marty. I better be careful with you or you will be my competition someday. The renovation will cost about $95 thousand per unit. It still pencils out to a great deal as a rental. Wouldn't you agree?" said Kyle.

"I think I could rent these up with an aggressive marketing campaign in about twelve to fourteen months if—and this is a big if—the drywall issues are completely satisfactory to the public. If they perceive a problem, you're finished," warned Marty.

"I agree with that. That's why I will subcontract the drywall to a firm recognized by the government with strict guidelines and procedures on how to mitigate 100 percent of any of the residual sulfur from the Chinese crap. They have successfully completed remediation of thousands of Fannie Mae and Freddie Mac government foreclosures that contained Chinese drywall. Plus, I will have a money-back guarantee for rental returns if someone feels uncomfortable or gets sick from any unit, perceived or otherwise. All of this with my reputation on the line and proper awareness should do the trick," said Kyle, strongly optimistic of his own words.

"You're not quite preaching to the choir, but I'm getting there," said Marty.

"Listen, if you are my leasing agent, you're going to have to jump on board here," said Kyle.

"I'm on board. I haven't been at this as long as you. I just need to study it a little further. You can always count on me," said Marty, exuding more confidence.

"OK, now all I need are the apartments signed over to me. After, of course, we pay for them," joked Kyle, sensing a triumphant gambit.

"What's the bottom line here all the way around? I mean, what will you net in rental money per year, and what are you projecting the sellout to be four to five years from now?" asked Marty.

Kyle was close to the vest on all of his financial dealings, but today he felt like bragging; after all, Marty was part of the family. "You know what confidential means, Marty, right?" asked Kyle.

"Please, Kyle, no lectures on secrets. I know how to keep mine just fine," expressed a slightly pissed-off Marty Burns.

"OK, sorry. I'm getting carried away with my own greatness," remarked Kyle.

"Cut the bullshit," answered Marty, growing impatient with the normally modest Kyle. He detested self- adoration from Kyle.

"Yeah, yeah, OK. As you can see by the affordable rents, I should net about $4 million a year even with a 5 percent vacancy. In five years, if I can get the same depressed prices that Secur is asking now, I will net after replacing the shit drywall and fix up when the renters are gone, about $285 million. That's gross. If the market recovers even slightly, I will net over $330 million. I have complete confidence I can do this, and so do my partners," said Kyle.

"What partners?" asked Marty.

That I cannot say right now. But I am close," lied Kyle. His partners had been lined up for months. He wasn't telling Marty everything.

CHAPTER FORTY-ONE

P enn was being pressured by SAC Thorne for more information about the murder of Sonya Michel on the high seas east of Miami. He was particularly troubled that other murders and missing persons were beginning to multiply around the Secur, Teamster, and Sonya circus. The FBI resources were being spread thin as multiple agents were following multiple suspects. Two people had blown the FBI tails, and their whereabouts were unknown. Thorne had called a special closed-door meeting with Ronnie and Penn in his office.

"I know it looks bad, sir, but we are beginning to get a picture of what is occurring more on a global basis," said Penn, wishing he had not used the word *global*.

"Ah, we're global now. How much of the globe are you tackling, Randall?" answered Thorne sarcastically. He always called Penn by his first name when he was pissed at his top agent. Ronnie sat still, fearing that she would soon be addressed as Ms. Feldman for the same reason.

"OK, give me a break. Global means multiple players are surfacing as potential Sonya murder suspects. Also, we believe that the Artone Gomez murder that occurred five years ago in a duplicate fashion may be back on the table, since several of our suspects may have had reasons to murder him as well," said Penn.

Thorne cut Penn a break and locked eyes with Ronnie. "And Ms. Feldman, would you agree with lover boy here?" said Thorne, spreading the sarcasm around.

Ronnie hated it when Thorne brought their relationship into any conversation. She glanced down nervously with her hands clasped resting on the table. "Mostly, sir. We both have worked on this investigation on our personal time and are committed to solving the case as soon as we can; however, new players are constantly surfacing as we dig deeper. You know how that happens," said Ronnie, defending her turf. Penn looked on with admiration.

"Enough. Let's hear some facts and credible theory," asked Thorne, ready to listen.

"Here's an executive summary of the facts as we see them. Someone wanted Sonya dead for a reason. According to her sister, Sandrine Michel, a mysterious text came in just before the time when we believe she was shot in the head and left floating in the Atlantic. The text said that Secur killed building inspector Gomez," said Ronnie.

Thorne cut her short. "Do you believe the source that told you this information? And do you believe the text was from Sonya? Did we ever find her cell phone? Does one really send a text just before they are killed? Agents, this is flimsy," said Thorne.

"We don't know if we believe the text was from Sonya. Her sister Sandrine gave us the lead, and I believe she was telling the truth," said Ronnie. Penn was nodding in agreement. Ronnie continued before Thorne could interrupt. "We are developing consensus on the alibis of Secur and Biagio LoPrendo. One seems solid; the other seems iffy," said Ronnie, sensing Thorne wanted to ask another question, but Penn spoke first.

"We think Secur is where he said, but we don't believe Biagio is telling us the truth," said Penn.

"Wasn't Biagio in love with Sonya?" asked a puzzled Thorne.

"Yes. But we think he is an accessory," said Penn.

"I thought you told me with some certainty that you believed Moto Seanu was the trigger guy. The guy, incidentally, we lost sight of the other day, correct?" said Thorne, getting impatient.

"That is correct as well, sir. As you know, one of our agents lost Seanu about four days ago on Highway 27 not far from where we found the body of Moto's friend from the Mia Kai restaurant. If you recall, he was buried in a shallow grave. He had been decapitated, presumably by a high-ranking Mexican cartel member named Armando Nacion. We also believe, based upon the testimony of a cartel member captured by Agent Lopez the night Moto was brought to that gravesite, that Nacion told Moto that if he didn't kill certain people he would be killed and so would members of Moto's family; not only a threat, but these promises are generally carried out to create fear among competing cartel members and members of the same cartel," said Penn.

"I am well aware of those tactics. Please carry on with your theory," said Thorne.

"We continue to tail Moto, hoping he leads us to the killer of his friend, and suddenly he dumps our guy. We formulate that Moto was ordered to kill Secur and Biagio. Secur borrowed millions of dollars from the Mexicans as loan shark money thinking he could pay them back because of a giant vulture sale that was under contract to Secur. The sale would be for over nine hundred units. The inspection of the buildings under contract showed that most of the units have tainted Chinese drywall in them. Signs of the corrosive impact are now showing up, so rather than buy at a lowered price and correct the problem after the closing, the vulture group elects to walk away from the closing. Secur has no way to pay off the Mexicans or the Teamsters, who were willing to take far less than their original loan. Friends of Secur, presumably the Teamsters or Biagio, shuffled Secur to a safe house somewhere on the west coast said Penn. Ronnie took notes.

"Do we know the whereabouts of Secur or Biagio?" asked Thorne, who was also taking notes.

"Secur gave our guys the slip, but Biagio has checked into the Ritz Carlton in Manalapan, Florida, about an hour north of our offices," said Penn.

"What agent is on Baigio?" asked Thorne, not looking up from his note taking.

"Ron Delano, sir, along with female agent Janice Patrick. Biagio's group is camped there for now, so we needed an onsite couple to avoid suspicion."

"Good. What has he reported?" inquired Thorne.

"Information and photos are still streaming in. We have confirmed that Secur's wife is living with Luc LoPrendo, Biagio's uncle—a dubious fellow on the outskirts of crime families in Brooklyn, Queens, and Newark. He was a Teamster president at one time. According to my old law firm in New York, several of his mob buddies have invested in Secur's projects," answered Penn.

"Did you say living with Alicia Secur? Like cohabitating?" asked Thorne with a confused tone.

"Yes, sir. Can you blame her?" said Penn.

"Luc LoPrendo is an old fart. What does she see in him?" asked Thorne.

The question was more personal than relevant, but Penn answered. "I don't know sir. I'm five years older than Ronnie. She thinks I'm terrific," kidded Penn as Ronnie giggled in embarrassment.

"Frankly, I don't see what she sees in you, Penn, and her lack of good judgment may cost her a promotion," chided Thorne, kidding him right back.

"Oh, Penn, are you going to let him get away with that?" said Ronnie, joining the fray.

"Actually, sweetheart, I agree with the man. I don't know what you see in me either," said Penn sarcastically. Ronnie shot Penn the finger as Thorne chuckled at his two lovebirds.

The tone returned to business. "So Luc and Alicia are together, and Biagio shows up too," asked Thorne.

"Yes," said Penn.

"All right, I've got the global picture now; give me your hunches. I assume one reflects the other?" asked Thorne as Ronnie and Penn both nodded.

"We believe that the same someone murdered Gomez five years ago and Sonya last month," proffered Penn.

"Why are these murders tied together in your mind?" probed Thorne.

"They're not so much tied to the same events, but they're so strikingly similar that I believe the same person or persons killed both people. But the circus surrounding Sonya's murder was coincidental to her murder. By that I mean that all the confusion of the Mexicans and the discovery of the

Chinese drywall were not related to Sonya's death. They happened later and had to do with circumstances unforeseen," said Penn.

"Not so fast, Rand. I disagree with you on this one small point. The Chinese drywall just doesn't make sense to me," said Ronnie.

"Go on, Ronnie," said Thorne.

"I can see how the Mexican money thing is not related to Sonya. It wasn't a great secret. My gosh, Marty Burns knew as well as others. But I don't think over 900 units get Chinese drywall accidentally. Bad drywall was a hot potato back then, and too many eyes should have caught it," concluded Ronnie.

"Interesting point, Ronnie. Don't you think so, Penn?" said Thorne. Penn was staring at Ronnie. He continued before Penn could speak. "Thanks to both of you for today's meeting. I appreciate your preparedness and the quality of the work. I think you're onto something. I'll leave you two to solve this puzzle. Find Secur, and I think you find out where you're headed. Great job," said Thorne as he rose from his seat and went to the door.

Penn looked at Ronnie with curiosity. "When were you going to share the drywall suspicions with me?" asked Penn.

"Right now, honey. It came to me in this meeting as you and Thorne were speaking. Think about it. That's a lot of smelly drywall to go unnoticed. Would you not agree, sir?" said Ronnie.

CHAPTER FORTY-TWO

Reginald Gambrel had used one of his ace cards to trick his Mexican prisoner into getting needed information about the whereabouts of one or more of Armando Nacion's safe houses—safe houses filled with not only food and computers, but ammo, guns, explosives and more. He interrogated the Mexican man he had captured at sea the night of the big bust. However, once he had a lawyer, the prisoner clammed up like a bank vault. Instead of meeting in the interrogation room at DEA headquarters, he went to the prisoner's cell. He explained to him that he did not have the evidence to hold him any longer and that he would call Armando to send a man over to pick him up and give him a ride. The prisoner's eyes opened wide at the mention of Nacion. He could not withhold his fright. The act by Gambrel was so convincing that the prisoner dropped to his knees, begging Gambrel not to release him. All of a sudden, broken English flowed unevenly, and valuable facts spilled into the air.

Over the next hour, Reggie and an interpreter questioned the prisoner about Nacion's methods, his demeanor, his habits, and anything else they thought would be helpful. Gambrel had two people taking notes; one in Spanish and one in English, just to be sure. Two hours into the interview, Gambrel signaled everyone to stop. He had all the information this prisoner knew. It would take days to decipher and interpret. But he was confident he had gotten it all. Reggie had promised the prisoner he would keep him in jail for a very long time if he fully cooperated. Gambrel left the interview to call Penn and give him the details.

"Hello, Reg. To what do I owe the pleasure of the director of the DEA's call?"

"Good morning, brother Penn, it's me. I got the Mexican prisoner to talk," said Gambrel.

"Which one?" inquired Penn.

"The one in Miami. Your guy's still in Lauderdale at the hospital, right?"

"Yeah," said Penn.

"This is the dude we picked up on that successful drug bust at sea. Remember?"

"Oh. And what information did you squeeze out of that poor soul, Reg?" asked Penn.

"How would you like the whereabouts of Nacion's safe house?" asked Gambrel.

"Don't tease me, Reg. Of course I want to know," said Penn.

"He has a number of safe houses from Coral Gables to Hollywood. Most are on the water, generally with fast boats parked behind them. They are also heavily fortified with secret gun ports and loads of handheld firepower," said Reg.

"So we start looking for homes on the water with cigarette boats behind them, huh?" asked Penn.

"I said fast boats, not necessarily cigarette boats. I asked specifically. These are mostly center console boats with three to four big outboards crowding the transom and probably a little cubby cabin up front for weapons stores," said Gambrel.

"Interesting. What else can you tell me? Any exact locations for us?" asked Penn.

"I didn't get an exact address, but I think I know the area. It is in south Key Biscayne. Near the end of the island overlooking the old Stiltsville houses," said Reg.

"I thought they were all gone," said Penn.

"They are, mostly. Still some concrete piles left, but I know this area. Boats like that will stick out down there. The water's shallow as hell at low tide."

"OK, are we doing this together?" asked Penn.

"I assumed so," said Reg.

"You can task with us but if we get him, he's mine on suspicion of murder connected with an assault by one of his guys on a federal officer. You OK with that? I just want him for a while to clear up this whole Sonya Michel-Alain Secur-Biagio triad," said Penn.

"Let's find him first. I'm OK with you getting him, but I want to be in the room during interrogations," said Gambrel.

"Don't expect too much; he'll be lawyered up for sure," reminded Penn.

"For sure," said Reg.

"Come by this afternoon, and we'll form a plan. Bring your key guys with you," asked Penn.

"Two o'clock OK?"

"See you then," said Penn as he viewed his calendar on the computer.

Alain Secur was bored out of his mind. He was also worried. He had been at the Marco Island retreat for almost a week with only occasional contact with Biagio and even less news from his wife. In the few times they had spoken, he could tell a distance had developed between them. He was also concerned about her being around Luc LoPrendo so much, protector or not. She had always spoken so highly of him when she reminisced about her father. Even though he was fifteen years her senior, he was dashing and sophisticated for his age. Perhaps it was the realization that he and Sandrine were finished and now Alicia had the leverage. This paranoia and his boredom were driving him crazy. His phone for today was ringing inside his pocket. Even though there was no caller ID on his untraceable phone, he was sure who it was.

"Alain, I know you must be bored out of your mind. Sorry about that, but we are all being careful," said Biagio.

"Goddamn it, Biag, you've got to get me out of here. I'm losing it here. I don't want to catch one more fish or read another book. What's going on?" asked Secur in desperation.

"I know you're anxious, but that crazy Mexican is on the loose. We think he killed Moto. His shot-up body was found this morning by a truck driver in a canal off Highway 27 just west of the Broward-Palm Beach

County line. His car, and I assume his body, was riddled with bullets," explained Biagio.

"The good news is he's dead. The bad news is that the Mexicans will be looking for us even more now," said Secur.

"Well, we moved again yesterday, but don't ask me over this line, OK?" said Biagio. He knew that the phone was untraceable and no monitoring of an unknown number would be possible. He was telling Secur the truth. Moving out of the Ritz yesterday, they had relocated two miles North in South Palm Beach to the Four Seasons.

"Are you with Alicia now?" asked Secur.

"No, I am not. She's fine, though. Uncle Luc is keeping an eye on her."

"I'll bet he is. How's Bennett? Is he still at school?" asked Secur, desperate for any family news. He didn't bother to ask about business. That was too far from his thoughts, and nothing good was happening there, he knew.

"No, we had to hide him up north, away from his campus. Alicia and Luc told him what was going on. He's too old to lie to," said Biagio.

Secur was frothing about the Luc- Alicia remark Biagio had let slip out. However, he was grateful his son was safe. "That's the best news of all. Thanks for watching over him," said Secur .

"I gotta go, buddy. We have a lot to do still, with our reinforcements showing up from Jersey. You just stay put and don't give our guys a hard time. I promise to call as often as I can," said Biagio, clicking off the phone before Secur could ask ten more questions. Biagio hated leaving him in the dark, but it was safer for all that way. Luc had been in the background the whole time monitoring his nephew's conversation with Secur. Alicia was napping in Luc's suite.

"Nice job, kid," said Luc as Biagio hung up.

"Thanks, Uncle. Have you heard from Anderson?"

"Yes, I have his proposal right here."

"Good. Now let's find that fucking Mexican," said Biagio.

"No, my young nephew, let's lead the FBI to him. Besides, my guess is they are already after his ass. They must know that he killed Moto. Just before we kill that son-of-a-bitch, I will thank him for that," reminded Luc.

Biagio knew his uncle could be a brutal and calculating bastard. He was clear on that. But where did Alicia fit into this equation? Biagio worried about how far Luc might go with Secur if he had permanent designs on Alicia.

CHAPTER FORTY-THREE

The chief medical officer, Grey Wong, performed his second bloated and waterlogged autopsy in the past three months with Ronnie in attendance. She had just left the morgue after reviewing the bloated body of an already-huge Moto Seanu. Ronnie called Penn to report her findings.

"His body was riddled with bullets, all semi-automatic from one gun. It looks as if he was shot while driving and his car swerved into the drainage ditch along the highway after he was killed. It sunk like a rock until a passing semi spotted the roof of the car just visible below the water's surface. The trooper who wrote up the investigation said there were gators all over the banks where the car was found. Looks like part of his right arm and shoulder were eaten away. Not pretty. You want all this, Penn?" asked Ronnie.

"No, not really. Bring me the report. Sounds like a Mexican kill. Looks as if they ran out of patience with Moto?" said Penn.

"Seems that way. Are you on your way to the suspected safe house?" asked Ronnie, standing outside the morgue leaning on her car.

"Yes I am, but I am not expecting to find Nacion. My guess is he's one step ahead of us. Might be some stragglers we can question. Probably a waste of time," concluded Penn, on his way to Key Biscayne.

"Any word on Secur?" asked Ronnie.

"Nothing. He gave us the slip and stayed under. He'll surface sooner or later," responded Penn.

"See you tonight, honey," said Ronnie, getting into her car to head to her office.

Within thirty minutes Penn reached the suspected safe house. By the time he arrived, several agents who had preceded him were milling around outside the empty house sans boats and artillery. Richard Melnick, senior field agent, waved to Penn. Penn coasted toward him in his Tahoe, rolling down the window as he came to a stop.

"What's you got, Dick?" asked Penn in a matter-of-fact tone.

"Not even close, Rand. They've been gone for days. I'll have forensics take over in an hour, but I'm not hopeful," said Melnick.

"Watch for surrounding surveillance. You know the drill, people peering from behind their curtains, drive-by folks going too slow. Check every possible lead," said Penn. Melnick acknowledged his instructions and returned to the house to wait for the crime scene van. Penn headed north, pondering his next move. His cell phone rang as he pulled away from the safe house.

"Rand, it's Lopez."

"Hey, Tony, where are you?"

"The Four Seasons in South Palm Beach."

"Biagio?"

"Yep."

"Anything you want to tell me?" asked Penn.

"Guess who showed up here just a few minutes ago?"

"Secur?"

"No, but you're close. Kyle Anderson."

"Not surprising. Word has it Anderson is trying to steal the two buildings where they found the Chinese drywall. He's probably there to negotiate with the Teamsters," said Penn.

"These guys are close."

"Whatdaya mean close, Tony?"

"You know, hugs and big handshakes like long-lost buds. That kind of close."

"Well, stay on Biagio and keep me informed." Penn hung up the phone and reconstructed the conversation, thinking of the possibilities-close.

He shook his head in amazement, recounting the incestuous relationship of the developers, their employees, their lender reps, and Uncle Luc and Alicia. One big, happy family feeding off one another's misfortunes. *What a screwed up group*, he thought. As he droned north on I-95, he thought about what Tony Lopez had said. Penn had assumed that Anderson was never in contact with Secur's lenders. He was conservatively financed through banks and insurance companies that had a long and successful history with Anderson. The last person he would associate with would be a lender like the Teamsters. He decided to run it by Ronnie that night.

CHAPTER FORTY-FOUR

Armando Nacion had located Biagio LoPrendo's whereabouts. If he could not find Secur to collect his $39 million, he figured Biagio was the next best thing. After all, Biagio had been present and assisted Secur when he acquired the loan from the Mexicans. The buildings still had residual value at a much-reduced rate, and Nacion wanted first position on the collateral and in any super discounted sale that may be concluded in the future; one way or another, he was getting paid.

Nacion arrived in South Palm Beach to research the area. He decided to stay down the street for a few days at the Ritz Carlton, one town south in Manalapan. It was the very same hotel that, just days before, Biagio and Luc had moved from. He needed time to get the lay of the land and see who else might be observing his mark. He was quite certain the FBI knew Biagio's location and had its own men in the area. His surveillance of Biagio was his priority, but his awareness of periphery people watching Biagio worried him. In Mexico, Nacion was so famous he could never be alone on the streets carrying on surveillance. He would be cut down like a wild dog by competing cartels. His maneuverability in America was far easier.

He was impressed with the FBI for knowing that he was now a person of interest in the Moto killing. Since his slave assassin Carlos Rodrigo Secundo had never shown up or called, he presumed that he had ratted him out. He made a mental note to call Juarez headquarters and have Secundo's family eliminated. Nacion checked into the Ritz with his platinum American Express card under the name of Hector Bias. After dropping his luggage in his hotel room, he returned to the valet stand to retrieve his car and begin his reconnaissance. As he waited for his car, his cell phone rang. He answered the phone, stepping well away from the crowd. It was his first in command, Jorge Anthony, reporting in.

"I got your text; what can I do for you boss?" said Anthony.

"Contact Juarez and have Carlos Rodrigo Secundo's entire family eliminated. Make it messy, and make it public. We must send a message to our slave forces," said a cold Nacion.

"Yes, sir," was all Anthony could say. He hated this part of the job. He had once been a slave himself and had to kill and pillage against his will or his family would have been destroyed. He had known Secundo and his family since their days in the Juarez little league baseball system together as teammates. While Anthony was no longer technically a slave, he had to carry out Nacion's request or he would be killed for insubordination. He had been smart about one thing, though: soon after he became a non-slave cartel member, he was allowed to move his family—a kind of reward for killings well done. His entire family was in Texas, in a small town friendly to illegal ex-slave immigrants. He made the call reluctantly, giving the order he had been instructed to give.

CHAPTER FORTY-FIVE

K yle Anderson was working late as usual, alone in his penthouse over Miami. A blustery rain was hitting the windows with varying degrees of force and unequal sounds dictated by the gusting winds. He was absorbed in the new numbers his CFO had provided him that afternoon on Secur's old properties. For Anderson, examining complex pro formas required the solitude and calm that evenings alone in this office gave him. The rain was cathartic, relieving stress even while he perused complex financial statements. The lights outside along the distant shorelines were blurred by the raindrops covering the glass. His eyes became blurred as well. He rubbed his eyes and heard a sound. Looking down, he saw his private line light up on his phone console. The phone ring blending with rain sounds created an unusual sound. His eyes stared at the blinking light for several seconds before he reached for the phone—it was either Sandrine or his wife Sheila. He answered the phone expecting a beautiful woman's voice. Instead it was a man.

"Working late, I see, Kyle," said James Foster, momentarily surprising Anderson.

He quickly recovered. "Hello, Jim. How's Costa Rica?" inquired Kyle warily.

"It's great, thanks. How's the plan coming?" asked Foster.

"What plan, Jim?" answered Kyle, sensing the reason for Foster's late-night call.

"Don't bullshit me, Kyle. The plan you're probably working on right now. The two Secur properties, buddy. Remember?" reminded Foster.

Kyle sensed what was coming from his former business partner. "What is it you want, Jim? We agreed to part company, settled the finances, and agreed not to contact each other ever again. Do you remember?" said Kyle with absolutism.

"I remember, Kyle. But I was reading about the demise of Secur due to the Chinese drywall our company installed. Then I started doing the math in my head about what you stand to make on the retrofit and resale of all of those units. What is it, 950 condos?"

"Yes, I am sure you do remember. But I paid you to forget, remember?" said Kyle, now irritated with Foster. He saw it coming as Foster began to shake Kyle down for more hush money.

"Have you heard from Ed Jenkins, Kyle?" Jenkins was the purchasing agent for Secur when Glisten and Claughton Island were being built.

"Of course not. He's honoring his commitment," responded Kyle angrily.

"Well, someone needs to compensate me for that windfall, or should I say that little bit of sabotage. You sure showed the old Mayor of the Skies, didn't you?"

Kyle was livid. He did not want to act in or converse in this state. He decided to put Foster on hold. "Jim, my wife's calling me on the cell phone. Can you hold for about five?" asked Kyle, putting Foster on hold before he could reply.

He calmed himself down and began to formulate a plan while Foster was on hold. It would only be a matter of time before authorities began pursuing Foster and his defunct company, demanding answers from him about the Chinese drywall—not to mention Secur's lawyers. After a four-minute break and a preliminary plan, Kyle reconnected to Foster.

"OK, Jim, where were we? Oh yes, you were trying to extort money from me. Ostensibly you want to blackmail me. Is that about it?" said Kyle, assuming Foster had remained on line.

"Pretty much, Kyle, or *The Miami Herald* gets a juicy story about your little charade in South Beach," threatened Foster.

Kyle had expected this and made an unemotional response. "I don't suppose you would come here for a meeting about this?" asked Kyle, expecting a no.

"What? And be killed by you and one of your henchmen? We'll do this through an intermediary, Kyle. I have someone in mind," said Foster.

"No to that, Foster, for basically the same reason. How about we meet in a neutral country close to both of us? Would you consider the Caymans? Plenty of banks and tight-lipped lawyers," responded Kyle.

"Lawyers. What do you need them for?" asked Foster, completely surprised.

"Because we are going to do this my way on the paperwork end or you can take your broke ass to *The Miami Herald*. Yes or no, Jim. What will it be?" said Kyle, dictating the conditions.

"OK, OK, you win. When and where?" asked Foster. He was not anxious to travel to the Caymans.

"I cannot meet you until I have this deal finalized with the Teamsters. It will take another three weeks, which puts us into mid-September," said Kyle.

"That's too long. We need to get this done now."

"It doesn't need to happen at all unless I can make this deal. No deal with the Teamsters, and whatever you want to tell whatever newspaper, go ahead," bluffed Kyle, knowing Foster was running out of money. He knew he would have to pay something for the delay.

"OK, when and where?" said Foster.

"Grand Cayman Island at the Ritz Carlton, the fifteenth of September. Do you know it?" asked Kyle.

"I'll find it," said Foster.

"I have a friend in San Jose near you. I will send him $10 thousand cash so you can get through this. Don't lose it at the casinos, either. Got it?" said Kyle. Foster was surprised by Kyle's offer of immediate hush money. His temporary plan was working.

"Thanks," responded Foster.

"And keep your mouth shut about this. Understand?" With that, Kyle hung up.

This was not good, thought Kyle, frozen at his desk, no longer capable of reviewing his pro formas. Now he needed to figure out how to get Foster out of his life for good. The trip would be tricky, and any agreement would be an affirmation of his involvement with Foster's drywall company. *Well, at least Sandrine can join me for a couple of days*, thought Kyle. His next call was to his private detective and cousin Jack Sanders.

"Jack, can we meet tomorrow for lunch at Tucci's in Coral Gables?" requested Kyle.

"Sure thing. What's up? Can you say?" asked Sanders.

"I'll explain tomorrow. Hey, you're not still tagging Sandrine, are you?" asked Kyle.

"No. You told me to lay low, remember? Is this about her still?" said Sanders.

"No, nothing like that. I forgot I called you off. See you tomorrow," said Kyle.

"You've been working too hard, Cuz. Don't lose that edge," responded Sanders. But Kyle had already hung up.

CHAPTER FORTY-SIX

Secur was growing impatient. He wasn't sure if he was being protected or held as a prisoner by Luc LoPrendo's men. He had been cooped up in a beautiful Mediterranean estate on Marco Island for over ten days. It had been over two days since his last conversation with Biagio, and he had yet to speak with Alicia. He spent his day talking to his guards as they followed his every move throughout the walled, fifty-acre estate. At first he marveled at the strolling paths flanked by multi-colored English gardens. Each wall was lined by incredibly symmetrical royal palm trees over fifty feet in height. From the moment he was dropped into this palatial estate, he thought he had been transported to the Tuscan Hills of Italy. Everything inside and out spoke of first class. But enough was enough, and individual freedom trumped even this beauty.

Secur had been planning his own exit for the past two days. He was not sure where he was, but he suspected by the length of the trip that he had traveled west and not north. Two and a half hours north of Miami put you near Melbourne. He was quite sure nothing like this existed there. It was hotter and more humid than Miami, which was typical of the west coast of Florida. He felt reasonably sure that he was on the west coast of Florida, but where—Naples, Fort Myers, or Marco Island? The TV had only cable networks, so no local stations were shown. The house sat in the middle of the fifty acres. The lush foliage and height of the trees around the perimeter prevented him from seeing what the neighborhood was like. It was also dead quiet at all times, leading him to suspect that beyond the walls, he was no longer near modern civilization but somewhere in the country. The daily paper delivered to him was *Investors Daily*, which was also nonspecific. The house contained no radios, and his cell phone had been purchased in Miami by Biagio. Since being issued three days before, and with no charging device, the cell phone battery was dead as well. The obvious nature of these restrictions led Secur to the conclusion that he was as much in danger here as he would be out there—wherever "there" was.

He had over six hundred dollars in his wallet and three changes of clothes to his name. Getting over the wall would not be difficult, but beyond that the unknown cast a huge shadow of doubt. In a few hours he would pack a sheet with clothes and enter the unknown. Because it was dark, he would need to travel in a straight line. If he deviated too much and became disoriented he could lose his way. He had tracked the sun during the day and knew east from west; east would be his direction of travel initially. He was alone in his room after eating a hearty supper knowing this could be his last meal for some time. At 11:30 p.m. Secur climbed from his window descending with a sheet he had ripped into strips and tied into a fifteen-foot length. Like a modern day Hobo he use another sheet to pack his clothes and a few belongings. His plan was to shimmy up the royal palm tree like a telephone lineman, using the leverage of the sheet wrapped around the tree's trunk. The trees were less than three feet from the wall. Once above the ground by fifteen feet, he would climb onto the top of the wall and hang along the opposite side of the wall before dropping the final ten feet. This was the most dangerous part. He could be landing in spiked-edge plants or any number of other dangerous items. The good news was that it was only a crescent moon that night, so the cover of darkness was in his favor. The bad news was that with so little light, he could see only about a two-foot area of his landing zone and nothing beyond. He dropped to the ground and used his sky diving training to execute a perfect PLF—parachute landing fall. First he hit with his feet, then did an immediate turn-and-roll to his calf and thighs to break the fall, and finally slowed with a slight roll to the torso and shoulders. The one, two, three method worked to perfection, breaking the fall without sprains or pain.

He quickly jumped to his feet, smelling his surroundings and touching the plants. As a builder he knew his landscape material well. The smell was that of brackish water with a slight sulfur twinge. The plants and stems were like mangroves, as expected, with brackish, tannic waters. He quickly processed the cues, concluding he was in an area near swampland and isolated from civilization. He established his position as facing due east with his back to the wall. Secur knew that a road led to the entry of the compound, and that would be his way out.

He moved to his left in an arc toward north, fighting through mosquitos and spider webs. He broke off a branch about five feet in length and swatted the air in front of him to clear the webs ahead, but there was nothing he could do to combat the annoying buzz of the large swamp mosquitos. The swarm was so loud he could not hear his feet walking along the ground. Ten minutes later Secur could see the road leading to the compound entry. He approached quietly. To his good fortune, there were no guards at the entrance to the compound. The light from the wall lamps at the entry gates cast a short shadow that Secur was out of in an instant. He walked the first thousand feet along the edge of the trees lining the street so he would not be spotted. Once a safe distance from the walled compound, Secur broke into a steady run. The excitement of the moment and the adrenaline rush enabled him to keep up the pace for over fifteen minutes. Ahead, the horizon over the treetops showed light in the distance—a good sign. Suddenly his body cast a slight shadow from behind. Instinctively he jumped into the ditch next to the road, landing on something cold and alive. The twelve-foot gator was as frightened as Secur, immediately flipping him off his back. The gator then scurried into the brackish abyss. Afraid of being caught, Secur lay face-first in the muck, keeping his profile as short as possible. He froze as the car rumbled past.

Secur waited several minutes to make sure the car was well out of sight before rising to his feet. His entire front was covered in black swamp muck. His face and hands were also covered with the liquid sludge. He had kept the tied sheets and used them to clean his soiled extremities. Next, he changed clothes from the sheet duffle bag he carried and resumed a light trot. Within thirty minutes he began to hear vehicles traversing a road. Cars and trucks rushed by as he carefully approached an intersection. On his left at the intersection, he saw an all-night convenience store. In the parking lot was the car from the compound that had passed him thirty minutes earlier. As he carefully rounded the building corner, he spotted two of Luc's men inside at the cashier station. Once they left to return to the compound, Secur made his move. From his soggy wallet he pulled out the business card of Randall Penn and entered the store. Since there were no pay phones anywhere to be found, Secur was forced to give the night clerk five dollars to use the store phone. He dialed Penn's cell phone.

Ronnie Feldman picked up Penn's ringing cell phone and looked at the window face as a 239 area code showed up.

"Who the hell is calling you from Naples at this time of night," she remarked, handing Penn his phone.

"Randall Penn speaking," he answered.

"Mr. Penn, it's Alain Secur, and I need your help right away."

CHAPTER FORTY-SEVEN

Kyle Anderson had decided to take lunch in the conference room of his office. He had invited Sandrine to join him. They sat at his sixteen-foot-long Malaysian mahogany table in the burnt orange leather chairs he had special ordered from Milan. For appearance's sake Sandrine sat across from Kyle as both dined on salads from the caterer in the ground-level shop in the same building. Kyle ate quickly, as if he were in the military. He was excited to tell Sandrine about the latest project he was about to acquire. She was dressed in a moderately seductive red silk suit, sporting an open white blouse with red trim adorning the edges of the collar—subtle but mildly sexy. Kyle was so love struck with her that whatever outfit she chose to wear would be one he thought extremely sexy. The room was filled with pictures of past projects hanging from the walls and a trophy case filled with design awards, small trophies for little league teams Anderson sponsored, and marketing awards for website and graphic excellence. In short, it was the equivalent of the home team's locker room.

"So tell me, Kyle, what's the next great project for us here at Anderson Development LLC?" asked Sandrine. This was the first time she had said it feeling like part of the team and not a scheming turncoat. It felt good to say it. Her remark did not go unnoticed by Kyle. He beamed proudly and could hardly wait to tell her his plans.

"This may sound a little funny, but I have struck a deal with the Teamsters at a ridiculous price to take over the two contaminated Secur properties—Glisten and Claughton Towers."

"What?" she responded with utter amazement, not believing her own ears.

"I know it may be a little uncomfortable, but it's a hell of a deal and comes with no personal loan guarantees. We are writing our own ticket, Sandy," explained Kyle.

Sandrine was still in shock but managed a response. "I am not uncomfortable for the reasons you may think. I am uncomfortable with the association with a bad building, dubious partners, and the financial risk that the public will never forget the Chinese drywall and won't take a chance on the eventual purchase. We are doing so well right now. Do we really need this?" said Sandrine, nearly pleading with Kyle.

The statement gave him mixed signals. He was definitely impressed with her concerns as a top executive, one he admired and listened to. He was also mildly upset that she was not on board. But he had not broached one single term of the contract with her in advance, a contract with more upside and less risk than any recent deal he had done.

"Sandy, 930 units at fifteen cents on the dollar. That gives me enough room in costs to bring in a Chinese drywall restoration firm with a stellar reputation to fix the problem. I also have lined up an insurance policy against any future long-term effects from their repairs. This will be the heart and soul of our awareness campaign," said Kyle. He was selling the merits hard, wanting Sandrine's approval.

"But what about those Teamsters and the Biagio baggage?" she asked.

"What baggage?" questioned Kyle.

"The fringe people who also invested. Mob guys from the Northeast. That baggage," pleaded Sandrine.

"I am their only chance for any return, Sandy. You've got to trust my judgment here. Give it a chance, please," begged Kyle, wanting her on board.

"Well, all right. I'll give it a chance, but you better have our attorneys comb through every detail and every word in the agreement multiple times," said Sandrine. She was about to return to her office when Kyle surprised her.

"By the way, I have a meeting with a friend in ten days on Grand Cayman. Would you care to join me? It's a short meeting. Normally I would come back the same day, but with you there, I would stay a couple of extra days," asked Anderson, blushing as he spoke.

"You are a naughty boy. Of course I would love to go, but..."

"No buts, Sandy. I take that as a yes," interrupted Anderson.

"Seriously, Kyle, how are you going to explain my absence from this office at the same time you are gone? We are a nonpublic item, and I am sure we both would like it to stay that way. How would it look?" Sandrine said with disappointment in her voice.

"I thought about that, so you're going to be gone a week before I leave. You can go anywhere you want before we meet, and I will pay for it," said Kyle, nervously awaiting her acceptance.

"You are not only naughty, you are a shady customer, Mr. Anderson. I like the Caymans. Why don't I just check in early and await your arrival? I can get some scuba dives in and relax until you show up," answered Sandrine with a big smile.

"Then we are good? Make your own arrangements down and back and tell me the amount it costs. I will take care of it from there," said Kyle.

"Who are you meeting?" Sandrine questioned.

"An old friend who used to work for me. Some unfinished business, so we decided to meet halfway," said Kyle without mentioning names. He wondered if Sandrine had ever met James Foster. *I need to remember that detail*, thought Kyle.

The invitation had worked to perfection. It not only made his day romantically, it squelched her doubts about Glisten and Claughton Towers. He sat at his desk after Sandrine left and pondered his new challenges. First, get the Teamster purchase resolved and the buildings in the name and title of the new company. *This may have to be done offshore*, thought Kyle. That would be another appointment while Kyle was in the Cayman Islands. *Perfect*. Getting the title away from Secur, the current and rightful owner, would not be easy. *Biagio had the power of attorney, but could the transfer be legally challenged as not being an arms-length conveyance?* Wondered Kyle. He would need to talk to corporate counsel on that one.

Second, and just as important, was keeping a lid on his affair with Sandrine. His desire to spend more time with her would eventually leave a trail. It always did. Secur obviously had an understanding with his wife, but Anderson would never have that luxury, nor did he want it. Moreover, his wife was on most of the loans with Kyle and was a partner in nearly every deal he did. That realization gave Kyle the cold sweats as his brow became moist.

CHAPTER FORTY-EIGHT

Alain Secur was at a safe house provided by Ronnie and Penn. Since his escape two days prior, he had met several times with the FBI pair and discussed various concerns and peculiar activities surrounding his recent demise and his protective disappearance. His last remaining untraceable cell phone had been ringing off the hook ever since he had escaped. He presumed it was either Biagio or Luc. He gave the FBI permission to deny information to anyone asking about him, whether or not he was alive and safe. For the FBI and their case, it was best for all concerned that he appeared to have vanished or been killed.

Secur was fresh and humble as he answered the door at his safe house. Ronnie Feldman and Randall Penn strode by him after good morning pleasantries and headed for a small table in the kitchen. The drab 1970s apartment had matted-down shag carpet, and everything spoke old and outdated. The kitchen had sheet vinyl floors with a seashell design, emblematic of that era. A case of air freshener had actually cleansed the stale Florida smell that existed when he arrived. It was bearable and a far cry from his Star Island mansion, which seemed like an eternity ago. Secur was glad to be alive. His only concern was Bennett away in school at Dartmouth. He now believed that Alicia was aligned with Luc and his friend Biagio. He briefly recounted how it had all gone so wrong and how stupid he was not to have seen it coming—the typical self-reflection every individual goes through in life when things go badly.

As Ronnie sat down with her pen and paper, she carefully laid her jacket to rest on the chair back. Secur took his seat opposite Randall Penn. Secur laid his notes in front of him as he began to go over all he felt to be relevant.

"Mr. Secur, perhaps it would be best if you told us what you believe to be the most pertinent facts that you know and we probably do not. These facts should relate to the Sonya Michel murder, or the Moto Seanu murder, or even the Artone Gomez murder over five years ago. We believe these murders are all somehow connected. Do you understand this?" said Penn.

"Yes, I do."

"And further, do you understand you are still under oath and Miranda still applies?"

"Yes, I do."

"I just want you to be aware we are recording your conversation, and Ms. Feldman will be taking occasional notes. You may begin," said Penn.

Secur began to detail his early beginnings as a developer, replete with mentors, old girlfriends, and tangent facts barely relevant to the case. Penn decided to let him ramble because eventually something relevant and useful would surface. As his story became more near term and related to the era at hand, Penn and Ronnie sat up in their chairs, expecting gold nuggets of facts to begin flowing. He detailed how careless he had become when anything he built would sell at ever-increasing prices. Sales were so easy he had become lax with his organization. Second-tier people at the superintendent and purchasing levels in his company were making decisions on the fly without checking with Secur. There was so much work to do to service the amount of construction related to high volumes of sales that normal, prudent business decisions were being shortchanged or ignored entirely. The ship was moving ahead very fast, but no one was in the wheelhouse as they sped on a collision course toward a looming iceberg. It was Secur's own version of the Titanic. Penn had heard enough filler information to begin to direct Secur to the answers he needed. He was curious about Secur's lack of oversight.

"So you admit that your lack of leadership caused these problems? But what I don't understand is how, after so many successful buildings, your two most current projects ended up with Chinese drywall and all of those construction problems. Don't you think that is odd, Mr. Secur?" asked Penn.

"Yes, I find it disturbing that almost one thousand units in two buildings escaped my superintendent's normally good scrutiny," answered Secur.

"What about your scrutiny?" said Penn.

"Yes, that too," Secur nodded, looking to the floor for answers.

"I presume that superintendent has since been let go due to lack of new work," asked Penn.

"He left after the last building received its certificate of occupancy; a CO."

"CO?" asked Penn. "Explain, please."

"After the building received its certificate of occupancy—a CO. Ready for people to move in," explained Secur.

"The building is finished at this point. Right?"

"Correct."

"Why did he leave?" asked Penn.

"He had an opportunity in Denver for new work. I was going to let him go, anyway. We had no work," said Secur.

"So he is no longer here? What is his name?" asked Penn.

"Jerry Kajohns," answered Secur.

"Did anyone else at the superintendent level leave after the COs were issued?" said Penn.

"Yes, our purchasing agent, Ed Jenkins," Secur answered. He was beginning to see Penn's logic and where he was headed. A frown appeared on his face.

"Where did he end up, and would you have let him go as well?" asked Penn.

"I would have kept him on for a short time. He could do other jobs as we wound down our work load. But really, Mr. Penn, it was clearly over for us condo guys. Everyone was vulnerable."

"Where did Ed Jenkins end up after that?"

"Kyle Anderson was always trying to get a few of my guys, and Ed was one of them. He ended up with Kyle, but it only lasted a few months and he left. I heard he moved to Costa Rica," answered Secur.

"What drywall company did you use for each tower? Was it the same company that had done all of your work previously?" asked Penn.

"We used Foster Brothers. They were a new sub," answered Secur, frowning once again.

"I would like to check them out. Do you have a company contact for Foster Brothers?" requested Penn.

"No. They are no longer in business. James Foster was the owner, come to think of it. He moved to Costa Rica, too," said Secur.

Penn looked at Ronnie, and Secur observed their cues. In Penn's mind, Secur had been completely out of touch with his last two jobs. He regrouped his thoughts and continued. Penn noticed a distant stare on Secur's face. The wheels were turning, and Penn sensed an opportunity.

"What are you thinking Alain?" asked Penn, more relaxed and informal, hoping Secur would react spontaneously. Secur kept the blank stare.

"Mr. Secur, did you hear my question?" repeated Penn. Secur quickly turned to look at Penn.

"I was just thinking it odd that Foster Brothers went out of business almost immediately after we completed Claughton Towers. He had all of Anderson Development's work. Kyle had just started a new condo on the water in North Miami."

"Do you recall if any of the Anderson condos had Chinese drywall in them?" asked Penn suspiciously.

"No. Kyle was a detail guy. I envy his systems and quality. He'd never let that slip by," answered Secur in submission.

"Word has it that Biagio and Anderson are contemplating a joint venture. Anderson will remove all of the drywall and refurbish all 930 units," said Penn, looking to get a read on Secur's face. It was an unexpected bomb, as Penn could see Secur hesitating.

"Well, I would do the same. He'll probably get the building for pennies on the dollar with easy payback terms and rent the completed building until the market comes back. Then he will convert the rentals to sales, and eventually the Teamsters might make some decent money back. It's the smart play. I would have done it if the roles were reversed," answered Secur as he looked up at the loft above his head, not wanting Penn and Ronnie to see his disgust. But Ronnie and Penn saw the anguish. Obviously Secur was hearing this news for the first time. They observed a beaten man.

"Where did you get that information?" asked Secur.

Penn hesitated giving his source, but felt it was fair. Secur had answered every question honestly, and a little reciprocation was in order.

"In a roundabout way through Marty Burns. He agreed to do all of the leasing. You were spot on about their intentions," said Penn.

Penn had some thoughts of his own about the construction process and Secur's poor performance, but that was not getting him closer to Sonya's murder. He switched directions, with Secur surmising that his mental condition had to be at an all-time low at this moment. Penn actually felt sorry for the man.

"Let's go back to your whereabouts on the night Sonya was killed. Not the night we found her but the night before, June second," asked Penn.

"I stand by my previous statement, Mr. Penn—home with my wife asleep," answered Secur without hesitation.

"How much money did the Mexicans loan you?" asked Penn.

"Thirty-nine million dollars," said Secur without hesitation.

"What kind of paperwork was signed, and what were the terms?" asked Penn.

"I think it safe to say that since there were no terms and no paperwork, this is the reason I am here with you today struggling to save my life," answered Secur as Penn nodded in agreement.

It was clear to Penn that Secur was distraught and becoming more so as painful issues were replayed in the questioning. With that, Penn decided it would be a good time to take a break. He and Ronnie decided to get some fresh air, leaving Secur inside alone.

CHAPTER FORTY-NINE

Penn and Ronnie were standing outside the apartment building shaking their heads about what Secur had just revealed. It was difficult not to feel sorry for the man. Even though his morality was in question, both agents agreed his only transgression was poor judgment and not murder. He trusted others and they took advantage of him, and his payback was the loss of everything he had worked so hard to attain.

"Pretty sad, isn't it, Penn? He's not a bad guy—almost likable," said Ronnie as she walked alongside Penn.

"He's clean on this one. But what are we going to do with him? If we let him loose, the Mexicans will be all over him. I give him two days, and he'll be dead," said Penn, shaking his head.

"What else can we do?" asked Ronnie.

"For now let's get Thorne to let him stay here," offered Penn.

"Don't you find it odd that the same sub who installed Anderson's drywall cleanly without the Chinese wallboard goes to Secur's job and installs that foreign trash?" said Ronnie.

"Yeah, and no one caught it over the entire time nine hundred and some apartments received the drywall," agreed Penn.

"Then everyone leaves Secur and either goes to another city or ends up in another country," added Ronnie.

"And now nobody wants anything to do with Secur. In fact, it looks as though the whole world wants him dead. Now Biagio and Anderson are working on a deal together. What's that all about?" said Penn, asking more questions than giving answers.

"Did you see the look on Secur's face when you mentioned Biagio and Anderson working together?" asked Penn.

"Oh my God. That was heartbreaking. You know he didn't know. I hate it when you're the first person breaking bad news to someone," said Ronnie.

"We should get back," said Penn. They returned to the front door as Ronnie gave Penn a quick butt squeeze.

Ronnie opened the door with Penn following her. A strange vision appeared before her eyes. A vision surreal and out of place. *What's this?* she thought. The brief disconnect reconnected instantly in her mind as she wailed uncontrollably. The surreal sight was two dangling feet partially showing from under the foyer ceiling, hanging from the loft.

Penn's vision was blocked, and he thought Ronnie was hurt. He grabbed her shoulders and quickly turned her toward him, inspecting her body head to toe as Ronnie pointed in the direction of a lifeless body hanging from the loft railing. Demoralized, distraught, and without apparent will to go on, Secur had hung himself while the agents were outside. Penn momentarily shielded a sobbing Ronnie from Secur's hanging body. Then he sprinted up the stairs. He felt for a pulse, looking down on Secur's cold, pale face. The life-enriching blood that had given pink color to the face just moments ago while Penn sat face to face with Secur had already pooled in the lower extremities. He was dead, hanging by his belt from the iron railing.

Penn instinctively reached for his cell phone to call for an ambulance. Then he bounded down the stairs to Ronnie. She was sitting on the outside stoop crying uncontrollably. All Penn could do was gently wrap his arm around her shoulders. She leaned into him, burying her reddened face in his chest. Both were stunned. Every dead body is gut wrenching and the two of them had seen many. But this was different. It was more personal—so soon after seeing Secur alive, and then the knowledge that what they had said in that kitchen may have tipped the scales and contributed to the taking of his own life. This moment and the graphic images would haunt Ronnie and Penn forever.

CHAPTER FIFTY

Luc, Biagio, and Alicia Secur had returned to the more friendly confines of New York to get ready for their meeting with Kyle Anderson. They had the private jet coming down in two days. Everything was set with Kyle. Anderson would immediately take ownership of Glisten and Claughton Towers under a quit claim deed from the Teamsters to a new corporation that contained the entities of Luc LoPrendo, Biagio LoPrendo, Kyle Anderson, and Alicia Secur. It was a slick deal for each partner. Alicia agreed to deed over Alain and her marital assets for a 15 percent interest in the newly formed LLC. Biagio and Luc negotiated buying the note from the Teamsters at fifteen cents on the dollar in exchange for a back-end kicker of 20 percent of the profits at the eventual sale. For their services Luc and Biagio received an 8 percent interest in the deal; all of which Luc assigned to his bad-boy mobsters, several of whom had threatened Luc personally if they were not made whole. The notion of being made whole quickly faded when the Chinese drywall was uncovered; reality sank in, and the bad boys were happy to get anything. Luc's 8 percent bought their silence and their assurances that no harm would come to any of the three.

Kyle Anderson stroked a check for $65 million and got two very important items in return. Foremost, he and his partners received clear title to the two towers. In addition, he received a new construction loan from the Teamsters for an additional $95 million to fund the removal of the corrupt drywall and the reconstruction of all units after removal. His contract with the renowned Chinese drywall repair subcontractor and his own construction work came to $82 million. The remaining $13 million would be used to pay the interest carrying charges on the debt until the two towers leased up. Marty Burns had estimated the lease time for 95 percent occupancy to be twenty months. Both towers' combined cash flow after debt service was $9 million per year. Anderson's split was 77 percent on the rental income until it was time to reconvert the apartments back to condos when market conditions changed. When the reconversion and sale finally occurred, Anderson's estimated profit after repayment of loans and capital at the current retail prices just before the drywall was discovered would be approximately $227 million.

Anderson's tax attorney and his in-house attorney had carefully crafted the deal. The partners argued over the meticulous calculations for only two days, and time was of the essence. It was a coup for Kyle and his team. They had the cash and the leverage, and no one else was willing to take on the uncertainty of the Chinese drywall and the myriad of negative situations that could occur even after the removal. Anderson had led the sheep to slaughter, but in a most gentlemanly way. Immediately after Kyle had heard about the drywall problem, he astutely put together his estimators, purchasing agents, attorneys, and accountants to assess the risk and the potential reward. Now he could reclaim the title *Mayor of the Skies* he had lost nearly seven years prior. The one thing he could not quantify in his risk examination was Armando Nacion and the Mexican cartel. Luc and Biagio were back in town and Kyle's first item of business with them would be the Nacion threat and what to do.

Luc and Alicia were at the pool bar of The Four Seasons discussing the complexities of the deal when Biagio appeared just outside the entry doors of the hotel. He wore a worried look on his face as he waved Luc over to speak with him. By the look on Biagio's face, Luc sensed the matter concerned just him and not Alicia. He asked Alicia to await his return. As he left her side, she turned to the bartender and ordered another Bloody Mary. Luc spoke quietly to Biagio as he approached.

"Is something wrong?" asked Luc, gesturing with his hands.

"Alain Secur hung himself this morning at an apartment in North Miami," responded Biagio as Luc gently grabbed Biagio's elbow, turning him toward the entry doors; they opened automatically. Once inside the hotel and out of sight of Alicia, Luc expressed his astonishment.

"What did you say? He's dead?" asked a confused and saddened Luc.

"That's all I know. It was on the Internet, and the details were minimal. I let the boys in Marco know so they would call off their search," said Biagio. Luc was looking down, still trying to process the unexpected news.

"Do you think the Mexicans had anything to do with this?" asked Luc.

"I doubt it. They do horrible things to a corpse in a revenge killing. It would have been much worse. It wasn't them," answered Biagio.

"How can you be so sure?" asked Luc.

"No one knew where he was. This is what I think. He escaped, not knowing whom to trust. His body was found suspiciously close to FBI headquarters in North Miami. I'm guessing he called Randall Penn asking for safe harbor. They put him in a safe house, and he killed himself there," said Biagio.

"I admit it sounds plausible. How can you be sure?" asked Luc.

"That's what I would have done," remarked Biagio. The door swung open a few feet from where Biagio and Luc were standing. A shrill scream caused them to turn their heads. It was Alicia, crying and screaming. She clumped in a heap at their feet. She looked up at both of them with scared eyes.

"Alain is dead. He killed himself. What have you done," she screamed. As Biagio looked up, his eye caught a picture of Alain Secur on a television news show with the caption *Prominent developer takes his own life.*

CHAPTER FIFTY-ONE

"I saw it too. How is she doing?" asked Anderson, referring to Alicia Secur while on the phone with Biagio. Biagio had called Anderson after he and Luc were able to get Alicia settled. Anderson knew Alicia from various real estate functions that he and Secur had attended with their wives. Anderson's relationship to Alain Secur was understandably cool. However, Alicia and Kyle's wife seemed to enjoy each other's company when forced to attend their husband's business functions. Kyle respected her and felt compassion for her position as the other woman, something he had only recently learned from Sandrine.

"Not very well, I am afraid. The entire episode surrounding the recent fall of her husband and the loss of their lifestyle, and now this, have made her an emotional wreck," said Biagio.

"I like Alicia, although I don't know her well. What about their son?" inquired Kyle.

"He's being watched by Luc's family," said Biagio.

"Thanks for the update. From a business standpoint, our agreement is not affected. I'll call you tomorrow," ended Anderson quickly as he hung up the phone.

Anderson was concerned about Sandrine's reaction to Secur's suicide. It was unlikely she had heard the news since she was in a closed-door meeting with marketing and ad agency executives discussing their new venture. Anderson wanted to be the one to tell her, so he arranged to have his secretary deliver a note to Sandrine asking her to see him once her meeting was over to discuss her upcoming trip. He wanted containment within his own staff. Forty minutes later Sandrine entered Kyle's office with a big smile on her face. *Good. She doesn't know*, he thought. She bounded to his desk and slumped in the chair.

"So did you change your mind?" she asked as Kyle became confused, forgetting about the note.

"What?"

"The trip. Are we still going?"

"Oh. No. We are still going. Will you come with me? I want to discuss something away from this office and the prying ears," Kyle asked.

"Oh, Mr. Mysterious. What are you going to tell me now?" Her good-natured attitude was killing Kyle inside. Normally she was not so flippant. This would be harder than he had thought. He wanted to get her to the sub-floor parking deck and tell her there, where no one could see her reaction.

"Come with me to the parking lot," he asked.

She cocked her head to one side and narrowed hear eyes. "Am I getting fired?"

"Shut up and just follow me. No, you're not getting fired," answered Kyle, playfully losing his patience. Sandrine agreed and followed Kyle to the elevator bank outside his office. He pushed the down button. As soon as the door closed, she grabbed his head and attempted to French kiss her boss. He did not immediately respond. She pushed back from him and looked him in the eye. He was serious, she could tell something was wrong.

"You are firing me, aren't you?" she repeated.

Kyle decided to end Sandrine's giddy play. "Again, the answer is no. I love you; why would I fire you? But I have something serious I want you to know," he said just as the elevator bottomed out at their level. Both stepped from the elevator as Sandrine's emotions suddenly changed.

"We're here. Now what is it?" she said in a more demanding tone. Her posture braced for bad news.

"Earlier today Alain Secur took his own life in an apartment building in North Miami."

Kyle could see she was confused as the information was heard but not processed. The grief, confusion, and recent death of her sister short-circuited her brain, causing a complete relaxation of her muscles. She fainted in Kyle's arms. Kyle stumbled momentarily as she slumped over his arm, almost dragging him to the concrete floor. Kyle heard a woman yell his name. To his horror it was Sheila Anderson, his wife.

"What's going on here, Kyle? What's wrong with Sandrine?" said Sheila with disbelief and surprise in her voice. Kyle thought about what to say, knowing he had only a split second to come up with a credible answer.

"She asked me to come here away from the employees and discuss her sister and how she was not coping well. All of a sudden she collapsed. It was a good thing I was standing so close. Did you see it?" asked Kyle, breathing heavily and hoping Sheila bought the lie.

"I did. I could not believe my eyes. Should we call an ambulance?" she asked.

"I don't know. I've never had anyone faint in my arms. She almost pulled me over," said Kyle, convincing his wife he was a hero. He gathered his senses and thought quickly. "What brings you down to the office? Is something wrong?" he asked.

"No, everything's fine. I was in the area when I heard that Alain Secur committed suicide. I didn't know if you had heard."

"Yes, I heard this afternoon. Can you dial Jack Sanders on your phone and put it up to my ear, please?" asked Kyle as the dead weight of Sandrine was making his whole body ache. Sheila did as she was told and raised Sanders on the phone.

"Jack, are you close to my office?"

"Yeah, what's wrong? You sound like you are straining. Why do you have Sheila's phone?" answered Jack.

"Sandrine fainted in the parking garage, and I am trying to hold her up with both arms."

"How'd you manage to call me?" asked Jack.

"Sheila happened to be coming by to tell me something, and she is holding the phone to my ear. Are you close by?"

"Five minutes away. Do you need my help?" asked Jack, starting to get the picture.

"Yes. Come to the lower level garage near the elevator. You can help me lift her into your SUV, and we will take her to the hospital. Hurry up," said Kyle. Then he asked his wife, "Honey, will you run up to the office and get a couple of wet towels?"

She immediately did as she was told. Once Sheila was inside the elevator, Kyle could hear tires screeching. Seconds later Jack Sanders leapt from his SUV and opened the rear hatch, making sure to fold all seats flat. He ran over to his cousin, helping him lift Sandrine into the SUV. They wheeled quickly out of the garage and headed for the hospital. Kyle's quick thinking had worked so far with Sheila. He knew he would be gone before she returned, giving him time to speak with Sandrine when she came to.

Just as they pulled into the emergency room parking lot at Jackson Memorial Hospital, Sandrine struggled to awake. When she opened her eyes, she was looking up at the headliner of Jack's SUV. She was disoriented and had forgotten briefly why she was just now awakening. She pulled herself into a sitting position and saw Kyle Anderson first.

"Are you OK, Sandy? You passed out," said Kyle in a reassuring voice.

"Yes, I think so. Is it true, Kyle? Is he really dead?" asked a despondent Sandrine. She was careful not to show her true emotions with Jack Sanders present. The car was now stopped in a parking space. Jack, understanding their need for privacy, quickly got out of the car.

"I'll be over near the entrance if you need me," said Jack, seeing that Sandrine was awake and appearing lucid and alert. He left the SUV.

"You're fine now. I know how traumatic these last few weeks have been. Alain's death was the catalyst that put you over the edge. That's why I insisted we be alone when I told you," said Kyle. He noticed Sandrine was starting to understand what had recently occurred.

"What happened?" she asked.

"You fainted as soon as I told you about Alain. My wife was coming to the office to tell me about Alain's death, thinking I had not heard. She saw you faint and rushed over. She called Jack and went to get cold towels as we waited. Jack arrived before she got back, and here we are," explained Kyle.

"Your wife saw me in your arms?" she asked in surprise.

"Yes. But she saw you faint and me catch you. Nothing more," said Kyle, seeing Sandrine getting confused again.

"Why are we at the hospital emergency room? I'm fine. Can we go back to the office, please? I need to get my things and go home," asked Sandrine.

"Sure thing," said Kyle. He waved over to Jack to get his attention. He reset the rear seats so Sandrine could sit normally, and all three of them left for the office once Jack returned to the truck. The short trip back to Kyle's office was silent and tense. Jack dropped Sandrine at her car. She opened the door and left without thanking Kyle or Jack.

CHAPTER FIFTY-TWO

Armando Nacion's head was about to explode. At every turn he was being denied his usual attempts at mayhem. In C. Juarez the AFI, Mexico's equivalent to the FBI, had somehow found the location of the Trinolea Cartel's collateral person's slave compound—a place where parents and relatives of the slave assassins were held until a slave achieved actual cartel membership and won the trust of its directors. Nacion knew this was the result of his captured assassin Carlos Rodrigo Secundo as he attempted to chirp his way to freedom with the FBI. He would have to deal with him later.

Further thwarting his plans was the fact that Biagio and Alicia were too well protected . This, and their constant movement, complicated Nacion's plans for revenge. The difference between a businessman and a madman was that a businessman would exhaust all efforts to collect a debt. A madman like Nacion had such a large weekly cash flow that replacing money owed from borrowers quickly morphed from practicality to revenge. His debt recovery process was short, intimidating, and effective, based on life threats and harm to one's family. His patience was short, and when debt collection took too much time, the money became secondary—as was the case now. He was out for revenge in order to set an example. But only he knew his plans. To the outside world, including Biagio and Luc, who did fear him, he was still in the patience and charm mode.

Unfortunately his charm had worn thin in recent days, especially with the implications of an article in the morning business section of *The Miami Herald*. It pushed him over the top. The avalanche of his failure to secure repayment had turned him into a fanatic bent on destruction and revenge. *The Herald* reported that the Teamsters pension fund and local developer Anderson Development LLC had reached an agreement to repair two condo towers infected with Chinese drywall and to reopen them as luxury rentals after completing all renovations. The article went on to explain that the Teamsters agreed to loan more money for the repairs in exchange for a portion of future incomes. *That's my money*, he thought. Kyle Anderson had just become a new target for his revenge. But first, before he would introduce himself to the new partner and outline his demands, he placed a call to Biagio from an unknown clean cell phone.

"Good morning, Biagio, and congratulations on your new venture. It's Armando," Nacion said in his charming Latin accent in a near-perfect English voice.

Biagio, wise to his charms, played along with the human dynamite keg. "Thank you, Armando, but it came at a terrible toll," said Biagio, suspicious of Armando's apparent good nature.

"Yes, my condolences to your former partner. How is Alicia taking it?" asked Armando. This did affect Biagio; hearing her name from his mouth gave him chills. He pretended not to show emotions.

"Not well, as you can imagine. What can I do for you today, Armando?" asked Biagio, having his fill of the false charm and compassion.

"I saw your deal in *The Miami Herald* today. Quite informative. Is the article accurate?"

"For the most part," said Biagio, knowing where this was going.

"Well then, I see there is a chair short. My loan was not covered in that deal; $39 million is a meaningful amount. It kept the projects from your own default, and most of that money went to you. Are you going to tell me that I am not a creditor here?" said Nacion as his voice began to anger.

"I know, it's unfortunate there are no more positions left in this deal, but I cannot name a partner as a creditor whose money was cash, to be laundered and considered blood money. Do you have a suggestion? You know your repayment was based upon the success of the vulture sale. Then we could have done some creative accounting. But here, we took losses far in excess of your investment and there is nothing on the bone left to divide," said Biagio. He could feel Nacion holding his temper and disgust over what he had just explained.

"Nothing on the bone. Interesting metaphor. I'm not impressed with your explanation. You and your uncle Luc and Alicia had better find a way to save a little on that bone for me. I don't foreclose on buildings—only on people's lives," said Nacion in an ominous tone.

"I could set up a meeting with Luc and me if that would help," said Biagio, hoping Nacion would take the bait.

"How about in C. Juarez next week at my office?" toyed Nacion.

"No. But I will meet you at the local Teamsters office in Miami," answered Biagio, staying calm and cool.

"I am a wanted man, Biag. Wanted by many men and by many governments, including yours. I will not fall for that trap. But I will give you a chance to live. Amass the 39 million, and I will let each of you carry on. Ignore me and you will end up like Moto and his friend," said Nacion with a click of the phone, ending the call. He threw his cell phone on the floor, watching it burst into shattered pieces. He would call in the reinforcements today.

Ronnie and Penn were putting the finishing touches on their plan to hunt down Nacion. Several near misses had led them to three safe houses, all vacated before they arrived. The last safe house was a bonanza as far as information went. They had just missed the Mexicans at a waterfront house and thought they spotted Nacion's men a mile away out on the bay, headed for the cut by speedboat. The Coast Guard was alerted, but the boat was long gone by the time the Coasties mounted a chase. Valuable information had been left behind: a ledger book, two forged passports, and a laptop. The laptop was in a drawer covered with towels and was probably forgotten in their haste to leave. The ledger book and passports likely fell from a folder as the men ran for the boat.

Ronnie had cracked the password on the computer with the help of the cyber boys down the hall. Much of the information was in Spanish and was being translated to English by Cyber as well.

"It says here that the Secur debt was $39 million, and it was paid to Secur in cash. Interesting, Penn; do you think we can RICO the two towers?" Ronnie said enthusiastically, looking to Penn for his support.

"You are a cute little thing, and what a great idea, too. My guess is no. The money was used probably to pay interest to the Teamsters. The building was built with legitimate funds, so it technically may not qualify under the definition of racketeering as outlined in the RICO statutes. But anything can be alleged," said Penn.

They pored over the laptop, looking for something that would lead them to any location they might try next. Names and places of people and companies they had loaned money to were listed. Each new folder they discovered on the laptop required a separate password in order to open the data files. Cyber had discovered that the passwords were Spanish names for men and women, which made code busting easier.

"Here it is, Penn," said Ronnie excitedly. She had come upon a list of locations. Some were restaurants, some were hotels, and others appeared to be individual homes. Penn began to review the lengthy list.

"Here are the addresses of the three places where we just missed them, but they are listed in no particular order," Penn remarked while scrolling through the lists. He was able to eliminate all but twelve addresses. He opened Google Earth and pinpointed each location. One location was a corner gas station, but the other eleven were homes in varying neighborhoods. All were on waterways with quick access to ocean inlets.

"Let's get Thorne in here and brief him on our plans," said Penn. Ronnie left the room to find Special Agent in Charge James Thorne.

CHAPTER FIFTY-THREE

Sandrine had reservations about going to Grand Cayman to meet Kyle, but if ever she needed time alone in a blissful locale, this was it. She preceded Kyle by one week and stayed at the Ritz Carlton as he had arranged. She had brought her golf clubs hoping to convince Kyle to play with her at the Blue Tips Golf Course, directly east of the Ritz. She had vacationed here from France with her mother and father over twenty years ago. It brought back memories of her playing the same course with her father during that visit. It was to be the last vacation she would have with him before he died six months later in a boating crash near Monte Carlo. Just before she entered the lobby of the Ritz, she turned to look at the entrance sign of the Blue Tips course behind her. It was just as she remembered it.

As the bell captain set her luggage in place in her suite, she examined the exquisite room that Kyle had reserved for them. It was island chic. The entry door into the hall was paneled in whitewash maple trimmed with articulated moldings. It was begging her to enter. Once inside the bedroom, her eyes went straight to the Caribbean Sea at the far end of the room. The double French doors were open, announcing the waves clambering on shore. The ceiling was set into an inverted pyramid with crown molding edging around the perimeter and bead board planking on each of the four pyramid sides. A spectacular ceiling fan was perfectly positioned in the inverted peak with four thatched, wide, leaf-like blades. The flooring was all marble, and every wall had wainscoting up to four feet high trimmed on top by a Charleston rail. The bedding and furniture had matching colors of lime, orange, and grapefruit accenting the teak furniture. Sandrine was used to all forms of luxury, but island chic was her favorite, and this was the best she had ever seen.

She tipped the bellman and headed for the wide balcony directly off the living area. It was sunny with just the touch of a sweet breeze. The turquoise water faded into a deep blue color close to shore, which was typical of the Cayman Island coast. The oceans surrounding the island just offshore were deep. As she took in the sights and sounds of the idyllic landscape, her thoughts and anguish disappeared. Her blood pressure and pulse were in the relaxed mode as the few remaining signs of stress quickly disappeared. She glanced at the balcony off the master bedroom and saw a basket of fruit sitting on an occasional small table. It had a card attached. She moved quickly back into the bedroom and onto the second of three terraces in the four-room suite. She picked up the card and opened it, knowing whom it was from. *"Dearest Sandrine, enjoy paradise until I arrive. Looking forward to golf and your company. All my love, Kyle."*

Typical Kyle, she thought. *Not mushy, but all the right words.* Her heart began to pound.

Sandrine was spending her days without Kyle in Grand Cayman shopping, exploring, reading, and unwinding at night. As a French woman with an independent personality, she was not averse to dining alone at fine restaurants. She decided she would try assorted restaurants near the Ritz before Kyle arrived so she could share her findings with him.

The men would gawk at her beauty, but none tested her by approaching her single vulnerability; they all wanted to. She was observant, feeling the stares and noting the smiles. One gentleman looked familiar, and his return look signaled similar recognition. She was at a local hangout up the beach from the Ritz, where supposedly every local had eaten at one time or another. The food was similar to that found in a sports bar, yet it was fresh and delicious. She was about to test the BBQ grilled chicken wings when she saw the man approaching. Two steps from the table it became obvious who he was—the drywall subcontractor on several of Kyle's buildings. *What was his name?* she thought. Before recognition occurred, he was offering his hand and his name.

"Sandrine Michel, what brings you to this lovely island? I'm Jim, from Miami. We did all of your drywall work until the bottom fell out," he said as he offered his hand.

This could be awkward, she thought, *Jim who?* She offered her hand in an attempt to stall while she tried to recollect more clearly who he was. At first she attempted to avoid asking the question but thought better of it, deciding instead to beat him to the punch and answer in her own words. After rebounding the same question back to Jim, she immediately remembered who he was, *James Foster*. She also recalled that he had fallen off the map fairly quickly when things began to slow. Then it hit her: he had also been the drywall sub for Secur's two infected towers. She had heard that his company disbanded when he suddenly moved away. *No wonder*, she thought. Sandrine decided to hit him right between the eyes with part of the truth.

"My sister tragically passed away a few months ago, and my boss, Kyle Anderson, sent me here for a couple of days to get my head on straight," said Sandrine, telling a half-truth.

Foster's face quickly flashed embarrassment. *She is here, and Kyle is due in a couple of days; interesting coincidence,* he thought. He knew about Sonya's death but decided to play dumb.

"Oh my, I am sorry to pry. I am sorry for your loss," he answered, attempting to exit the awkward moment. He was surprised by her answer. It was nearly three months since Sonya had passed and just now she was here. *I may have something for old Kyle boy*, he thought. But as he was about to say his good-byes, Sandrine turned the tables on him.

"Jim, where are you living these days?" she asked, not so innocently.

Foster could not lie. One way or another, she would mention this chance meeting to Kyle, along with details of the meeting. "I've retired to Costa Rica; San Jose, in fact," answered Foster, feeling an ambush.

"Lovely country, and so many Americans living there," she responded. Sandrine was about to set her own trap. "Well, I am a fisherman, and it's the best there," said Foster, beginning to enjoy the meeting.

"What brings you here, Jim?" asked Sandrine, looking Foster in the eye for telling signs.

He did not disappoint, although he did lie. He looked down, then glanced away, giving away his next answer as a fabrication. "Change of scenery, really. Meeting some friends from the States, golf. That kind of thing," he answered.

Sandrine fell upon the words *meeting some friends from the States* and knew whom he might mean. Puzzled, she treaded lightly. "Well, enjoy your stay. I'm leaving the day after tomorrow. It was really nice seeing you," she said as she shook his hand good-bye.

The suddenness of her exit told him all he needed to know, but he played along and nodded to her in return.

CHAPTER FIFTY-FOUR

N acion was on the run. He had nearly been captured by FBI agents at his last safe house in Hollywood, Florida. The home was less than a mile from the Port Everglades Inlet. He was coming into the inlet after a longer-than-usual visit to the mother ship when he noticed two long barges flanking either side of the jetties protecting the inlet channel. They looked like dredge barges, so he thought nothing of it. He motored into the channel at a leisurely pace to avoid any unnecessary attention. Five of his men onboard stayed out of sight in the cabin below. These were his standard procedures when entering an area of police boats and Coast Guard vessels.

The remaining men had stayed at the safe house awaiting his orders. The house was strategically located on an end lot facing the intercostal waterway, with quick access to the inlet. The street leading to the house was long and pencil straight. Anyone entering the street would be spotted by Nacion's lookouts at the far opposite end of the street. Every Nacion safe house was rented to an American corporation on a canal or waterway near an inlet. The FBI were excellent trackers, but they had not anticipated the level of sophistication Nacion's men possessed regarding electronic surveillance and their lookout network. Two spotter houses were rented in as close proximity as possible, depending on availability.

The warning was given to Nacion's men at the safe house as the government vehicles approached the first spotter house two blocks to the west. Important documents and computers usually stayed on the high-speed cigarette boats unless they were being used for a meeting or when surfing the Internet. Documents and computers were only allowed in the room closest to the rear exit doors leading to the boats. As the FBI approached the safe house, a meeting was underway, and cartel personnel inside the house were using documents and computers. Once the message came through about the imminent arrival of the FBI, cartel members in symphony executed their preplanned emergency exit procedures. Two men went to the boat, untied the lines, and started the engines. Boats were always faced in the direction of the escape route. Two other men scooped up documents and computers and quickly placed them in large canvas carrying bags. The remaining two men quickly scanned the meeting room, checking for missed objects. By the time the feds were halfway down the long street, all six men with their belongings, computers, and documents were away from the house at high speed. When the FBI arrived at the house, the boat would be a speck on the horizon, turning into the inlet heading for freedom and the open ocean in a boat faster than any one could catch. Today would be different.

As Nacion cleared the jetty entrance on the inlet channel, he happened to glance behind himself to the east. His heart skipped a beat as panic flushed his face. The twin barges appeared to be moving toward each other, establishing a blockade of the inlet he had just passed through. Nacion's survival senses feared the worst, and then it happened. Screaming around the corner of the intercoastal and the inlet channel came the second of his boats, manned with six of his members. The boat's driver was the only man on deck, as protocol required, and he was focused on his own escape and not Nacion slowly motoring into the intercoastal from the opposite direction. A split second later, an FBI cigarette boat and a DEA boat flew by Nacion, wetting him with their wake. He was so close he could see Penn and Gambrel in each of the vessels. Three agents had automatic weapons in position pre-aimed at Nacion's number-two boat. Nacion observed another agent was filming the entire chase from the south shore.

Nacion feared the outcome but remained calm. His men on the second boat were not slaves; they were company men who would take a bullet to the head rather than be captured. They headed east at over ninety five miles per hour hoping to cut between the closing barges. For a moment a space wide enough between the barges gave Nacion hope his men would be able to get between the barges and accelerate to 120 knots and flee to international waters before an intercept was possible—even if they had to run to the Bahamas flat out in doing so. Federal officers positioned on the barge in prone position began to fire at the boat's engines in order to halt the fleeing Mexicans. The sound of gunfire brought the five men from the cabin up on deck with their automatic weapons as gun barrels blazed at the barges. The opening was large enough, and they would make it through.

Instantly, the driver's head exploded as red vapor left a crimson trail wisping behind the boat. His corpse pushed the steering wheel left, directly into the side of the north flanked barge as the engines remained spinning at full power. The agents on the barge had seconds to react; they dove overboard on the opposite side of barge, away from the impending collision. The boat had turned sharp left before a full-speed impact, lowering the bow just enough so that it drilled into the side of the barge at a slight angle. Fiberglass met steel, and a fiery explosion filled with shards of fiberglass burst into flames. Three of the remaining cartel members were gunned down moments before the impact; they were the lucky ones. The one living member on the lower left side of the boat was thrown from the boat. Leaving the boat like a missile, he exploded onto the rear conning tower of the barge just below the pilot's window. He was killed instantly falling onto the deck like a ball of blood. The final living member on the right side of the dipping cigarette boat was launched as well. His fate was sealed when his flopping body skipped across the steel deck of the barge, skidding at high speed into the three-cable guardrail. He was diced like an onion. Mangled bodies and soggy evidence sank to the bottom of the deep inlet.

There was no human life to save, but within seconds the DEA boat carrying Gambrel and a scuba diver were at the site where the crushed cigarette boat had sunk.. The DEA diver entered the water among several opportunistic sharks. In less than ten minutes, computers and water-drenched papers were aboard Gambrel's boat, soon to be examined by the DEA and Ronnie Feldman.

It was painful for Nacion to witness the mayhem and destruction of his crew members. The intelligence recovered was of prime concern to him. It was all he could do to keep the five men below deck on his boat from aiding their compatriots. They would have been massacred as well. Nacion had witnessed many deaths in his life, most at his hand. But this short burst of blood, explosions, and violence had happened so quickly that his breath was taken away by the lethal attack of the federal officers.

Revenge surfaced immediately within Nacion, then respect, and then reality. He was never going to see his $39 million, and repeated attempts would deliver diminishing returns. He motored peacefully north to his new safe house in Fort Lauderdale. It would be his final retreat in South Florida before he returned to Mexico empty handed.

CHAPTER FIFTY-FIVE

Penn was meeting with Ronnie to review the evidence from the Mexican firefight the previous day. His cell phone rang, and the name 'REGINAL GAMBREL DEA' splashed across the glass face.

"Good morning, Reg. What's up?"

"I just looked at the film from the firefight yesterday. I think we have an ID on our boy Nacion," said Reg.

"Based on what?"

"Do you still have that slave assassin in the area?" asked Gambrel, painting a picture that Penn did not recognize.

"OK, you gonna tell me what's going on, or do I have listen to your forty questions? Yes, he's in the Broward County jail. Why?"

"Easy does it, Penn. We passed by a cigarette boat yesterday during the chase, and I didn't notice the driver in the heat of the moment," said Gambrel.

"I remember that boat. You almost ran me into him. Don't tell me your on-shore cameraman got pictures of Nacion?"

"It wasn't that cameraman who got the pictures; it was one of the guys on the barge. The one where the two Mexicans got diced and sliced. He was in the pilot's house filming our chase looking west when he saw this guy turn to watch the action from his boat. Out from under him, coming up from the forward cabin, are these guys with automatic weapons. The boat captain, presumably Nacion, pushes them all back into the cabin to get them out of sight. Then Nacion continues to watch the firefight with extreme interest. When it's over you can tell by his look that he had just lost some good men," said Gambrel.

"You can tell all that from the body language from a film that was taken five hundred yards away?" said Penn.

"I got to hand it to this guy, he saw something suspicious, and he stayed with it. He missed the firefight in front of him except for the human missile that almost came through his window. Very messy stuff," said Gambrel.

"I assume the other barge had a cameraman as well to film the action?" asked Penn.

"You got it. So I'm thinking we need to see that slave assassin and have him ID Nacion," explained Gambrel.

"You're thinking clearly now, Reg. You want to meet this character?"

"You bet. When?"

"This afternoon around 3:00. Does that work for you? Hey, did you ID the boat?" asked Penn.

"No. I mean we have the color scheme, but the boat is not named and the registration numbers were not visible in the film. What's the slave's name again?" said Gambrel

"Carlos Rodrigo Secundo. Come by here at 2:30, and we'll all go together."

"Penn is Ronnie going too?" asked Gambrel.

"You want answers, don't you? He talks more when she's around."

"I dig it. See you then." Gambrel hung up as Ronnie perked up, hearing her name. She knew that Penn had just volunteered her tits again. She gave him the lover's frown when he turned toward her.

"What?" asked Penn, already knowing the answer.

"So I'm jailbait for your Secundo interrogation? Is that about it, Penn?" spoke Ronnie deciphering Gambrels comments.

"Not in the usual terms, but I guess you could say yes," Penn said with a big smile.

"I'm feeling a little unappreciated here Penn."

"Listen, I'd bring along your tits, but since you're attached to them, I guess I gotta bring you too," kidded Penn as Ronnie blushed.

"Seriously, fill me in on the Nacion theory," asked Ronnie, ignoring Penn's last remark. Penn sat across the table and explained what Gambrel had found on film and where they were going in the afternoon. They needed to discuss other issues regarding the larger mess that was growing into a violent cauldron, seemingly spawned by the murder of Sonya Michel.

"Penn, we got to get this Nacion fellow. We got a dead Samoan, followed by a suicide prompted most likely by Nacion's collection tactics. Now having found his first safe house, six dead Mexicans are being fished out of Port Everglades inlet. Any ideas how this ties into Sonya Michel's murder?" said Ronnie, asking Penn to connect the dots.

"All great questions, sweetheart, here's what I think. Sonya definitely knew something had gone down or was about to. And for that her life was taken. The Biagio alibi does not compute on the night she was murdered. Now this drywall mess you brought to my attention has got me wondering what these individual anomalies have to do with all of this," said Penn.

"I found out more about the drywall guy," said Ronnie.

"Tell me. Don't make me beg like I had to with Gambrel."

"His name is James Foster of Foster Brothers Drywall."

"In business still?"

"Hell no, Penn. The shmuck disappeared shortly after he completed installation of Claughton Towers. He had already completed Glisten the month before."

"When did his business fold?"

"Interestingly, almost immediately after he finished Claughton. He didn't even come back to do the punch-out work. Vanished."

"Huh," muttered Penn in deep thought. He continued, "Where to?"

"He moved to Costa Rica and has not been back since."

"Lots of Americans down there now, I hear," said Penn.

"Foster Brothers did all of Kyle Anderson's work as well," said Ronnie. Penn hesitated as the wheels turned in his mind.

"That's odd. Did you see if Anderson ever had Chinese drywall issues, my dear?" asked Penn.

"Yes, I did. Never."

"You and I don't believe in coincidences, do we?" asked Penn.

"No, we do not."

"Do you have the whereabouts of Biagio LoPrendo?" asked Penn, looking Ronnie in the eye.

"He's back in Brooklyn with uncle Luc and Alicia Secur," responded Ronnie.

"Who's tagging that trio?"

"Melnick."

"Next time you talk to Melnick, give him an attaboy for me," said Penn. Melnick and Lopez were the FBI's best bloodhounds. Both could blend into snowy terrain in a black coat.

"Anybody else you need to know about?"

"Where is Anderson?" asked Penn.

"I don't know. Is he now of interest?" asked Ronnie.

"Everyone's of interest. Get me his twenty when you can." The meeting ended. Ronnie adjourned to her office to review the Secundo file for their upcoming meeting at the Broward County jail.

CHAPTER FIFTY-SIX

Gambrel was right on time for the Secundo meeting and supplied Penn and Ronnie with a disc of the firefight. The three reviewed the carnage in the jail's computer room and noted the footage showing an interesting Latin boater believed to be Armando Nacion. Gambrel paused in freeze frame and enlarged Nacion's face. Penn downloaded the FBI's sophisticated version of photo-shop to process the evidence. Using the FBI viewing tools to eliminate grainy features, he produced a final portrait that was crisp and clear. Several copies were printed on photo paper to show Carlos Secundo. If Secundo positively identified Nacion, immediate APB's would be sent to all law agencies up and down the east and west coast of Florida. Staying underground would be next to impossible for the Mexican Wonder Boy.

With photos in hand they headed straight for the interrogation offices. As Secundo entered the room, his smiling face focused on Ronnie. She sighed and rolled her head, watching as Gambrel and Penn each gave her a slight smirk. Seated around the table were Penn, Secundo, Ronnie, and Elaine Johnson. Johnson had been the interpreter for Secundo's' intake the day after his capture. Today Penn had given her a list of standard questions to ask Secundo.

As he sat down, Secundo looked Johnson in the face and began to babble in Spanish. At one point he gently clutched her hands with his cuffed hands, bent over, and kissed her hand as a grateful gesture. The attending guard immediately approached Johnson and Secundo to break up what initially appeared as a mild assault. When he realized it was an act of honoring Ms. Johnson, he took a step back, waiting for the grasp to be released.

Johnson was blushing and confused by the conversation.

"What did he say to you, Ms. Johnson?" asked Penn.

"I'm not sure. He thanked me profusely for saving his family back in Cuidad Juarez or words to that affect," she answered.

"Oh, I see. Now I get it. We received information on the whereabouts of his family from Secundo and promised if he cooperated with us, we would have them evacuated from a collateral family's safe house where they were being held as hostages. This had been ordered by Nacion to motivate Secundo to keep killing cartel targets against his will," said Ronnie, looking directly at Ms. Johnson.

"Ah, yes. I recall part of that slave arrangement from his first interrogation," said Johnson.

"Now would be a good time to show him the photos of Nacion and see if, in fact, it is who we think it is," said Penn. For a brief moment they spoke of how she would preface her remarks pertaining to the pictures and Secundo's obligation as *quid pro quo* seeking his cooperation. It had been reported by jail officials that Secundo was quite the personality among fellow Latins housed at this jail. Everyone around the table could see he was relaxed, jovial, and slightly cocky. They hoped he would not forget the debt he owed Penn and Ronnie for saving his family.

Elaine Johnson saw the opening and casually mentioned she had a photo of a man Secundo may know.

She spoke to Secundo in Spanish while handing him the photos. The response on his face told the story before he spoke a single word. He babbled on again in Spanish, but this time every trained ear heard the name Armando Nacion muttered from his lips. Elaine Johnson quickly gave Penn and Gambrel the thumbs up.

"He has identified your suspect as Armando Nacion. Furthermore, he will do anything he can to help you capture this scoundrel. Apparently several of his friends and their families were not so lucky."

"Ronnie, can you finish up here with Elaine while Reg and I head back to Miami?" asked Penn, eager to get back to his FBI office and start the all-points bulletin using Nacion's picture and other personal data.

"Elaine, can you take me back to Miami when we're done here?" questioned Ronnie.

"Certainly. It's on my way."

"I'll see you tonight," said Penn, talking to Ronnie as he left the room.

Penn and Gambrel headed for the elevators as another deputy entered the room to fortify the security of the women remaining alone with Secundo. Once in the car, they conversed about strategies. Penn also wanted Reg's perspective on a couple of hunches he was feeling.

"I don't get it, Penn. Why would the Teamsters purposely sabotage Secur's two towers? They had the loan on the damned things, for Christ's sake," said Gambrel after hearing several of Penn's hunches in the elevator.

"I never said the Teamsters. I said Biagio LoPrendo," corrected Penn.

"I thought he was a Teamster," countered Gambrel.

"No. He's their loan correspondent. He works for them to place their pension money in real estate. But he is not a Teamster."

"What's his motive? And what does Kyle Anderson have to do with Biagio? That limb you're out on is about to break under the weight of these outsized hunches, my man," said Gambrel, kidding Penn.

"First question: motive. Biagio had seen six or seven no-brainer condo deals go through with Secur and the Teamsters over the good years before the bottom fell out. He's theoretically made the Teamsters lots of money and in turn has done well himself in fees earned, right?"

"Yeah, go on," encouraged Gambrel as his interest in the story started to pique.

"You and I have seen guys like this before. We call it the second-in-command theory. Biagio begins to think his role has made all this success and that he is worth way more. More than he would ever make in fees alone. You getting this, Reg?" said Penn.

"I've seen that theory many times before. Only on DEA deals, someone usually just kills his boss," said Gambrel.

"That's it exactly, Reg. Only Biagio can't kill anyone to get rich. He's a slimy bastard and a schemer," Penn said.

"Biagio can't run a construction site. He doesn't determine what drywall goes in a building. He's a suit. There goes that little hunch, Brother Penn."

"Enter Kyle Anderson, Brother Gambrel."

"What? I say the same thing about Anderson that I said about Biagio. He doesn't run Secur's construction jobs," said Gambrel.

"That, Mr. Gambrel, is the first truth you have spoken. But here's what that beautiful Jewish babe from Texas has discovered: Ronnie found out that Secur and Anderson both used the same drywall company during the boom times," said Penn. He was sucking Gambrel in little by little and was enjoying the banter.

"Again, my little white buddy, it could have just been a coincidence. Secur was unlucky he got the bad batch, and Anderson was lucky he did not. Besides, how does this involve Biagio and Anderson together? Do they even know each other?" inquired Gambrel.

"I believe they knew each other before, and here is why; Biagio knew that the timing of the towers starting as they did gave the projects very little chance of ever being successful. The boom had started to peter out. But the money was already committed, the land was already bought with Teamster funds, and everyone was in denial about the housing bubble. The moment they broke ground on those towers, the market was in free fall and they were unlucky to be at the zenith of the housing bubble just weeks prior. Biagio knew before the shell was completed that they would be upside down on the values as housing prices tumbled dramatically. His opening selling prices had nowhere to go but down. He also knew the pre-sales for the towers were bogus—typical in that marketplace. He gets an epiphany one night that goes like this: He knows Anderson was beaten out of those two sites by Secur. It's no secret the two despised each other. So he goes to Anderson and makes a deal. He also knows that Secur had stiffed this drywall contractor on numerous occasions, claiming poor workmanship. Remember, this guy is doing all of Kyle Anderson's work to perfection. Biagio gets Anderson to pay off the drywall company, who is about to go broke anyway because of Secur not paying the entire fees. Anderson and his drywall contractor despise Secur, and Biagio tries to profit from it by suggesting his own ruse. You with me here, my little black buddy?" asked Penn sarcastically as Gambrel cracked a big smile. Penn was the only one who could say that to his friend.

"Yes, honky, I get it," answered Gambrel as Penn laughed out loud.

"The drywall guy gets enough money to shutter his business and retire to Costa Rica. He purposely supplies and installs Chinese drywall as part of his agreement and flees the country. Shortly thereafter, Secur's purchasing agent retires as well.

"Now fast forward to today, and Biagio and Anderson pen a deal to strip out all of the old drywall, refurbish the units, and turn both towers into rentals. This is all possible because Anderson is not only buying the units at fifteen cents on the dollar, but the Teamsters agree to fund the refurbishment for a part of the deal. And since Biagio orchestrated this whole ensemble of characters, you can assume his take will be millions. We got our accountants running the numbers, Reg, and there could be several hundred million dollars in profits to split up," said Penn, reaching for bottled water from his cup holder. The story had started on Broward Boulevard, and Penn was just two miles from his exit in North Miami. Gambrel became an immediate convert, congratulating Penn on his outstanding sleuthing; mentioning as well that Ronnie Feldman, that beautiful Jew from Texas, probably fed the pieces of the giant puzzle to Penn.

"Well, I must say that is some story you got there, Penn, and quite believable. Our involvement at DEA is done here except for Nacion and his offshore smuggling operations, which of late seems to have been put on hold. But if there is anything we can do, let me know."

"You already have, my friend; thanks for listening," acknowledged Penn as they pulled into FBI headquarters. They exchanged a firm handshake as Gambrel left to find his car. He was calling it a day as darkness began to envelop the Miami skyline.

CHAPTER FIFTY-SEVEN

Sandrine decided to be a little naughty for Kyle's arrival. She visited the island's equivalent of Victoria's Secret, called Special Girl. What she paid $112US for could be carried in a small clutch with room to spare. Her change weighed more than the skimpy outfit she purchased. It was a sheer pink thong almost as clear as glass, with a mini bikini bra that had at the most four threads of material—inadequate to cover her crimson nipples. Earlier in the day, she had a touch-up Brazilian wax to cap off the soon-to-be-realized fantasy.

After getting back to the room, she checked Kyle's flight to see if it was on time. He had insisted on taking a cab. The flight was on time, and he would be coming to the room in about twenty minutes. *He's no fool*, she thought.

She shed her clothes, hanging her resort wear neatly away in the closet nearest the bathroom. The mirror was behind her, and as she turned, she admired her naked, forty-two-year-old body. She tried on the nano bikini for the first time to see how it fit. She had been too embarrassed to try the bikini on at the store. This was show and tell time for her, and she looked fantastic. As she gazed in the mirror, she chuckled at her own vanity. *This guy better appreciate the hard work that went into this body*, she thought. The visual of her own body was turning her on, and she considered masturbating in order to warm up for Kyle. She looked at the clock and decided there might not be enough time to finish before Kyle arrived. That possibility suddenly became exciting to her, but reason gave way to sexual mischief, and she decided against it. Their lovemaking was so torrid that she didn't need a warm up. *Better not break anything with too much of a good thing*, she fantasized. She decided to lounge on the bed in her nano bikini, reading her book waiting for Kyle. She had told Kyle to get his own key in case she was on a small errand. The disappointment in his voice that she might not be there when he arrived added to the excitement of her surprise.

Within fifteen minutes a knock on the door signaled Kyle's arrival. It was show time, and she could sense a moist condition between her legs in anticipation.

Sensing the possibility and hope of a sexual ambush, Kyle slowly opened the door and peeked his head around the door. He was slightly disappointed to find that Sandrine was not lounging on the sofa in the living room of the suite as he had fantasized on the plane trip down. Hope sprung optimistic as he headed toward the bedroom after dropping his luggage on the floor. The shades were drawn as he approached the dark room. Sandrine had the overhead reading light shining down on her near-naked body as Kyle came in. His eyes immediately locked onto the French bombshell he so coveted. She returned the sultry glance as Kyle's erection snapped to attention in three seconds flat. Instead of ripping his clothes off like an animal as he had done that first time in her South Beach apartment, he stopped to stare and pay tribute to her body. This completely fooled Sandrine but made her desire for him even more heightened than before. Even more seductive was the fact that neither had spoken a word, as if this moment had been tele-graphically rehearsed.

Kyle stepped to the edge of the bed and sat within inches of her throb-bing body. He looked her over from head to toe as he began to softly rub her muscular, tanned thigh. He kept his breathing relaxed and controlled while Sandrine was about to burst with anticipation. She clutched his hand, spread her legs, and moved his fingers to her moist vulva. That was too much for Kyle to endure. He stood up and stripped his clothes off, talking to her in mushy half sentences that made her giggle uncontrollably. She was near laughter as Kyle's boxer shorts pointed to the ceiling like a hid-den missile. Before he removed his boxers, she had slipped gently out of the

Nano bikini, showing her bare, smooth skin in that area. Kyle lost control and nearly crushed her, falling into a love-crazed lump over her naked body.

They made love for hours, as if their days were numbered and the world was ending at any moment. Kyle had never experienced a woman like Sandrine before, and her physical attractiveness and lovemaking skills had brought him to a total love of her soul. How could he carry on in his wife's bed with these powerful feelings? For the moment, exhausted and drenched, he felt himself drift into a trance, too tired to move but wide awake. Sandrine had already stepped into the shower, equally satisfied.

CHAPTER FIFTY-EIGHT

Armando Nacion was resigned to the fact that the $39 million was as good as gone and that his persistence to extract revenge would put his own life in danger. His smuggling operation was on downtime thanks to the undying efforts of Reg Gambrel and the DEA. It was so much easier in Arizona, Texas, and California, he thought. Mexican cartel members had established a beachhead in those areas after years of trial and error. The misguided and underfunded steps of the US Border Patrol could not cover that vast area. Things would only get better for him as the US Congress flailed away indecisively, actually making smuggling easier with their nonsensical policies. To make matters easier, his resources and manpower were much greater than the individual states and federal agencies.

He was holed up in another safe house, this time in Fort Lauderdale, in an area known as Coral Ridge. It was an older section along the intercostal area near the Coral Ridge Yacht Club, filled with beautiful waterside mansions and quiet streets. Unfortunately, this was a short-duration safe house because it was too far from an ocean inlet. If he had to make a run for it, his escape route would be along narrow canals two miles north of Port Everglades; the ocean inlet where he had recently lost a boat and six valuable men. He was down to his last six men and himself. Nacion was awaiting a new safe house, but his realtor could not deliver the house for another two weeks. This new home was less than two minutes from an inlet in Lighthouse Point, Florida, six miles north of their current Coral Ridge location.

While his crew was playing dominoes in the family room, he was lying in the master bedroom watching the big-screen TV. The weather had just played, and business news was next. Nacion had just finished reading *The Miami Herald* and *The Wall Street Journal*, catching up on local news and his investment portfolio. Relaxed and half dazed, he heard familiar names that brought him out of his trance: Secur, Anderson, and the Teamsters. A real estate editorial on a local TV news station was revealing the extraordinary new deal between a former rival developer and that developer's team of lenders. There it was, like a bad penny—a story that seemed to follow him no matter how hard he now tried to forget.

A sudden realization came over him. He would lay low in this house until they moved to Lighthouse Point. He knew he had been made by the authorities. He also knew that they filmed all of their chases, and he had certainly been in the crossfire of several cameras. DEA and the FBI were super diligent about film forensics, combing over each frame many times looking for additional clues. His thoughts were forming about how to get back part of his money. A lucky break had come his way by coincidence. As he watched the details of the new condo collaboration, a gift fell into his lap. The exclusive realtor he was working with on all of his safe houses turned out to be a member of the new Anderson team: Marty Burns. His goal to retrieve the $39 million was immediately rekindled.

Nacion was not only smart, but he was highly practical. The lack of a formal education had made Nacion a voracious reader of financial newspapers and magazines. He needed safe havens for his money but trusted no one but himself when it came to investing. He had lots of down time in his safe houses and used that time wisely to read about stocks, bonds, derivatives and gold. He quickly learned that there were more crooks on Wall Street than his hometown of C. Juarez. Being from a tough Mexican family, he was fearless of intimidating drug lords generally more brutal than brainy. It was then that he decided that if he was going to be a crook, he should do so where he already had connections and family support. In Mexico he quickly rose to a leadership role in a leading cartel due to his personality and investment skills.

As he relaxed with his crew he began to hatch a new kidnapping plan revolving around Burns and his family. Marty Burns was a devout family man with a wife and three kids. Nacion would brush up on his kidnapping skills and requisition more men from Mexico for this next operation. It was mid-September in Florida and the height of the hurricane season. Hurricane Manny was skirting the east coast of Florida just sixty miles to the east. Nacion viewed this as a good sign; his childhood nickname was also Manny.

CHAPTER FIFTY-NINE

The morning after Kyle and Sandrine's torrid love fest, Kyle was scheduled to attend a mid-morning meeting with James Foster. He knew Foster wanted to renegotiate his deal , and Kyle was struggling with how to proceed peaceably in a conversation in which he fully expected to be blackmailed. He was lying in bed staring up at the ceiling in deep thought while Sandrine bathed in the next room. What he did not know at that moment was that Foster, having seen Sandrine days earlier, had hired a local island PI. The evening before as Kyle arrived on the island, Foster's PI had followed Kyle to the same suite where Sandrine was staying. It was valuable information that might get Foster some extra bucks.

Kyle gazed to his left just as Sandrine's naked body filled up his sight lines. Sandrine caught him staring and blushed uncontrollably as she gently shut the door. They had hardly conversed at all during their marathon lovemaking session the evening before as each fell silent to exhaustion. Kyle decided to break the ice, wanting to know how she had enjoyed the week she was alone in the Caymans.

"Hey, sweetheart, can I come in?" teased Kyle.

"Sure thing, stud, come and see me," she answered, playing along. "Who are you meeting today?" asked Sandrine with a hint of suspicion.

Kyle had come to the Caymans with a prepackaged lie, not wanting her to know it was James Foster he was meeting—a person she may remember. Sandrine waited, expecting to hear James Foster's name.

"Roy Jansen. He was one of my first investors, and he wants to see me about a project he is planning in Ecuador," said Anderson. He had rehearsed the lie so often that it sounded like the truth.

Sandrine accepted his explanation thinking it was just a coincidence bumping into Foster. She knew Jansen had moved to Ecuador after finishing his investment positions three years ago with Anderson Development.

"Oh, it's been so long since I have seen him. Why don't you invite him to dinner tonight with the two of us? I don't think I can repeat last night," she said.

Kyle chuckled as he held his composure. "OK, I'll ask him. Where shall we go?" Kyle answered, trying to get out of the discussion. He would merely call after the Foster meeting and say Jansen had to depart for Ecuador immediately. Since Jansen had his own private King Air, the lie was plausible. Kyle had thought of everything.

Sandrine was satisfied. Her suspicions seemed baseless, and she felt guilty for questioning Kyle with unannounced motives. She decided better of it, but had one last question. We can go to the Wildflower Café here in the hotel. Where are you and Jansen meeting? inquired Sandrine as she stood in the doorway, scantily covered in bubbles but otherwise naked and desirable.

"I got to go, babe. I can't stand here next to you while you're like this," said Kyle, leaving the room and feigning a lack of self-control without directly answering Sandrine. He quickly stopped just before opening the door and shouted back. "We're going to meet at the Cayman Island Bancshares Building and then figure where to go from there. I'll call you," said Kyle, disappearing out the door.

Now Sandrine was certain he was meeting Jansen; Foster was a coincidence. She would tell him about that night and her chance encounter.

Sandrine had her own plans for the day. An hour later she was dressed and headed for town and the island boutiques. She closed the door to the hotel and caught a glimpse of a white piece of paper on the ground directly outside their suite. She bent down and saw an address written on the paper in Kyle's handwriting. Lighthouse Restaurant, Bodden Town and Cliff Hill Lane. Her heart was confused. Kyle had sounded so convincing. Could this be for tomorrow, their last day on the Island? She wondered. She walked back into the suite, Googled the address, and saw that it was way east of Georgetown near the Queen Elizabeth II Botanical Gardens. She had visited the Gardens two days ago and knew the route. Her doubt and curiosity were getting the better of her, so she decided to drive by the location.

Thirty-five minutes later Sandrine reached a white building shaped like a lighthouse on the beach highway. She made a pass and saw Kyle's rental car in the parking lot. The restaurant was just west of the intersection of Bodden Town and Cliff Hill Lane. She turned left on Cliff Hill and parked along the road facing north, with the restaurant clearly visible in her rear view mirror.

Foster had chosen a relaxing spot for his meeting with Kyle. It was a wonderful late August day in the Caribbean. Soft waves with small white caps spread across the sandy beach at regular intervals. The restaurant where the meeting was being held was a converted white residential house with a lighthouse turret situated atop the gable roof. It was a bit contrived but believable, except for the fact that it was on a straight stretch of beach with no threatening rocks or a dangerous inlet. However, the food was excellent and the service was impeccable, impressive for an eating establishment so far out of the way.

Kyle was not enjoying his visit with *old businessman* Foster. Apparently, his personal financial management was no better than his business acumen as a former drywall subcontractor. But Kyle was enjoying the restaurant and the unlimited southern ocean view. He knew it was a shakedown, and he wanted to end their relationship once and for all.

After fifteen minutes of painful, irrelevant reminiscing about old times, Kyle finally broke the ice. "Foster, I didn't come all this way to discuss old times. Why don't you get right to the point," Kyle suggested firmly. He was now anxious to hear what the number would be.

"You always were right to the point. I guess it has served you well, so I will be equally as short. Two million tax-free dollars wired to my Costa Rican bank account. Here's the wiring instructions and account number. In three days or else," said Foster.

Kyle was impressed. Usually he could manipulate Foster. *Gutsy move*, he thought. It infuriated him, though. He liked the old, easygoing James Foster better. "And what does that get me in return?" said Kyle, barely able to stop from reaching across the table and strangling his pudgy friend.

"It gets you my complete silence and me out of your life forever."

"I seem to recall that was what we agreed upon before about two million dollars ago. Are you mad? For half of that sum I can get the best hit man money can buy, and you will disappear so fast no one will know you are gone. Need I remind you of who my new partners are now?" answered Kyle, mixing his tone.

Foster's grin turned upside down instantly. He was suddenly off guard in confusion and fear. *Was he bluffing?* Foster reconsidered his options as the table grew quiet.

Kyle could see he had made an impact. *Did I really just threaten to kill him?* Kyle thought.

"Well, make me an offer," was all Foster could say, still surprised at Kyle's veiled threat—*or was it veiled?*

Kyle was surprised at the effect his threat had on Foster. "How about I forget we had this conversation and get back to my hotel room?" said Kyle.

"You mean with Sandrine Michel?" came Foster's uncontrollable reply. He had said it and he regretted it immediately.

"What? How do you know about Sandrine?" said Kyle, turning defensive.

Foster picked up on the effect of his remark. It emboldened him. He'd recovered. "I saw her the other day, and I put two and two together. I don't blame you, but I doubt your wife knows about that exquisitely fine woman who is here in the Caymans with you. Does she? Make it two and a half million, lover boy. And the next time you threaten me, I'll be coming after you," said Foster. Again silence.

"All right, you've got yourself a little confidence now; don't be foolish," advised Kyle, not sure how to bargain with this obviously desperate man who possessed an important chip on his stack of influence. His mind was spinning. Had Sandrine seen Foster?

"Look, I'm serious. This is the last time, I promise. I'll go back to two million," answered Foster in a conciliatory tone.

"I need to think about it. I want to consult my attorney first."

"What? Are you crazy, Anderson?" reacted Foster.

"No. I need to be sure that it's done with complete discretion. I'm being watched by all of Miami now, and I cannot move that quickly. I'll let you know in about a week," said Kyle calmly as he got up and left abruptly.

Foster followed him to the parking lot in close trail. As Kyle moved to open his car door, Foster stepped in front of him, pointing a finger at Kyle. "You can't leave; I'm not done with you," said Foster harshly as Kyle stepped back.

"We're quite done here. And if you want your sugar daddy to send you any money, you better get out of my face right now," yelled Kyle at close range. He gently moved Foster aside as he got in his car. "Don't worry; you'll be hearing from me," said Kyle as he drove away.

After forty-five minutes staring in her rear view mirror, Sandrine saw Kyle leave the restaurant and briskly walk to his car. Surprised and deeply disappointed, she saw James Foster bidding Kyle a not-so-sweet good-bye; it did not appear to be a friendly parting. Kyle sped out of the parking lot heading for Georgetown. Sandrine sat a while trying to understand why Kyle would lie to her. More puzzling was the less-than-friendly departure. *What was that all about?* Her cell phone began ringing; it was Kyle. She quickly pushed the red button, putting Kyle to her voice mail. She needed to compose her thoughts. She would need to call him back soon.

"Hey, honey, I couldn't get to the phone before it went to voice mail," she said to Kyle after she dialed him back ten minutes later.

"Hey, babe, looks like Jansen is on his way out. He wants to beat some weather moving over the ocean between here and Ecuador. I'll be happy to meet you in about thirty minutes downtown. Where are you now?" he asked.

"I took a drive up the north coast to West End. I'll see you at LeBouqet Café, OK? she said.

Kyle agreed to the meet and would need to slow his pace in order to arrive around the time he said he would. Sandrine was misty eyed as tears melted down her cheeks. *Have I misjudged this man who was so kind to me? Is he another selfish man like Secur? What went on in that meeting?* She beat herself up for about two more miles and then decided to reason through the meeting between Kyle and Foster. She decided to try a chronological self-examination of events, current and past, dealing with Foster and Kyle the past three years.

Before beginning her arduous memory exam, she took one last moment to gaze south over the shimmering, light blue waters of Grand Cayman. It relaxed her momentarily before she resumed the inevitable. As she placed past events in their order, a pattern emerged. Foster fled the country shortly after Secur's last tower was completed. Now Kyle was meeting Foster in a meeting he denied, and he and Biagio were ending up with Secur's failed buildings. Was this a mere coincidence? Then it dawned on her as soon as the two events trickled from her memory in sequence. *No, No. Would he do such a thing? Was Kyle capable of this?*

That day she was barely able to look Kyle in the eye. She complained of a phantom stomach virus, thus avoiding any social outings or sex with Kyle. She tried her best to subdue her anger toward Kyle and still stay affable as before. Rather than accuse Kyle of what she felt was now a certainty and face an argument, Sandrine just wanted this trip to be over as soon as possible and manage to keep Kyle at bay until it was time to leave.

The next day they left for Miami. Sandrine knew what Kyle did not. They were through for good.

CHAPTER SIXTY

Biagio was informed by several sources about the violence in Miami that he knew had a link to his actions. After reading about the gunfight at the Port Everglades inlet between the FBI and Mexican smugglers, he assumed Nacion would be on the run and he would be reasonably safe. But he was careful coming to Miami this time, bringing a security detail of four men, each deadly in his own right. He was looking forward to staying at Alain Secur's home on Star Island. The Teamsters' newest home was for sale, but until escrow closed, he would be using the home on this and all future visits. Alicia Secur had removed her personal items and placed them in storage. She was living a materially reduced lifestyle with Luc back in New York; she was healing with Luc's help and affection. Her son Bennett had temporarily left Dartmouth and was at his mother's side in New York. For Biagio, his deal with Anderson Development was a brilliant move in a precarious market with a dysfunctional asset. Unfortunately for him, Penn and Ronnie had received news from agent Melnick that Biagio was back in Miami to discuss his new venture with Anderson. He agreed reluctantly to meet with Penn and Ronnie at their office. He arrived at the FBI building in North Miami hoping this would be his last interrogation. While all was finally well in his life, he was nervous about this meeting.

Inside the windowless conference room, Biagio sat fidgeting. This was an informal room with dull government-issue paint, flooring, furniture, and complete blandness. There was no one-way glass panel, but there was a carefully disguised camera leading to a bank of video displays being currently viewed by Penn and Ronnie.

"He looks a little nervous today, Penn. You've got the poor boy scared already," she lightly quipped. Penn was more serious and focused on Ronnie's observations. She was right. "It's not me, my dear. It's the guilt by deception. Eventually it wears down the best. He ain't the best," said Penn, using his tough-guy voice with Ronnie.

She just smiled. "OK, bruiser, go in there and get a confession," she said.

Penn's look said it all as he glanced back. They had seen enough and walked into the room where Biagio sat nervously awaiting today's questions.

"Good morning, Mr. LoPrendo. Thanks for coming in early. I believe you know Ms. Feldman?" Penn remarked cordially as Biagio nodded to Ronnie. He asked to be called by his first name. Penn obliged.

"Mr. LoPrendo—check that, Biagio—as you know, we are still investigating the murder of your girlfriend, Ms. Sonya Michel. Will you please acknowledge you have previously been Mirandized for the record? Ms. Feldman will be the scribe today, and I will be asking all of the questions. Do you acknowledge?" started Penn quite formally.

Biagio was feeling pressure over both eyes as his vision of a tough day of questioning seemed a reality right from the get-go. "I acknowledge everything you said," replied Biagio.

Penn began quickly. "I see you and Mr. Anderson have struck a deal on the contaminated condo towers in Miami. Congratulations."

"Is there a question in there?" asked Biagio, somewhat confused.

"No, it's just that your two little projects seem to be murder magnets. Sonya was with you, and she's gone. Secur was your friend, and now he's gone, and we recently whipsawed a boat of Mexicans rumored to be working for an unofficial lender of the same project. And I'm betting the Artone Gomez killing five years ago may have been the very first casualty, not Sonya Michel. So let's cut to the chase, Biagio LoPrendo. For starters, where were you really on the evening prior to Ms. Michel's discovery?" asked Penn quickly, ratcheting up the heat in a put-out, impatient, fed-up tone.

Biagio sank noticeably in his chair. "We've been over this before, as you know. I was with Alain Secur."

"No, you were not. The night of the discovery of Sonya's body, you were with Secur. I'm talking about the night before the discovery of her dead body. You said before that you were with Secur, but Secur swears he was with someone else. Again, where were you?"

Biagio, confused, struggled to remember what his alibi was supposed to be. His lengthy hesitation looked bad, he felt extreme anxiety, and he felt lost. "I, ah, I cannot remember. I've hit a blank. I'll have to think hard about that, Mr. Penn. I'm sorry; I just don't remember."

"Where are you staying while you are here?" asked Penn, shifting gears and catching Biagio off guard.

"I am at the Secur home on Star Island. It's technically our asset now, and I'm on official business."

"Mr. LoPrendo, you are officially a person of interest in this murder. That's fancy for suspect. So I don't want you leaving this town without telling me. I am about to wrap this case up, and I want you nearby for one reason. I think you know what that is," said Penn with focus and pressure on his new suspect.

"I did not kill my own girlfriend, Mr. Penn."

"Maybe you did not pull the trigger, but you know who did. Don't you?" said Penn, eye to eye with Biagio.

"I'm sorry you feel that way. I will answer your question in a day or two when I have time to reconstruct the dates. But I will not be calling you. My attorney will deliver the answer," said Biagio.

Just then Ronnie's cell phone rang. She glanced at Penn just before she was about to cancel the call to voice mail. It was Sandrine. She quickly excused herself, nodding at Penn as she left the room.

"You may go, Mr. LoPrendo. Have your attorney call me." With that, Penn got up and left the room in search of Ronnie. Biagio was left alone as the cameras recorded his demeanor. It would be telling.

Penn saw Ronnie huddled in a corner with her hand over the phone to privatize her conversation. As he approached she looked back and whispered two words to Penn: "It's Sandrine." Sandrine was hysterical and insisted she be able to meet Ronnie for lunch as soon as possible. The meeting was set, but this time Ronnie would pick up Sandrine.

Two hours later Sandrine left her apartment, hailed a cab, and was dropped off at Bayside. She took the parking lot elevator to the top floor of the garage. It opened to a nearly empty, open-top floor with the clear, blue sky as its ceiling. Ronnie was in Penn's black Tahoe in the handicapped space next to the elevator door. As soon as Sandrine walked from the elevator, she strode quickly to the open door of Ronnie's ride. The windows were tinted FBI black. Ronnie quickly drove the length of the parking lot and took the other exit down.

The nose of Jack Sanders's car emerged just seconds after the rear of the Tahoe descended to the streets below. Sanders had been slipped by Sandrine.

"What's with all the drama, Sandrine? Is that guy following you again?" asked Ronnie.

"Yes, I'm certain of it."

"Why? I thought you and Kyle were real tight?"

"I'm afraid that is history. I gotta stop falling for these builders. They're all the same; smoke and mirrors. Oh, I'm so mad at myself," she said, shaking her head in disappointment.

"What happened? Let me guess: he went back full-time with his wife?" Ronnie said.

"No. Worse. That's why I called you. I'm getting real bad vibes about Kyle and this whole new deal with the Teamsters and Secur's old projects."

"Well, let's drive to a new place near our office and have Randall meet us there. In the meantime, we will have some drive time to talk," said Ronnie in a calming tone. She reached over and gently squeezed Sandrine's hand.

"You're the best, Ronnie."

"My job is your welfare and safety. I'm happy to do it. Tell me what you know."

Sandrine began to explain to Ronnie, starting with the strange meeting in the Caymans that Kyle had with James Foster. "He never told me he had the meeting, but I saw it with my own eyes," said Sandrine.

"On what terms did Foster leave Miami permanently?" asked Ronnie.

"I'm not sure, but I know that Secur was bragging that he got a better price on the drywall job than Kyle was getting on his jobs. Typical builder brag and testosterone bullshit. I cannot say for sure why he left since things were closing in for everyone and construction had ground to a halt," she said.

"Let's say this for a minute. Suppose that great price Secur got for his drywall job was subsidized by Anderson. Further suppose the Chinese drywall was purposely installed by Foster, after which he split the country. My guess is he had a pocketful of money from your boy Anderson," said Ronnie as Sandrine put her head down in her hands. Something clicked and it wasn't good.

"My God, Ronnie, you're right. You've nailed it."

"Now hold on, girl. It's a story that I deduced from thin air, but we don't have any facts," cautioned Ronnie.

"Yes, we do—or maybe we do. I was so depressed when we returned from the Caymans that I did something I had put off for weeks. I went through Sonya's belongings at my apartment. That's the other reason I'm here. I found a diary and her cell phone."

"Oh no," said Ronnie, expecting the worst.

"I'm afraid so, Ronnie. I know what you're thinking. How could she have texted that distress message when she was just about to be dumped in the ocean and killed?"

"Go on. What else has you so suspicious?" asked Ronnie.

"There are some very loving words about Biagio; at least at the start of their relationship. Later on in the relationship, she seemed anxious to move on. I could tell by her writing she was becoming afraid of Biagio. She also made numerous entries about Biagio and Kyle. Biagio was impressed with Kyle, and his association with Kyle made him feel like a big shot," explained Sandrine.

"Why is the competing builder hanging out with his competition's lender?" asked Ronnie.

"Maybe I stumbled onto the truth after all," said Sandrine. Ronnie looked at Sandrine. She was beginning to weep.

"What's wrong, honey? Get it all out; clear your mind while you are with me," reassured Ronnie as Sandrine composed herself.

"I think Kyle may have had something to do with the disappearance of Artone Gomez and the Chinese drywall showing up in Secur's two buildings. Secur was questioned once about Gomez, but he could have never done that," said Sandrine, rambling from one idea to another.

"Was that in the diary?" asked Ronnie quickly.

"She wrote that it was a possibility that Kyle may have been involved in the Gomez mess based upon Biagio's discussions with Sonya. She also wrote that she grew to disrespect Biagio because he was always trying to impress her and shock her with outrageous claims and stories. I think she realized she was dating Mr. Second Place. The guy was always trying to portray himself as something bigger and better than he really was."

"So how does that make Anderson the potential murderer of Gomez?" asked Ronnie, a bit confused.

"Biagio had mentioned to her that her sister's boss would have the last laugh with Secur, just as he did with Gomez," said Sandrine.

"Go on. What else?"

"Apparently Biagio has a reputation for being a big-mouth blab, especially when he's a little tipsy and in bed with my sister. She was over his head, and he felt as if he needed to impress her all the time. I think they killed her because she knew about the drywall scam and Gomez. I have no doubt that this whole drywall scam is playing out now just exactly as Biagio and Kyle planned it out months ago. Now Kyle looks like Mr. Clean coming in to save the Teamsters' ass," said Sandrine, sobbing more rapidly.

Ronnie again gave her a comforting squeeze. "Now you've hit on the weakest part of the story, Sandrine. Why would the Teamsters purposely allow their building to have Chinese drywall installed in the first place? My understanding of this new deal with Kyle is that they will get at the very best forty cents on the dollar. And that won't happen for years—if at all. No one goes into a deal to lose that kind of money," said Ronnie.

"How did you get that cost information?" asked Sandrine, impressed and confused.

"We have a wide range of specialists in our bureau. Our accounting guys are said to be better than the IRS. All of this information is public knowledge. They just put everything together and gave me the summation," said Ronnie.

Sandrine was not giving up easily. "Yes, but Biagio is not a member of the Teamsters. He is their loan correspondent, a lender's rep. He is only out for himself. Even though he tries to be a big shot, he's a wimp without Luc. Luc got him the job with the Teamsters. Besides, it was the perfect time to pull this off. The economy was changing, and the Teamsters probably knew by the time the shell was finished that they were screwed on both towers. Secur had made them millions and millions of dollars over the preceding six years. But for Biagio, he made just a fraction in fees. He was jealous and wanted more, so he hatched the Chinese drywall scam with Anderson. You would think from the writings in Sonya's diaries that Biagio is the genius of the Teamsters' success. Why are men are always like that?" said an angry Sandrine.

"Go on, Sandy, you're on a roll. I must admit I'm starting to believe your theory has legs," offered Ronnie. The storyline was more reasonable than she had originally thought.

"There you have it, Ronnie. Biagio the wimp cuts a deal with Anderson. Anderson subsidizes Foster and pays him a healthy reward to sabotage Secur's towers, knowing he and Biagio will split a risk-free payday down the road. I think Biagio got scared and called in his bodyguard to kill my sister. He sent the text from her phone knowing the exact time when she would be killed in order to steer you and Penn toward Gomez," said Sandrine.

"So why didn't he trash the cell phone? Anyone would know better than that," questioned Ronnie.

"Yeah, I must admit, that has me stumped too," said Sandrine.

"What is your relationship like with Kyle now?" asked Ronnie.

"In a word, uncomfortable. We have been back for three days, and I have managed to tactfully avoid him. I knew I needed to stay away, but how could I since I work there?" said Sandrine. Ronnie continued to fish for answers. "How are you handling that?"

"I made love with him two days ago, but have put him off by telling him I have my period. Obviously that won't last much longer," answered Sandrine.

"That's an oldie but a goodie," chuckled Ronnie, lightening the moment.

Sandrine was finally able to relax. She pondered her reply to Ronnie before answering. "When I am at work, I can be out in the field away from the office. I have carried on a good ruse so far. But, it's harder now because I believe he knew about my sister. I can never forgive him for that."

"I don't know how you can go to work every day, Sandy," answered Ronnie, shaking her head at the thought.

They were turning into the restaurant in Aventura as Sandrine and Ronnie finished their discussions. Penn was waiting for them outside the front door as they parked across from where he was standing. He acknowledged Sandrine with a polite smile and kissed Ronnie on the cheek before turning to enter the restaurant. The trio took a table in the back of the upscale Italian café to review Sandrine's new discoveries. Over the course of lunch, Ronnie gave Penn the summary of her conversation earlier with Sandrine on the way to their meeting. On many of the points Penn had drawn similar conclusions. It became clear to both agents where and when to incorporate the pool of FBI talent and resources they would need to conclude this ever more complex criminal investigation. They left the café grateful for Sandrine's cooperation, yet at the same time worried for her well-being. Penn vowed to protect her.

CHAPTER SIXTY-ONE

"I don't know. She must have known I was on her. She's up to something, Cuz," said Jack Sanders.

"Why didn't she just drive over to Bayside and leave her car? What's up with the taxi?" asked Anderson.

"It's easier for her to watch who may be following her out the back of a taxi, for one thing. And it makes me wait for her at her apartment, which is not ideal for trailing folks. What are you going to do?" asked Sanders.

"I don't know. She's been a little standoffish since we returned from the trip. She hasn't been in the office much and tells me she's having her period in order to avoid any physical contact. She had her period two weeks ago, so that's a lie," said Kyle.

It was late at night, and Kyle and Jack Sanders were trying to figure out what Sandrine was up to. For Kyle, he was in love with the French beauty. He also worried about her brainpower and her powers of deduction. Sandrine always figured out how to solve problems, reach solutions, and turn enemies into friends. Kyle had to be careful when speaking to Jack of Sandrine. He could not risk telling his cousin too much. He decided to call it a day.

" Cuz, I'm beat. Why don't you head home while I check my e-mails before I leave? We'll talk tomorrow," said Kyle, wanting to be alone.

Jack said good night and headed for the elevator.

Kyle wanted to see if Sandrine had responded to any of his e-mails. He saw only one, which had been sent just twenty minutes ago.

My dearest Kyle. It has been wonderful, but I can no longer be with you. Effective immediately, I hereby resign from Anderson Development. I wish you continued success. I will send someone for my things in a few days. Be well, Sandy.

He was stunned.

Biagio was on his way over to see Anderson the morning after Sandrine had tendered her resignation again. He was continually looking over his shoulder to see if he was being followed. Paranoia had set in since his last meeting with Penn and Feldman. Miami was becoming toxic to his mental state. He could not wait to finish his business with Kyle and return to New York and the safety of Luc's army. The distance also gave him a sense of safety. He parked in the garage of Kyle's office building and noticed a car slowly glide by as he exited his vehicle. It was a black Dodge Charger with darkened windows. It kept going and eventually left the garage. He hurried to the elevator and stood with his back to the elevator door, scanning the sparsely filled garage for activity. As he reached Kyle's office, the door opened and his pale expressionless face glistened with sweat beads. He sat briefly in the lobby with a motionless gaze, awaiting Kyle. Minutes later he was shown to Kyle's office.

"Look at you. What did you do, walk up the entire flight of stairs?" asked Kyle, noticing Biagio's sweaty demeanor.

"No. I think I'm being followed by the FBI."

"What?" responded Kyle with surprise.

"That's why I am here. I have a problem."

"Tell me."

"Randall Penn of the FBI has questioned me now for the second time. He is questioning my whereabouts the night Sonya was murdered."

"I thought you told them you were with Secur," said Kyle.

"No, that was the night after she was killed. The night they found her, I was with Secur."

"Well, then, we do have a problem," said Kyle. They both paused, thinking the inevitable. After a couple of minutes of reflection, Kyle broke the ice, changing the subject. "Sandrine has left Anderson Development for good," said Kyle in remorse.

"Why?"

"I think she knows about our little gambit with the drywall," answered Kyle.

"That's not good. She just left?" asked Biagio in disbelief.

"Yep."

"How did she figure that out?"

"I could tell the change in her attitude the moment we got back from the Caymans. That spark was gone, and she began working more and more in the field to avoid my presence. I think she may have seen James Foster in the Caymans. The big-mouth puke might have said something, or she may have put two and two together. I'm not really sure."

"What else do you think she knows?" asked Biagio, leaning forward in his seat.

"No telling at this point. My cousin started following her again. She knew he was tailing her and slipped the tail at Bayside in an elaborate scheme," said Kyle.

"Whatdaya mean scheme?"

"She took a taxi to the main lot, then rode an elevator to the top level of the garage, where someone was waiting for her. When Jack got to the top level, she was gone."

"Who was she meeting?" asked a nervous Biagio.

"I don't know for sure. She doesn't have a lot of friends," said Kyle.

"Didn't you tell me that she was friendly with that FBI gal?" reminded Biagio.

"Oh shit, that's it. She knows," said Kyle as a grey cloud formed in his head. He was instantly depressed and stunned. Somehow she knew about Foster. *Does she also know about her sister?* he wondered. Minutes went by as he recalled his most recent actions with Sandrine.

"Hey, snap out of it. We've got work to do," reminded Biagio. "This is not good."

"If she went to the FBI, they will start to look more closely at us and our deal. Who knows what they will uncover," said Kyle with quickness and uncertainty in his voice.

"Just relax. Nobody is going to find out anything unless you tell them," said Biagio. He was used to pressure and brushes with the law. He attempted to console Kyle, showing concern over his partner's nervousness.

"That's easy for you to say."

"It is because I have been where you are before," remarked Biagio. He was beginning to lose patience with his whining partner. Another moment of silence transpired as each reflected on their mutual worries.

"Let's just review the paperwork we planned to go over tonight so we can move to more productive matters," said Biagio in a measured tone. Kyle agreed and picked up the documents he needed to review with his newest partner. He had reviewed hundreds of documents like this before and had very few comments. Kyle turned to a page in the agreement he had marked and refreshed his thoughts about his new deal with Biagio and the Teamsters.

"I noticed in article seven subset (C) that if something happens to me, you have the right to take over the job and acquire my percentage position. What's with that?" asked Kyle.

"It's perfectly logical when you think about it. If you are unable to complete the building, then we are assuming we will need to hire a new contractor, or at least have the option to do so in order to complete what you started. We will also need to hire a management company to oversee the rent-up stage and run the operation. That's only fair, don't you agree? We had this same clause in all of the Secur loans as well," reassured Biagio.

Kyle remained skeptical but he continued to review several other points with Biagio. Getting his head back into business had changed his attitude, and he shook off his previous worries about Sandrine. He was beginning to understand his new partner. After all, they were in in this thing together.

CHAPTER SIXTY-TWO

"Randall, please come in here right now," shouted Ronnie from her office.

Penn's office was in earshot, and he came immediately to her door. "What's wrong?" he asked, thinking she was in pain or some danger.

She motioned him over to her chair, where she was sitting with her phone to her ear. "It's Marty Burns from that real estate company. He saw the composite picture of Nacion we floated in all the papers the other day," said Ronnie.

Penn reached for the speaker button. "Mr. Burns. How nice to speak with you again. It's Randall Penn sitting with Ronnie. Do you have information on Armando Nacion?" asked Penn, taking over the conversation.

"I think so, but his name to me is Roberto Perez," said Burns.

"Can you tell how you know this man?" asked Penn.

"He's a client of mine. Actually a very good client. I have rented him several waterfront homes over the past few months," answered Burns.

"Did you rent him the home that burned down last month in South Miami?" inquired Penn.

"No, that was another broker. Now that we are talking I just realized that no one has heard from that broker in over a month. Oh my God. Do you think..." said Burns without finishing his sentence.

"Mr. Burns, when did you first rent a home to Mr. Nacion, ah Perez to you?" asked Penn, not wanting to discuss a possible missing person at that time. He made a pencil note on his pad: *missing broker.*

"About two days after the house in Key Biscayne burned down," Burns answered with a touch of fear in his voice.

"When did you last hear from Mr. Nacion?"

"It has been about four days since I last spoke with him. He rented a home in Lighthouse Point; a very large home, in fact. It's right off the inlet," volunteered Burns.

"Exactly how many homes has he leased from you?"

"Three homes."

"Is he current on the rent? And what did he tell you he wanted with all of these homes on the water? What's his story?" asked Penn.

"None of my owners have complained about his rent. It's generally in cash and three months in advance. He doesn't say much except that he films movies in Miami and he needs homes for actors and crew members," said Burns.

"Could you give me the addresses of each of these homes for our records? Also, I want to send an agent over to keep an eye on you for a couple of weeks for your own safety. If Mr. Nacion calls you, please give me a call on my cell phone right away. Now, Ms. Feldman will finish up some standard FBI protocol and take down the addresses of the homes. Will you please hold on? Thank you for this important information," said Penn.

"No, I don't mind the agent stopping by at all. Very thoughtful of you, Mr. Penn. Thank you," said Burns.

Ronnie finished up some basic FBI questions of her own with Burns. This took about fifteen minutes. She hoped the FBI could keep him from the same fate as the other broker Nacion had used up and apparently killed. Ronnie was sure to get the name of the missing broker along with additional information about Burns and his relationship with Nacion. Penn came back in the room just as Ronnie hung up with Burns.

"I knew we were going to get something from those composites," offered Penn, stepping over to Ronnie and massaging her shoulders. She reacted by touching Penn's right hand, acknowledging the tenderness.

"It never fails. Great work by our photo ops crew," she confirmed.

"I sent Melnick over to Marty Burns's office to get acquainted. You got those addresses he mentioned?" said Penn.

"Yep. Right here, babe," Ronnie answered.

"All right, let's book it up to Lighthouse Point. That seems to be a favorite spot for bad guys with boats," reminded Penn.

"I think Nacion is getting desperate, don't you?"

"Maybe, or he's just a fearless young Mexican who apparently values money more than his life," said Penn.

They walked out of the building toward Penn's Tahoe. Their next stop was Lighthouse Point. Before leaving they checked their ammo and slipped into their Kevlar vests. They smelled a capture.

CHAPTER SIXTY-THREE

Biagio took the elevator down to the second floor of Kyle's office building. He then walked down the final floor via the fire exit stairs. He peered through a slit in the exit door, gradually opening it wider and eventually walking to his car once all was clear. His paranoia was at a high level, but not so high as to render him a complete basket case. He quickly moved around his car to the driver's side when suddenly he heard a familiar voice. A voice he feared more than anything. He grimaced, bending slightly, expecting to receive a life-ending bullet. He waited for almost ten grueling seconds. He slowly turned his head like a lizard trying to surprise a fly hovering behind him. Instead of death he heard laughter from the car parked next to him. His body faced his car while his head finally turned enough to see a chrome gun pointing directly at his head. The man behind the gun was Armando Nacion. Biagio summoned enough courage to straighten up and face the potentially fatal situation. He quickly focused on what he should say to save his life. Something he had done once before.

"Armando, I have tried to reach out to you so we could settle up. I guess you haven't been getting my e-mails," he said, trying to bait Nacion into his humor. It appeared to work. Nacion lowered the gun slightly and broke out laughing. Biagio remembered that Nacion had a twisted sense of humor, morbid at times and took a deep breath. Sweat poured from his forehead as his death sentence was lifted for the moment.

"My little Italian buddy, you do have balls. But we do need to settle up. I want you to meet my friend Franco Santore," said Nacion. Biagio looked inside the Dodge Charger at the man in the back seat.

"That's him," said Santore.

"Who's he?" asked Biagio.

"Someone who knows you very well. But that is a story for another day," said Nacion as he leaned over to open the door for Biagio, the muzzle of the chrome revolver still pointing in the general direction of Biagio's head. Biagio got in the car and looked at Santore. He was not a swarthy Mexican soldier. He was clean cut, well dressed, and spoke perfect English. Once Biagio turned around, Santore left from the rear seat behind Nacion and disappeared into the dark shadows of the parking garage.

"Now shall we take a little ride, Biagio?" asked Nacion, tucking his gun into a shoulder holster under his left arm pit—hidden, but in a very accessible place if needed in a hurry. Biagio was thinking about his options. He knew Nacion had a plan. *Listen, and then react slowly*, he thought.

"I thought we would ride for a while and talk. Don't be stupid. I'm not going to kill you. I need you alive to execute our plan," said Nacion.

"Our plan? What exactly is our plan, Armando?" asked Biagio, feeling more confident.

"Don't get smart. I need you, but I am not beyond killing you for all the problems you and your friend Anderson cost my associates, and me" said Nacion in a menacing tone.

"OK, what do you want?"

"It's what I will demand, and you will deliver. Right now my men are in the same towns around New York and New Jersey as your mother, your brother, uncle Luc, and your sister Sheila in Denver. But here's the thing about your sister. We have her in custody, and nothing will happen to her as long as you play ball with us. The rest of your family thinks Sheila is away on a familiarization trip to Europe. Being a travel agent was a lucky break for us.," said the relaxed, maniacal Mexican drug lord. Nacion was prototypical in today's sophisticated business of drugs. Biagio was shaken by the mention of his sister from the lips of this madman.

"I get it, Armando. Now what do you want?"

"What? No negotiation, no banter, no smoke and mirrors, Biagio? Thank you for going public in the papers with your new deal with Anderson. How stupid. Anyone with half a brain knows what the two of you cooked up. I'll bet you even suspected poor Secur would kill himself. How fortuitous for your team.

You rigged the game, and you crapped all over your Teamster buddies. I don't know your split, but here's what we want. Simple. We want half the deal now for the lack of fair play on your part and for trying to cut us out of the old deal."

"That's not true. I tried to reach you. With everything you've been doing to draw attention to yourself I have to be careful too. The FBI is all over me, and I can barely move around this city. How was I supposed to get to you?" pleaded Biagio.

"It does not matter now how we arrived at this moment. What matters is that you need to get me fifty percent of this deal. I leave that to you. That man you met is a legitimate American businessman with a Mexican heritage. He will be your new partner as our shill. Now, I am going to leave you off here. This is a satellite phone. If you need me, dial this number and leave a message and I will call you back on its local number," said Nacion, handing Biagio a phone the size of a BlackBerry.

"How much time do I have?" asked Biagio.

"I will give you one week to wrap this up. Then if it is not done, I will move on each of the family members we discussed. We will also take out your current partner, Kyle Anderson," said Nacion as he pulled over to the curb.

"All right. I'll get you your half, but I need a grace period if I am close and running out of time," pleaded Biagio.

"OK, if you are late I will only kill your sister and give you and extra three days," said Nacion as he reached across Biagio and opened his door. He pulled his gun from the holster and pistol whipped Biagio across the skull. In a dazed half stupor, Biagio was pushed hard to the curb by Nacion as the mad Mexican drove off.

Biagio, stunned and bleeding from his temple, struggled to his feet in a foggy, dreamlike state. He heard tires screeching in front of him. In a relaxed state with burning pain in his head and his vision blurred, he saw cars surrounding Nacion's Dodge Charger. Everything appeared in slow motion as Biagio struggled to process the scene as a bad dream or current reality in his injured state. With complete loss of time and clear vision, he heard small pops and a whizzing noise passing his right ear. Instinctively he curled up on the sidewalk, using his satchel as a pillow and covering his head with his arms. As he closed his eyes succumbing to the dream, his world went dark. Moments later, as if awakening from surgery still caught in the grip of anesthesia, he heard vague voices speaking his name and asking him if he was all right. He felt someone move his head but was too dazed to resist. *It must be a dream*, he insisted. Suddenly his nose breathed in an ammonia-like smell, causing an abrupt awareness. The face staring back at him was Randall Penn, and suddenly a woman's voice from behind sent his senses into complete confusion overload.

"Mr. Penn," he feebly said. "Where am I?"

He glanced down at the street away from Penn's stare and saw the man who had just kicked him out of a car lying motionless in a pool of blood. With his senses returning slowly, so was his reasoning. Panic enveloped his entire brain. His vision went double, and he fainted into the wonderful smell of Ronnie's arms, smearing her blouse sleeves with blood from his head wound. He went into a dream state once again.

Leaving a shocked and unconscious Biagio with his assistants, Penn turned to Ronnie with a disappointed glare. "Well, there goes the best witness we had," sighed Penn, weary from the mental toll that chases and shootouts produced.

"He's replaceable. The Mexicans will have a new leader installed in twenty-four hours. Don't feel bad about Nacion; he wasn't going to live much longer, anyway. He was a battery near the end of its life," added Ronnie without remorse.

"You are one hard bitch. No mercy for the dead?" Penn half kidded.

"They give no mercy. Forget it, Penn. He died in combat. What I want to know is what that wimp Biagio was doing in the car with this scumbag. Trying to get himself killed?" asked Ronnie.

"Call an ambulance, take him to Parkway Hospital near our office, and hold him on some bullshit charge. I know he was kidnapped, but he's dirty and we will find a charge before he reaches his senses. Have him guarded twenty-four seven, and don't let anyone know about this until I talk to Thorne and see how far we can bend the law to get this greasy piece of shit to talk," said Penn, suddenly out of patience.

"What happened to your mercy and compassion, Penn? Pretty tough on the kid, aren't you?" Ronnie remarked with a wry smile. Just then a white van drove up and began hoisting its spiral antenna. *Great, Channel Ten News*, thought Penn.

"I'm tired of these foreign slugs coming to our country and thinking they can get away with robbery and murder. I was kidding you before, but really, you are right. Let's get out of here before every news agency and beat writer in Miami and Fort Lauderdale shows up," said Penn.

As Penn and Ronnie were leaving, he called out to his most senior assistant, motioning to him by crossing his lips with a finger. The agent acknowledged back with the same motion and a thumbs up. Penn felt confident the press would be shut out of a story as he and Ronnie slipped away to their car. They would ride to their office and brief Special Agent in Charge Thorne about the day's serious events. Afterward they would pay Biagio a very special visit.

CHAPTER SIXTY-FOUR

Sandrine was sitting at home watching daytime TV for the first time in her life. She was depressed about the direction her life had taken ever since her sister had died. Her regrets turned to self-pity, and that self-pity had prompted the current forty-eight-hour bender she was now in the middle of. The self-proclaimed neat freak looked around her apartment. While she did care, she was helpless to pick up the half-finished take-out boxes and the empty pizza cartons. Her life was a mess. She decided at that moment to go on her next bender. But instead of food and booze, she would apply herself to cleaning her untidy apartment.

Over the next two hours she drank coffee, sobered up, cleaned and dusted the entire apartment, and capped off the event with a shower. It helped her lose herself for a couple of hours, but the thoughts and guilt came right back. She turned her attention to her sister's cell phone. It was a BlackBerry like her own. She decided to charge the dead phone and see what information, if any, it might hold. As the day wore on, she carefully pruned and sorted her sister's belongings. Staring at the box full of Sonya's belongings at rest in a corner of her bedroom for nearly four months relieved some of the hurt one day at a time.

She dozed off for several hours, awakening in the early evening. By then the phone had come back to life. She decided to sync the contents of Sonya's

BlackBerry directly onto her computer. Sonya's address book, her contacts, and her e-mails were placed on Sandrine's desktop. She then charged her body with a double espresso before starting her journey through Sonya's social life. She knew it would be draining, and she grew fearful of what she might find. Espresso would give her the energy to fight through the pain. Despite her gloom, Sandrine had the ability to draw from deep within her soul and do the unpleasant and necessary thing.

She had excellent powers of priority and was proficient at handling large quantities of data without getting bogged down in tedium. She listed a short outline of how her search would go. Within the first hour of e-mail and contact reviews, she was surprised to see that she and Sonya had traveled in similar social circles. She categorized Sonya's e-mails by individuals. Surprisingly, she had numerous e-mails from Kyle and Biagio. It appeared that she had asked Kyle for a job in sales at one of his condos. *Why wouldn't she have asked me?* wondered Sandrine. She created her own folder for all of the e-mails she wanted to re-review.

As she set up the new folder, she saw a folder Sonya had set up entitled NO-NO. Immediately Sandrine froze her stare on the title of the file. Her breathing increased, anxiety flooded her head as she developed an ache above both eyes, and within minutes beads of sweat formed on her upper lip; she was petrified. After what seemed like hours, she emerged from her trance, knowing a batch of rough air lie ahead in the discovery process.

She double clicked the file, and a list of e-mails from Kyle Anderson emerged. In her anal approach to nearly everything she did, Sandrine decided to read the e-mails in chronological order. It had been over three months since Sonya's death, so counting back to the first e-mail landed her in February, four months before her death. As she read the first few e-mails, it became obvious that Sonya was being paid by Kyle to keep tabs on Biagio. The e-mails were very businesslike for the first two months, almost boring. Sandrine's heart rate lessened, and her aches and anxiety subsided. She breathed a sigh of relief. Then, one by one, the e-mails took on a gradual flirtatious nature, started by Kyle and responded in like kind by Sonya. Now Sandrine's emotions changed to disgust. Her sister was cheating on Biagio with a married man. Her guilt got the best of her in self-examination—*but wasn't I?* thought Sandrine. The pain over her eyes returned. In May it was clear that Sonya was going out with Biagio and seeing Kyle on the side. Sandrine was exhausted by the mental conflict. She bowed her head and closed her eyes in an attempt to relieve her anxiety. She continued without relief.

Struggling to concentrate her mind took another jolt as her fears were confirmed about James Foster and the meeting with Kyle in The Cayman Islands. While Sonya was careful with her words, it became evident that Kyle had orchestrated the Chinese drywall switch with Foster's firm with the understanding that Foster would be rewarded. His part of the deal was compensation and leaving the country for at least five years.

Then, suddenly there it was, a mistaken e-mail that ended up on Sonya's phone when Kyle accidently hit reply all instead of reply. Sandrine rushed to the bathroom to dry heave in the toilet. She was gasping for air, as an unbelievable cramp began to knot her stomach. Suddenly her doorbell rang. *How did someone get up here without the guard calling me?* she wondered. She was now near delirium as she feared that it must be Kyle. He knew how to get around guards and the alarm system. He had the same equipment for security in his buildings. Luckily, the curtains were drawn, and no one could see in. She waited for ten minutes in the very place she had stopped when the doorbell first rang. She was motionless and dripping wet from fear, with an elevated heart rate beating so strong that she could hear it in the dead silence of her apartment. Finally, she moved to the curtains and peeked out, barely splitting the drawn seams. Looking eyeball to eyeball through the tiny slit was Kyle Anderson. She was so scared she jerked the curtains open as only a thin plate of glass separated the former lovers. Kyle pointed to the doorknob, asking for her to open the door. His eyes grew large as he focused on Sandrine's sickly appearance.

"Are you all right? Let me in, please. I am worried about you. What happened?" Kyle said in fear, running all of his sentences together.

Sandrine snapped together and attempted a smile. After what she had just read, she felt like getting a gun and shooting her uninvited guest.

"OK. I'm ill, Kyle, but just give me a second," she managed to say. Adrenaline replaced her fear and she quickly addressed her next problem:

hiding the incriminating evidence. *Does he know?* she wondered as she quickly closed her laptop and threw her note pages in a file in her briefcase. She quickly moved Sonya's belongings into the corner. Then she wiped the sweat from her face with her blouse; it barely helped since it was soaked with perspiration as well. She could no longer stall and decided her disheveled appearance could be of benefit in her discussions with Kyle. A discussion she could stall no longer. She opened the door.

Kyle was aghast. "What on earth is wrong, Sandy?" He seemed genuinely concerned.

Sandrine decided to fall into his waiting arms and take a chance even though she had slowly detached herself from his loving grip. *This has to be believable*, she said to herself as she embraced Kyle. "Yesterday it finally hit me. I have been unable to process the recent deaths of my sister and Alain. I started thinking how much has changed so quickly. I'm overwhelmed. It started in the islands, and every day since, it has gotten worse. That's why you haven't seen me much. I needed space to clear my head. I'm sorry if I hurt you," she said in between tears and gags for breath. It was an amazing transformation by Sandrine, and Kyle appeared to believe her; part of it was true.

"Sandy, why didn't you confide in me? I could have been a helpful shoulder to cry on. I knew you had feelings still for Secur, but I thought I could get into your heart and make you forget," he responded sympathetically.

"Oh, Kyle, you are so good to me. You don't deserve me. I'm a wreck," Sandrine said. The gambit seemed to be working.

Then Kyle focused on the box of Sonya's belongings. "Are you going through your sister's belongings?" asked Kyle. His tone was strange in a funny way.

Sandrine decide to confront part of the truth. "Yes, it's painful. I must do this, though, or I will never get closure," she responded.

Kyle now had both hands on her shoulders and refocused on her face. Looking through her messy hair, he leaned in to kiss Sandrine.

She turned to avoid the lips she had once longed for. "No, not like this. I'm an emotional wreck. I love you, but no, Kyle," she lied convincingly.

Kyle's attitude became upbeat. He was back in her life. Now as her protector, he gently guided her to the sofa and sat next to her, cuddling his love.

Sandrine played along. They just sat there without saying a word as he helped her grieve. The silence allowed Sandrine to think about how to get rid of Kyle. *Thank goodness he can't read my mind*, she thought.

Finally, after ten minutes of silence, Kyle spoke. "Come back to work, Sandy. I miss you."

"I'm not going to agree now, like this. Let me think about it. Can you give me a couple of days to regroup? I need that time."

"OK, then, I'll leave you alone to your thoughts. I love and miss you," said Kyle as he kissed her forehead. She stood with him and walked him to the door in a submissive posture. She kissed his cheek and thanked him.

Kyle left, quietly. He was glad that he had come and left with the hope that Sandrine would return to work.

She let five minutes pass for good measure before she finally opened her laptop. Then she typed a desperate e-mail to Ronnie Feldman: *I know who the murderers are. Please come quickly. Don't call. E-mail me when you can be here. Please come now. I'm scared.*

CHAPTER SIXTY-FIVE

Kyle was feeling sorry for Sandrine, yet he was hopeful that soon the grieving would be over so he could resume their love affair. He was just pulling into Marty Burns's office to meet Biagio. The three had a lot of work ahead of them rebuilding the two infected towers back to a level where they could be successfully rented. Marty had been in on the plan from the beginning; his role was perhaps the most important. Any number of contractors could fix the ailing residences, but only Marty had the network to tell the real estate world that Anderson Development had cured the ailing towers and that they were safe to occupy. His financial take in this real estate misdirection was almost as big as Biagio's, which, was an occasional cause of irritation between LoPrendo and Marty. When Kyle arrived, Biagio and Marty were conversing in Marty's office.

"Where you been, partner?" asked Biagio. Kyle was surprised to see the extent of damage to his partner's injured face.

"Hey, are you all right? I heard what happened to you the other day, but I didn't think it was this bad," said Kyle.

"That crazy Mexican was going to kill me. Thank God the FBI was tailing his ass or I would not be here today," said Biagio, talking tough to impress his friends.

Kyle leaned in closer to inspect the injured face. "Shit, he got you good," he said.

"Yep, twenty-three stitches. A little lower and the eye would be gone," said Biagio, taking his tough act up a notch and basking in the attention.

"Where ya been, pal?" asked Marty, repeating Biagio's original question. Marty was upset at Kyle for being over ninety minutes late without a phone call or a text to explain.

"Sorry, guys. I had to see Sandrine. I miss her," said a somber Kyle.

Biagio and Marty were surprised at what Kyle was saying.

"I thought that was over," said Marty, somewhat angered.

"I did too," said Biagio, glancing at Marty.

"The heart never gets over this. She's a wreck too," answered Kyle.

"Whatya mean a wreck?" asked Biagio, sensing trouble.

"When I went by to see her, she didn't answer the door for ten minutes. I knew she was in there. Then finally she comes to the door, and she's soaked head to toe in sweat, she's pale, weeping, and distraught. I could barely take it myself," said Kyle. Both men listened intently.

"Why was she so upset?" asked Marty.

"She had been going through her sister's belongings. That has to be tough. With our relationship on hold, I think she finally misses Secur too; it all just overwhelmed her," he said.

Biagio's fears became manifest. He was streetwise and knew the subtleties of Sandrine's deception. He hoped for the best at all times but planned for the worst. He became quiet as he tried to reason what might really be behind Sandrine's panic attack. *She could be grieving,* he reasoned, *or she may know something that she shouldn't. They were sisters; they thought alike, they were inquisitive.*

Marty saw that Biagio had dropped out of the discussion. Biagio's silence made Marty think retrospectively as well.

"What's wrong, Biagio?" questioned Kyle.

Biagio hesitated as he gathered his thoughts. "Maybe she knows something about one of us and she is scared. She could have reasoned herself into an emotional corner," said Biagio.

"What kind of corner?" asked a confused Kyle.

"The kind of corner you don't want to know about. Did you happen to see what she was going through?" asked Biagio, staring Kyle in the eye.

"No, I did not. What do you mean? Besides, I don't want to know," asked Kyle. He was not happy with Biagio's innuendos.

Marty shrank from the conversation, waiting to see if Biagio would reveal his cards. He knew Biagio could be trouble when he feared exposure.

"Let's just say, we all want Sandrine to get over her sister's passing without any more trouble," said Biagio, measuring each word.

His warning worked, as Kyle's face revealed that he now understood. The room became dead quiet for several moments.

Finally Biagio was compelled to speak. "We are not done with the Mexicans. Nacion's replacement will pose the same threat. We have to be better prepared," he remarked.

"I suggest we move forward without your presence here in South Florida. Marty and I can handle the day-to-day operation. Just keep the money flowing, and we'll take care of everything," said Kyle.

"How long do you think it will be before they put two and two together? That damn newspaper article laid out everything for the public to see. The only things they left out were our personal financial statements. Besides, to the Mexicans it's the same deal, just a few missing participants and a couple of new people brought on board. They'll want their money," said Biagio firmly.

"What?" asked Marty.

"No matter who goes forward on this deal, they are going to have to deal with the Mexicans. I suggest we find a solution," said Biagio.

"What about some of Luc's people? Does he know what we have done? Does he know your position?" questioned Kyle.

"He knows we are taking over an asset full of liabilities and paying the Teamsters more than anyone else would," said Biagio. He ignored Kyle's full question.

Kyle acknowledged the omission. "So the answer is no, they don't know your little game and the rather large fee you stand to make," retorted Kyle.

Now Biagio grew tense. "You got a problem with that?"

"Not at all. I just want to know the facts. I don't want to find out I have another partner, especially pissed-off Mexican drug lords," answered Kyle with a smug expression.

The meeting was getting tense, and Marty was rustling nervously in his chair watching his partners battle. "Hey, look, guys, this is counterproductive. Here's what we know. We have a Mexican problem, but we have one hell of a deal. Let's not get greedy. If we give a little from each of us, we may be able to compromise our way clear," offered Marty.

Biagio turned his attention to Marty. "Maybe we can compromise at a reasonable number."

"The term reasonable to a Mexican drug lord may be more than we can afford," said Kyle.

"I think we may need to involve Luc's friends for our protection. They have something to gain here," offered Marty.

"You start a war with two crime families and no one wins," answered Kyle.

Biagio was impressed but he had more bad news. "The FBI doesn't compromise either, and that's my problem at this moment," he said angrily.

Marty and Kyle looked at each other in surprise.

"Oh, you didn't know, guys? Penn and that Jewish babe had me in for another chat yesterday and want me to come back for another little chat and fill in some holes for them. Seems they have trouble with my alibi. Secur was supposed to back me up when Sonya had to be dealt with, but he got caught up with his own alibi once he was a suspect. That made me the odd man out," said Biagio calmly.

"Great. What are you doing about that?" asked a frazzled Marty Burns.

"Not a damned thing, Marty. I didn't kill her, and they know it. Just like what happened to Kyle and the Gomez death. Eventually when they can't prove anything, they quietly give up. Right, Kyle?" said Biagio.

"That was an accident, and you know it. Why the fuck did you bring that up at this moment with all the other distractions we have to deal with?" said an upset Kyle.

Biagio regretted saying it as soon as he spoke. "I'm sorry. You are right; that was uncalled for. Can everyone just relax?" said Biagio apologetically.

"I'm more worried about Nacion's replacement," said Marty.

"Can we please discuss how we are going to make this the most successful rental project in Miami? That's what we're here for," reminded Kyle.

Even though the meeting had gotten off to a rough start, the partners focused once again on the game plan for the twin tower restoration. Within an hour it was obvious the strong team would be capable of making a winner out of Secur's loser.

CHAPTER SIXTY-SIX

Ronnie and Penn had just traveled fifteen miles in just over eleven minutes after leaving their offices in North Miami for Sandrine's South Beach condo. They were extremely worried about her state of mind and her safety since receiving her cryptic plea for help. Ronnie feared that harm might come from someone connected to Sonya's murder, while Penn feared her unstable mindset could trigger something worse by Sandrine's own hand. Something that she had learned or something that had recently occurred had sent Sandrine into panic mode. Both agents hoped they would not find another tragedy.

As they pulled into the parking garage at Sandrine's building, Penn stopped directly in front of the elevator and let Ronnie out. She sped to the open door, going up first as Penn parked in a nearby handicapped parking spot. Five minutes later Penn appeared at Sandrine's floor. As the elevator doors parted, Penn observed Sandrine's half-open front door. As he eased closer to the entry, he could hear Sandrine weeping and Ronnie softly encouraging her. With no imminent danger present, he backed away, moving closer to the elevator loggia, not wanting to interrupt the cathartic emotions of the two bonding women. He glanced out the loggia window, admiring the fall weather that cast a different sun angle on the watery scene unfolding below. He took a rare moment to gaze upon the eclectic yet beautiful cityscape of South Beach. The sun-soaked bay and ocean were pond-like, with no discernible wind to ripple the surf. A seaplane was landing at Watson Island after a picture-perfect approach. He stood in awe of all the local beauty for ten minutes, not once noticing the time.

His trance was interrupted by Ronnie. "Rand, can you come in here now, please?" requested Ronnie, standing in Sandrine's doorway with her hands on her hips. Penn admired her sexy posture and obeyed his lover as he moved toward the entry. Ronnie had tears running down her cheeks, as if she had absorbed whatever agony Sandrine was sharing.

"Everything's OK, honey," said Penn gingerly. He walked past Ronnie, spotting Sandrine crumpled on the sofa wrapped in a blanket. Her hair was wildly mussed, and her eyes were red with raw emotion. She did not acknowledge Penn as she slumped looking at the floor in a dead trance. Ronnie closed and locked the entry door and took a place next to Sandrine. As she did so, Sandrine cuddled to Ronnie like a cub to a mother tiger. It was a touching scene, and Penn stood his distance as an uncomfortable third wheel.

Finally, Ronnie spoke quietly to Sandrine. "Sandy, do you mind if I speak to Randall about what you told me?" asked Ronnie with a light whisper.

Sandrine never looked up but nodded, barely enough to confirm the request.

With that, Penn sat across from Sandrine and Ronnie on the edge of his chair, not really knowing what to expect but anxious to hear.

"Three months ago, Sandrine went to a private storage locker Sonya had leased. In it was a single box full of her important papers, including Sonya's diary. Within the papers were pictures of Sonya and Biagio, as one would expect. But some of the pictures were also with Sonya and Kyle Anderson. These were more than occasional photos; they were very intimate pictures. As she read the diary, she placed pictures in an order that followed the same timeline," said Ronnie. She spoke deliberately as if telling a room full of FBI agents what she had found at a murder scene. Penn was impressed by Sandrine's adroit approach. She continued. "It appears from the writings and the pictures that Kyle came on the scene about three months before Sonya's passing." Ronnie hesitated to say murder.

Sandrine continued to sniffle and sob as Ronnie spoke.

"It became apparent that very little love for Biagio existed just prior to her death and that Kyle was winning her heart. Then, just days before her passing, she suddenly ended her relationship with Kyle," said Ronnie, giving Sandrine an extra hug in between her next revelation.

Penn was anxious. "Go on. What was the entry?" asked Penn quickly.

Ronnie put her finger to her mouth, signaling Penn to be quiet. "Kyle confessed to her that he had accidently killed Artone Gomez on his boat a year earlier, and he did not know how he could deal with his guilt any longer. Apparently Sonya had become his sounding board and therapist over the months leading up to his guilty confession. Sonya was uncomfortable with that surprising disclosure," said Ronnie.

Penn was livid, Ronnie could clearly see, but not for the reasons she thought. He could not control himself. "The son-of-a-bitch killed her. I knew it. I'm bringing that bastard in," ranted Penn.

Finally Sandrine raised her head, displaying a strange look on her face as if to question Penn's logic.

Before she could speak, he blurted out his suspicions. "I want a warrant served today on Biagio LoPrendo. He killed Sonya just as sure as I am standing here," Penn said in a rage.

Ronnie and Sandrine had thought Penn meant Kyle Anderson. Ronnie corrected him. "You mean Kyle Anderson, don't you, Rand?"

"No! Don't you see?" said Penn, ignoring Sandrine entirely as he spoke directly to Ronnie. "Biagio had his eyes and ears out. My guess is either Sonya mentioned it to Biagio, which I doubt, with her being the survivor she was, or Kyle spilled the beans to Biagio under the same pretense—a guilty conscience. Biagio saw the potential of his grand plan being blown away if Sonya, who had already stopped seeing Kyle because of the murder disclosure, blew the whistle on Anderson. Emotionally he had lost Sonya, and he knew she might just alert the police to Kyle's actions with Gomez. Kyle doesn't strike me as a murderer, but that slimy New Yorker does. Biagio did it. Excuse me; I need to make some calls," said Penn as he disappeared outside, dialing his cell phone as he left Sandrine and Ronnie speechless on her sofa.

Ronnie continued to comfort Sandrine. Her sobbing had ceased as she struggled to understand Penn's police logic. She began to think back in time, trying to identify clues she may have missed that would help her understand Penn's confident conclusions. Just then Penn reappeared.

"Ronnie, I want you to stay with Sandrine for a while. I'm leaving to meet Thorne back at the office and to get a warrant for Biagio's arrest." He was standing in the doorway.

"I'll drop Ronnie off, Randall. Thanks so much for being there for me," said Sandrine as she stood and moved toward Penn. Penn froze at the unexpected reply. Sandrine threw her arms around Randall, whispering her thanks to him again.

Penn was warmed by her touch and taken by her difficult mental state. He gently unwound her arms with a silent nod and quickly left for the office. Ronnie arose to meet Sandrine as the two shared a warm embrace. Nothing else was said.

CHAPTER SIXTY-SEVEN

Biagio and Luc were sitting under the veranda of the former home of Alain Secur, discussing their options for the upcoming revitalization of the two towers. The autumn sun tracking to the south warmed the air to a perfect eighty degrees. The bright glare on this cloudless day was intense; however, the low angle lit up the waters of the bay, creating a continuous sparkle on the miniature chop. Suddenly their heads turned in unison as each caught a glimpse of the tanned and lithe body of Alicia Secur walking across the pool deck to her lounge chair facing southeast into the direction of the autumn sun. Even Biagio lusted over the sensual distraction.

"Uncle Luc, you should be ashamed of yourself for dating a woman that young and beautiful," said Biagio, attempting to goad his uncle.

"When you become more mature and respected, you may someday have a woman this beautiful," said Luc, returning the light banter.

Biagio ignored the retort and jumped right to business. "We're all set with Kyle. He has signed the contract, and we are ready to begin the interior demolition in three weeks," said Biagio.

"Three weeks? Why so long?" asked Luc.

"Permits, Uncle."

"Permits. That reminds me, who knows about Artone Gomez and Kyle Anderson?" asked Luc in a nonchalant tone.

"Not so loud, Luc. Do you want Alicia to hear you?"

"She would not say anything. Besides, she doesn't know anything about that or Sonya," said Luc, hoping to elicit some information.

"Well she may be fine for now, but when you stop bedding her, she may not be so kind," said Biagio.

The "bedding" remark upset Luc, yet he let it go. "She knows nothing. Besides, I may marry her."

"Wow, I had no idea," said a surprised Biagio.

"She's a fine woman, and I plan on giving her what she deserves. Now let's get to the business at hand," said Luc.

"You're right."

"I have allowed you great profit latitude in this new deal that the Teamsters are financing. We are forced to wait for a mere fraction of the monies we originally loaned Secur. And while I think we have made a great deal, I have tremendous pressure from investors who basically put money into the same project I did just because of their belief in my investment prowess. So, in light of that one little secret we share, I need you to sign this document. It says in so many words that if you become incarcerated or die or are unable to perform your duties, your shares in the project will be immediately transferred to me," said Luc in an even and serious tone.

Biagio was stunned. His own uncle was using the same terms he had gotten Kyle to agree to, turning the knife toward Biagio.

"Uncle, I can't sign that. It's like an invitation to kill me. It makes me worth more dead than alive," said Biagio angrily.

"I can see one might think that, but this has to do with the incarcerated aspect more than anything," answered Luc.

"You mean the Sonya killing?"

"Yes, exactly."

"No one knows about that but you, Luc."

"Are you sure, Nephew? I mean, how am I supposed to know who may or may not know? What if Sonya told someone that you were going to kill her? Did you let on to her that you would ever do such a thing, possibly in jest?

"No. I killed her because she was going to tell the police about Kyle accidentally killing Artone Gomez."

"Accidental? They found two bullet holes in his skull. Just like Sonya," said Luc, continuing to bait Biagio. The answers were necessary.

"That was done after he was already dead. Me and Moto Seanu cleaned that one up," confessed Biagio.

"So, my greedy little nephew, that is why I need you to sign this paperwork. You see, the Teamsters have asked me to look after their newly downgraded asset. They have made it clear to me that if this deal hits a snag like the first time, I will no longer be protected from some of the boys who invested against my recommendation and have already lost millions. You know the guys I speak of, Biagio?"

"Hey, don't call me greedy, Luc. You went along with this plan in the beginning. I had the difficult task of executing it and steering it to where it is today. I should get most of the new deal," said an angered Biagio as he raised his voice.

Alicia looked over, sensing an argument. She rose from her lounge and wrapped a towel around her waist. She walked directly to Luc, bent over, and kissed him on the lips. "Everything OK here, darling? I think I'll go into town and do some shopping."

Biagio was embarrassed when she caught him looking at her sexy cleavage while bending to kiss Luc. She curved her lips in a wry smile, acknowledging his peep, then she turned and walked back into the mansion.

"She caught you," Luc chuckled.

"You are a dirty old man and a lucky sonofabitch," answered Biagio, making light of his dalliance.

"Read this over and sign here. Alicia kept her notary up from the early days of Alain's business. She can notarize your signature," said Luc.

"Really? How convenient," said Biagio.

"Yes. Say, let's go to Joe's tonight to celebrate. I'm buying. OK?" said Luc.

"Deal."

"I've got to go out for a while and get this document to our attorney and get the Teamsters set to go. Why don't you meet us at Joe's at 7:00 p.m.?" said Luc as he stood to leave.

"Sounds good. I'll see you then, Uncle Luc," said Biagio.

CHAPTER SIXTY-EIGHT

Sandrine was rested and composed as she dropped Ronnie off at FBI headquarters in North Miami. It was early evening, and she was exhausted and mentally spent.

"Thanks for the lift, Sandy. Hang in there. Things will get better," remarked Ronnie as she stepped from Sandrine's Mercedes.

Sandrine was focused elsewhere and in a confused state. "Isn't that Alicia Secur's car near that bench?" said Sandrine.

Ronnie was surprised and thought Sandrine was mistaken. "I wouldn't know, Sandy. Why would she be here?" asked Ronnie, looking at the license tag. It read *Secur2*. Ronnie looked confused as well and smiled at Sandrine, nodding good-bye. She knew that Penn had something to do with this and quickly left Sandrine as she headed for the back door of the building. She glanced back to see Sandrine leaving.

Once inside, Ronnie bounded up the stairs to Penn's office; it was empty. She quickly strode down the hall to SAC Thorne's office. Thorne's secretary saw the confused look on Ronnie's face as she peered at the closed door. She knew something big was going on inside Thorne's office.

"Good evening, Ronnie. Did you need to see Mr. Thorne?" she asked.

"Is he in?" said Ronnie.

"They're expecting you. Go right on in."

Ronnie approached the door with her head spinning in the possibilities of what she was going to find. This case had escalated into a soap opera of murder and international revenge. She gripped the door handle and took a deep breath before turning it, then she entered the unknown.

Once inside she saw Thorne, Penn, Alicia Secur, Luc LoPrendo, and one of the guys from the cyber group working on the recording devices they used on wire stings. Suddenly clarity arrived in her mind. Penn had gotten Luc and Alicia to wear a wire.

"Come in quickly, Ronnie. I think you know most of the people. Say hello to Luc LoPrendo and Alicia Secur," remarked Thorne as he stood to offer Ronnie a seat next to Penn. Ronnie glanced down at the wire, then instinctively looked at Luc, putting the two together. His shirttail was loose, hanging outside his slacks.

"What's going on here?" asked Ronnie, thinking through her own question while weighing the situation.

"Mr. LoPrendo and Ms. Secur have given us the break we needed in two unsolved murders: the Artone Gomez murder and the Sonya Michel murder. Last week Mr. LoPrendo came to us after hearing about his nephew's possible involvement in the murder of Ms. Michel. Through his lawyer and his cooperation, we were able to get Mr. LoPrendo to wear a wire today in discussions with him and Biagio LoPrendo. In summary, the recorded voluntary responses from Biagio, coupled with the lack of an alibi the night of Ms. Michel's murder, will be enough for the state's attorney and DA to issue warrants for his arrest. We believe in questions with Biagio after his arrest we will be able to get a warrant against Kyle Anderson for the Artone Gomez murder," said Penn into a live microphone in the middle of the table.

"I see. What is the nature of Mr. Luc LoPrendo's volunteering to do this? What I mean is, why would a tight-knit family member turn in his own nephew?" asked Ronnie, glancing at Luc.

"A number of reasons: guilt, cooperation, moral correctness, and the disappearance and dissolution of several pending actions in Brooklyn that

Mr. Penn's old law partners were kind enough to inform him of recently," answered SAC Thorne.

"I believe he will also inherit his nephew's position in some pending construction projects, but that is not our concern. In the end, for whatever reasons, justice to the victims' families will finally be done," said Penn, expressing the company line.

"Where is Biagio right this minute?" asked Ronnie.

"I just received confirmation from agents Lopez and Melnick that Biagio LoPrendo was picked up at Joe's restaurant ten minutes ago. He is being transported to the Metro Dade jail. His bond hearing will be this Monday," answered Penn.

Luc and Alicia were not the least bit nervous like most witnesses. In fact, Ronnie saw relief in their faces. They had made a pretty good deal after all: a murderer for two towers in Miami's finest residential section. *Justice comes in funny and unexpected forms*, she thought.

"Randall, will you and Ronnie finish the perfunctory paperwork with Luc and Alicia? I have another engagement I need to leave for," said Thorne.

"Sure thing, Jim. We'll take it from here," said Penn.

Ronnie sat silent, wondering what had just happened. The case was closed, and she and Penn would tie up the loose ends.

"I wonder, Ms. Feldman, if Alicia and I might ask a favor of you on a personal matter?" asked Luc very politely.

"Certainly. How can I help?" she responded, somewhat confused at the speed of events.

CHAPTER SIXTY-NINE

"We were fishing on my Robalo. It's a center console, twenty-nine foot twin-engine fishing boat with a mini tuna tower. We were trawling next to a weed line looking for dolphin and tuna about ten miles offshore. The winds had picked up, and a rogue wave out of nowhere laid my boat almost on its side. We were both in the tuna tower at the time, but I saw it a split second before it hit my boat broadside and grabbed the railing of the tower. I yelled to Artone, but it was too late. He flipped out of the boat like a rag doll and hit his head on the right side gunnel of the boat, eventually landing in the water. I was thrown against the chair so hard it knocked the wind out of me. By the time I struggled to find Gomez, he was dead, floating face down. I panicked and called Biagio on my cell phone," said Kyle. Kyle Anderson was sitting in the same room where, just two days before, Luc and Alicia had electronically indicted Biagio LoPrendo. Ronnie, Penn, and James Thorne were all in attendance once again.

"Can you tell me how he ended up with two bullet holes in his head, Mr. Anderson?" asked Penn.

"That was Biagio's idea, and Moto Seanu, too. They came out right away to my position, and we waited until dark to cover up the accident," said

Kyle. He spoke like a scolded child with his head down. Penn wondered if he was feigning remorse.

"How did Biagio get out there so quickly, and whose boat did he use?" asked Penn. Thorne and Ronnie were glued to every word Kyle spoke, looking for clues of the truth.

"He borrowed Secur's boat. He used it all the time. It was a little larger than mine, but the same class boat," answered a disquieted Kyle.

"Why were you and Artone fishing? Was this a perk for easy building inspections?" asked Penn.

"No, nothing like that. He was my friend. I always built straight up. No bribes. Artone had a gambling fetish that got him in hot water every now and then, so I tried to help him out," said Kyle.

"How does fishing equate to solving his money problem?" asked Penn.

"Well, I needed some information on Secur's building activities, and I knew he needed the money. Every time I paid him off, we would go to sea early in the morning before light and fish. I paid him in cash offshore," said Kyle.

It was obvious to Ronnie, Thorne, and Penn that Kyle was coming clean. They could see the burden of Artone's death lifting from Kyle's shoulders with every revelation.

"Let me get this right, Mr. Anderson. You not only paid Artone to spy for you, but you also made sure James Foster of Foster Brothers Drywall got the Secur job. Correct?"

"Yes, that is correct."

"How did you do that exactly? I mean, Secur had his own drywall crews, didn't he? Why would he use one of your guys?" asked Penn.

"Secur was always trying to steal my guys. My people had all worked for me for years. My subs were impeccable and I paid them weekly with no holdbacks. And, my quality was always better than Secur's. Secur was a bottom feeder. He always took the low bid, and his quality showed it. But that was only part of the story, I'm ashamed to admit. I paid James Foster $800 thousand over what Secur would pay him to install the toxic Chinese stuff. He went to Secur and told him I had fired him and as part of our settlement I had paid a large deposit for the drywall he had already ordered. He gave Secur an unbelievable price. I did actually pay for the bad batch that he used on Secur's job," said Kyle.

Thorne rose from his chair and finally spoke. "Mr. Anderson, this is an intriguing and very incriminating story you feel compelled to tell us. I want to ask you again, as I did at the beginning of this meeting: Would you like an attorney present as we go on?"

"No, sir, I don't. This has been haunting me for years. I need to get this off my chest."

"You remember we Mirandized you and you are under oath, correct?" confirmed Thorne.

"Yes, sir."

"All right. I hope the judge takes this confession into account when the time comes," said Penn.

" May I continue, Mr. Anderson?" asked Penn. taking over for SAC Thorne.

He nodded yes.

"So as I see this, you and Mr. LoPrendo had planned all along to set up Secur by installing drywall that was obviously contaminated, with the express plan of later taking the buildings back and reinstalling good drywall. You and Biagio then cut yourselves a sweet deal at the expense of Secur and his lender. Is that a fair summation of what you were trying to do?" said Penn, connecting his own dots.

"Pretty much, yes," answered Kyle.

"What did I leave out?" asked Penn.

"Armando Nacion. You left him out."

"Enlighten us, please," said Penn.

"Secur actually thought he could save the two towers. He needed to pay enough interest to the Teamsters until the auction date arrived. The Teamsters had funded their last drop of construction interest, and Secur was nearly insolvent. Somehow he found that wily Mexican doper and he loaned Secur the money to carry the two towers until the sale. That we did not see coming," said Kyle.

"What did you do next?" asked Penn.

Ronnie and Thorne were enthralled by Anderson's all out confession. They could hardly wait to hear what came next.

"Biagio had convinced Secur to put his assets up for sale in case we needed to pay the Mexicans from Teamster money."

"If the Teamsters were not lending money, how could you get the money to pay Nacion?"

"We had worked out a way to pay him out of the new construction money we were going to use to redo all of the tower units. Some of the Secur assets had already been sold at one price and marked down by the trustee for the Teamsters," said Kyle.

"Who was the trustee?" asked Penn.

"Biagio."

"I see. How did you think you would not get caught, Mr. Anderson? I mean, really?" asked Penn with a puzzled look on his face.

"After a while as things got out of control, I deceived myself into thinking everything would be OK. I never wanted Secur to kill himself. I never expected the Mexicans would not be paid, and I guess I was like the guy with the huge Ponzi scheme. You often wonder, what is their exit strategy? It's always one answer: jail."

"Does your wife know what you have gotten yourself into?" asked Penn in disgust.

"No."

"Here's what we will do for you. You have two options. Both are painful. First, you may call your wife and tell her you are not going to be home for a while. Although I think you will make bond eventually. We will go get her and bring her here and let you tell her face to face with Ms. Feldman in the room exactly what you have told us before we send you to jail. The other option is that you can call her from jail and explain this to her through your lawyer. What is your choice?" said Penn. He saw Kyle's face sadden when he mentioned Kyle's wife.

"I am ready for jail now. I don't have the strength to go through this again. Please put me out of my misery and lock me up now," whispered Kyle as he grabbed his head with both hands. He was a beaten man. His guile and cleverness had made him a success. Now the same ingredients, so deceitfully applied, had destroyed him.

As Penn stepped from the office, Ronnie hailed his attention, pointing to a blinking phone on hold.

"Its Reggie Gambrel on line two for you," said Ronnie.

"Hey, Reg, what's going on?" asked a tired Penn.

"Armando Nacion is back."

"I was there when he was shot dead; don't you remember?" asked Penn with irritation in his tired voice. Gambrel sensed the frustration in his old boss.

"Yeah, I know. You know how the boxer George Forman named all his sons George?" asked Reg.

"No, don't tell me. You're not serious?" begged Penn, afraid of the answer.

"Yep, old buddy, there's a new Nacion in town, and he's looking for the cartel's money," said Reg.

EPILOGUE

Luc's unusual request of Ronnie Feldman after the wiretap reviews was a touching offer. She was meeting Sandrine this Saturday at Bayside on a wonderfully mild late November day in a quaint Italian restaurant known for its thin-crusted pizza.

Ronnie placed the order just after wine was delivered and made a short toast in Sandrine's honor.

"I have a request from an admirer of your talents, and I am sure your beauty as well," said Ronnie.

"I am mystified and intrigued. Please tell me," requested Sandrine. Ronnie had now become one of Sandrine's closest friends.

"Kyle Anderson has relinquished his share in the twin towers. The sole owners are the Teamsters. Luc LoPrendo would like to make you an offer. He wants you to take over Anderson Construction, which Kyle agreed to, and finish the renovation of the two towers using all of your talents and the same staff you used to oversee. The staff of Anderson Construction personally asked that you come back and save the company and the towers. Also, Alicia Secur, who plans on marrying Luc, concurs. So, what do you think?" said Ronnie as a huge smile lit across Sandrine's face.

"Are you serious, Ronnie?"

"Yes, I am."

"Can I let you know after pizza?"

Made in the USA
Lexington, KY
22 May 2012